EXTINCTION

THE ENDING HAS BEGUN

SEAN
PLATT

JOHNNY B.
TRUANT

Extinction
Sean Platt & Johnny B. Truant

REALM & SANDS

To our Realm & Sands Outlaws.

EXTINCTION

THE ENDING HAS BEGUN

SEAN JOHNNY B.
PLATT TRUANT

CHAPTER 1

Clara didn't see the point of this.

The Den's games were definitely interesting at first, but quickly lost their luster. After playing those first few times, she kept with it mainly because Sadeem seemed to enjoy watching her. She'd turn the simple wooden puzzle cubes through the now-obvious patterns and he'd grow giddy, or she'd move the lights around on the electronic games and he'd gape in pleased astonishment. Clara felt like she was somehow deceiving him: claiming credit for something anyone could have done. But she kept on, because it pleased him, and the others. Though bored, she pretended to enjoy it. And while she didn't see why the others kept prompting her to play, there wasn't much else to do down here anyway.

"You do not wish to turn it in that direction?" Sadeem was watching her with his earnest brown eyes, brows raised. If Clara had to guess, he was probably in his sixties, but something in his manner — or perhaps in his movement — reminded her of someone much younger. A surrogate parent instead of a grandparent, perhaps. He had curious eyes that Clara hadn't seen in people his age. They said that Sadeem's mind was hungry to learn anything new — that discovery of something contradicting his worldview would be welcome rather than threatening.

"Do you want me to turn it that way?" Clara asked in reply.

She looked over in the dim. The place she'd been staying for the past days had seemed frightening and claustrophobic at first, but was now almost homey. Mullah made the earthen tunnels comfortable. The robe-clad men and women had always seemed so serious when they'd been tailing her topside group, but Clara had never been as afraid as the others, and now it seemed like she'd been right. They were focused, not scary.

"I do not *want* you to do anything," Sadeem said in his metered, precise English. "I was merely inquiring."

"You're sure?"

"Yes, of course. I only wish for you to play."

Clara looked down at the puzzle. The thing had been an almost indecipherable knot of small wooden shapes linked by threads when she'd started. It had struck her as being like the Christmas lights they'd strung for a few years in Heaven's Veil: a mess of gnarled wires, refusing to be straightened. But after playing the game for a few minutes, Clara had seen that there was order to the tangled lines connecting the cubes. It didn't take long to straighten them before she could reassemble them into a large wooden sphere, and already Clara was halfway there — where it always became worse before getting better.

Clara looked back at Sadeem. She wanted to ask again, but there was no point. He wasn't trying to guide her solution, but he obviously couldn't see it himself. She couldn't shake the feeling that her play meant something to the Mullah. They weren't merely eager for the out-of-place little white girl to entertain herself in their midst; her actions somehow mattered.

She looked down. Saw the next major phase in her mind but knew she'd need to backtrack. So, ignoring Sadeem's confused expression, she unraveled the puzzle and then began to assemble it again once the constriction was passed.

"Clara, what made you — " He paused as something boomed from the distance. It was a far-away sound, and his distraction only lasted a second. "What made you decide to approach it that way?"

"I was just playing."

Sadeem looked disappointed. His eyes ticked to the side, and again the ground seemed to tremble.

"Mr. Sadeem?"

"Just Sadeem."

"Sadeem?" Clara repeated.

"Yes?"

"Can I ask you a question?"

"Of course."

"I've noticed that none of the other kids play these games."

"That is not a question."

Clara gave Sadeem a look she might have given her mother. She felt the familiar divide form inside. Mom missed her — but didn't just miss her; was *worried sick* about her. Literally *sick*. Sometimes, Clara felt that illness through her mother's mind. But she was safe here; she knew this was, somehow, where she was supposed to be. It just felt right. And besides, Piper knew she was okay. Clara had seen her wake up inside the darkness like a torch coming alight not too long ago. She could probably talk to Piper if she tried, the way Grandpa spoke to Kindred. She meant to try once this round of play finished. Because there were questions Clara wanted to ask, too — like why she'd felt punched right before Piper had appeared, and Mr. Cameron's mind had suddenly changed, to become part of something Clara didn't fully understand.

3

"All right," Sadeem said as Clara held her assessing look, "it is because they are not games for children."

"They're for grown-ups?"

Sadeem nodded.

"Is it okay for kids to play them?"

"It depends on the child."

"Me, I mean."

"Obviously," Sadeem said.

"But why ... " Clara trailed off, hearing an argument down one of the tunnels, in Arabic. She'd probably have been able to understand if the speaker came closer. She didn't speak Arabic, but languages felt to Clara like these puzzles. You just needed to see how the parts fit together.

"What is it?" Clara asked of the commotion.

"Nothing to worry about. You were asking about the toys."

"Why do you want me to play with them?"

"Because you wanted to play with them."

Clara watched him, considering. It was chicken and egg. She liked to play with them because the Mullah, for some reason, took such joy in her doing so. But without their interest, they barely held her attention. Not the games made of physical things, not the games on the tablets and the computer in what the Mullah (jokingly, Clara thought) called the Nerve Center. The Nerve Center was an interesting place, filled with screens of places both seen and unseen. Clara saw views of the palace (including the occasional shot of her family and friends), but also cities she'd never been to. A place of lush green, of ancient ruins so different from Egypt's and yet so similar. There was one man, Quaid, who monitored the Nerve Center. Once she'd heard him mention Ravi, the boy she'd met up top and who, Clara gathered, had broken contact with the others. And in that conversation — too whispered to be helpful — she'd heard Quaid mention Peers.

Clara, watching Sadeem, called him on his crap. "C'mon."

"What? You do not believe me?"

Another booming from above, much larger than the last, came rolling down one of the longest tunnels. If Clara's sense of direction was intact, it was coming from the palace. In the other direction, Mullah tunnels seemed to yawn far into the desert beyond the wall. She'd considered following them the way she'd once followed what she'd thought was Peers Basara's dog, but there were always polite guards barring her in the central area. Keeping her with the toys, playing with apparent purpose.

Shouts — urgent but distant enough to dismiss — followed the boom. A big one, enough to sift dust from the tunnel ceiling.

"What's going on?" Clara asked.

"Nothing unanticipated."

"They sound like something's really wrong."

"The fact that it was anticipated does not mean it is pleasant. Or that it will be."

"What is it?"

"Tell me about the games."

Behind Sadeem, someone ran by, shouting. A woman, yelling as if giving commands, gone before Clara could try and translate.

"I think I'm done for now."

"Then just explain. How do you see the solutions?"

"What's going on, Sadeem?"

"Let the others worry about that. We will be moving, but nothing should concern you."

Quaid rushed into the room, white robes rustling, shouting at Sadeem in Arabic. Clara focused. Saw the words in her head. Rewound her memory, hearing the syllables that had eluded her. She played forward, listening to Quaid at different speeds. She turned the words like blocks. A cypher formed. Unlocked a corner of the language — enough for Clara to get an alarming glimpse.

"*Explode? What* exploded?"

"It's not your concern," Sadeem said.

"You said, 'Charles.' Are you talking about Charlie?"

Quaid ignored her. This time Clara heard "Coffey." A word with no translation, said in English.

"*Mr. Sadeem?*" Clara said, her voice closer to demanding than concerned. Almost righteous. She heard it herself, and wondered.

"Return to your games, Clara."

But this irritated Quaid further. He raised his voice, and with a greater sample of the language to twist and turn, Clara found herself able to understand even more. She disengaged part of her mind and allowed herself to drift — toward her mother, toward Piper, toward Mr. Cameron. And when she pulled back and spoke again, her objection came in a shout.

"*What happened to Cameron?*"

"Calm yourself," Quaid snapped. "We said nothing of Mr. Bannister."

But Clara hadn't drawn only from their discussion. She'd plucked that right from Piper's distraught mind, from Cameron's absent — or distantly altered — one.

Quaid continued. Clara didn't bother to try understanding; his clipped Arabic came out in a string of rapid-fire nonsense. At the end, Quaid's eyes were huge and waiting. Sadeem's were wide and worried. Almost frightened.

"Clara. Gather your belongings. Hurry."

"I don't have any belongings down here."

"All the games. Anything you've touched. Anything there." He gestured toward the collection in front of her then kicked a bag , his message clear. "Hurry. Please."

Clara wanted to ask but did as instructed. Thirty seconds later she had a bag full of Mullah puzzles plus a cup she'd been drinking from, now drained. Sadeem was behind her, practically shoving, his urgency clear.

"What is it?" Clara demanded.

"They cannot see your mind. It is important that they do not see your body down here, either."

"Who?"

Sadeem's hand was on her back, shoving Clara into a small, cunningly concealed door. He'd shown it to her before with a wink — a man conveying something he wasn't supposed to. Behind the door was a closet beneath a subterranean set of stairs, but without a special key, you'd never know the closet was there. The place was full of secrets. Mullah tunnels reminded Clara of Derinkuyu. No wonder the Mullah had pursued their group so handily there. They were treading familiar turf.

"Stay inside until someone comes for you. Do you understand me?"

Clara nodded. He pushed the door, but she spoke again before it was fully seated.

"Sadeem?"

"We must hurry, Clara."

"I'm scared."

He looked for a moment like he might shut the door in his rush, but Sadeem paused long enough to meet her eyes. His look was soft. Sympathetic.

"Now is not the time for fear," he said. "That comes later."

The door shut. Clara was suddenly in full dark, the obsidian curtain pierced only by a tiny sliver of light at the short door's upper corner.

She heard a growing hum. She put her eye to the slit, squinting, trying to see through the minuscule crack as the sound mounted, buzzing like a massive swarm of angry hornets.

She saw Sadeem. She saw Quaid.

She saw them pause their rushing about then turn to face something unseen, hands raised as if facing policemen.

Then Clara saw nothing more as the chamber filled with tiny buckshot-sized metal balls, the entire mass surging like a swarm — buzzing, frenzied, and furious.

CHAPTER 2

Chaos reigned beyond the glass as Ember Flats tore itself apart.

The Ark was open. Every human soul could feel the psychic buzz as judgment began and ended, as the Astral verdict was decided, as humanity failed its biggest test. Reptars prowled the streets. Shuttles obliterated any who crossed their path. There was a hum in the air, resonating between every human mind and the stone repeaters beyond the city: citizens all looking inward, seeing their faults, realizing the betrayal of Heaven's Veil with its phony viceroy and the city's ensuing destruction. Knowing they would die betrayed and could do nothing to stop it. Gulping each breath in fear and outright panic. Seeing, finally, that the time had come for the human race to be decimated so the few who remained could start all over again.

It had happened in the past, and it was happening now: an extinction-level event, unfolding before them. Kindred, standing beside Mara Jabari, gazed furiously up at the massive ship hovering above Ember Flats, hands balled into fists at his sides.

How hadn't he known the Deathbringer was on its way? He must have seen it at some point, before the change.

But more and more, Kindred found it hard to tap into his Astral side. Ever since he'd woken to his true identity back in Heaven's Veil (an Astral in human form, somewhere between the Titan he'd once been and the man Meyer Dempsey still was), he'd been an intruder in an odd middle ground, able to touch the planet's human and alien halves. He'd sensed nearby motherships; he'd felt the collective and Divinity inside it; he'd always been able to operate his old species' technologies when he encountered them. Yet at the same time, he'd been as human as Meyer, complete with all his old memories.

But over the past months, Kindred had begun to feel his two halves like water and dye. The two wouldn't stay separate; eventually, the dye claimed everything. Humanity's imperfections had swirled throughout Kindred until there was no Astral left within him. And so now, standing before the big window, Kindred could still sense the Ember Flats mothership — but he couldn't feel the colossus. Whatever the huge ship was, he was as clueless as the humans.

And it made him livid.

"*What is it?*" Piper asked, looking upward, her voice full of dread.

Kindred looked over, realizing that his anger extended to Piper. She suddenly struck him as an idiot. Cameron was dead, pitched right into the Ark's fucking abyss. Cameron's humanity had polluted it the way humanity had soiled Kindred — and now he was barely Astral while the Ark was coughing, choking on mankind the way Divinity had retched on Meyer's emotions. If he'd not infected the collective, it wouldn't have squeezed out the Pall like pus from a zit. And if Cameron hadn't died in some vain attempt to confuse the archive's judgment — or at least *bias* it, making it emotional rather than objective — then Piper wouldn't suddenly be an obvious, shining, white-hot empath. The answers were all so obvious. And yet here she was, gaping as if her mind could see nothing despite her new gifts, asking the stupidest questions.

"It's a ship," Kindred snapped.

Piper didn't look over. Instead she said another dumb thing: "It's bigger than the city."

Kindred clenched his fists harder. He felt the very human sensation of pain, fingernails cutting tiny moons into the heel of his palm. Piper sounded like this was all a big surprise — and yet it was obvious that if she'd just get out of her own way, she could see much more than him.

But *Kindred* was supposed to be the knowledgeable one, the man in charge. But now he was as low on the totem pole as his daughter — if that's what Lila was. The panic and fury he felt at the loss of control was ...

Well, it was very *human*.

"You said you had a plan," Kindred said to Mara Jabari, ignoring Piper.

"It's too late."

He felt his control slip another notch. "What do you mean *it's too fucking late?*"

"I didn't know this was coming. None of us did."

Goddammit. Kindred didn't like standing still, motionless by the big windows with the others, lined up like targets in a shooting gallery. Beyond the palace wall, the city was killing itself. Every human was suddenly for himself as Titans pursued them, becoming black creatures with teeth and claws. But it was all shock and awe. The Astrals wouldn't carry out their extermination hand-to-hand or one-by-one. You didn't need to be an empath to see that.

This was about creating fear.

This was about preparing the city — and likely the planet — for whatever the ship would soon unleash.

"What *was* the plan?" Kindred asked.

"It doesn't matter."

"What was the plan?"

Jabari looked over at Kindred's raised voice. For a moment she looked dumbstruck, but then she sobered and answered him straight.

"There's an escape vehicle."

"Great."

"But we'll never reach it now."

"Why not?"

"We weren't counting on something like this." Her eyes ticked toward the window, and Kindred knew she had to mean the enormous ship, which looked like a moon in low orbit. "Every projection we ran at the Da Vinci Initiate only considered motherships and shuttles. This is unprecedented. All the historical records mentioned ships of two sizes, never three."

"Probably because by the time the big one shows up, everyone's dead."

Kindred, annoyed, swiveled toward Piper. Jabari saw his face and raised a hand.

Stop it, Jabari's eyes seemed to say. *Whatever is wrong with you right now, get a grip and try to help, or we'll never get out of here alive.*

"At the Initiate, we looked through dozens of mass exterminations — those suspected by the Ancient Aliens theorists and a few known only by us. The pattern is always the same. Every time the aliens come, we fall into some sort of equilibrium. There's always a period of cooperation, where it's as if we've formed a dual society. You'll see great inventions: machines that fly, create food, help humanity wage war. But then all of a sudden the records stop. There's a plague. A flood. A meteor strike. And afterward, only a small core of humans remains. Evidence of the new inventions vanishes, and it's as if humanity's clock is reset."

"We knew this." Meyer didn't sound as impatient as Kindred — just the normal amount of restless agitation he always had under pressure.

Jabari nodded. "We collaborated extensively with Benjamin's lab. He and Charlie would both tell you the same things I'm telling you now. But what they didn't know — what *nobody* knew other than the Da Vinci Initiate — was that the Astrals left behind a record of their version of events, too. And those records told us that — "

Somewhere unseen, a massive explosion struck, shaking the floor and glass in the mansion's windows. Kindred heard several crashes from elsewhere as fragile items toppled and broke.

Jabari looked back, toward the commotion. "We have to get below. Come with me. There is a basement."

Kindred grabbed her arm as she moved away. "Is that the way to your escape plan?"

"It's the way to hide."

"Hide from a global extermination event?"

"You don't understand." She was tugging against Kindred's grip, but he held her firm. "This is a show of might. They won't reset the human clock by killing us one by one. We must hide and wait for this phase to finish. Then maybe we can recalibrate and find a way out before they do whatever they're planning next."

"You said there was a way out. An escape plan."

"Forget it. The records showed us what we thought were predictable patterns. They'd move the motherships to create a sort of global antenna, like what was happening with the Apex and the array in Heaven's Veil before Cameron stopped it with his key. I don't have time to explain, but they seem to have layered redundancies — and Cameron shutting down their first antenna wasn't just something they knew was possible; it was something they practically encouraged. And — "

Meyer moved to Jabari's other side. Her eyes weren't as panicked Lila's or Piper's, but she was clearly pulling against

Kindred, eager to run and hide. Meyer's eyes, however, were furious.

"What do you mean, they encouraged it? My wife died shutting down that antenna. Did you know that would happen? Is this all some sort of ... some *game* you didn't bother to tell your former collaborators about? If the motherships are going to do the same thing now that the pyramid did and it was all for nothing – "

Another explosion, larger than the first. Deeper in the house, someone screamed. When the shaking ceased, new cracks had formed in the plaster. One of the smaller windows had shattered without breaking away, its clear surface webbed and opaque.

"We need to get below! The basement is a reinforced bunker. It will protect us if they level the mansion!"

"We're not hiding. We're getting out of here if there's a way out," Kindred told Jabari.

"You're not listening! We knew the mothership would move away when the judgment event began. The shuttles would likely be too occupied to follow. But we have to travel in the open; do you understand? We can't move unseen with the big ship above. They'll see. They'll know! If we blow our only chance now, we'll never have another!"

Jabari tugged again. Kindred tightened his grip, turning her dark skin red beneath his fist. Kindred's ambient anger – whether it came from inside himself or from the archive and the stone repeaters – made him feel powerful. He'd go outside and fight with his fists if he had to. As the expression went, it was better to die on his feet than live on his knees ... or to hide, in a stone bunker, like a coward.

He'd done that before. Even if it was just inside of Meyer Dempsey's memories, he'd tried that once, in Vail, and it had turned out to be exactly what the Astrals wanted him to do.

"We're getting out of here. Your vehicle. Where is it? *What* is it?"

Jabari met his eyes, then Meyer's. There were more flashes from outside. Screams were audible even through the reinforced glass. Screams — and Reptar purrs. She seemed to be weighing their mettle — trying to decide if there was any point in continuing to protest.

"It's not just one vehicle. It's a fleet of small vehicles. Taken together, we call it 'the Cradle.'"

"What kind of vehicles?"

"The only thing we thought might be able to move unseen from above."

"Cars in tunnels," Meyer guessed.

"Submersibles," Jabari corrected. "Like miniature submarines, able to skim the surface when it seems safe. The river isn't deep. But it was the only chance we saw."

"Who else knows?" Kindred fought his rising temper. Jabari had this plan all along. *All along.*

"Only a small inner circle. And the other viceroys."

"Not *all* the other viceroys," Kindred said.

"We didn't know if we could trust you. Heaven's Veil was special. It was the only site without Ancient Aliens significance. The only capital with a Money Pit." She swallowed. "The only viceroy who seems to have been replaced by an Astral shapeshifter."

Meyer and Kindred shared a glance. Then both turned to Jabari, fury thick in the room's thin air. Was it possible that Meyer was the anomaly rather than Jabari?

"Where is it?" Meyer growled.

"You'll never make it," she said simply.

"*Where!*"

"On the Nile. Upriver, near the first of the jade monoliths. Away from the capital, at the end of the Orion Road. It's an area we've protected from the freaks and cannibals in Hell's Corridor, but you'll need to cross their land to get there. We have an understanding with them, but you do not. Do you understand what that means?"

"We made it past the crews before," Meyer said.

"It's not just them. You can't travel out of sight. Even if the mothership has moved away as we predicted, the colossus will see you. You're a fool if you think the Astrals inside it don't know exactly who you are and how to spot you. Not after what we pulled out there. You understand now why they let us tell the world about Heaven's Veil and the two Meyers, don't you? Every human mind inside the neural network is a collective we can broadcast on screens, so you can just bet the Astrals can tap it. All we did out there today was blow your cover. We turned every person in this city into another pair of eyes that will follow you wherever you try to go."

"We'll take our chances."

"There are three submersibles. Each holds only four people. They run on diesel. We didn't think we could trust electric; we didn't know for sure how often we'd be able to surface to let solar panels charge the batteries. They have full tanks, and there are spare cans in each. But Meyer, they won't get you far. It's over 250 kilometers to the river delta, but traveling into open sea was always a last resort. The plan was to stop once away from Ember Flats, raise a satellite antenna, and use a signal we've pirated to get in touch with the others. But with the big ship up there with all its interference, you'll never — "

"Which others?"

"*The other viceroys!*" She seemed threadbare, nearing panic. There was a fire burning beyond the wall now. Another window must have broken in a subsequent crash because now sounds from outside were obvious — including purring Reptars, and the discharging weapons of shuttles.

"But we always knew there might be unknowns!" Jabari continued, forestalling Kindred's response. "Plan A was to establish contact viceroy to viceroy — something we could only do once outside the cities, after judgment began and Astral eyes turned toward us while they rallied their troops for global extinction. Plan B, for Ember Flats, was to make it all the way to the open water if communication couldn't be established. We'd take the submersibles to Lesan Area, possibly to Alexandria, then into the Mediterranean. Again, we'd try to establish communication once away from population centers. But there was always the chance that we'd have to scrap it all — that something unexpected might happen like a giant *fucking ship taking over half the sky!*"

Kindred looked up at Meyer, his temper temporarily diffused. He'd never heard Jabari swear. Didn't know she could. She looked wild-eyed, and wasn't alone. Lila had shut down, practically in a ball on a chair across the hallway. Piper was mute, gazing at the descending chaos beyond and the unmoving, ominous eclipse of the mammoth alien ship. Cameron was dead. Charlie and Jeanine Coffey were probably dead, too. Peers was missing — probably dead as well; why not? Clara was still gone. Leaving the city meant leaving her behind, wherever she was.

Safe. That's where she was. That's what Piper had said, and what remained of Kindred's internal sense agreed. They shouldn't be worrying about Clara. Time had come to make sure *they* were safe, too.

An itch made Kindred turn. Piper and especially Lila had both looked up and were now staring at Kindred, Meyer, and Jabari. It was as if the women had heard his thoughts about Clara. Probably had.

"Please," Jabari said. "Try and understand. We ran every possible scenario. We couldn't know this big ship was coming, and for all we know there are ships like this over every one of the capitals. We might *never* reach the other viceroys. You might end up out of fuel, bobbing around in open water in a tiny tin can. We're all safer here. This was always — " She patted the wall beside her, indicating the entirety of the mansion. "Our last, best option if it all fell apart."

Kindred watched her. Trying to see all the way down to the floor of her soul. This woman — unlike Meyer Dempsey but possibly like every one of the other viceroys — had been allowed to rule as herself rather than an alien puppet. What did it mean that she'd turned on the Astrals? What did it mean that, apparently, all of the *other* viceroys had turned on the Astrals, as well? Were the Astrals really that stupid? Were they really that ignorant of human nature, to fail at truly converting even one of their eight turncoats?

"We're going," Meyer said. "I'm not going to curl up in a hole in the ground and hide from the aliens ... *again*."

A rushing shout echoed from behind them, making Kindred jump. Feet coming fast, like someone mounting a sneak attack from the rear.

Kindred turned.

The newcomer struck.

CHAPTER 3

"Howdy."

The hairless, alabaster-skinned Titan turned toward the sound, its expression the same as the one that seemed permanently affixed to the face of every Titan — vaguely surprised but eager to help whoever had sneaked up behind him, like a maitre d' caught unaware.

The Titan watched the middle-aged man who'd approached him while he stood outside the Ark courtyard. The human was dressed in a rumpled but clean button-down shirt and blue jeans. He wore a brown belt, and the tips of scuffed brown boots protruded from the bottoms of his pants. He had a long, lean face that other humans would see as equal parts weathered, like old cowhide, and ugly. His most distinctive feature was probably his hands, big and lean; they seemed to be made of bone and leather. As the Titan watched, he used the index finger and thumb of one of those big dextrous hands to pluck a reed or thistle from between his teeth. Then he spoke again.

"You're not very talkative, are you?"

The Titan cocked his head.

"I know this is a cliché, but I wonder if you'd be willing to do me a favor." The man chuckled, creasing his forehead in wrinkles. "*Take me to your leader.*"

The Titan said nothing.

"I know you've got shuttles around the Ark. Maybe you could let me knock on one of them doors."

Still, the Titan was silent.

The stranger shifted as if settling in. He moved his weight from one boot-clad foot to the other. His mouth worked, as if assessing the mute conversationalist before him. Then he returned the reed to his lips like a smoker with his cigarette and fished something from his pocket. A tiny clack filled a convenient auditory pause between an explosion and a loud grinding from beyond. Then there was a banging, like a gunshot. Someone screamed, and the evening sky lit with the flash of a shuttle blast. The man didn't flinch, as if deaf and immune to the shaking earth.

"I think I know what's going on here," the human said, his manner serious. "I'm being rude, aren't I? Expecting to get a favor without giving anything first. That's not the way my mamma taught me. Promise. Not that my mamma was an ordinary lady. You know what I'm talking about, don'tcha?"

The Titan moved slightly, blocking the courtyard from view, angling his large body between the strange human and the courtyard where the archive was still pulsing and glowing, from which shuttles had been ferrying back and forth since the city had started its dying.

The human held up a hand, fingers splayed. There were shiny black spheres the size of smallish golf balls between his index and middle fingers, between his middle and ring fingers, and between his ring finger and pinky. One big hand with three black balls, palm forward like a greeting.

The man moved his fingers. The balls rolled down into his palm. It happened slowly, the movement precise and controlled. The balls didn't touch. Then he closed his palm only slightly, and they did, each one rolling against the edge of the other. Subtle shifts in his hand muscles moved in circles. Tiny chime-like sounds filled the air.

"I'll bet it's boring, being out here all by yourself," the stranger said. "Just standing around. Gawking at nothing. They tell you to stand guard, but really it's mostly just you being here, doing nothing. Or is it more like you're just part of the bigger group? Not really by yourself at all, but part of that big ol' alien *collective*. Am I right?"

The Titan's eyebrows rose, curious. He watched the balls move in the human's hand, chasing each other in circles. The movement was hypnotic. Slow. Taking its time.

"You'd think I'd know, wouldn't you?" the man asked. "But I don't. Just like I don't know you, friend. But I could, if I tried. What do you think? Here. Take this."

The Titan looked down. His own hand was out, powder white. One of the black balls was resting in his palm, like a diseased eye against the pale backdrop. He didn't remember taking the ball but had apparently done so.

The air between them seemed to blur. An observer, watching the two figures from the outside, would have seen a drooping of eyelids. A sagging of heads. And then nothing, except that each looked up when the moment was over, understanding somehow clarified.

"You can keep that. I have plenty."

The Titan's eyes moved from the black sphere in his palm to the three balls still in the stranger's hand. The stranger hadn't gone into his pocket again. It was as if he'd summoned the new ball from nowhere.

The man put one hand over the other to cover the balls. When he parted his hands there were two black balls per palm. Then he did it again, and this time there were three in each hand, circling with tiny chimes. The city soundscape seemed to have gone mute. Not far off, a red beam lanced into a building, and it detonated, throwing brick like shrapnel into the air. Debris rolled between the Titan and the man, but neither looked down to see it.

"Thing about being me," the man said, "is that there's always plenty to go around. I can be where I was or I can be where I stand. I can be what I used to be or what I am now. It's not always easy. Not like you forgetting where that gift I gave you ended up."

The man nodded toward the Titan's palm. The ball was gone.

He raised his right hand. Combined it with his left. There were six balls in one hand, no balls in the other. Then five, four, and the original three. Nothing hit the ground. Nothing rolled up the man's sleeves. The balls circled fingers and thumb as if mocking gravity. He splayed his fingers with the balls between them, rolled the balls from back to front, clenched them in his fist, and made them vanish. Then he opened the opposite hand and the balls were now there, still moving.

"Funny thing about all of this," the man said, closing his hand and opening it again to reveal four balls instead of three, then five instead of four, "is that I think we both know there's more happening than meets the eye. The question isn't about yes or know. It's not really about win or lose. It's about *how*, ain't it? There's what you see and what you don't. But it's hard for anyone to guess what's going to happen if they don't see the *how* and the *why*. If they only see a slice, is what I mean."

The man pressed his hands together. The balls vanished as if they'd never been.

"If you thought you knew how I did that trick, friend, you'd be wrong. Just like if you think you know all that's in play this time you came to visit your little ant farm." He held out his large, empty hands and smiled — a strange expression on his long and leathery face, which seemed far more suited to scowling. "Now how 'bout you let me in to have a chat with the man in charge? Or the thing in charge; sorry."

The man stepped forward, toward the shuttles. The Titan moved to block his way.

"I just want to talk. And despite how you won't stop yammering on, I don't think you're the fella to talk to."

He tried to move around the Titan again. Still, the alien blocked his way. So the man said, "Think you can see all that needs seeing? Think you've got it all figured out?"

The air shimmered between them. A thought, finally lubricated and frequencies duly tuned, shot from one mind to the other, handily translated by the black orb, their minds finding resonance like clacking spheres:

It doesn't matter.

"Of course it matters."

Judgment is at hand. Selection is coming. Extermination will follow.

"Same as always?"

Same as always.

"What about me?"

You don't matter.

"What about the *kids*, fella?"

Nothing changes. As with earlier epochs, they will self-select, and some will remain.

"To perpetuate the species, huh?" the human said, nodding knowingly, hands on his hips.

Yes.

"And no other reason. No other point in considering the kids. Even those your stubborn asses can't see?"

The Titan's head cocked.

"I'm on your side, friend. Which is to say I'm on no one's."

The man tried again to circle around but this time didn't stop when the Titan moved in front of him. He pushed

23

against the alien's strong arms. Fought him. Punched at him, determined to pass.

A rolling, gravel-filled noise percolated from the Titan's throat. When the man looked up, he saw a blue spark blooming inside the Titan's mouth.

Instead of backing away, the man pushed harder. And as he pushed, the Titan changed. Shining black carapace covered smooth white skin. Limbs elongated and cracked, becoming multi-jointed, creaking with stretching tendons. The man stepped back, seeing the half-Reptar thing, watching it shift.

"Let me through," the stranger said, "or this time, everyone loses."

The Reptar didn't hesitate. The psychic bond had soured; the man could feel its animal cunning replacing calm Titan logic. He felt its bloodlust and primal anger. He seemed to see himself through the Reptar's eyes as it stretched out, jaw unhinging, and bit him in half.

Only the man wasn't bitten at all. He was standing, fully intact in his blue jeans and dress shirt, rolling three black balls in his big right hand.

The Reptar pulled back, confused. It had tasted flesh. It was still swallowing something that wasn't precisely there when the human signaled to a pair of Titans who'd come to investigate the Reptar's purr, to see what was at the courtyard's perimeter. The Reptar didn't turn to look, but both Titans trained eyes on the human, polite expressions on their faces.

"You there," the stranger called. "Did I ever tell you about my cousin Timmy?"

The Reptar coiled its panther-like rear legs and leaped, but as it launched itself at the man, there was a low yet horrible popping, and it detonated in a flesh bomb of black shell and gore.

The stranger looked at his shirt with distaste, reaching down to flick away wet pieces of the Reptar's body, then strolling nonchalantly forward, toward a trio of shuttles. The door of the middle one was open. The human made for it, nodding toward the two newcomers with a tip of an invisible hat.

This time, the Titans did not interfere.

CHAPTER 4

Clara stirred, found herself blind, then remembered that she'd fallen asleep in the tiny, cramped closet under the subterranean set of stairs in the Mullah tunnels. That realization led to a question: Why, exactly, had she fallen asleep? Sadeem had shoved her into the secret cubby, and she'd watched what looked like millions of flying Astral spy BBs swallow them whole.

Even thinking back on what she'd seen through the slit around the concealed doorjamb made Clara's head feel garbled. The scene had been like watching swimmers in undulating metallic waves, except they never surfaced for air. There was only the slow — and yet somehow furious — ebb and flow of massing drones, moving in tandem as if they were one thing rather than untold numbers of individuals.

Kind of like the Astrals themselves.

Or *humans*. Because that's something that had been clear to Clara from the start, though it often felt like she was the only one who truly got it. Sadeem and the others were fascinated with how she solved puzzles years too advanced for her (or perhaps years too advanced for even the wisest adults), just like how Mom and Dad and Piper and all the others had once been fascinated by how she learned anything. They seemed enthralled that Clara had walked when she had, that she'd talked when she had, that she'd spoken in full sentences from the start and understood even what her parents tried to protect her from. But how could a girl *not* know how to do all those things? It was all so obvious. She'd known most of it from the start, before she really even had a body, before she left her mother's womb. What was the big deal? Did "normal" kids just decide not to walk and talk and be who they obviously already were? That had never struck Clara as particularly *normal*.

After swarming the room for a while, the balls must have left. She could hear no commotion outside. But *that*, Clara had no memory of. Because she seemed to have fallen asleep, watching the lazy rhythms, feeling the sights and sounds of shifting silver waves working on her mind like a lullaby.

She put her eye to the crack, peeked out, and saw nothing but an empty room beyond.

"*Sadeem!*" She said it in a harsh whisper.

There was no response.

Clara twisted her face all she could, shifting from one eye to the other, laying her nose to the side and pressing her cheek to the door, hoping to see more than her limited panorama. But she could only make out that tiny sliver of the room.

"*Sadeem! Quaid! Anyone!*"

Nothing.

Clara touched the knob. Turned it slowly so as not to make sound. Opened the door a hair and peeked out the new crack, still seeing and hearing nothing. She opened it farther, millimeter by millimeter, until there was enough of a gap that there was no longer any point in stealth. She opened it the rest of the way and looked out into the Mullah's underground chamber, tunnels branching left and right.

The strung lights were still lit, black cords tacked to the walls and ceilings in long ribbons.

The rooms were utterly silent. Even when Clara had first followed the dog that wasn't a dog to this place, they hadn't been so still. But now, she'd be able to hear a pin drop from the complex's other end. The echo, in all this stillness, would have seemed titanic.

But: nothing.

"*Sadeem!*"

Nothing.

Clara closed the cubby behind her, aware that if something was quietly amiss, she might still need a place to hide, and crossed into the far tunnel, then the next chamber, and beyond. There was no one around.

She stifled her fear. Sometimes — most times, really — Clara could sense the emotions of others around her, even if they weren't there. That's why she didn't worry about the Mullah's intentions once she'd met them, and why she didn't fret much about her mom or the others. Clara understood that the Mullah would finish with what they needed and then send her home. Mom would get past her worry. But right now she sensed an emotional void. The ever-present knowledge— served up, it seemed, by some sort of invisible censor for Clara to sample — had gone missing. She couldn't stretch her mind to try look. It simply wasn't there.

She didn't know where the Mullah were or what they might be thinking.

Before, even when she'd had that strange feeling about Cameron and the city's mood had soured like bad milk above them, she hadn't been too concerned about her family and friends because she'd known they were fine and would — for at least the time being — remain so. But now she couldn't sense any of them, either.

She couldn't see or feel or hear her mother inside her mind.

She couldn't feel Piper.

She couldn't feel either of her grandfathers.

She could only feel herself.

That never happened. She felt acutely, intensely alone, as if she'd gone deaf and blind in unison and was being forced to navigate her world by touch.

She forced herself to breathe slowly, and stay calm.

Chill out, Clara. This must be how it is for most people every day. For Mom. For Mr. Cameron. For all your Mullah friends. Everyone but you and the other freaks seem to do just fine without a window into anyone else's head. You're fine.

She moved on, feeling as if she were groping through the dark.

Just keep putting one foot in front of the other.

Before long, Clara arrived at a section of tunnel she recognized. Only now the slab at the hallway's end was open, and she could see muted fluorescent light beyond. She walked out, found herself in a more traditional-seeming basement, then moved up a quiet set of stairs. She was in a dwelling, also vacant.

She moved to the window. And that's when it hit her.

The wave of intense emotion — not bubbling up from inside this time, as usually happened when she was alone and her mind traveled to those she cared about most. This was raw and forceful, beaten into her from the outside.

Now that Clara could see the city streets, she couldn't help but feel them as well. The entire world, so recently quiet, was now stuffed full of noise. It was like the time she'd borrowed Uncle Trevor's music player back in Heaven's Veil then hit play without checking the volume. With her walls down and her sensitivity all the way up to catch any whiff of emotion, intensity from the streets was a tsunami of mental

29

clatter. For a few terrifying seconds, it felt like it might blast the brain right out of her ears.

Clara winced, bit down on the feeling, and gripped the windowsill until she found herself able to breathe again. Then her muscles relaxed, and she looked out on the city, realizing she could see and hear and feel and sense and taste *everything*.

While she'd been playing games, Grandpa Meyer and Grandpa Kindred had made some sort of announcement. Clara could hear snippets of that announcement deep beneath the raw fear that rode on the surface. That's what had started this all — or maybe more accurately, that had been the first in a chain of events that had caused whatever had gone wrong.

Betrayal.

Terror.

Confusion.

Meyer Dempsey was supposed to be dead, or at least disappeared. There was only supposed to be one of him — the one wasn't far off from a modern Hitler or Stalin — two names Clara didn't factually understand but knew plenty from mental context. But now there were two, and they were very much alive. Now Heaven's Veil wasn't his fault at all. Now blame belonged to the Astrals, and the aliens weren't doing much to contradict the story.

The Ark is open.

The inner whisper made her flinch. She'd been there, at Mount Sinai. She'd seen what had come out. She'd known what it must mean. How had she missed this? Had the Mullah really kept her mind so occupied with the endless puzzles? Had they done it on purpose, to keep her blind?

But it was true: Cameron had opened the Ark. And what she'd sensed seemed to be true: The Ark was an archive of all humanity had done and said and felt and intended and explored and rejected and exploited and committed since the Astrals had left the last time. It was a record of humanity's good and evil, and popping its top had called the Astrals to sort through the evidence and render their judgment.

The judgment was in.

And the verdict was *guilty*.

Ember Flats knew it. Even if the people couldn't spell it out, they felt it in their bones.

Clara moved to the door. Looked up. And found that the presence she'd felt wasn't all in her mind. She could see the enormous low moon exactly where she'd expected, for the last thirty seconds, to see it.

The Dark Rider. That's what the Mullah's minds called it. The final Horseman. The bringer of death, the one Mullah legend said started the plagues.

Clara ducked back behind the door, closing it most of the way, as a Reptar patrol galloped by on their strange insectile legs: half-distorted black mammals, half *things*. The horror of seeing them was more immediate and visceral, less predictive. Knowing what was happening made it no less terrifying. Seeing the entire picture did not, Clara realized, make her any more prepared or unafraid to face it.

Clara closed the door, slumped against the wall, and slid down until she was sitting on the floor of the unknown stranger's empty house. She didn't feel special. She didn't feel Lightborn.

She felt like a seven-year-old girl who wanted her mother.

Clara began to cry.

Then there was a knock on the door.

CHAPTER 5

Piper saw it coming, but there was no time to stop it.

Peers, in a dead sprint but looking behind him as if being chased, collided full-on with Kindred's back. The pair didn't crumple so much as slam flat onto the floor. Kindred managed to break the fall with his hands, but Peers wasn't as elegant. His momentum rolled him along Kindred's body like a stuntman toppling across the hood of a parked car. He ended up crashing shoulder first into the floor beside Kindred then sliding across the hardwood until he wedged into the corner where floor met wall.

Kindred was up in a second, every inch the intimidating physical specter Meyer — or his duplicates — always managed to be. Meyer himself was two feet away, his eyes also on Peers, his hands also raising to fight. It seemed to dawn on them both that Peers hadn't tackled; he'd bumbled in like a fool. And as he was standing, rubbing his shoulder, his eyes were so wide, they were like giant white saucers with circles of spilled tea in the center.

"Meyer!" Peers blurted. "Thank God. You must come with me."

"Where?"

"There's a way out. There's ... " His eyes went to Jabari. "She has a plan. I need to get you out of here."

Meyer's eyes narrowed. "*You?*"

"We know about the escape plan, Peers," Piper said. "But Mara says we can't make it."

"We can make it," Kindred mumbled.

Jabari sighed. "You'll just hold umbrellas over your heads and run there, I suppose? Hope the giant ship that knows your name doesn't notice or care?"

"We have to hurry." Peers kept looking backward, as if still fearing the arrival of whatever had him running. "Come with me." He tugged at Meyer's blazer. Meyer, disgusted at the base gesture, shook him off with disdainful eyes.

"We're not leaving without Clara."

All heads turned toward Lila. Piper — and the others, apparently, judging by the group's puzzled looks — had forgotten she was there.

"Of course we're not." Piper looked at Peers but cast much more meaningful looks at Meyer and Kindred in the doing. "Peers? We're not going anywhere until we find Clara."

"The Mullah have her. Come. We have to hurry."

"We *know* the Mullah have her,. That's why we need to find her. Cameron did what they wanted. So they'll let her go. Right, Piper?" Lila's look was pleading, begging for knowledge Piper couldn't possibly have. Though she did, sort of — after Cameron's mental presence had vanished from her mind, she'd had an intense flash of emotional knowledge. She'd known he was gone, and that Clara was safe. But now she couldn't access the feeling or be sure that Clara was still safe, let alone where she might be. And she hadn't a clue as to the Mullah's intentions. Trying to restore her flash of empath's sight was like trying to move a new limb: she could do it, but not entirely on purpose and certainly not reliably.

She'd sensed Clara, a little.

She'd sensed the city, a lot.

But now she could still feel Ember Flats, and the Ark summoning some sort of power. But she couldn't feel Clara. Where had she gone? Was she still okay?

Peers saved her from responding, cutting off Piper and ignoring Lila.

"Come. Hurry! There's a new ship. It's — "

"I think we figured that out," Kindred said.

"Its purpose is to *destroy*. It's their wrecking ball. We can't be here when it starts doing what it came here to do. Do you understand? There are not several of these large ships. There is only one. And it's here, right above us. Ember Flats is where it all begins. We can't be underneath it when Armageddon arrives!"

Piper was sensing something new from Peers. There was fear, yes. And urgency, for sure. But there was something else as well. He'd been keeping one secret, she saw, and now he was keeping another. It was guilt atop guilt, and the deepest layer was miles thick. The kind that had gripped Peers by the spine, to never let go.

What had he done? She narrowed internal eyes, trying to flex that new limb. But focus eluded her. Piper's mind was too preoccupied with what he'd said about Ember Flats, about plagues. And about what she'd seen — or, more accurately, had stopped seeing — about Clara.

"We are safer in here than out there," Jabari said.

"We are *annihilated* in here, whereas out there we at least have a chance!" Peers was practically heaving, his body language pleading. Piper wondered again at his intent. He seemed more than eager to leave. This was somehow personal. If nobody listened, Piper sensed, Peers would fight tooth and nail until they did.

He was behaving as if he needed to right a terrible wrong. As if this was all his fault. She could see it in his manner and sense it in his emotions.

"Peers?" Piper asked. "Do *you* know where Clara is?"

"They've made their judgment already," Peers rushed on. "Now they're stirring panic to squeeze out the last of our poison — to make sure there's no corner of us they haven't seen. Meyer and Kindred's announcement made everyone angry, and now all of that rage is streaming into the Ark, adding to what they know and believe about us. But it won't hold for long. Soon it'll all be shaken out. They'll return to their ships, and the lottery will start. We can't count on that. Not for all of us. *We have to get out!*"

"Where are you getting this information, Peers?" Meyer asked.

"It doesn't matter!"

"It matters to me."

"There's no way to move unseen," Jabari said. "We will be safest below."

Peers turned to Lila, then Jabari, then Piper.

"Please," he said, his voice softer. "You *must* trust me."

"But Clara ... "

"The Mullah didn't leave that note, Lila! Ravi did. Jeanine and I got him to confess. There's no time to explain. But she's fine. I *know* she's okay."

"How can you possibly know that?"

"Piper thinks the same thing," Kindred said. "She said that Clara is safer than us. Going is our only sensible option. We might not get another chance."

"She's your granddaughter, Dad!" In Lila's emotional state, she didn't seem to know which Meyer she was addressing.

"She's fine, Lila!" This time, it was Meyer.

"Is that what your superbrain tells you? You two being Sherlock?"

35

"Honestly? Yes. Based on what we know, getting out is our best-possible scenario. We'll circle back once the big ship is gone. If Peers is right, it'll move on eventually. We can get Clara then. She and Piper both seem to have ... *something*. We'll find her if she's as safe as everyone seems to think. But we can't find her if we're dead."

Lila turned away, somewhere between angry and terrified. Piper felt a jolt watching her, wondering if she should speak up. She'd felt Clara was plenty safe when this started, yes. But they'd been paralyzed with indecision, watching Ember Flats implode through the windows and gate, for the better part of an hour. Did the fact that she couldn't really feel Clara now mean she was having a hard time finding the levers on her new psychic gifts? Or did it mean that Clara had moved out of safety and into peril?

"We're going," Kindred said. "*Now.*"

"Yes," Peers agreed. "Now."

"We're not going anywhere," Jabari said. Beside her, Lila nodded. And Piper, almost unaware of her own actions, realized she was nodding as well.

"Don't listen to her," Peers said.

"*Listen to me,*" Jabari countered, her stare even and firm. "I don't care how many 'scenarios' Meyer and Kindred have run. We thought out every tiny piece of this at the Initiate. Other than the big ship, everything else has gone according to predictions."

"You mean other than the planet-sized thing above us? Is that the small, failed prediction you're referring to?"

Jabari ignored Kindred, facing Piper, whom she seemed to see as her biggest potential ally — the one in the middle, whose swing vote might make all the difference.

"*All else has gone according to predictions,*" Jabari repeated, eye to eye with Piper. "We're excellent at prediction and planning. I got from where I was to here without incident. I had a plane ready, with redundancies. Other people's trips to their capitals went less smoothly, I hear, due to poor planning and poorer in-the-moment decisions."

"Wait just a goddamned minute," Meyer said.

"Who plots a road trip through Chicago?" Jabari said. "What sort of prepper does that?"

"My plane was grounded."

"And you had it at an airport where a crew *listens* to groundings? Not a private strip where you make the rules? That seems like the poorest of choices." Jabari was speaking to Meyer, but her eyes were on Piper. She paused, seeming to gather courage. Then her eyes flicked to Meyer and back to Piper. "No wonder they felt the need to put an Astral in your place."

Meyer lunged at her, but Jabari had put herself behind Lila. She moved back as Meyer, control effectively lost, reached and stuttered behind his daughter. Piper stepped between them, holding her hands out like a referee separating fighters.

"Enough! Knock it off, both of you."

"We're not leaving without Clara," Lila said.

"We're not leaving at all," Jabari added. "It's not just Clara. Leaving under that ship's eye would be idiocy."

"*You* set the plans in place." Kindred seemed agitated but not nearly as much as Meyer, who was stepping back as his fury subsided and — true Meyer, to the last — straightening his tie.

"Yes. *Plans.* Plural. You make plans and you nest them, with backups in case things happen, as they have. We also have a network with the other viceroys, on that pirate signal, that lets us meet from time to time, but the signal is blocked. So we're cut off. It's just us. And do you know what that means we have to do?" Jabari didn't pause to let Kindred answer. "We do *the best we can.* If we could reach the Cradle, we'd have headed north on the rivers to make contact away from the city. If we couldn't make contact, we'd go to the sea. And if we couldn't leave, we'd stay in the city. There's a well-stocked bunker below. This was *always* part of the plan, in the event that we couldn't leave the palace without being watched from above ... which, if you'd like to look outside for a second, *we can't.*"

Peers stepped up to Jabari.

"What if I told you we could?" he asked.

CHAPTER 6

The man in blue jeans sat on a white bench, reflecting that Meyer Dempsey would think this place resembled an Apple Store. Surfaces were white and rounded. It was the definition of minimalism, if *minimalism* really meant *nothing*. From where he was waiting for his appointment, the room's walls, ceilings, and floors were an undifferentiated expanse of white. Light seemed to come from everywhere, so there weren't many shadows. It seemed entirely possible to be walking through a place like this and run into a bench you hadn't known was there.

He squinted. These human eyes were so limited. It had been easier when he was able to shift shape, to become smoke or Astral or any human he'd touched. Even that black dog. Now it seemed he was stuck in this shape, doomed to be human for at least a fair spell. There were worse things in the universe. He'd seen as much before being squeezed out of the collective: Meyer Dempsey's humanity distilled, forced through a matrix of Astral assessment. He'd been the piece that didn't fit when they called him the Pall, but now he fit even less. He wasn't sure why he had this shape. Was this how Meyer's mind saw rebellion personified? If so, why hadn't he coalesced into a punk rocker once the Ark's opening ceremonies had finished assimilating him, once done with Cameron Bannister? He could be pierced and tattooed, sporting a two-foot, egg-white-stiffened mohawk.

He looked down at his blue jeans. At his boots.

Well, this would do. He was nothing if not a strange wanderer in a strange town.

A featureless door opened across the white space. It looked for a moment as if the first Apple Store had opened into a second Apple Store beyond. Maybe Hell would be an endless chain of white rooms where you could buy glossy electronics. Or Heaven, depending on your take. Either way, he supposed humanity would discover what was waiting beyond mortality's curtain soon enough. The answer had definitely surprised Dempsey's expelled emotions — or himself, if a finer line was to be drawn.

A woman stepped through the doorway, and the second Apple Store disappeared. She approached him on sensible heels — the stranger found himself wondering if she was about to offer him a discount on an overpriced mobile phone.

"Who are you?" The woman would have been in her late twenties if she were actually human. She had a pleasant, pretty face, but it seemed almost as if she didn't know how to use it. She wore her pleasing features sternly, pleasantries left in the box.

"I guess that's a matter of opinion," he answered.

"What is your name?"

"I suppose you can call me Stranger."

"What do you want?"

"Got the new iPhone?"

"We do not understand."

"'Course you don't." Stranger stood, shifted his weight, felt as if he'd subconsciously adopted the stance of a waiting gunslinger. He leaned against a wall to make himself friendly, but that pulled up Meyer Dempsey's image of himself as the old-time Marlboro Man. "Who are *you*, if we're getting friendly?"

"We are Divinity."

"You look like a woman to me."

"You would not understand our native form."

Stranger sent his mind back. He'd been created, as the Pall, after the first false Meyer's death by Meyer's son-in-law. If he concentrated hard, he could almost glimpse memories from the Titan who'd become that first replacement Meyer.

"I've seen it. I'd understand it."

"You would literally *not understand* it," the woman said. "We communicate mind to mind, whereas you require speech."

"Do we? I've seen the trick you pull with those big rocks. Wakes up even the dumb old human mind, doesn't it?"

"Irrelevant."

"You're such a pleasant conversationalist anyway," Stranger said, kicking one leg up so the sole of his boot rested against the wall. "Don't suppose you'd like to get a cup of coffee?"

"Why are you here?"

"You brought me here."

"On your demand."

"I asked kindly. Your Titans allowed it after seeing my trick. Sorry about the Reptar, by the way."

"Irrelevant."

"And yet, my condolences."

"How did you do what you did?"

"Even the Great Divinity wonders at my petty tricks? I'm flattered."

"You haven't answered the question."

Stranger reached into his pocket, then his hand emerged with three golf ball-sized silver spheres. He flexed the muscles of his hand, and the balls rolled in circles against each other, emitting light chimes. A subtle shift of pressure made them climb higher, into the branches of his fingers. He held them splayed, balls between each digit, then closed his palm and made them vanish.

"Like it?"

"We do not understand."

"You asked to see my trick."

"It's not what we were referring to. We meant — "

"I know what you *meant*, darlin'. Problem is you're attempting to judge a people without understanding them."

"We now know all we need to know."

"Because of the Ark, you mean."

The woman finally expressed surprise. Which, Stranger thought, was a wonder in itself. All he'd seen of the Astral mind spoke of emotional inertia. Surely the Astrals *had* it, but they kept it contained and didn't allow feelings to affect what they saw as work and duty. But that had changed, and Stranger was proof. The idea was supposed to squeeze all contaminants from the collective — the pollutants dripped by one Astral replacement's overeager participation in a human's peaks and valleys. Kill off one kid and force a guy to decide between two women he loves, and things get messy fast.

"What do you know of the archive?"

"Same as Bannister. *Both* Bannisters. Same as the various Dempseys — Meyer and Piper, even Heather, God rest her soul."

"Heather wasn't a Dempsey."

Stranger reached for his lips, realizing only once his long fingers touched them that he wasn't chewing on a toothpick. But he gestured as if he'd plucked one from between his lips anyway and spoke in a *gotcha* tone. "See? Now, you shouldn't care to point that out."

"You haven't answered our question about the archive."

"And you haven't answered my insinuation about Heather. Tell me. Who did Meyer Dempsey love more?"

"Irrelevant."

"Is it now?" Stranger smiled secretively then moved away from the wall and stood with a hand on one hip. "Well then. I don't want to be rude. To tell you the truth, I don't know much more about the Ark than you planned for them all to know."

"You mean what their research told them."

"Mmm-hmm. Yeah, that's exactly what I mean. It wasn't what you'd intended. Like Cameron Bannister being able to open the thing. Just like how he could reach the archive without problems, whereas anyone else would have been pushed back by your Titans and Reptars."

"Why are you here?"

"I see. You'd rather be direct. I like that in a woman. Then I'll just say it. 'Course I know about the archive. I know you wanted it open, and I know it was *the choice to open the archive* — not what it contained — that mattered most."

"The archive contains records of all that has happened in the last epoch. It is the evidence by which humanity will be judged."

"And judged guilty, no doubt."

"It is none of your concern."

"What about the viceroys? Is *that* my concern?"

This time, the woman paused with her mouth open. A curious affect for a species that normally communicated without using mouths at all.

"I know that *you* know they're plotting against you. All of those disobedient, individual-minded folk. Even Dempsey, who you replaced, is a loner. You'd sure be stupid not to see the way they've been sneaking around behind your back. So of course you know. You know that all of those loyal human leaders you put in place to run your cities actually aren't loyal at all. You know about their secret communication channel, which really ain't so secret from where you're standing. You know about Mara Jabari's Cradle, stashed outside Ember Flats. And ... " Stranger paused, wishing he had a toothpick or a cigarette to play with for effect. "Let me guess. If they run to the Cradle, you won't stop them. You'll let them leave, shooting lasers at their heels to pretend you're chasing them, although you never really have."

The woman's mouth worked, but no words came out. Did being in a human form color the way her mind worked? Was she a transformed Titan, like both replacement Meyers? Or some sort of projection? Stranger knew better than most what *taking human form* did to an Astral intelligence. Flesh had a way of getting its emotional hooks into you.

"Did I ever tell you about my cousin Timmy?" Stranger asked the woman.

"We do not understand."

"Well, actually, he was *Meyer's* cousin Timmy. He wanted to be a musician. Everyone was supportive. *Really* supportive. Like, *too* supportive. You know how everyone supports a retard? That's about how everyone supported Timmy. Folks in the family told Cousin Timmy how good he did in everything having to do with his music. They went to all his shows. They wore shirts he made for shitty gigs in pissant little clubs. You know why? Because they didn't really believe in him. They faked enthusiasm because they felt they had to, and when you fake it, you don't need to believe. And do you know who Timmy became?"

"No," the woman said.

"He became Tim Whitney."

The woman just stared.

"Not a country music fan, I see."

"Why are you here?" To Stranger, the woman sounded stuck in a loop.

"Tim wasn't the biggest name, but he definitely made it on the professional music scene. Pretty big time, and he made a great living as a semi-famous singer until you killed him along with most of the planet. But his family couldn't see his fame even when he had it because to them he was their stupid Cousin Timmy, who thought he could play guitar. 'Good for poor, dumb Timmy,' they said. You get me?"

"What is your intention? What do you want?"

"Friend, it's not a matter of what I want. It's a matter of what I can give you."

"How did you destroy the Reptar?"

Stranger held up his hand. He pinched a silver ball between thumb and forefinger and ring finger. He made it dance, put his other hand to it, and suddenly had a pair rolling across the backs of two hands. Then three, then four.

He waved his hands theatrically, and all the balls were gone.

"I have many tricks I'd rather not share."

"Then what do you have to give?"

"Let's start," Stranger said, "by discussing the Internet."

CHAPTER 7

The knock repeated.

Clara waited, knees to her chest, arms around them, pulling herself into a ball. The sound beyond the home's walls was *loud*, both inside and out of her head. Inside, she heard fear and begging and bargaining, soul searching and loss and abject panic. Outside, she heard screams and pops and bangs, crashes and Reptar purrs.

And yet the knock, when it came a third time, was soft and polite. Respectful. As if the person on the other side hadn't noticed all that was happening at the end of the world and was doing her best to not wake the home's occupant from a nap.

"Clara?" It was a young voice, but she couldn't tell how young because the door muffled it. "Clara, open up."

Clara crawled forward. She tried to peek through the window near the door but couldn't see the porch. Then she crawled to the other side and managed a glance — two kids on the steps: a boy and a girl. The boy looked about twelve or thirteen with hawklike features and a lock of hair that wouldn't stay off his forehead. The girl was maybe ten, black-skinned, strong-looking and tall, her hair a messy halo around her head.

His name is Nick. Her name is Ella.

[We know you're in there. Don't be afraid.]

Clara recoiled, looking around as if someone had shouted. And someone had, outside near the home's rear. While the main part of Clara's attention had been on the visitors at her front door, part of her had been listening all around. A Reptar purr had preceded a shout of pain and surprise. It didn't take much imagination to guess what had happened.

(Maybe she can't hear us.)

[Of course she can hear us.]

(I didn't mean your out-loud voice.)

[I know what you meant. But she talked to us, too, didn't she?]

Clara ducked, feeling watched. She hadn't spoken, but the sense that she knew these kids — specifically, that the boy was Nick and the girl was Ella — had been like her own voice speaking inside her mind. It had been stronger and somehow different from her normal internal voice — almost as if it were somehow coming both from within *and* from the kids themselves.

"Clara? We're friends, okay?" came the boy's

(Nick's)

voice. "Let us in, will you? Nobody seems to want to eat us, but I get a bad feeling about those little flying balls."

"Who are you?" Clara said.

"We're like you."

"Like me how?"

And then it was like someone had shut off Clara's sense of vision. For a split second she saw only blackness, then in the dark, a sort of mental video show began to play. Whoever had spliced this particular film had been manic and low on attention; it was composed of second-long clips, possibly images, that seemed to fly toward her, like a rush of speeding traffic: an Astral ship above a city, a baby cradled in its mother's arms, a hive filled with swarming honeybees, a series of beams of light in a web that seemed to be streaking toward each other like contrails of jets, only much faster, a chasm opening in the earth to expose a pit like Hell come topside, a group that seemed to be family, a wad of garbage washed from dishes and sliding down the dark maw of a running sink.

Images blasted into Clara like a strong wind, and then, when it was over, she felt their residue: the meaning behind all that had at first seemed only visual.

The children were Lightborn, same as her.

Clara turned the deadbolt and opened the door.

"How did you know I was in here? How did you know my name?"

The boy shoved past her, followed by the girl, who turned to shut the door and re-lock it. He was taller than Clara had imagined, and perhaps a bit younger. Eleven instead of twelve or thirteen.

"You know what you are, right?" the girl asked.

Of course she knows, the boy said without opening his mouth.

"You don't know that," the girl said, turning to the boy with juvenile disdain. A snippy response that said that he should have known better.

"Clara," the boy said. "What's my name?"

"Nick."

"And her?"

"Ella."

"That's how I know your name. That's how I knew you were in here."

"I knew, too," the girl said self-importantly.

"How long you been in Ember Flats?" the boy asked.

"Few days?" And then an out-of-control addition blurted from Clara's mind: *We've been in the palace.*

The girl nodded at the boy, hands on her hips and mouth pursed, as if she'd won a point in an argument. "*That's* why."

"Why what?" Clara asked.

Still speaking to the boy, the girl said, "I told you so."

"You didn't tell me so. Winnie said it first."

"Winnie and me." The girl raised a finger in victory. With her finger still up, she said, "There. Did you hear that?"

"Hear what?" Clara asked.

From Nick, Clara heard a mental voice say (to someone apparently not present), *Stop encouraging her, Win.*

"What are you guys talking about?" Clara asked.

"Hang on," Nick said.

Clara heard chatter, like people arguing, barely there. Like something coming through on a fuzzy station, a fraction from being on frequency. Nick and Ella — neither of whom had introduced themselves, Clara realized — didn't seem to be having trouble. Both had their heads cocked as if listening to an inaudible argument. Like crazy people.

"Hey!" Clara said, waving a hand. "*You* came to *me.*"

Ella broke from whatever was happening and turned to Clara. "You're related to someone, aren't you?"

"Aren't *you?*" Clara replied, her patience wearing thin.

"No — I mean you're really close to things up here somehow." The girl tapped her head, managing to find it through all her black hair. "Like, you're close with an alien. Or your mom is part of a hive or something."

"What's a hive?"

"When you were still in your mom's stomach, you were near one of the ships. Is that it?"

"Is that *what?*" Clara felt lost in this discussion yet sure that Ella was also involved in several other conversations and effortlessly managing them all. Nick, who was now paying attention to Clara and Ella, was clearly doing the same.

Although based on mental fragments that Clara seemed to smell wafting off of Nick, she was somehow certain that he wasn't just conversing but figuring something out as well. Each was doing five other things at once, and Clara was only doing one, and yet she was the one having problems following along.

"Let's spell it out," Nick said, half to Ella and half to her. Clara, sure she was about to be condescended to, tried not to be insulted. "You know what you are, right? In the city, they call kids like us 'Lightborn.'"

"Of course," Clara said, keeping her shoulders back and proud.

"We can do all these mind tricks. Like talking without really talking. Like having a really good feeling about what's happening even if nobody tells us. Sorta-kinda predicting the future."

"*Sorta,*" Ella added. "Maybe."

"I was reading adult books when I was three. I guess that's not normal. My mom was funny; she tried to keep me from knowing about Hell's Corridor. But I knew who was there, and what they did. I knew what a cannibal was without ever having to learn. It didn't scare me. It just made me want to stay inside the walls. You know what I mean?"

"I can do all of that stuff, too," Clara said.

"Yeah, but I can barely hear you. And now you say you've been in the palace since you've been here."

"Are you deaf? And why does it matter that I was in the palace?"

"I mean, *I can barely hear you.*" Then Nick tapped his head like Ella already had. "In *here.* You're part of that group that came in a while ago, right? So you were out in the desert. Is that where you were born?"

"Why does that matter?" Clara fought frustration, still sure that each of her new companions were doing ten other things while speaking to her, handling each effortlessly while watching her flounder.

"You're not used to being around other Lightborn, is all. Right?"

"No."

"And the palace shields everything. They know some of what we can do, and they don't want us peeking. The Astrals, I mean. So the palace walls are made of that same rock that dark minds use."

"*Dark minds?*"

"Sorry. I mean normal people. That's what we call them, since we're *light*. It's not like they're bad people." Nick looked for a moment like he thought he might have offended her, then pressed on. "They need the rocks to hook their minds up, and we don't, but the same rocks can keep us out. Sorta."

"What do you mean, *sorta?*"

"If you haven't been around a bunch more of us Lightborn kids, that's probably why you're bad at this. It's okay; you'll get better." Ella said it as if offering Clara a gift.

"I've been around plenty."

"In an outpost or something?" Then, speaking to Nick out loud for what was clearly Dumb Old Clara's benefit, she added, "You know many Lightborn in outposts? I thought they were mostly in capitals."

"I grew up in Heaven's Veil," Clara said, trying to gain any credibility she could muster. She felt like a yokel: a poor country cousin who knows nothing of the civilized world.

"Really?"

"Yeah. In the mansion there, too."

"Your dad an ambassador or something?"

"No, but my grandpa was the viceroy."

Nick and Ella looked at each other. Finally, Clara had drawn an ace.

"*That's* why she stuck out so much," Nick said.

(She's lying.)

[No she's not. I can feel it. Can't you feel it?]

(She's just saying it because he did that whole speech. It's crap.)

[Why would anyone claim to be related to Viceroy Dempsey who wasn't?]

"Hey!" Clara said. "I can hear you, you know."

"Sorry," Nick said. "It's just that … " Images followed, all about Heaven's Veil and her grandfather, none flattering.

"It's not true. My grandpa is a good man. Kindred, too."

"Who's Kindred?"

Clara tried what Nick had done, using her mind to push out a string of images and feelings. It was easier than she'd imagined, once she offered her full attention. Just being around these two for five minutes had fortified her. She felt her eyes opening, her mind getting stronger. They were right; she *had* been isolated — in one shielded palace, then in the desert away from other Lightborns, followed by yet another palace. She'd heard there were plenty others like her in the world, but she'd never met any face to face. Being around them felt powerful, like one plus one making five. Or ten.

"He's the … clone? … they made to replace my grandpa when they had my grandpa prisoner up in their ship. Actually the second. The first replacement was killed." Clara stepped hard on the following thought, suddenly sure she didn't want Nick and Ella to know it was her own father who'd killed that first doppelgänger. It felt shameful, like something best relegated as a skeleton in the family closet. "Kindred came after that. Nobody realized he wasn't really 'Viceroy Dempsey.' Not any of us. Not even himself. But then he figured it out and saved my grandpa from the ship, and now they're kind of like twins but not really."

Nick and Ella traded a glance, a stream of communication moving between them like a whisper that Clara couldn't catch.

"Saved him, huh?" Nick said.

Clara nodded.

"But he's an alien?"

"Was. I think he's stuck as a human now."

"So it really *is* like there are two Viceroy Dempseys. Like on the broadcast."

Clara tuned her mind and saw what they were talking about: something she'd missed while with the Mullah. But one of the children had seen it, or someone they were mentally linked to. A full record of the broadcast, complete with many emotional interpretations, seemed to be right there in the middle of some sort of shared Lightborn archive.

In that archive, Clara saw something else about the broadcast. She leaped upon it.

"And it really is like they said. Astrals destroyed the city because they were looking for the Ark. It was still hidden back when I was little, but still sorta listening to the world's feelings. I was there when they blew up the city, and then they just listened to the sounds of all those people dying, and followed the screams so they could figure out where the Ark was. That's why they did it, I swear. It wasn't Grandpa's fault."

Nick was nodding. "It's true. You're right." Clara could feel him rooting around inside her mind, sifting through memories of the event. Clara's words weren't convincing him. It was her personal firsthand account, which Nick and Ella now seemed able to see.

"And he's your grandpa?" Ella said.

"Uh huh."

"What are you doing out here? You stuck out to all of us like you'd set the house on fire. It sounded like you were in here crying."

Clara wasn't sure if Ella meant it literally or metaphorically, but her agreement didn't seem necessary, so she kept her mouth shut and answered the question instead.

"You know the Mullah?"

"Mullah?"

"They're — "

But then all of a sudden, inside Clara's mind, everything was strobing red. A mental klaxon blared, and all three children slapped their hands over their ears. It wasn't a literal alarm that anyone could hear, but it was *something*, all right. A decision being made, perhaps. Something horrible about to begin.

"Tell us later," Nick said. "Right now, I'm thinking we'd better get the heck out of here."

CHAPTER 8

"Did you hear that?" Peers asked.

Lila turned to look at Peers. He wouldn't stop pacing the bunker. The room reminded Lila of so many places she'd hoped to never think of again: her father's Axis Mundi, Derinkuyu, their hidey-hole in Roman Sands, even Mount Sinai, where they overnighted in a cave once before seeking the Ark's original location. Life, it seemed, had become one long series of dark holes. Although the alternative — the viceroy's palace above — wasn't much better. It was plush but reminded Lila of their mansion in Heaven's Veil. And that had its own horrible memories.

"Stop it, Peers," said Meyer.

"Stop what?"

"I don't want to be here any more than you do. But we made our decision, as a group."

"I just asked if anyone heard anything."

"Stop it, Peers," Jabari said.

"Jesus fucking Christ! What's wrong with you people?"

Peers shouted too loud. His accented voice echoed in the concrete chamber. But it also proved Meyer and Jabari's point: Peers was pacing because he was agitated and angry, not because he was stir-crazy. There was something going on with their fearless desert wanderer that he wasn't saying, and ultimately that had been the nail in his otherwise reasonable plan's coffin: too much unknown, too many frayed nerves, too many secrets that Peers obviously held and refused to divulge.

There are tunnels below Jabari's mansion that even Jabari doesn't know about? How do you know that, Peers?

How can you possibly know how to get into those supposed tunnels, Peers? And what makes you think you have any idea where they go ... if they can get us to the Cradle to escape or not?

Why are you so sweaty, Peers? Why so jittery?

What are you hiding, Peers?

Lila stayed quiet, not liking the bunker more than anyone else (although she liked the decision to stay where Clara had gone missing an awful lot more), taking it all in. She didn't feel as timid as she probably appeared. She was actually feeling bold, now that they'd made the decision to stay. She was turning over what Peers had said about Ravi: how he — not the Mullah at large — had written the note demanding the Ark be opened. It meant that Ravi was rogue, and that there was an outside chance that the enemy of her enemy might turn out to be her friend. Could she approach the Mullah, if she found a way to contact them? What was she willing to do if it meant getting her baby girl back?

Just about anything, really.

If action had to be taken — if someone needed to push Peers into danger so that no more of her people would fall to harm — Lila thought she could do it. Same for Jabari, if worse came to worst. She didn't trust either of them. They both announced that things were done after they'd happened and nobody could verify anything one way or the other.

Oh, Clara was kidnapped? Sure, I'll believe you weren't involved even though you benefitted. And oh, the Astrals always just kind of paved the way for you despite your claiming not to be in league with them? Sure, no problem – I trust you.

Peers especially irked her. She didn't have the deductive genius that her father and Kindred had with their blended minds, but she had her mother's intuition. For some reason, everyone was taking Peers at his word. They'd *always* taken the man at his word. He'd shown them his Den full of Astral technology, but everyone believed that he and Aubrey had simply stumbled upon it. The Astrals didn't chase Peers's big, obvious bus through the desert, but everyone believed it was luck. Peers could yammer on and on that it happened because the Astrals *wanted* Cameron to use his key all along, but who was left to corroborate his story? Not Cameron, who was dead. Not Charlie, who knew all the Ancient Aliens lore – also dead. No. Their only expert was Mara Jabari, a woman whom – let's not forget – Peers came to kill because her troops had murdered his son. And everyone sort of ignored that the conflict had vanished with their arrival.

Peers, Lila felt sure, was hiding something.

Something *big*. And *bad*. He'd been sneaking around most of the time like a teenage boy hiding porn. The fact that nobody had called him on his late arrivals, wild eyes, or flimsy excuses seemed ridiculous to Lila. He'd been around the night Clara had vanished, but nobody wondered if he'd been in any way responsible. Oh, it was the Mullah, Peers? I believe you. And yet the man seemed to know a *lot* about the Mullah.

He had plenty of reasons for them to hightail it to these alleged tunnels: The ship above was the "Dark Rider" and would "bring plagues." It was the last in a long string of Astral dominoes. He seemed to feel it was his duty to protect Meyer and Kindred, but not really anyone else. He talked about those two as if they were men of legend then forgot about Lila, Piper, and Clara. Like they were all pawns in some big plan that everyone was turning away from and pretending not to see.

Sure, Peers argued to leave. But who stopped them? Who convinced the group to stay? Why, Jabari, of course. An admirable ploy: Peers got to look like he was against staying, when their secret partnership would keep them where they were. Perhaps so aliens could eat them.

Stop it, Lila. You're being paranoid. And besides, you got your way. You wanted to stay.

The thought reminded her of Peers and his incessant pacing and mumbling, the way he kept saying things that implied the situation was turning bad (like "Did you hear that?" when there was nothing to hear). At least the others were calling him on his transparent protests — or, in the case of his maybe-partner-in-crime Jabari, kept *pretending* to.

"Look," Peers said after taking a long few minutes to calm himself. "At the risk of being shouted at again, I'm telling you, I actually did hear something."

"And? What do you want us to do about it?" Meyer glanced at Kindred, but his twin seemed to be stewing even more deeply than Lila. Kindred had been strange lately. Angrier. A shorter fuse. More bent on logic and intolerant of any emotion-based decision — which was ironic, considering his own ramped-up emotion (anger) was half the problem.

"Check to see what it was," Peers answered.

"No point," said Jabari. "Whatever happens, this is still the safest place."

Peers looked like he might reiterate his supposed opinion that *the Cradle* was the safest place, accessible through these tunnels he'd have to be a Mullah spy to know about. Instead, he said, "If we wait until their plagues are too far along, we'll never escape in time. You can't flee natural disasters and disease by hiding out in the epicenter."

"You're free to leave if you want," Meyer said.

"You have to go with me."

But even as another round of mumbling circled the group, only Lila seemed to see the subtext. That *you* wasn't a collective. He didn't need to take the entire group. Only Meyer and maybe Kindred. Why? And why was nobody questioning him?

She watched him, eyes narrow. He'd been the last person to see Jeanine alive. The last person to see Charlie, other than possibly Jeanine. He might have been the last person to see Clara before she disappeared. And now he had all sorts of insider knowledge about what was happening that even Jabari — who had credentials at a bona-fide alien think tank — didn't.

"We're staying here," Kindred mumbled.

Peers stopped pacing. He perked up then put his hand behind his ear as if listening. His posturing was so annoying, Lila came close to standing up and punching him to the floor.

But she paused when Piper's head cocked, too.

"You hear it, don't you?" Peers said, eager.

"Maybe."

"It could be anything. The big ship opening and sending something down. Shuttles flattening the city."

"Well, if shuttles are flattening the city, let's definitely run right out there."

Peers's head flicked toward Lila. She'd been a quiet hole in the group, so her speaking now — and with such vitriol — was like a knife.

"We have to get out of here. Trust me. I know! If we stay, things will be so much worse!"

"*How* do you know, Peers?" Meyer asked.

Piper stood. Touched her temples. Seemed to listen.

"She knows. She can feel it," Peers said, pointing at Piper.

Then Piper sat.

"Maybe. But maybe not."

And Peers, his composure shattering, screamed, *"We have to leave! We have to get the fuck out of here before Armageddon begins!"*

"What's coming, exactly, Peers?" Meyer asked.

Lila stood. Faced Peers. She was a foot shorter than him, but she moved very close, nearly chest to chest, and stared.

If you had anything to do with taking my daughter and keeping her from me, she thought, *I'll slit your throat.*

Peers looked down at Lila, blinked, looked away. Lila stared for another three seconds, basking in his discomfort.

"I'm going to take a bath," she announced and walked away.

She made it to the basement's surprisingly well-appointed bathroom, turned on the water, and started to scream.

CHAPTER 9

Clara ran through the streets trailing Nick and Ella, realizing she'd apparently decided to trust and join them without ever making a real decision. They ran fast and Clara followed. After several blocks she finally stopped to look back and see that they weren't just heading away from the small, vacant home the Mullah tunnel had opened into, but away from the palace as well.

She thought of her mother. She thought of Piper, who for some reason she could feel much more than usual, but who she doubted could precisely see or feel her. She thought of the others. And for the scantest of seconds Clara considered running back to them, knowing she wanted them, and that they must be worried about her. But the Lightborns' pull was stronger.

Every second she stayed with them, Clara's mind seemed to strengthen its connections to theirs — and not just to Nick and Ella; also to the people they were linked to and those peoples' first-degree connections as well. She couldn't focus while running, but to Clara's expanding mind the potential of this new Lightborn kinship felt like a closed bud opening to bloom. She would, in time, be able to touch any of them, anywhere.

She imagined the feeling of a drug. Like the psychedelics that Grandma Heather and Grandpa Meyer had taken, which Clara discovered after exploring their past feelings. Like the mental trip to another place. And like a drug, the sensation was addicting.

Clara wanted her mother. But the thought of severing herself from these others now that she'd finally found them struck her as intolerable, impossible, unthinkable.

Inside her head, boxes opened. Tight knots unwound themselves without effort. Avenues opened, and puzzle pieces slotted into place. And she thought: that alarm we all just heard. It means something — but not what the rest of the people in Ember Flats would think it meant if they were able to hear it, which they weren't.

It wasn't a public signal.

The alert the three children had felt? The thing that had been like a flashing light and a blaring klaxon? That had been Astral. Something the aliens were sharing with each other, not meant for general consumption.

Clara saw a branching tree of light, with other Lightborns at the end of every limb.

Where are we going? Clara shouted to Nick and Ella, inside her mind.

[We have a place.]

The voice wasn't a voice but still had something like a sound, a tone — sharp-edged, matter-of-fact, direct, yet understanding. Nick.

And then a softer presence showed Clara what Nick had spoken of. She saw a large room with little flair and a lot of warmth: couches in varying stages of disrepair arranged haphazardly around a large, open space, most carved into semi-personalized nooks. One was claimed with posters, stuck to the wall behind it. Another was piled with pillows in cat-patterned fabric. One had been painted — a couch, painted. The surface of the paint had been hard at first, probably, but now it was cracked and softened from use: small islands of upholstery bearing tiny isles of paint rather than a big unbroken expanse of color.

But the Astrals ...

As if in answer, Clara's thought was cut short as the trio ran up on a large patrol of Reptars. The scene had not been made ready for children's eyes. The things were eating, and what they were eating was, in at least two cases, still alive. Limbs and blood were everywhere, painting the walls like a macabre mural. As they arrived, practically skidding to a stop on their sneakers, two of the black animal things flicked their insect legs and rushed off between a row of broken-windowed buildings. There was another human scream from that direction, then it was severed as if with a blade.

(Don't run, Clara.)

Clara fought her muscles. She turned to Ella, whose eyes repeated the same thing her mental voice had whispered: *Don't run.*

But although Clara herself understood, her legs and arms did not. When you encountered Reptars, you ran. It's what their group had always done. It's what had kept them alive.

Images flashed through Clara's mind, all from Nick, attempting to convince her in the fastest way possible not to move. Words were too slow. Pictures and feelings and other people's memories spoke millions of words in slivers of seconds.

She saw a group of children surrounded. She saw them exit without a scratch, practically elbowing their way through the frothing Reptar circle as if politely excusing themselves.

She saw a representation of an old-school circuit, with a component missing.

She saw images from stories Clara remembered from when she'd been younger and Mom had read out loud from her Vellum, all now coming from Nick's memories: Br'er Rabbit who'd fooled the fox; a pirate with two blind eyes. Then seeming thousands of personal recollections from within the Lightborn network, each showing a Reptar or a Titan or a shuttle, and a child walking heedlessly by.

[They'll see you if you run.]

But now Clara understood. The Reptars wouldn't precisely *see* her, would they? They'd see her emotions. They'd see the panic that accompanied running.

Which meant that right now, looking the black things in their alien eyes, the Reptars weren't seeing them at all. Not in the way they saw normal children or adults. Not in the way they saw targets or food.

Clara found herself remembering the Mullah tunnels. The way Sadeem had shoved her into the closet so she wouldn't be discovered. The way the threat that time hadn't been Reptars but the tiny BB drones.

She looked to Ella, a question on her lips. But Ella shook her head, took her hand, and led Clara away. Then, away from the Reptars, she said, "They don't seem to notice us. You didn't know that?"

Clara fought a hammering heart and shook her head. "I've always been with someone else."

Nick held up a hand. The *Shh!* Clara heard came from Nick's mind, not his lips.

A low chattering came from every direction at once. It was like one long, low Reptar purr. The sound of a thousand horrid things emerging from dark closets in the middle of the night.

More Reptars emerged from the shadows. They came in rough pairs, two-by-two like soldiers in formation. Seeing it reminded Clara that although Reptars looked like animals, they were beings with brains and thought and logic — Astrals as much as Titans. Watching so many enter the street around them was chilling. They moved with an icy precision, each pair moving to a dwelling and camping at its front like guards at a palace.

A door across the street banged open. The middle-aged woman who emerged had a front covered in red, as if she'd spilled something across her chest. Her eyes, even from where the children were standing, were wide enough to see whites all the way around.

Maybe the Reptars couldn't see the children, but the woman could. She stumbled three steps toward them with her hand out, failing to notice the new Reptar sentinels flanking her house.

Then she fell to the sidewalk and didn't get up.

A scream. Another scream.

More people emerged, many grasping their throats, most with the same curious red wash down their front. Some had the same red on their hands, and one old man had it all over his face, as if splashed there.

Some of the people collapsed as the woman had, frozen. Those who didn't came toward the children as if drawn. But then the Reptars moved out between them, and the people stepped back, stopping when they encountered the other Reptars behind them, surrounded.

The surviving and red-painted people of Ember Flats stared at the children, but the Reptars seemed not to notice.

Two words entered Clara's mind — maybe from Nick or Ella, maybe from within herself, maybe from the air as an intercepted Astral thought, or maybe even from Piper, all the way back at the palace:

Gathering.

And *Plague.*

The warning siren the children had heard in their minds wasn't something these people had heard. Their shocked faces told Clara that they'd seen something different. Something that had terrified them to the core.

65

No, the siren had been Astral to Astral, telling the others that it was time.

Time for what? Clara wondered.

Ella said, *I'd rather not find out.*

CHAPTER 10

Peers sat on one of Jabari's couches, then Nocturne came and sat with his head on Peers's knee. He looked down, and then, after a few seconds, ran his hand along the dog's head and neck in long, slow strokes. Poor, dumb dog, with no idea of what was going on. Lucky animal — still occupied only with comforting his master, playing with toys, tugging on ropes, and chasing thrown balls.

He looked around the room. The tension was practically visible. Meyer and Kindred were angry. They wanted to leave — to try whatever it took to flee the city and reach the escape vehicles Jabari had planned for but had given up accessing. But he didn't have allies in Meyer and Kindred. They — like Jabari, Piper, and Lila — were untrusting. He couldn't blame them. He wouldn't trust himself right now, either.

Peers couldn't tell them how he knew about the tunnels, how to get through them, or where they almost certainly went: because he'd once been Mullah, and knew how they thought.

He couldn't tell them all he knew about Clara because that would implicate him in her abduction.

And he *definitely* couldn't tell them how he knew about the Dark Rider ship. Even Jabari hadn't known about that, and she'd made a career out of analyzing past visits and, apparently, predicting and mapping this one's probable course. The Da Vinci Initiate had been among the first to weigh in when the Astral app had spotted the approaching ships, mincing few words in what they believed them to be. And yet even she had no clue what the big ship meant — including reasons why they needed to flee and why it wouldn't care if they did. Hell, the reason he knew half those details was something he couldn't even admit to other Mullah.

Why yes — I know the ship has come to fuck us up because the Astrals told me as much when I told them to go ahead and hightail it here to judge us.

Peers felt a churning in his gut. He could barely swallow. It had been that way since he'd seen the memory sphere's record of his juvenile transgression in the Temple. Arrogant, stupid little boy, eager to see what secrets the Elders had kept from him — and now he knew he'd caused the end of the modern world.

Great going, asshole.

Peers looked around before putting his face in his hands, knowing how it would look. But then, when he saw that Meyer and Kindred were deep in discussion, with Jabari across the room talking to Piper, he did so anyway. It was all too much. He was the guiltiest man in history, and he couldn't even confess. They'd kill him if he did. They'd skin him alive and leave him to slowly die.

Just like all those people out there ended by Reptars and lasers.

And just like the coming plagues. The legends were all metaphorical and written like poetry, but as long as there'd been a civilized humanity, there'd been Mullah. Even thousands of years ago, record keepers had known times would change and that stories warped through millennia, so they'd been careful. The Astral visitors of the first epoch had *told* them to be careful. And because those first Mullah had been precise in their descriptions, the modern Mullah had always felt relatively confident, in the broadest strokes, of what would happen.

There might be a literal plague, or perhaps a massive kill-off.

There might be an illness, or maybe the Astrals would activate some ancient Earth-moving machine and tilt the axis enough to fuck up the ice caps and flood the shorelines.

Perhaps the Astrals would split the planet in two. Maybe they'd somehow excite the sun and trigger massive, deadly solar flares.

Peers only knew two things for certain: First of all, what came next would be worse than devastating. All traces of modern society would be destroyed or buried. And second, some people *would* survive. That was the way it had always been: a new seed cluster meant to reboot the human race so it could try again, and maybe prove the planet more worthy the next time around.

Meyer and Kindred would be among them. According to the scrolls, the King survived the cleansing. Were they really going to "survive" while hiding in a bunker? It didn't feel right. They had to get out — try for the Cradle and a rendezvous with the other viceroys beyond their exodus. But how could he get them out? And when?

Peers longed for a window, but there were none in the bunker. But when they'd been topside he'd been able to feel the Ark's judgment like static in the air. What the first group had seen at Sinai would be nothing by comparison. Everyone out there would be facing their own personal demons — perhaps literally, as Cameron had faced Morgan Matthews. Or maybe the Ark would spare them the soul-searching and simply eliminate most of them. The verdict was in, and humanity was — as it had always been — guilty as charged.

Guilty of being an inferior race. An inferior representation of the seeds the Astrals had planted untold ages ago.

Guilty of being barbaric. Of thinking only of the one, never truly the whole. Guilty of living disjointed, isolated lives. Even birds could think as a group intelligence, and yet humans could not. All signs pointed to Egypt and Ancient Maya as finding harmony in a collective subconscious, but current Earthlings hadn't pulled it off. Instead, they'd created email and instant messaging. They'd created social networking. There was no collective on the surface the way there was in the Astral motherships — the way, even, that humans had managed mental collectives before.

Why wouldn't *they be guilty?*

This iteration of humanity was a failed experiment.

How many people would die because Peers told the Horsemen to saddle up and ride?

He'd earned his role. Ravi thought Peers was "the Fool" the scrolls talked about, and Peers had to agree. Fool indeed.

Saving this group was the only road to redemption. To get them out. And not just Meyer and Kindred. His actions had killed Cameron, Charlie, Jeanine, maybe even Clara. If he couldn't save every one of the people in this basement, they wouldn't need to string him up. He'd do it himself.

Peers ran his hands through his hair, elbows on his knees. When he looked up, Piper was looking directly at him.

"Peers?" she said. "You okay?"

He shook his head — not that he wasn't okay but that he didn't need her attention.

She came closer. Meyer saw her move and raised an eyebrow. Kindred, watching Meyer, saw his head turn and turned his own: a chain reaction of attention, headed right where Peers didn't want it.

Piper looked back at Meyer and Kindred. Then, glaring until they looked back at their own business, she settled in and spoke more softly.

"You can tell me," Piper said.

That's when Lila, in the bathroom, started to shriek.

CHAPTER 11

"You have something I want, and I have something you want. That's the way this works."

"Unacceptable," the woman said to Stranger.

"Were you not listening? About the Internet?"

"It's meaningless."

Stranger laughed. Astrals were, in the end, like people. You could separate beings into three classes, and the highest could be a giant anemone creature that called itself Divinity — but rules were still the same in the end. There was still posturing. There was still pride. And even though Divinity in its normal form didn't carry weapons or have a torso, there was still a lot of saber-rattling and chest-pounding.

"Listen to you," Stranger said, leaning back on a thing that, here in the new section of the ship, looked like a giant white lozenge. "You brought me to White Castle. Unless you're stupider than any human, you know you need to at least hear what I have to say. But now we're here, and you've got to put up the same front as any man or woman *Unacceptable. Meaningless. Irrelevant.* Everything is beneath you, ain't it? I could psychoanalyze the *shit* out of that. Would you like to have your matter-transporters or whatever manifest you a couch to lie back on?"

"We do not understand the need for a couch."

Stranger waved his hand dismissively. "Let me see it. Let me see the stream."

"Tell us more about the blind spot."

"So you *are* interested? I *do* matter?"

"The Mullah. Tell us what they were hiding. Tell us what you believe our drones missed."

"Not until I see what I want to," Stranger countered, becoming serious.

"You would not understand it."

"Then there's no reason not to show me."

The woman seemed to freeze. Her eyes moved in small ticks, and Stranger took this to mean she was discussing something with the hive mind. Or perhaps the big lit-up anemone thing using her like a puppet was having trouble working her controls. He wished they could have done this in person, Stranger and this ship's Divinity. But nope — even intergalactic visitors had their gatekeepers.

"A window will open to your side," Divinity said through the woman's mouth.

"I'm afraid of heights."

"It is not a hole in the ship. It is a window based on a human display screen. The same hybrid technology used to communicate with the viceroys."

"I know. I was kidding."

The woman stared at him.

"Open your window." Then, because he knew she wouldn't understand: "I'll try not to jump through it."

A panel slid open. The large lozenge thing he'd been perched on began to hum. Maybe it was some kind of computer or database; Stranger didn't know. He was more human than Astral and — almost by definition — always had been.

The panel filled with squiggling lines, white on blue.

"I don't understand this," he said.

"Put your hand on its surface."

Stranger did, and for the first seconds he was sure he'd made a stupid move — the Astrals were about to trick him. But that was pesky human insecurity, which Stranger wasn't immune to. If Divinity wanted him dead, there were easier ways to do it. And what he knew was more valuable to them than whatever they had to offer. *He* was mainly curious. But for the Astrals, this was a matter of success and failure, of cost and consequence. They didn't understand the Internet thing, for sure. But that was the point — and *the fact that they didn't get it* was, interestingly enough, something Divinity *did* seem to understand.

With his palm to the glass, Stranger found his vision blurring. The room dissolved and became like mist. He could move his focus around if he tried: reaching out with his mind to see the woman's face, the smooth white surface of the Titan-sized door where they'd entered, the presence of his own boot-clad feet. But unless he directed his attention, Stranger saw nothing beyond the haze.

It was as if he were smoke again. Just the Pall, free to roam and meddle and become — free to urge the Ark open, because opening a wound was the only way to see it clean.

"Do you see what you seek?" said the woman's disembodied voice.

Stranger couldn't find his mouth. He thought his answer instead. But since he was in the Astral memory stream — the source of spheres like Peers Basara had found, containing a vision of his unfortunate secret — his mind seemed to touch the Astral mind again. He was back to the Pall, able to communicate without any words.

I don't see it.

"Recall the donor."

You mean Meyer Dempsey, Stranger thought/said.

"Turn your mind toward his vibration node."

He wanted to make a sexual joke — Stranger had inherited plenty of lust from Meyer — but he refrained, instead expressing his continued lack of understanding.

"Stop thinking like a human."

Kind of tricky .

"Stop looking for an individual. All individuals are peaks in the species' vibration. Individuals do not normally matter. We direct you to one peak or node because of your fixation on a specific individual, but to us the differentiation is meaningless."

Meaningless, huh? So is it also irrelevant?

"Yes," the woman answered, not getting it.

He thought of Meyer Dempsey, who'd been an unwitting part of the alien collective for two years. He'd never been Astral, but they'd still managed to suck most of his personality out like milkshake through a straw and implant it into a pair of Titan clones. The feeling of Meyer was still here somewhere, like a copied file. The Astrals wouldn't understand that metaphor (ironic, really, considering the circumstances), but it was true enough for Stranger.

Okay, he thought/said. *I think I found Meyer's brain in here.*

"Move out one node."

Then I'll put my right leg in and shake it all about.

"One node to the first iteration," the woman clarified, ignoring him. "The iteration flagged as an imperfection."

All right.

He didn't know what it meant until he tried. But once he did it was simple. There was a blob of energy in the stream that seemed like a backup of the original Meyer Dempsey, but just past it Stranger could feel something that qualified as a "node," all right. Like a lump in space.

Now what?

"Enter it."

Stranger focused. He felt himself putting this new node on like a jacket. Meyer without being Meyer. And that made sense, because the node just past the Dempsey file was logically Kindred's predecessor — the nameless Meyer who'd lived between the true man and the one who named himself Kindred. The man who'd never realized he wasn't a copy, even after being killed by Raj Gupta.

Stranger didn't bother to ask Divinity anything more. He hadn't told them what he was looking for because he didn't really know. Part of this was sheer human curiosity: the need to know where he, when he'd been the Pall, had come from. But another part of this seemed essential for a reason Stranger felt but couldn't quite articulate.

He knew the Pall had come into being when the Astral collective had done their psychic autopsy on the first Meyer clone and determined that he'd been somehow "infected" with too much of Meyer's raw humanity. But the issue wasn't just academic to Stranger. The question of how and why the Pall had been born was central to all of this — to what was happening with Clara and the way the Astrals couldn't see her without their BB drones, to the ant farm experiments the Astrals were performing while pretending to be doing something entirely different, to the way the Internet had changed everything for everyone.

It *mattered*.

He shook mental arms and legs, feeling the first Astral Meyer's psyche settle on his mental shoulders.

What had gone wrong with this first clone? What had the Astrals found so threatening that they'd cut it away before making Kindred — then flushed it out so it could coalesce, roam free, and return in boots?

Through the old Meyer's memories, Stranger saw conflict in duties. Saw family. Saw Trevor, and the news of his death. He saw Raj and Heather and Lila and Piper.

Heather.

And Trevor.

Heather.

And Trevor.

Those two mattered most. And as Stranger rolled the old memories back and forth, examining what had been cut out, he began to understand. Maybe he could even comprehend it in a way Divinity couldn't.

Because after all, he was in a unique position to understand. He'd *been* the Pall. He *was* what had been cut out from this man and discarded.

Heather.

And Trevor.

Something began to transpire that hadn't precisely happened to Stranger before.

He began to get angry.

But not just angry. It was a righteous sort of rage. Desperate. An itch that couldn't be scratched, because what made him angry was long since finished. There was no making things right. Only loss. Fear. Fury. And love.

Love.

The difference between this first copy of Meyer and Kindred — that's what seemed to matter most.

Stranger looked around with mental eyes. Tried to remember all he could. Then he realized that, with some effort, he didn't just need to *remember*; he could actually take it in. These were records, after all. They were files, in a sense, that could always be copied.

He pulled back once finished and found himself standing in his old body, boots firmly on the floor, head now decidedly out of the clouds. He felt a bit dizzy, but otherwise fine.

"Satisfied?"

"Not at all," Stranger said.

The woman acted as if he'd given an affirmative, nodding as if she understood humans. But she didn't. The woman couldn't see the change on Stranger's face. She couldn't tell read his red-hot fury, or see how this time, when he said *Not at all*, he wasn't joking.

Heather.

His fists in balls at his sides, fingertips turning white from the pressure.

And Trevor.

"Now," Divinity said, "tell us why the Lightborn matter."

Stranger opened his hands. Made himself breathe.

"Because what you're doing down there right now, they'll see right through it."

"What is there to see?"

"That's it's not a plague," Stranger said. "It's kabuki."

CHAPTER 12

Lila ran out with hands that looked dipped in dark red paint. She was screaming, waving them around, spattering the floors and furniture and walls. Meyer stood and rushed over, and when he reached his daughter found that she'd dripped onto her feet as well, and was leaving prints. Her chest was spattered with thick droplets. Her pants were half-covered. Her neck looked like it had broken out in new red pimples.

She was screaming. Shrieking. Out of her mind. And that's when Meyer's nose recognized the smell in the air — dank, coppery, heavy like mildew, thick and rotten like meat.

It wasn't paint or dye on her hands. It was blood.

"What happened?" Meyer demanded, taking Lila's wrists and eyeing her thrashing body, resisting an impatient urge to shake her back to sense. "Where are you cut? What happened?"

"The bathroom! The bathroom!"

Piper had rushed over, but already Meyer knew he wasn't seeing things quite right. Lila's head was dry, and a scalp wound was the only thing other than a chest shot that might bleed anywhere near this much. She looked like she'd assisted in impromptu heart surgery, massaging someone's heart to get it beating.

"LILA! What happened?"

Behind them, something fell to the floor and detonated like a bomb. Meyer could hear shuffling and waited, still trying to calm Lila, for the others to finish their scrambling and rush over. But whatever was happening back there apparently wasn't about Lila and all this blood. Meyer could hear Jabari, Peers, and Kindred — he thought he could hear the television Jabari had left on to watch the city, no longer muted. Why? Why now?

"Lila!" Piper said. "Hold still!"

Checking her scalp, even though there was no blood in her hair. Checking her wrists for signs of desperate escape, but the blood mostly stopped above her palms, except for spatters. It didn't look like she'd hurt herself; it looked like she'd been in front of someone when they'd exploded.

"Check the bathroom, Piper."

"Lila? Where are you cut?" Piper's head ticked around, and she seemed to count, as if sure another member of their party had met their doom. But all six were accounted for, including the dog. Other mini-bunkers throughout the palace might be occupied, but even aides and employees hadn't come down here with them.

"Piper! The bathroom!"

Piper rushed around the corner, and there was another scream. Meyer decided that his daughter would remain upright without him and that whatever was in the bathroom required his attention more than Lila did. So he went, distantly sure that both Jabari and Peers had shouted urgently at his retreating back, fear as present behind him as it was in front.

Piper was in the bathroom doorway. Beyond her, a horror show. Blood wasn't coming from a person or a some macabre aftermath. It was coming from the shower head, which Lila must have turned on and then left running.

The tub was draining but still heavy with an inch or more of red syrup. Tiles were covered from shoulderheight down on the far side, and the curtain, which hadn't been tucked in, was soaking from the other side. Blood from the curtain spatter had dribbled to the floor, leaving a puddle like a murder scene. There was no drain outside the tub, so the gore had already made it nearly to Piper's feet, inching toward the threshold.

The sink was dotted. So was the mirror. The walls had long streaks where Lila must have brushed them with her red fingers on the way out. The room wasn't tiny, but the spray had made its way to half the nooks and crannies. It looked like someone had walked to the middle, swallowed a stick of dynamite, and let fly.

"What the hell is going on, Meyer?" Piper yelled.

"*Meyer!*" came a voice from outside. From Jabari, he thought. "*Get in here!*"

Then Lila: "Dad! *Dad?*"

Meyer forced himself into motion. Moving slowly across the slick tile, he made his way to the spigot and turned it, suddenly irrationally sure that the flow would refuse to shut off. But it did, and the noise of the clotting surge (coagulating in the nozzle, fanning the spray even farther out) ceased, and the shouting and yammering and general freaking out continued from all sides as Meyer stood with his hand on the switch, heaving breath, his fine suit and shirt — and, he was sure, his face — wet with gore.

"Done," he said.

"*Done?*" Piper said, as if she didn't understand the word.

"MEYER!" came Jabari's voice.

There was a stomping of feet, then a slamming as if someone had struck the wall. Then Peers's voice: "What happened?"

"Dad?"

"Meyer!"

"Just a goddamned second!" Then to Piper: "I have to see what's happening out there."

"What about what's happening in here?"

"It's off now, Piper. It's not going anywhere."

"THE GODDAMNED SHOWER WAS SPRAYING BLOOD!"

Meyer pushed past her, fighting an uncharacteristic wave of nausea. His sinuses felt packed with meat. He could feel the greasy, organic slick of blood on his neck and hands and cheek, crawling across his skin, trying to cover him, filling his world with its rotting, suffocating reek.

"Meyer!" Piper shouted from behind.

He saw Lila, stock still and wet with more of the disgusting, stinking flow. It was easier and more useful to be annoyed than sympathetic, so he moved her aside, his eyes telling her that now wasn't the time, blood shower or no. He'd come back. In ten seconds, after he was done with the squeakiest wheel.

Peers wasn't far from Lila, looking at her with shock, somewhere between concerned and disgusted. Everyone heard her scream, but something on the TV seemed to have grabbed the others' attention while Meyer and Piper reacted. Now Peers was seeing what had caused Lila's commotion, but it was clear by Kindred and Jabari's echoing stares that whatever had happened on the television must be more pressing than the screams.

"What is it, Peers?"

He didn't answer, but Jabari said, "Meyer. Come here."

She didn't add *hurry*, but it was implied. Meyer crossed the room, dimly aware that he was leaving his own awful trail of red footprints, and faced the television.

On the screen were shots from cameras in the city above — fixed-position feeds. A corded phone was lying beside it, as if someone had called Jabari on the antiquated hotline.

"What?" Meyer said.

"From the Nile to the pipes," Jabari said, "every drop of water in Ember Flats has turned to blood."

CHAPTER 13

"Clara!"

Clara was stopped in the middle of a street filled with commotion, people running hither and yon around her as if she was invisible. Her ears were perked, listening for something she'd almost — but not quite — heard. There were so many voices in her head already; adding Nick and Ella's wasn't too big a deal. But this was different. Like it was someone who mattered a lot, calling her home.

Nick came and took her by the arm. Clara didn't shake him away, but her muscles seemed to do something that baffled his grip. It was like she was a big inert dummy and he was making the mistake of grabbing her like a seven-year-old human girl.

"*Clara!* What are you doing?"

Clara's concentration broke. The summons or call or whisper or whatever it was had faded the way desert radio broadcasts always did while on the move. It was a lonely sensation in the desert and struck Clara that way now: something anchoring her to a place or a person, dissolving like mist.

She looked at Nick, his face so very urgent. Non-Lightborn citizens of Ember Flats were streaking by on both sides, many with red hands, red fronts, even red hair and faces. None of the three children knew what had happened — but Clara, at least, kept wanting to tell the frightened, crimson-covered people that what they thought was happening actually wasn't, and that they needn't be afraid.

At least not yet.

"I thought I heard something." Clara was still trying to focus, hoping to pluck the voice or sound or whatever it had been from between human shouts in the panicked streets. Whatever it was, she felt desperate for more. It was like a song she couldn't place, or a face once seen and mostly forgotten. She didn't know what she'd heard or which slot it occupied in her mind. She only knew it was somehow meaningful or precious, and that she longed to hear it again.

But it was still gone, and Nick pulling for her to get out of the traffic was impeding her concentration.

"You didn't hear anything?" she asked.

"Same thing we heard back at that house," Nick said. "You really want to be out here with all these people after that?"

Clara thought back to the mental klaxon — the one that had sent them running for the Lightborn Hideout, wherever and whatever that was. It had been like a siren in their heads, but that hadn't been the scariest thing. Clara was freaked out because it was closer to an alert than a warning. She had this weird sense that it wasn't meant for human ears (or brains) at all. It had the feel of Astrals calling to other Astrals: "Hey, wake up, you aliens ... *it's time.*"

But time for what?

Not for this laughable horror show. Clara knew it was all supposed to be terribly frightening, but it just *wasn't*. Seeing people cavort around covered in goo wasn't scarier than the old supposedly scary movies she'd seen on any of the jukes she'd ever had access to. Splash a bunch of red stuff around, and everyone screams. It wasn't real blood. Looked like it, smelled like it, probably even tasted like it for the folks who went for cups of water without turning on a light. But Clara could tell the difference.

No, that klaxon had meant something else was coming. Something the Astrals maybe didn't want the humans to know about just yet.

"Come on. You seem cool and all, but we'll leave you behind if we have to." Nick smiled a little when he said it, but Clara wondered if that might be true. She could see fear in his eyes and hear it in their shared thoughts, and that fear had nothing to do with horror show. It was about something wicked that had yet to reveal itself: something involving the blood, but not the blood itself.

Clara let herself be led. She moved to the side of the street, out of the flow of shouting, rushing people. She and Nick joined Ella, and they tucked back so they wouldn't be trampled. In front of them, people were fleeing left and right. There was no true bearing in the chaos. It was unadulterated panic, and the only direction any of these people seemed to be headed was *away.*

"What was it, Clara?" Ella asked.

Clara watched the girl's curious, dark brown eyes, wondering what it meant that even her two Lightborn friends hadn't heard ...

Hadn't heard ...

Clara flexed her mind, still trying to hear the presence that had appeared so suddenly and vanished so soon. But it was gone.

It had the feeling of wanting to lead her but hadn't seemed to know how. It was reluctant and afraid, yet made her feel bold. It had been as scared as she was but felt stubborn enough to bully past its ignorance and lead anyway.

It was friendly. Comforting. A safe presence she felt used to following.

Sort of like Mr. Cameron.

CHAPTER 14

In the middle of watching Meyer jam an oversized hiking backpack full of food and water and assorted gear, Piper felt a sudden, crushing need to cry. The feeling came out of the blue. But she had no choice, if she wanted to remain upright, other than to sit and let it come. So she did, and it washed over her, and Piper's eyes watered without her having any idea why.

She looked up. Nobody was paying her any mind. The room's attention was squarely on Meyer (who was shouting orders like his old self, though without the harsh edge), Kindred (who was shouting similar, aligned orders, *with* that old edge), and Jabari. They were yelling. There was much profanity. Many threats, and options offered, like when Kindred told the viceroy, "You can come with us, or you can go fuck yourself."

Lila, off to one side, was dabbing her face with a beige washcloth that looked like it'd been used to clean the world's worst nosebleed. She'd changed clothes and had done a fair job of cleaning herself considering that the only water left was frozen as cubes, but she still looked like she'd taken a run through a dripping meat locker. She wasn't looking at Piper. Lila's eyes were on Peers as he tossed in his own two cents, reasserting that he could get them safely to the Cradle, but Lila looked like she didn't believe him. She looked, in fact, like she might jump on the man's back and stab him with a nail file.

Piper's head sagged with the weight of an unknown feeling. She couldn't find anything to hold in the emotion, so she waited for it to subside. It could be about Clara still missing; it could be about Cameron; it could be about something else entirely. Somehow, it felt like it might be about both Clara *and* Cameron, but that didn't make sense. She only knew her own heavy sorrow. And yet there was hope in the sadness, as if it had meaning. As if some of the horror they'd lived through in the past hours and days and months and years had been worth it. As if there'd been — and maybe still was — purpose behind it all.

The feeling passed, moving on like low-hanging mist dissolving in the sun, and then there was only the sound of arguing.

"I don't give a shit what you want to do," Meyer was telling Jabari. "We're going."

"You can't get away! Where are you going to go?"

"To your submarines. Then to the sea; what do I care?"

"You can't just go out into open water! You're safer here."

"You mean where the water just turned to blood? You know we're in Egypt, right? Any of this seeming familiar to you? What comes next?"

"Frogs," said Peers.

"Well, fuck that," Meyer said. "I'm not going to sit around and wait for frogs. You want to wait for frogs, Kindred?"

"I hate frogs."

Jabari moved a foot closer, too far into Meyer's personal space. Her eyes darted to Kindred then back. "What a shock that you agree with yourself."

"*You* don't have to agree with me, Mara! This is a simple proposition. Whoever wants to come with me can come. Whoever wants to stay can stay. You want to wait for lice and boils and locusts and shit? Go for it. But if there's a chance we can walk through the sea once parted by Moses, all the way to some vehicles you put in place specifically to escape this, *then we're going to take it.*"

"We have to stick together! For protection!"

"Only one not going is you. *We'll* be fine."

Lila tossed her washcloth to the floor. It landed with a splat.

"I'm not going, Dad."

"You're *goddamn well* going, Lila!"

"Why?" Jabari said, advancing another inch. "You said whoever wanted to stay could stay."

"She's my daughter."

"She's an adult. And her daughter is here."

"You don't know that," Meyer said.

"You don't know *anything!*" Jabari screamed.

"Peers," Kindred said. "The tunnels. Where are they?"

"I have an idea. I'd have to go up into the palace to see."

"Great escape plan," Jabari said, looking around. "You don't even know where you're going. Maybe I shouldn't worry about it after all."

"I can find them," Peers said.

"How?"

"It's ... complicated."

Attention left Peers when Jabari started pacing, but Piper noticed that he'd grabbed his backpack and was holding it in his lap. A subtle change, but to Piper it looked as if he had something he meant to protect. He'd hugged it tighter when Jabari asked her question. What was in that backpack that would tell him the tunnels' whereabouts?

Piper's eyes went to Lila. She'd seen Peers grip the backpack, too. She noticed Piper watching her and looked away.

At the room's center, Jabari shook her head, glaring at Kindred and Meyer, gesturing overtly at Peers.

"He doesn't have a clue. He won't tell you what he knows or how he knows it. And you're just going to trust him to get you out so you can hook into the satellite and talk to the other viceroys?"

"Fuck the other viceroys!" Kindred said. "I don't care what happens as long as he can get us out of the city."

"You'll draw the ship's attention! Bring it down on us all!"

Meyer rolled his eyes, shaking his head. "Do you really think we're hiding from them? The Astrals know *exactly* where we are."

"This building is made of repeater stone, same as the monoliths," Jabari said. "They can't see through the walls in here. It was part of the truce when we founded Ember Flats."

"Don't be naive."

"We studied this! We did our research!" the viceroy shouted, her careful control starting to unravel. "You just dropped acid and followed the motherfucking godhead!"

"Actually, Benjamin's people inside Heaven's Veil told me that Ayahuasca — "

"Stay out of this, Piper," Kindred said.

"I'm on your side!"

Meyer raised his hands, palms out. "Okay, okay. Calm down, everyone."

"I'm plenty calm," said Jabari. "In fact, I'm the only sane one here."

"I said I'm staying, too."

"No you're not, Lila," Kindred said.

"How can you not care? She's your granddaughter!" Then it looked, for a second, as if Lila might add, "Sorta."

"We might have a better chance of finding her once we're outside the palace walls anyway," Meyer said, hands still halfway raised. "You heard what she said about the stone in the walls. Piper's obviously tapping into something now. Right, Piper?"

Piper fought down annoyance and indecision. Finally she nodded.

"If Clara is outside, maybe that's why Piper can't really *feel* her now. Maybe if we go outside — "

"You'll find yourself covered in frogs and boils and locusts?" Jabari said.

"Logical," Kindred said. "The *Bible* is just a story. It's not a field guide to what's going to happen next."

Jabari jabbed an accusing finger at the TV screen, now showing a feed of the Nile. The river looked as if someone had filled it with tomato soup.

"The shuttles have mostly retreated," she said. "I'm not seeing nearly as much here about Reptars or anything else, other than my people stampeding each other. They turned the water to blood. They did that once before. Did you ever stop to think that they're not doing it because 'the *Bible* says so,' but because this is *what they do* and the Christian *Bible* is just one record of something that actually happened, for other reasons?"

"You're guessing," Kindred said.

"You're guessing!" Jabari retorted.

"Just ... relax. We're leaving."

"I'm not leaving, Dad!"

"Goddammit, Lila!" Meyer said, his temporarily calm mood snapping like a twig. *"We're all going, and that's all there is to it!"*

He turned to Jabari in the following silence.

"Do whatever you want. Stay or go. I'm sure there are some of your people left around in other bunkers, hiding in rooms, wherever. Maybe you can get a clear frequency and talk to the other viceroys. I like you, and I'm grateful to you for taking us in. But you will not tell me what my family can and cannot do. *We are leaving.* I'd prefer to do so with a plan once we leave Peers's tunnels. But we'll go however we have to, even if that only means running. God knows we've done it before."

Jabari sighed then nodded.

"I'll unlock a tablet for you. If the feeds are still showing up down here on the TV, that probably means the house server is running. It'll sync with maps to the Cradle's location. It'll walk you through how to de-dock the submersibles, how to pilot them, where to find and how to access the rendezvous checkpoint, everything. If I can reach the viceroys before you reach the broadcast hub, I'll let them know you're coming and that they should speak to you as they would to me. If not, the fact that you're authorized by my fingerprint should convince them to at least hear you out." Jabari looked earnestly at Meyer, her rancor gone now that she saw the futility of her cause. "But there are no guarantees. Even if you make it to our broadcast hub, *they* might not reach theirs. I've seen nothing at all that tells us what's happening in other cities. They might all be dead. They might all have ships like this overhead, and water turning to blood might be nothing by comparison."

She looked at Peers, but he didn't take the bait. Watching them, Piper felt sure that he had a response — knowledge about the possibilities of other big ships, perhaps — but the man said nothing.

Meyer looked at Lila, Piper, and finally Jabari.

"Thank you," he said.

But Piper felt the echo of her earlier sorrow deep inside, and the way it resonated with the news that they'd be leaving the palace was troubling.

She couldn't shake the feeling that even as the world fell apart, the process of judgment wasn't yet over — and that by running, they were doing exactly what the judge, jury, and executioners expected them to do.

CHAPTER 15

"Welcome to the Hideout," Ella said, smiling, as they reached a nondescript spot behind an alley dumpster.

She extended her hand to knock on a graffiti-covered door, but it opened before her knuckles could touch the metal surface. To Clara, the whole thing looked like an empty ritual. Ella didn't look like she'd expected to actually knock (her fist wasn't even clenched) and the red-haired boy who opened the door didn't seem surprised to see them. *Any* of them, including Clara.

He stepped aside, allowing their entry.

When Clara saw that they meant to let her in without so much as a nod, she extended her hand to the boy.

The boy took it, but did so limp-handed, halfheartedly, as if irritated by the distraction that had required him to open the door. It seemed like he wasn't a greeter so much as the person closest to the door when he'd felt their presence beyond it.

"I'm Clara."

"I know."

After a pause, her hand already dropped, she said, "What's your name?"

The boy looked at Nick. Then Nick, not the boy, said, "This is Cheever."

"That's an unusual name."

"It's a nickname," Nick said. His real name is — "

"Don't say it," Cheever said.

(*Eugene*), Clara heard in her mind.

Nick smiled like a little devil.

They were still standing around awkwardly, Cheever looking as if waiting to be excused. He seemed to be a year or two younger than Nick, not much older than Clara but with a teenage-sized chip on his shoulder. His hair was the color of a dirty carrot, and his eyes were green. He had a sloppy, slouched look about him, his blue T-shirt rumpled.

"Nick and Ella found me in a — "

"In that house on Divinity Avenue," the boy finished. "The one with the broken rear window and the busted fence. You're Viceroy Dempsey's granddaughter. You've spent most of your life in a palace or wandering, so you're new to communicating in a network. And right now you're trying to figure out how I know everything you told these two, even though it should be obvious. And — "

He stopped then turned to Nick. "What's this?"

Clara looked at Cheever, expecting to see something curious in his hands. Instead, she saw nothing, except that she could feel mental fingers poking at the memory of the strange voice she'd seemed to hear — the one that had stopped her dead on the street on their way here.

"Something she kinda remembered on the way over. It's not important."

"Sure seems important. *She* thinks it's important."

Clara's mouth opened. She was considering an objection but wasn't sure what to protest. Was it more offensive that they were casually discussing a personal mental event that she'd shared with no one, or that they were talking *about* rather than *to* her?

"She's just getting used to things. Give her a break, huh?"

"I dunno. Feels like something she's hiding."

"I'm not hiding anything," Clara said.

"And she's ... " He trailed off, focusing, and Clara felt the mental fingers digging deeper. The sensation was intrusive. She tightened instinctual muscles and found she could push him back. But not before he reached something else.

"She's been with those guys. The whatchacall'em?"

"Mullah," Clara said, preempting her blown not-really-a-secret.

"Did you know that when you picked her up?"

"No," Nick said. "But what, were we supposed to *not* go out and get her? You felt it same as me, asshole."

"It's nothing," Clara said.

"I knew," Ella said. "She told me all about it."

Clara hadn't, but she *had* been thinking about Sadeem and Quaid and the others. Reliving the ... the *attack?* ... in the Mullah tunnels had felt like a conversation with herself. Maybe she'd been chatting with Ella without even knowing.

"It's no big deal," Ella said. "They kidnapped her."

"They didn't really kidnap me."

"What then?" Cheever asked. "You know the reputation those guys have? We've been dodging them since we made this place. Now they've probably followed you here. Great job, Nicholas."

"They didn't follow us," Nick said.

"You know she's hiding something. You saw it same as me."

Clara decided she'd better defend herself before someone else had to do more of it for her.

"It was just something I was thinking about. On the way over here, it was like I sorta heard something, or remembered it from a long time ago. The way you'll hear someone hum and not remember what song it's from. You know?"

Cheever was still half frowning, unconvinced.

"And the Mullah didn't do anything bad. Mostly they wanted to know about me. About us."

"Right. Us. And you told them, did you?"

"Relax, *Eugene*," Nick said. "It's not like she could have told them about the Hideout or any of us anyway."

"No, but she cooperated. And now they know how we think."

"Why is that important?" Clara asked.

"I dunno," Cheever said, crossing his arms. "It just is."

Nick rolled his eyes and pushed past the boy, leaving him behind. The space ahead was just as Clara had seen it in her head, but seeing it physically brought it to different reality. It was large and open, like a converted warehouse. She saw the poster nook and even the paint-covered couch, but with proper eyes she noticed countless details. Industrious inhabitants had somehow strung lines from the high ceiling to suspend privacy curtains. Some had fancy beds that no kid could carry alone — and that two couldn't carry other than piece by piece.

She had so many questions, but the decorating scheme was too far down the priority queue. She followed Ella and Nick through the cavernous space, mentally itching at the spot Cheever had been so suspicious of. Heads turned as they walked. Could everyone see it? Were they all as suspicious as Cheever?

I don't even know what it is. How can they blame me for something that came at me out of the blue?

And Ella's voice answered, even though she'd meant to talk only to herself.

(Lightborn aren't used to secrets.)

I don't mean to keep a secret!

(It's not your fault, Clara. There's just never anything we can't all share, is all.)

The idea made her skin crawl. Was there truly nothing personal here? Did they all mentally see each other changing and using the bathroom? When a girl got a crush on a boy, was he able to laugh at her affection right away rather than the girl being able to stew for a while first?

"Ella's right, Clara," Nick said aloud. "Don't listen to Cheever. He's a dick. All that matters is what Logan thinks."

Clara was about to ask who Logan was, but by looking inside herself she found the answer. He was this group's leader. And by looking deeper, following mental branches like a river delta, she could see more of him: Logan was sixteen, wore glasses, and had grown up in Austria before being shuttled here by his now-deceased family. She had his whole dossier. It was there for the browsing, open as a book.

"Logan's sixteen," Clara said.

"It's okay. He's cool."

"No. I mean ... " She stopped, realizing her question would apply to Nick, too, as well as many of the assembled Lightborn. "I thought Lightborn kids came from being born near a ship."

"There's a few kinds. You'll learn. We all think sorta as one big brain, but at different levels. And we all shine a bit different. Ella's pretty bright, I'm a bit dimmer, Cheever's unfortunately pretty bright considering he was born before Astral Day, Logan's okay ... Look around once you're settled, and you'll see."

"What about me?"

Nick laughed. "You're super-bright, Clara. Like, really *light* out of all the *Light*born. It was kind of hard *not* to see you the second you came out from the palace or those tunnels or wherever you were. That's the reason Cheever's all up your butt about that thing in your head. We can all wall off parts of ourselves, but usually it's not something we notice unless the rest of our brightness is turned up to eleven, like yours."

"I swear. I'm not trying to keep a secret."

Nick nodded shortly. "I know. I'm not Cheever."

He moved ahead. But the feeling of needing to divulge — of needing to make amends for the secret she hadn't asked for — was pressing.

"Nick?"

"Yes?"

"I think I can hear the Astrals. There's this sensation of whispers. It's English in my head, and it sounds to me like whispering kids, but ... well, I'm new to this, but I don't think it's you guys. I think it's them. My way of imagining them."

Nick waited a second before nodding again.

"That's what Logan thinks, too. That we're tapped into them, and they might not even know it."

Clara looked around, searching for their sixteen-year-old leader. But among the Lightborn, people didn't need speech to agree.

"So that loud alarm thing we heard? It was, like — "

"Like a timer going off," Nick said. "It was right before the water became like blood. So ... "

"Right. A timer. *Time to unleash the plagues.* That must be it."

He started to walk away again with Ella by his side. But Clara, unmoving, still felt an itch. Something else bothered her about this. Something she'd been rolling over inside her mind — somewhat guarded since she'd realized how easily her thoughts were being read. And now here in the Hideout, she realized it was something she didn't sense in the hive mind. Something that rang funny about all of this.

About the plague they'd already had.

Abut the plagues the citizens seemed to be anticipating next.

There had been a King James Bible in the craphole they'd stayed in outside Roman Sands, and Clara, then just six, had read it cover to cover. She knew what came next. By now, in these apocalyptic times, pretty much everyone knew what to expect once the rivers turned bloody.

"Nick?"

Nick and Ella turned.

"There's more. I don't know if it's just a feeling or if someone told me and I forgot, but I've sorta been ... hiding it, I guess. Not on purpose, but ... "

"What?"

"I can't shake the sense that they gave us plagues *because we expected plagues*. Because that's what people think happens when the world ends."

Nick turned fully around then walked back. The mood on his face was unreadable.

"What does that mean, Clara?"

She swallowed and said, "What if this is all just a show — and that whatever they're *really* doing and whatever they're *really* after is something totally different?"

CHAPTER 16

It wasn't easy for Stranger to see the world through Astral eyes, now that he had a fixed and unchanging human body.

He thought this as he focused on the Reptar at the bottom of the big dune. The thing couldn't see Stranger as he watched from the perch where the shuttle had left him — beyond the city limits, at the desert's edge. But Stranger could see the Reptar just fine.

And he focused. Attempted to see the world through Astral eyes.

Stranger squinted, trying to do the thing he'd done before. Trying to pop the Reptar like a big purple zit. But it was no use. Taking in all that new Meyer Dempsey on the mothership had been like drinking a bottle of liquor. He was drunk on Dempsey. The last of the Pall's floating, ephemeral nature was gone now that he had all that extra humanity. Now he wasn't Pall at all, as he'd been when he'd turned the last Reptar to mincemeat. He was this new thing, through and through. Now he was Stranger, from mouth to asshole. Just like any of the others.

Well, not *just* like any of the others.

He pulled a pair of silver balls from his pocket and revolved them in his palm. They orbited like twin suns. Technically speaking, the balls hadn't existed until he'd pulled them from his pocket. How could they? His jeans weren't loose, and the balls were big enough to play ping-pong with. You could never fit them into tight pockets without looking like you had tumors.

Two balls became three.

Became four.

Became five.

He clenched his hand, and the balls were gone.

What was different between the balls and the Reptar? He'd blown that last Astral soldier apart just by looking at it. Simple enough at the time. He'd merely needed to realize that the thing was energy and so was his mind. It was the way the Astrals saw the world — as one big pool of energy where the line between "individuals" was fuzzy at best. Astrals couldn't blow stuff up just by looking at it — that particular marriage of talents was his alone. To do what he'd done to that Reptar, you had to see the patterns then use feedback to *disrupt* the patterns from within.

It helped that Stranger, at his core, *was* feedback as far as the Astral energy pool was concerned.

And now he'd seen the stream. Now he understood what he was — what the Pall had been before him. He understood why the Pall had become Stranger when the Ark had opened. He understood what the Pall and Stranger had in common: that both were made of the all-too-human traits that had caused the first Meyer Dempsey replica to malfunction, turning from its Astral cousins toward the human side of the coin. The Astral collective, when it made Kindred, had squeezed out those negative traits and made a "better" copy of Meyer Dempsey by doing so, but the process created waste as well.

And the Pall had been born from that waste.

Then Stranger had been born when the opened Ark had turned that human waste into something even more human. Something that could walk around on two legs and tell Divinity what was what.

And now, having taken in a new dose of Astral Meyer's emotions — the same emotions that had caused all that feedback inside the hive mind — Stranger had become a bit too human to pop Reptars by thought. What a shame.

But he could do other tricks, too. Stranger wasn't out of magic just yet.

He could still make inanimate props — silver balls, say — appear from thin air. All it took was intending for them to be there. Easy as pie. Things like little silver balls didn't have brain enough to disagree, so they appeared and disappeared whenever he wanted them to.

And he could see the truth. About the Lightborn. About the puzzle. *About the ant farm.* Hell — even about Cousin Timmy.

And he could open windows.

Stranger squatted down. He sat, wondering where he should open a new one. The Reptar was too far below to see as he came to rest on his ass; it dropped out of sight. Now Stranger could only see sand and horizon beyond the dune. Not far off was the lush edge of the Nile valley. Then the river itself, crimson with blood.

Soon, the Astrals would make their next play — maybe their *real* play — or maybe more jazz-hands bullshit designed to frighten the humans. *Probably* the bullshit. There was so much these days. And after the bullshit with the blood was over, the Astrals would probably try some other cockamamie "plague" or scare-fest to get the humans jumping. It'd be funny if it weren't so pathetic.

Eventually they'd kill everyone on Earth, save a few to start over and try this whole thing again. It's how it always happened, if the memories he still carried from his more

Astral days were correct. But before killing them all, they'd play and watch the frenzy.

To most humans, blood and locusts and other such bullshit was all worth fretting over. But to Stranger and the Lightborn, rivers of blood and other bullshit like it were obvious for what they truly were: yet another way the Astrals were shaking the planet-sized ant farm so they could see what the insects did next.

It was cruel. And unfair. Ants were ants, and could never know you were fucking with them.

His thoughts turned to Mara Jabari, who thought she was so clever. The Astrals knew she was plotting against them. *Of course* they knew, just like they knew the other human viceroys would plot against them. That was *why* the viceroys existed. That was *why* the Astrals had chosen the people they had to become viceroys in the first place. They were all leaders, thinkers, and rebels at heart. *Of course* they'd play along — then try to wiggle out.

Just about everything that had transpired around the Ark and the key and the group that carried it had been *allowed* to happen. That group, like Jabari, thought they were so clever, too. Peers Basara, given his big cave full of Astral technology so he could find and assist Meyer's party, then left alone no matter where he went or what he did. Cameron Bannister, who as the Key Bearer had never truly understood — except perhaps at the end — that *what he chose to do* with the key mattered far more than *actually doing* it.

But the Astrals thought they were clever as well. They thought they were smart, staying out of sight and watching the ants. They thought they knew it all, and that the humans couldn't surprise them.

Well, the Astrals hadn't known about the Lightborn. Not what they meant. And in the ways that mattered, the aliens still didn't truly know why the Lightborn were so incredibly important. The Mullah seemed to suspect, but the Astrals hadn't a clue. They simply weren't human enough to get it.

And the Astrals didn't know what the Pall had been. What Stranger now represented, now that he truly understood what he was and why he'd been born — now that he'd soaked in so much more of the emotion that had caused him to be here in the first place.

Maybe the newfangled breed of humanity hadn't developed the New Age mental kumbaya that the Astrals expected, but another thing Stranger knew (that the Astrals had missed): they were mentally connected all the same.

Meyer Dempsey proved it with drugs. He proved it by taking ayahuasca with Heather. At the time, Stranger knew by looking inside his own memories, Heather had thought they were tripping out and having fun. But even back then Meyer had suspected their journeys were something more. He'd known even all those years ago that by speaking to "Mother Ayahuasca," he'd been talking to some kind of universal unconsciousness, composed of all the minds the world — all the worlds — had to offer.

That had opened one kind of window — the one that had let the Astrals see Meyer's world through his eyes, and begin to judge it while their ships were still on their way to Earth.

But there were other kinds of windows to open, just like there were other ways in which universal unconsciousnesses were formed.

Stranger crossed his legs.

He closed his eyes.

And as the window opened in front of him, he said to the New Human Collective: "What they tell you next, friends? It's only smoke and mirrors."

He felt the collective's minds turn to listen, even if they didn't understand what they were hearing.

And Stranger told them about themselves. About who they were and what they represented. And about how Cousin Timmy might just have his day after all.

CHAPTER 17

Whatever was happening, things were getting worse rather than better.

Kindred followed Peers through the upstairs hallways, not so much oblivious to the frenzied, all-too-human panic visible through gaps in the fence as mindfully defiant of it. All that was happening in Ember Flats struck Kindred as stupid and annoying. So the water had turned to blood? It wasn't like the Astrals were killing everyone, which is what was supposed to happen in the aftermath of rendered judgment. The entire population — especially after Meyer and Kindred had told them about Heaven's Veil and the massacre there — had been primed for a bloodbath. Instead, the Astrals had given them a bath in blood. Context made all the difference. Blood water smelled bad, but it didn't hurt anyone. And yet even now that the shuttle lasers and Reptar patrols had mostly stopped (so far as Kindred could see, and so far as Jabari reported from her monitors), everyone kept right on panicking.

Kindred kind of wished the Astrals would get on with it. At least that would shut everyone up and stop their whining.

He clenched his fists. He couldn't close his eyes or he'd run into Piper's back, but he forced himself to breathe. And again he recited, for the thousandth time:

It's just the Ark. Cameron opened the Ark, and you're feeling its negative energy, not just your own. Cameron dropped his dumb ass into the Ark as some sort of a mindless sacrifice, and for some reason that's a goddamned problem. For some reason Cameron's issue became your issue. You were supposed to make a speech. You did your, part and Cameron was supposed to do his, but he did it wrong (or maybe too right) and now the world is filled with bad juju. It's not you who's pissed off; it's the world, thanks to all this bullshit with Cameron and his inability to follow a simple set of fucking instructions.

Kindred's fists didn't unclench. He wasn't calming. At first, the self-talk had seemed to remind him that he was being influenced by the Ark's bad energy — all the judgment in the air and whatnot. At first, he'd felt a bit better with every reminder, telling himself that he felt angry because the planet felt angry. But not anymore. Now whenever he thought of the Ark, he got pissed at Cameron for botching his part of their carefully laid plan.

Meyer's hand on Kindred's upper arm, surprising him enough to make him jump.

"What's wrong with you?" Meyer asked, his voice a near-whisper.

Kindred, startled enough that his emotions fell to neutral, turned to Meyer. It was like looking in a mirror except that Kindred, during their time in the basement, had shaved whereas Meyer hadn't — probably planning to regrow his salt-and-pepper beard. But why *wouldn't* Kindred shave? Life went on. And if he needed to shave again now that things had gone red, he'd lather up and shave with blood. It'd be very pagan. Very manly.

"Nothing's wrong with me."

"Bullshit. You're all pissed. You're making it hard to concentrate."

"What do you need so badly to concentrate on?"

"Peers."

"What about him?"

For the second Meyer spent glaring, Kindred thought his double might slap or shake him. But then Meyer's incredulous look became words, and he said, "I've been in your head for a half hour at least about this. You haven't noticed?"

"I've been preoccupied."

"I gathered. About the Ark? But who cares? It's open. It's over."

Even having this discussion was proof of how much things had soured. Normally there was no need to whisper because anything that required whispering could be done in their shared mind. Meyer had gained intense human insight during his time in captivity, and Kindred was supposed to be their Astral half, able to access the motherships and Divinity, even if only partway. Together their shared headspace was like a room full of supercomputers. At least that's the way it was *supposed* to be, with interoffice memos passed between them below the level of conscious thought. Meyer's presence in that shared space — borrowing from Kindred's mind, basically — without him noticing? That was troubling. And the way Meyer seemed not to understand why the Ark still troubled Kindred? That was troubling, too.

"Tell me why you're concentrating on Peers," Kindred said, deflecting Meyer's question.

"You've seen the scenarios. You've seen the conclusions."

Kindred looked inside. Yes, Meyer had begun assembling their usual scenarios, but the quiet part of Kindred's mind didn't seem to have been terribly involved. They'd be weak logical arguments at best, but it also meant that Kindred wouldn't have a clue, without delving in, as to what they even were.

"Pretend I haven't."

Meyer gave him a look.

"Just spell it out. I'm an auditory learner sometimes."

The look persisted. But after another few steps down the long hallway, lagging farther behind Piper, Lila, and Peers at their group's head, Meyer complied.

"Peers is hiding something."

"We knew that."

"He knows far too much without logical roots. He's making assumptions about Clara and the Mullah with nuances that would only come from experience."

"You think he took her?"

"No."

"He was in on it," Kindred said.

Meyer paused. Apparently he was having trouble accepting that now was the first time Kindred was hearing any of this. "Not necessarily."

"What, then?"

"He might be Mullah."

"In which case?"

"We're headed to tunnels only Peers knows about. *Tunnels.* Tubes underground in which we could be easily surrounded. The Mullah have been trying to catch us, but we've always managed to get away. Maybe this is their chance, and Peers is their tool."

"So we shouldn't go."

"You really haven't looked at the scenarios?"

"Just tell me, dammit."

"Given the alternative, it's still the best option. But there are other questions. His nerves, for one. And some of his biometrics. He's sweating too much. His pupils are dilated. His pulse is up. I can *hear* it, for fuck's sake. And that makes us think that he's hiding something beyond being Mullah. Something more present than a plot to trap us."

Kindred noticed Meyer's use of the word "us," as if Kindred had been involved in the analysis. He let it go.

"What's the assessment?"

"Guilt."

"Guilt over what?"

"It's hard to say. That's why we're concentrating on watching him — so we can see if it's guilt that makes him dangerous or guilt that will make him helpful. Perhaps he's guilty because he was involved in Clara's abduction and now he plans to make amends. Or maybe it's something bigger. My money's on something bigger. But I can't really tell because I keep trying to concentrate, and all I hear is your bitching. About the Ark."

"It's been on my mind."

"Why?"

Kindred glanced at Meyer. If there was one person he could be honest with, it was Meyer. But in the end they *weren't* actually the same person. Meyer was human, and Kindred — despite all he'd been forced to go through — was still Astral. The minute he admitted to being more angry than sympathetic toward humans, the group would turn on him. What was happening in Ember Flats? It was Us versus Them. Only perimeter security had kept the hordes out of the palace so far, but the power wouldn't stay on forever. Then the obnoxious, panicky human assholes would come inside, too, with little patience for Astrals of any shape or size — *especially* if they seemed to be losing a grip on what had made them human-ish in the first place.

"It's just another datum for our scenarios," Kindred lied.

"Seems like a big datum. And I'm not even seeing your mind inside."

Kindred forced himself to focus. He entered the mindspace. He felt Meyer join him, and together their mental selves moved to the cognitive planning tables to work scenarios about Peers and his potential plans.

"Better?" Kindred said.

Meyer watched him for a long moment. His beard was already noticeably back, stubble dark and obvious. Humans were so damned *hairy*. This one in particular.

"Good enough," Meyer answered.

At the group's head, Peers stopped. Piper and Lila paused behind him, and Meyer and Kindred brought up the rear. They all looked forward at nothing. The wall at the group's head looked ordinary enough to Kindred, but it seemed special to Peers — and after a few moments' searching he popped open a concealed panel under the baseboard. Kindred bent forward to assess it. Inside the panel was what looked like a very strange keyhole: an inverted triangle made of three smaller inverted triangles.

Peers pulled a keyring from his pocket. Kindred half expected him to brandish a key to match the strange hole, but instead he made three of the normal-looking keys into tips and touched them all to the contact points as if hoping to short-circuit a mechanism.

There was a grumbling of stone on stone. A section of wall moved back, separating from its neighbors at cleverly concealed gaps in the panels.

Below was a tunnel lined in ancient-looking stone, lit by what seemed to be dangling, naked bulbs.

One by one they descended.

Then, as they walked the tunnel at a fair clip, Kindred's natural ability to mesh with Meyer's mind returned, and they both repeated the same conclusion, one to the other.

There is only ahead and behind. There is no way to escape if we are surrounded, and none of us but Peers knows where we might be going.

This is a Mullah place.
And even now, I can hear them stirring.

CHAPTER 18

The Lightborn children moved toward one end of the big room with all its tiny, nomadic living spaces, centering on a tall teenage boy that had to be Logan. To Clara, the movement seemed to be unspoken, unannounced — almost instinctual. Nobody had called them together. It was simply happening.

But the message hadn't reached Clara and didn't seem to have reached Nick. Ella had moved on with the others, but Nick was still facing Clara as the others passed them, unheeding. The others must not be hearing either of their minds, either, because none perked up as they passed. They were all focused on something, and no distraction, for anyone, seemed loud enough to cause a diversion.

"What do you mean, 'expected plagues'? What kind of a 'show'?"

"It's just a feeling I get."

Nick moved closer. He used his voice, but Clara could feel his thoughts reaching out as well, grabbing her by a mental arm, gripping it too tightly.

"I get it. I'm asking, *what's the feeling?*" It was more a demand than a question. Like Clara herself, Nick acted older than his years when compared to non-Lightborns.

They were like a tribe of stunted adults. Pods grown to age fifteen or more before the day they entered the world.

Clara looked around, uncomfortable. Her words were like a confession to clear the air of secrets and mental withholdings, but she hadn't thought it would strike Nick as a surprise. They were all gifted. They could all see, hear, and sense things on the air that the others couldn't. Clara had wanted to toss in the helpful information that seemed missing from the Lightborn Collective, but it hadn't dawned on her that they'd have sighted none of it.

Clara stammered to catch up.

"The ... the voices I hear. They seem to say ... "

"Like the voice from earlier? From on our way over, when you stopped on the street like you were listening?"

"No. This is different." And yet *that* voice was back as well. Or one an awful lot like it. Something inside her mind was rising, building steam. Did the others feel the same thing, or was she alone in that, too? She'd finally found a group of like minds who wouldn't see her as a freak. But was she strange even within the Lightborn? A freak among the freaks?

"*Clara?*" Nick prompted when she stalled. There was urgency in the air, like the building of a static charge. *That*, all of them seemed able to feel. Clara saw it in her mind like a timer ticking to zero. It was why the others were going to Logan, the reason Nick sounded so rushed and impatient.

"Chatter. You can't hear chatter?"

"I hear the others in this room."

"What about the others outside this room?"

"You're saying you hear other Lightborn?" Nick's raised eyebrows told Clara all she needed to know: They only knew those in the city. Another reason she'd never sensed collectives before now. They were local. Except that now that Clara knew what to listen for, she could swear there were ever more on the air.

Freak among the freaks.

She shook the thought away.

"No. I mean like the siren. From before the blood. When we knew something was about to happen?"

"Yeah ... "

"That's it! That's all I mean: like before, when we knew it was coming."

"Ella and I knew *something* was coming before the blood. Not what it was."

"What's the difference?"

"Did you know, Clara? Did you know the water would turn to blood?"

The technical answer was *no*. She hadn't know that the citizens of Ember Flats were turning on taps and stepping into baths made of liquid that would clot at the edges. But the story behind the story had been clear as day. The gist of her mind's translation?

Let's see how they react to this.

Even now, thinking back, Clara could see those moments from a distance. There weren't specific words — at least not in English — but there was meaning and intent. There was curiosity, and dispassion. It hadn't felt like punishment. It hadn't felt like the *Bible's* portrayal of ancient Egyptian plagues. Even now, it felt more like a science experiment. The mood behind the chatter was investigation and analysis, not retribution.

"No."

"But you knew something."

"*You* didn't?"

"I told you. No."

"Why is it a big deal?"

Clara jarred something in Nick. Maybe he sensed her agitation — the feeling of being accused. So he let go a little, and the mental grip Clara felt on her mental arm relaxed.

"Look. You're different. Ella already sorta told you that, but the more time you spend here, the more obvious it becomes. To all of us."

Clara looked toward the assembling knot of Lightborn. Logan must have been standing on something in the group's middle because he was above them all, his head as high as someone seven or eight feet tall. The others kept glancing back at her. Curious, yes. But maybe afraid.

"Maybe it's because you haven't been around other Lightborn, or because you're Viceroy Dempsey's granddaughter. But you shone so bright we *had* to go out and get you. It's not like light from the others. I can see into you just fine. But there's ... more."

"More how?"

"That kid? From earlier? Cheever. He's gifted. And nosy. Normally, people can't keep secrets from him if he really wants to know them."

"I'm not trying to keep secrets!"

"I'm not saying you are," Nick said, subtly patting the air between them. "I'm saying that you puzzled him the way you're puzzling the others whether you realize it or not."

"I realize, all right," Clara said, again looking toward the group. Toward Logan, who was now looking right at them.

"Point is, whatever you're talking about with the plagues and the Astrals, I haven't seen it in our hive. That means the others haven't either. From where I'm standing, there was a warning, then the water turned to blood. But now you're talking about a *show*. You're talking like there's something else behind it all."

"I don't know. Maybe there is."

"Like how?" Nick asked.

"I don't know, Nick."

"You brought it up!"

Clara's patience broke. Her voice rose, and heads turned. "I don't know! I don't know! I just get a feeling, but I can't tell you what it is, okay?"

"Try. Just ... try."

"Okay. Do you know how people say, *It's not what you said; it's how you said it?*"

"Yeah. My mom used to say that to my dad all the time. Usually right before he got himself in trouble."

Clara smiled; the tension softened. "It's like that. I don't really hear words, but I get the vibes behind them. And with the siren thingy we heard ... I can't explain why, but I was pretty sure it was *them* talking to *them* like it was time for something to happen."

"For water to turn to blood."

"No." She groped for the internal word then found one that would make her mother's eyes roll, because it sounded like something a twentysomething might say. "It was more meta than that."

"How?"

"Like it was time for the test to start. Or the *next* test."

"What test?"

"I don't know. I only get little bits."

"But ... you think the blood is like a test?"

"A test or a show."

"A *show?*"

"Yeah. Like a performance. That's what I meant when I said the plagues are *expected*. They're like something out of an old movie about Judgment Day. Or at least Moses and pharaohs and stuff. And I just ... " She shook her head, frustrated. "I can't say why, but it's like they're all whispering behind their hands, like, *Don't let them see the wires.*"

"Wires?"

"Like in an old space movie where the fake spaceships were held up by wires."

"I've never seen any old movies. I didn't grow up in a palace."

Clara wondered if that was a jab. She let it go. "But you get the idea?"

"Kinda. So what does it mean? What do we do?"

That was a great question. Clara didn't know how to answer, and the strange voice she'd sensed all day offered no help. Even the new, distant collection of others she seemed to hear — human, not Astral — had no idea. The last was new. Just one more thing she couldn't integrate, that made her feel like she was losing her mind. Maybe telepathy-blocking stone walls weren't a bad thing. Maybe, in the past, they were the only thing keeping her sane.

"I don't know."

"If the blood and stuff is only an act, what's behind it? What are the Astrals really up to?"

"I don't know."

"Clara, I can't help if you don't — "

Nick stopped when the great grinding came from above. All the electronic devices in the room emitted a squeal so intense and piercing, every child winced and curled inward, fingers jamming into ears, faces contorting in pain.

There was a bark of static. A roar of electronic disruption belched from every tablet, every tiny juke — even, seemingly, the light fixtures keeping the warehouse space from darkness.

There was a pregnant pause while everyone stopped to listen, from Logan to Ella to Cheever. Inside Clara's mind, she heard Nick whisper, *Clara, what should we do?*

Another tiny bark of electronic disruption. Then three short beeps, like a forthcoming communication clearing its throat.

Clara gave the only answer she could, fake plagues or no:

Whatever they're about to tell us.

Then the lights went out, and Clara saw only blackness.

CHAPTER 19

Peers felt the memory sphere's weight, clunking against his back with every step. It looked heavier than it was. That was good. The way it kept wagging around in his pack — alone except for a few small supplies and the sheet he'd wrapped it in before making his way from his palace room — it'd be crippling. But as things stood, it was merely uncomfortable.

Uncomfortable because it kept whacking his shoulder blades.

And uncomfortable because with each passing minute, it became clearer and clearer that the others knew he was keeping something from them.

Lila and Piper kept eyeing his pack. They wouldn't demand he open it — yet. But the deception had gone on for too long — he couldn't reveal the sphere now. Without a reason to broach his secret, it would come off terribly. Even *with* an excuse it would probably be awful. Lila kept staring at his pack as if it held a bloody machete, and with the big, fat, round way it looked, there was little denying he had something more than toothpaste. The longer nobody asked him to open it, the longer he didn't show them. The longer he didn't show them, the more it would look like he'd been deliberately hiding it when the secret finally came out.

Which, of course, he was.

Because as things turned out, there was one person responsible for ringing the Astral dinner bell eleven years ago, and his name was Peers Basara. He'd tried to bury his guilt, to assure himself that even if he hadn't gone into the Temple that day and spoken through the portal, the Astrals would have come eventually. But time and research had shown him that the *point* of the Temple and portal — of the Mullah's stewardship in general — was that humanity was supposed to choose its time of judgment. They were supposed to make themselves worthy, then call the masters to check their work. But whenever Peers tried to justify his younger self's actions with those ideas, he felt like a rationalizing asshole. Humanity *hadn't* been ready for the Astrals' return. Peers, because he'd been an idiot kid who couldn't leave well enough alone, had called them early. And now everyone would die.

Well, not everyone.

The scrolls said that at the end of each epoch, a small group was chosen to carry the race and try again. The past was somehow erased (the scrolls said "washed away"), and it all started over.

Meyer would survive. Kindred would probably survive as well. The legend of the Seven Archetypes said there was a King, and that he had two heads, and that the King survived to lead the next epoch. That's how Peers had known it was his duty (as the Fool who *did* happen to know a way out of town, so long as he could find its entrance) to shepherd the King toward safety.

Either that, or he was a coward. Either heroism made him lead Meyer's exodus, or the hope that staying by Meyer's side would keep him safe as well.

Because the scrolls said nothing about the Fool and his fate.

"I hear something," said Piper from behind him.

Peers turned. He'd heard things, too, but it was just Meyer and Kindred chattering like the two-headed being they were.

He looked down. It wasn't Nocturne making noise. Years of desert living had ground the dog's claws so they no longer clacked when he walked.

"I think it's our echoes," Peers told her.

"It's not just that." She looked around, flustered, but seemed to let it go. "What are these tunnels, anyway? How did you know they were here?"

"Just a hunch."

Peers winced. They deserved a better lie. Guilt had its hooks in him. His gut was churning, and he could barely think. He was a man with a hideous secret and no one to take his confession, because even the most forgiving priest would strangle him for the truth.

"You must have a guess."

Peers glanced at Piper. Met her big blue eyes. She wasn't an idiot, nor was Lila beside her. They were choosing to pretend they believed his bullshit, but Peers knew they didn't — and in turn, they knew he knew. A game of chicken with Peers in the middle. Everyone knew he'd betrayed them, but no one spoke. They were sharpening knives, waiting. And right now, Peers could see the hatred on Lila's face, more fierce from the blood still matted in her hair and in the creases of her skin.

"They must be Mullah tunnels."

She didn't ask how Peers had known how to enter a Mullah place. Everyone knew it, just like everyone must know he was carrying a stolen alien artifact — that he'd lied with every breath for hours, that he'd caused the human race to meet its end, that he knew a whole lot more about Clara's disappearance than he'd let on. For a while there, his secret had been mercifully out. But then Jeanine Coffey had got herself killed, and it had again been easier to curl up and lie than admit to the shameful truth.

"I can feel them," Piper said. "The Mullah."

"Me too," said Lila, looking right at Peers. "So close, it's like they're right here with us."

Peers pretended not to notice Lila's stare. "Come on. It's this way. It must be, I mean."

"Only makes sense," Lila said. "Of course, none of us knows for sure."

"Of course," Peers said, fighting to steady his voice. It wasn't Lila getting to him. It was *himself*. Guilt, a million-pound weight. He shouldn't be fleeing the city. He should let the Astrals take him if they wanted — maybe die heroically, like Cameron seemed to have. But every time Peers considered a hero's exit, he found it easier to keep his mouth shut for another few minutes. To keep on walking.

"Where do you think Clara got to, Peers?" Lila said it like a question, but to Peers it sounded like an interrogation.

"I don't know."

"The Mullah have her."

"Yes."

"And this is a Mullah place."

"Maybe."

"So maybe she's here."

But she wasn't, and Lila knew it. The tunnel had been mostly straight so far, with few branches. The chambers and jaunts they'd passed were open and straightforward with no one inside. No Mullah, and no little girls.

"I don't think so."

"Is that because she's dead, Peers?"

Peers stopped. Piper almost ran into him.

"Lila!" Piper said.

"Don't say that," said Peers.

Lila shrugged. It was a businesslike gesture. "If she is, I'd rather just know. It's worse to keep hoping if that's how it ends."

For a moment, Peers couldn't respond. Lila's eyes were spheres of ice. Her irises were brown instead of Piper's blue, but in the tunnel's dim light they looked black. Her skin was still stained with dried blood. Her hair was a clotted mess, and she smelled like rancid meat because there'd been only an ice-dampened rag to clean herself with. Her stare was hard. She wasn't looking at Peers like a human. At least not a rational one. He could barely hold his space without falling back.

"You have to keep hoping," Peers said. "I'm sure she's fine."

"*How* sure?" Lila's voice held almost no emotion. Like she'd been bent too far and had finally broken. "Sure like you've *seen* her?"

"Of course not. But I'm sure nonetheless."

"Sure like you've talked to her kidnappers? As sure like you *are* one of her kidnappers?"

"Lila," Meyer said from behind, trying to break the strange standoff.

Without turning, Lila said, "I'm just asking, Dad."

"They wouldn't hurt her if she was held for a reason," Piper said.

"But the reason was a lie." Cold eyes turned to Peers. "He said so, and we trust him."

"We'll find her," Piper said.

"Except that you can't feel her anymore, can you?" Lila asked Piper. "You were so sure before that wherever Clara was, she was *safer than us*. But now you're not."

"Lila. Knock it off."

Lila turned to her father. To both of her fathers. "I'm just being logical and unemotional so I can make the best decisions, *Dads*. Just like you do."

Again, her stare turned to Peers. He was so focused on Lila that he didn't hear the rush of feet coming right at them.

CHAPTER 20

By the time Peers saw the Mullah, they were surrounded.

It happened in a blink. Peers had no idea where the men and women at their front and rear had come from, but judging by the others' faces, he wasn't alone. Meyer and Kindred were supposed to be the logic-makers, and ever since Cameron had opened the Ark, Piper was supposed to be the empath. But nothing had seen them coming. They weren't there, then they suddenly were.

A hard, angry face stared at Peers. Other angry faces stood behind him, all atop long, off-white desert robes. It took Peers a minute to realize that he wasn't imagining the sliding sensation at his throat. To realize someone was holding a blade to his skin.

"Who are you, and why are you here?"

The question was barked in accented English. The man who'd shouted, who by virtue of being first had been assumed the leader, had rough, sun-toughened skin. His lips made a scowl.

Peers realized his hands had come partway up. He didn't want to turn and look around. The others in his party could be doing anything.

"Please. Let me explain."

"I am telling you to explain! So tell! Who are you? How did you find this tunnel?"

Peers exhaled. There was no way out of this other than shaded truth.

"I used an Elder's Key."

The blade — a long scimitar, by the look — retreated a fractional inch. There was muttering in Arabic.

"Show me!"

Peers moved his hands slowly, palms open. He didn't have an Elder's Key, of course. Fools didn't seem to need them. But the phrase had grabbed the man's attention, and Peers only needed a second to show him something else that might change his mind.

Instead of reaching into his pocket, Peers raised his sleeve. He turned his bare arm to show the man his Mullah brand, tucked high near his armpit.

"You are Mullah?" the man said.

"Yes."

Something shifted behind him. The sound came from where he knew Lila was standing.

"What is your name?"

"Basara."

More whispering.

"I know this name. But I do not know you."

"My Den is from Turkey. I only ask that you let us pass."

The man shifted to be more in his way rather than less.

"I would be a poor soldier to let you go with only a question and half an answer."

"Then follow us. See that we only want the way out."

"Maybe I do not want to let you go?"

"I wear the brand. I opened the lock."

"And yet you have not shown me your key." The man frowned. "You know, *Basara* ... you do not seem old enough to be an Elder among the Mullah, even if you gained access in the manner you claim."

"I'm not claiming anything."

"You claim to be friend. Are you a friend?"

"Of course."

"Then perhaps you can help us. Our Den's tunnels have been here since well before the palace atop them, and before now there has been no way to enter. *Nothing* could get in, not even those little balls the Horsemen send. And yet recently they came in force. One of our Elders was abducted. Like you, Elder Basara, he had a key."

"Oh," Peers said, unsure where else to go.

"Maybe you took it from him."

"I — "

"Maybe if you show me your Elder Key , I will tell you whether or not it was once Sadeem's."

"Look," Peers said. "I'm on — "

"Someone betrayed us," he said, cutting Peers off. "They told the Astrals where to find us, then let them in. Someone let them take Sadeem, and helped them steal something very important to us — something we thought was protected but has now gone missing. We don't know how it happened. They came, and we fell asleep. When we woke in our chambers, Sadeem and our treasure were gone."

The man smiled an unconvincing smile.

"I'm telling you this because you are a brother among the Mullah. But I imagine it is not news to you. After all, there have been betrayers in the Mullah before ... *Basara.*"

Peers met the man's hard eyes. Then there was another sound directly behind him, emanating from the parcel in his backpack.

It was a harsh, staticky sound, followed by three sharp beeps.

The man's eyebrows dove downward. His lips formed a scowl.

"What is in your backpack, my friend?"

But before Peers could summon an answer — one for the Mullah and another for his group — the tunnels trembled, the ground shaking like the world was reaching its end.

Peers's legs buckled. The scimitar at his neck retreated, the hand holding it needed for balance. Someone fell at the group's rear, ahead of Peers. Dust sifted from the ceiling. It was like that day in the Temple many years ago — the day, it seemed, when Peers had ended humanity's chances and Cameron Bannister had first heard his own key's calling.

Shouting behind them. Shouting from the group ahead. The man who'd been so bent on skewering Peers now seemed focused only on staying upright, holding the wall for balance.

"*Push. Now,*" came a voice in Peers's ear.

Meyer or Kindred. But whoever it was didn't wait for Peers to comply. The push came from farther back, not so much against him as using Peers like a ram. He collided with his interrogator, their skulls clacking together. More shouting came — either in alarm at the situation or that their captives were fighting back — but as the tunnels shook and rock began to fall, it meant nothing.

Peers was forced forward. Through the throngs.

Dust sifted, getting in his eyes, eclipsing vision. His teeth chattered. His brain felt unseated, rattling like a ball in an empty box. A dog barked: Nocturne, of course, nosing his own way through. Then there was a shout. A growl. A canine thrashing, as the gentle dog found motivation to snarl and bite.

"*Go! Go, Peers!*"

And they pushed, trampled, shoved. Peers's boots found bodies, reaching up and trying to grab him. His hands sought the wall for balance, trying to stay upright, knowing he'd be dead if he fell.

There was a tremendous grinding. An enormous roar from somewhere above, filtered through stone.

"GO!"

A figure in a suit shoved past Peers to take the lead. Peers turned his head in the confusion, seeing the Mullah knocked flat and shoved aside, now too concerned with the apocalyptic shaking to mind their quarry. Piper and Lila were behind him, faces pale and frightened, but focused. Nocturne was beside another man in a suit, this one claiming the rear. The man's tie was blue: Meyer, apparently.

They rushed. They scrambled. And miraculously, an exit appeared. Peers thought he should have seen daylight with it, but none came.

He could only see was the mammoth black ship, eclipsing the world.

It was moving. Somewhere. And the sound was like the vibrations of planets.

They came up outside the city. Beyond the wall, though Peers wasn't exactly sure where. A glance around showed that the peril of cannibal clans was still present, but none of the vehicles or painted men seemed threatening compared to the thing slowly crossing the sky.

They were all ignoring the newcomers. Looking away, mouths open as they gaped at the heavens.

Between the ground and the black ship was a wide bright area, like something projected in three dimensions.

The space carried a message, written in English in what had to be fifty-foot letters.

It simply read, *STAND BY.*

CHAPTER 21

Lila didn't even take time to stare Peers up and down before pushing past him. He had something in his bag that might be anything at all, and he'd been on the other side all along. But the ground was shaking like an earthquake and there was a bulletin hovering in the sky above Ember Flats. Even the cannibals were too transfixed to look away.

She stared into the sky.

STAND BY.

The message and presentation were so stark. So businesslike. It had all the character of a generic, black-on-white cereal box. And once the ship stopped moving — now directly over the city's center, a line of blue light arcing between the behemoth and the Apex pyramid — it sat there in letters tall as most of the buildings, rendered in three dimensions and, she had to assume, somehow readable at all angles, rotating slowly.

Lila felt a tug as her still-moist shirt pulled against her front. She looked back and saw Piper pinching the fabric between thumb and fingers, dragging her subtly backward.

Lila's mouth opened. Piper's index finger shot in front of her lips.

Shhh ...

As Lila looked around, Meyer turned to watch her. Then Kindred. Then finally Peers, who didn't seem to know where to aim his gaze.

Lila moved back, obeying the tug. She turned after a handful of steps before Piper let her go. The group followed Piper as she moved away from the tunnel's exit, which had come up in a rock scree. They hadn't surfaced among the cannibal clans, but were definitely near them. They'd be easily seen if any of the monsters turned their heads, once they stopped caring more about the big blue letters hovering above them.

Down behind a rise, the clans dropped out of sight.

Lila peeked at the Astral message. There'd been beeps to alert whoever had whatever Peers was carrying, followed by shaking and noise, then a placeholder note in the open air. A message must be coming, and they wanted everyone's attention. But for now, there was nothing.

"Anyone hurt?" Piper said, her voice low.

Heads shook.

"We need to get out of here."

Peers was staring at the sky. "Where?"

Piper looked at Peers as if he were daft. She didn't have the vacant look that Lila assumed must be on her own face. She appeared calm and in control. Even Meyer and Kindred seemed more shaken.

"To Jabari's subs. To the Cradle."

Lila was still staring at the message.

"Now?" she said.

"When else?"

"But ... " She looked skyward.

"We don't want to stand by."

"You can't know that."

"I can."

"How?"

"I just do." Piper touched her head. "It's too much to explain."

Meyer was looking skyward too, but his eyes were on the ship, and Lila could tell he was trying to look *through* more than at it.

"We don't even know where we are," he said. "None of the landmarks are visible, and I can't see the sun."

"We're much farther north," Piper said.

"How do you know that?"

She touched her head again.

"We can't trust your feelings," Peers said.

"We can trust them more than yours," Piper countered.

"Can you feel Clara again?"

Piper squinted, frowned, contorted her face. "Kind of. But I don't think it means anything. I can still feel Cameron, too."

"Is she ... ?"

Lila turned to Peers. All at once, something snapped.

"How dare you," she said.

"I had nothing to do with — "

"How *dare* you!"

"Lila, I swear, I want to find Clara as much as — "

Lila's hands flashed out in front of her. Before she knew it, they were clawing for his throat. Peers scrambled to back away, fell back against the dune, then rushed back like a crab when she dove again, Meyer's arm restraining her.

"You took her!"

"I didn't t — "

"You took her, you motherfucker!"

"Lila!" Meyer hissed. "Keep your voice down!"

"I don't care who hears me! Got that?" She raised her voice and shouted, *"I DON'T CARE IF THEY ALL HEAR ME!"*

"Lila!"

Lila turned to Meyer and Kindred. Tears obscured her vision. She didn't know what she was feeling. Sadness? Loss? Anger? Outright fury? It was all a soup inside her.

"He's with the Mullah. You heard them. He's got a tattoo to prove it!"

"It's a brand," Peers said. "And if you'll let me explain ..."

Lila lashed out, but Meyer and Kindred both moved to hold her. She could only flail one arm, and only halfway. A fan of loose sand sprayed at Peers, her fingers scrambling madly for whatever they could hold, finding nothing.

"He's Mullah! That's how he found us back in Turkey, when *the Mullah* were after us! That's why he had that big cave full of alien gear: because he was working with them! They're all in it together, and they *took my daughter!"*

"Lila! Quiet!" Kindred seemed agitated — furious, even. He kept shooting glances at the top of the dune, presumably at the cannibals beyond. It seemed as if he wasn't just worried that Lila would give them away, but angry about it.

"Let her get it out." The voice, strangely calm, was Piper's.

"There are clans *right there,* Piper," Kindred said.

"And they didn't come when she shouted. They won't come after us yet."

"Yet?"

"The message just went up. They're waiting for some sort of broadcast. The Astrals turned water to blood to set the stage, then shook the ground to get everyone's attention. Those people down there won't look away. *You* can barely look away. We're safe. For now."

"We're not safe, Piper," said Meyer. "Not until we reach the Cradle. And not even then."

"We're safe for now," Piper repeated.

Her gaze was fixed on Lila, and the effect was hypnotic. Lila suddenly understood: Piper wasn't guessing. She somehow *knew*.

"I can try and explain later," Piper said. "For now you need to trust me. We're going to get out of here if we follow instructions."

"*Your* instructions?"

Piper shook her head. "No. It's someone else. I can hear them. In here." A finger went to her temple.

"The Astrals?"

"No. Someone else."

"Clara?" said Lila.

"It's a man. In my head, he sounds almost like Meyer."

Peers shifted. Brushed sand from his shirt. He looked at Meyer and Kindred then said, "Seems like *everyone* is Meyer Dempsey these days."

The hold on Lila had shifted enough that this time when she lunged, she managed to break free, making a loose fist as she leaped at Peers, then connected with his left eye. The impact against bone sent a shudder through her knuckles, hand, and wrist. But the pain didn't bother Lila, as long as Peers felt it, too. After this long forcing herself to go numb, even pain seemed like a blessing.

"*Lila!*"

"Stop holding me back, Dad! What's wrong with you? You should be killing him yourself!"

"If you'd just let me explain!" Peers said, hand over his beaten eye.

"Explain what? That you kidnapped my daughter? That you've been ratting us out the entire time?"

"I didn't do either of those things! I'm — !"

"*Where is she? Where is Clara?*"

"I don't know! I swear I don't know!"

"He doesn't know, Lila," said Piper.

Lila stopped, sniveling, practically foaming at the mouth. Piper's voice shut her down like flicking a switch, and now there was only the worry and sadness she'd kept so tightly behind an internal shell.

Her head fell. Her hand caught it.

"I was with them when I was a child." She heard Peers from behind her curtain of black hair. "I made a mistake. A ... a *dreadful* mistake."

Lila felt hesitant fingers tap her back. When she didn't flinch, Peers touched her again. Fury bubbled inside. She wanted to lash out. To grab it. To break that hand like a twig. How dare he? How *dare* he touch her after what he did?

"He's telling the truth," Piper said.

She wasn't just talking to Lila. She was talking to them all.

Lila let her head hang. And she broke. Cried, until it was all out of her. She heard and saw nothing of consequence outside her own knees until she finally looked up, the Egyptian day still shadowed like dusk. The black ship hadn't moved. Its presence was everything, except for the static crackle of energy moving between it and the Apex and the whisper of a warm breeze.

Lila looked at Piper. Piper looked back, a question on her face. And when Lila nodded slightly, Piper rose to her knees. Both Meyer and Kindred looked toward her, deferring. Whatever analytical power they'd had, it now seemed diminished. Meyer looked spent, and Kindred barely contained. Peers was off to the side, penitent, with his dog. Only Piper seemed clear. Something inside — not Clara but a strange man who sounded like Meyer — was telling them all what to do.

"We need to go." Piper took a moment, seemed to reflect, then pointed. "That way. We need to find the nook where the Cradle subs are stored. Nobody has beaten us to them, and nobody will. They've not been discovered. The clans won't follow, and the Mullah have stopped trying. They don't care about us, only about recovering their man, plus whatever they lost. But they're wrong about the Astrals. The Astrals didn't take it. It's gone somewhere else."

"Is it Clara?" Lila asked. "The thing the Mullah lost?"

"I don't know, Lila."

"How do you know you can trust whatever's telling you all of this?" Meyer asked. It wasn't a challenge. It was simply a question.

"Because he gains nothing by lying."

"What does *he* want?"

"To exist."

"Who is he?"

"I only know he's not Astral. He's human, or something close."

"What does *that* mean?" Meyer asked.

Piper went on as if she hadn't heard him. "And he feels very familiar. And that I'd trust him in exactly the same way that I trust you."

"Trusting a voice you hear in your head isn't the same as trusting us," Kindred said.

"Not trusting *you*," Piper told Kindred. "Trusting *Meyer.*"

Kindred looked like he might protest but didn't. Piper said, "We have to go. We can't be here when the announcement comes."

There was a crackle from behind them. From the direction of the big, black ship.

Letters vanished from the sky, replaced by the projection of a young-looking brunette woman in a simple white blouse. She was cut off at the waist, but otherwise she looked as if she were really there above Ember Flats — not a hologram at all.

Her voice was like soft, pleasant thunder. "Please hold whatever you are doing, and pay attention to the following message."

Blue lightning crackled between ship and pyramid. Its activity seemed to increase, arcing to one side to form a tiny storm.

"This message is being shown to all eight of your remaining capitals, though anyone watching our broadcast channel from the outlands will hear it as well."

More sparking. More lightning.

"Humanity's current form has failed our tests. Your species, such as it exists, must be pruned back and allowed to regrow."

"Pruned?" Lila whispered.

Nobody answered, but the genocidal meaning was clear.

The tiny storm to one side of the line between ship and Apex increased its fury, becoming something like a ball.

"Each capital is being given a vessel," the woman said. "And as long as you are aboard the vessel, no harm will come to you in the days that follow.

The lightning ball seemed to stretch out. To take shape. To become something as long and as broad as the Apex itself. As the light show died, Lila could see that what had materialized there looked like a large boat, its keel nearly on the ground, its body propped up by blue-glass scaffolding.

"Each capital's vessel will hold approximately 1 percent of the city's population," the woman said.

Lila looked at Meyer, Kindred, Piper, and even Peers.

"But it is up to you to decide who lives and who dies."

Lila gaped. Watched the air, waiting for more. But then the woman in the sky vanished and the giant black ship began to move, ever so slightly, the blue lightning breaking its connection, an enormous blue spark churning in its metallic gut as it journeyed toward whatever it meant to destroy.

A killing storm.

A destroyer of worlds.

Beyond the dune and in the city, what remained of humanity began to panic and scream and rampage and kill.

CHAPTER 22

Mara watched the screen as the woman representing Divinity vanished. She didn't fade away. She simply cut out of existence. And then the chaos began.

Not Astral on human. The Astrals seemed, according to the monitors, to have piled into their shuttles and left the surface sometime between when Meyer, Peers, Kindred, Lila, and Piper left the bunker and when the rumbling began.

No. This violence was human on human.

Mara flicked the screen, half expecting the other city feeds to have been cut. But the Astrals and the city were full of surprises. They hadn't been cut off when Meyer and Kindred had been blowing the Astrals' secret about Heaven's Veil, and nothing had been cut during all the blood and proclamations of mass extermination. Even the house above still had power, thanks to its buried lines and Astral non-interference. And all the video feeds — along with the emotional co-signals broadcast by the rocks around the borders — were still live and perfectly clear.

It was as if the Astrals wanted her to betray them then lead Meyer and Kindred to that stage. It was as if they knew what she'd been doing all along — right down to hiding in this bunker, watching things go to shit — and were cool with it.

This wasn't in the Initiate's projections. At all.

A booming sound seemed to shake the room. But it wasn't another ship-moving earthquake. It was someone assaulting the outer door with their fists.

She tried to ignore it. Rioters had finally made it onto the palace grounds. It was fine; the bunker had been built on that exact assumption. She'd covered the bases, unlike Dempsey. She'd heard his story — both from the outside world and filtered through the Astrals' knowledge. He'd reached his conclusions through drug trips rather than logic and planning. No wonder he'd made so many mistakes. He was lucky to have reached his *Axis Mundi* at all.

Mara had planned better now, and better then. They wanted to flee the city under the big ship's unflinching eye? They wanted to try and reach the Cradle — then the broadcast rendezvous with the other viceroys — despite the interference introduced by the ship? They'd never make it without the Astrals' allowance.

Like their allowing her little resistance despite clearly knowing the entire time.

She blinked the thought away, ignored the pounding, and watched the monitors. Whoever was up there would either give up and go away (the door was impregnable by anything other than explosives, and good luck finding *those* in an Astral-run city) or would be leveled by other rioters who wanted a try. The house must be sick with them.

She clicked away from the feed showing the big ship created by the blue lightning. It was large but not titanic. They'd be lucky to stuff 1 percent of the Ember Flats population inside.

People had massed around the thing but weren't approaching. There was a force field or something surrounding the ship. The Astrals had apparently given each capital a Noah's Ark, but the citizens couldn't reach it to climb aboard. What a ripoff.

There was a beep from behind her. Mara hadn't heard the sound in so long, it took her a while to figure out what it was. Then she opened the charging laptop computer and scanned the bottom row of icons — sure enough, it had come from where she'd thought.

Just the Astral collective dropping her a line.

Because they were old buddies, Divinity and the human viceroy.

At first Mara didn't believe her eyes. It had to be an old message. Divinity had gone into a communication blackout around the time Cameron and Company entered the city. That's when she'd suddenly found herself on her own, sensing shit rapidly approaching the fan, increasingly certain that her well-thought-out contingency plans A, B, and C would be needed.

Fortunately, she'd anticipated this.

Well, all but the enormous ship that ruined her plans. And that the aliens were apparently playing with her all along. It cast doubt on everything. Mara found herself wondering what would become of Meyer's group as they headed toward the "secret" escape vessels. She wondered about the bunker, and if it was truly private or impregnable. She even wondered about the rioters banging on her door. And the force field around humanity's only hope of salvation, of course.

Divinity's message was the usual clipped, socially retarded brief:

Lifeboat perimeter deactivation code 091804.

Mara stared, her forehead wrinkled.

Lifeboat.

Deactivation.

Was this what she thought? It looked almost like a code to unlock the big Noah's Ark thing. It sort of seemed like they'd given Mara — traitor to her masters, rebel who'd actually gotten away with nothing — the keys to her city's only hope for survival.

For 1 percent of the population.

"MARA!"

She looked up. Toward the stairs. Toward the impregnable door where rioters were storming her gates.

She clicked the video feed to one showing the palace interior. It was empty, as it had been every time she'd checked. She'd seen some aides running through a giant hole in the wall, possibly blasted by Charlie Cook and Jeanine Coffey. Reptars had been chasing them. She'd seen others leave of their own accord, but certainly nobody was still here who was, once upon a time, supposed to be here. The place was open for rioters and had been for hours.

But still, the house was empty.

"MARA! LET ME IN!"

She climbed the steps. Turned all the right knobs and pulled all the right levers. She peeked tentatively out even after checking the screen beside the door, then opened it wide and stared slack-jawed at the black-and-blue mess across from her.

"Kamal?"

"So I *am* still as beautiful as I used to be," Kamal said, his words somehow unaffected by his fat lip.

Mara ushered him in, glanced through the hallway, and closed the door. She secured everything she'd unfastened then took his arm as they descended into the bunker. Kamal had a significant limp and fell down the stairs nearly as much as he was stepping.

"What the hell happened to you?"

"I walked into a wall."

"Were you out in the city? Were you attacked?"

"Your visitors did this. I never want to run a bed and breakfast again."

"Which visitors?"

"Jeanine Coffey."

"*Jeanine* did this to you?"

"I misspoke. I meant it was a gang of big, strong bikers."

Mara ushered Kamal to a couch and eased him onto it.

"Do you need a ... ?" She stalled, not knowing how to end her sentence.

"How about some Flintstones aspirin?"

"How can you make jokes at a time like this?"

"I'm a hilarious person. I can't control it."

Mara sat opposite Kamal. He seemed intact, just painfully ugly. Jeanine had done a number on him, but he wasn't acting like anything was broken.

"Where were you?" Mara asked.

"Bitch knocked me out. I woke up a few minutes ago, and everyone had left. Then I went to the window and saw. Checked the feeds and saw more. So your State of the City didn't go well?"

"Not so much."

"And the Ark?"

"Cameron opened it. That didn't go well, either."

"And the girl?"

"Clara? I don't know."

"They thought I was Mullah. That I'd taken her. Just because I'm Muslim? That's racist."

"What happened?"

"Ravi, I think. Hard to tell with all the unconsciousness, but our secondary surveillance got most of it."

"Ravi is *Mullah?*"

"I think. Shoulda known. He's Muslim."

"So why did Jeanine beat *you* up?"

"Because she's a bitch. Please tell me she's down here so I can punch her in the vagina."

"She's dead."

Kamal looked genuinely sorry. "Oh. That sucks." Then: "So who's here?"

"Just me. Charlie didn't make it. Or Cameron. I don't know what happened to most of our staff, including the insiders, but I think Reptars chased them out of the palace before they could assemble."

"Cowards."

"I was still with the Meyers. Ran into Piper and the younger one. Lila, the girl's mother? Then Peers Basara ran up at the last minute, and we came here."

"Peers?"

"Yes. And I think you're right about him. He had something in his pack that he wouldn't show anyone. Talked about escape tunnels but wouldn't say how he knew."

"Mullah?"

Mara nodded. "That's my guess."

"He and Ravi should hang out."

"But I still don't think he's dangerous. I wouldn't have let the others go with him if I had." Mara realized she wasn't fully explaining. Her mind was moving a mile a minute. There was so much Kamal might have missed. He hadn't asked about the bloody footprints in the bunker, but that didn't mean he knew about their new plumbing issues.

"They all decided to leave. I told them where to find the Cradle and how to hook up with the others at the rendezvous linkup. The big ship outside ... Did you see the big ship?"

"Yes."

"The big ship made me think it wasn't a good idea to go at all. Went with Plan C: Stay here. But now I wonder if I could've made it. If there was any chance they'd so much as try to stop me."

"What makes you think that?"

Mara waved a hand through the air like wiping an invisible windshield. "I'll tell you later. Did you see the broadcast?"

"Yours, or the one by Divinity just now, about how we have to play the lottery to see who lives or dies on that thing?"

"The second one."

Kamal nodded his puffy, bruised head. "Quite the conundrum. Although I don't know why they said we need to choose. People will kill each other for their spot. It's probably full already.

Mara showed Kamal the feed. Let him take it in until he squinted and frowned, seeing the force field.

"They can't get in?"

Mara shook her head. "There's a barrier. And they sent me the code, I think." She showed him the laptop with its new message.

"Why?"

Onscreen, a team of Reptars was entering the plaza by the Apex, moving in a slow line toward the mass around the boat.

"What are they doing?" Kamal's eyes moved upward on the screen. "And why a boat?"

Mara shook her head. "Maybe it's symbolic. It's not the first symbolic thing they've done."

"What do you mean?"

Mara's eyes flicked toward the blood on the floor. "Nothing. I can explain later."

Reptars moved toward the force field. Then they stepped right through it, though its energy still seemed to hold the humans at bay. They lined up inside, then marched slowly outward, inching the citizens of Ember Flats away from the field, forcing them to disperse somewhat.

Order restored. Chaotic situation controlled through might. But why?

Something blocked the camera. Then whatever it was stepped back, and Mara and Kamal found themselves looking at a Titan's overly pleasant face. It was a male, indistinguishable from any other Titan male she'd ever seen. She waited for him to move on and assist whatever the Astrals were doing in the plaza, but he stayed put, his face toward the camera.

"*What's it doing?*" Kamal's voice was low, as if the Titan could hear him.

Mara shook her head.

The Titan looked directly into the camera. He gave that maddeningly polite, neutrally bureaucratic look they all had, but did so right at the two of them, as if he knew where the tiny camera was hidden.

The Titan pointed. To his right, Mara and Kamal's left.

"What the hell is it pointing at?" Kamal asked.

There was another knock on the bunker door. Right where the on-screen Titan was pointing.

CHAPTER 23

In the Canaan Plains palace, Viceroy Jayesh Sai stood staring at his message from the mothership above. It was terse and simple, as were all communications from Divinity. But this time, it was also a mystery. What was a lifeboat, in this context? Why did it have a perimeter? And why did Jayesh — who wasn't even sure what perimeter needed deactivating — need the means to unlock it?

He was wondering if the lifeboat in question had anything to do with the message they'd seen broadcast above the Canaan Plains main square when the door opened. At first Jayesh was annoyed. But then his dark face cracked into a smile, and a grin too young for his years surfaced.

"Nitya! Have you come to visit your Daada?"

The girl padded across the office rug, thumb firmly in her mouth. Watching her, Jayesh felt a disconcerting mixture of sorrow and envy. Nitya didn't understand that the world was ending, didn't know she might soon be dying along with her Daada, if the message from Divinity was any indication. But still, the sinking feeling he got thinking of the odds (1 percent survived while the rest were killed, and even the viceroy had no clue where to find the "vessel") was counterpointed by the jealousy he felt when considering his granddaughter's ignorance and how, if she died, it would be without the fear to precede it.

How would it happen?

When would it happen?

And how were they supposed to make their attempt at escape?

Jayesh hadn't a clue. Between the time the still-alive Meyer Dempsey (and his clone) made their little speech and this newest announcement, his city had heard nothing. Canaan Plains grew agitated when they learned of Heaven's Veil, but things had been percolating back toward normal until this.

Nitya circled the room. She was only eighteen months old but walked as well as Pari, his assistant's five-year old daughter. Pari was older than Nitya, but Nitya had hat special spark. Sometimes it seemed like the girl could read minds. Always it seemed like she knew far more than she let on, as if she'd been an Elder since birth.

"Nitya? I would love to play with you, but now is not the time." Jayesh looked again at the message then at the girl, wondering if they'd ever have a chance to play again.

She took the thumb from her mouth and said, plain as a teenager: "There is a new ship in the desert, beyond the valley, perched on its keel in a cage of blue glass. A man in jeans and boots is at the palace door, wishing to speak with you. And the rain is coming."

In the empty land beyond Loulan Mu, a fisherman named Shen sat in a small boat, looking out at the western sky. Thunderheads were forming on the mountains like dark and ominous snow. A slight wind rippled the water. It wasn't like the normal breeze, in a way Shen couldn't place. This was different. This was new.

His line jerked. He looked toward the water, only now aware that he'd been staring into the distance for long vanished minutes. He doubled his grip on the rod, jerking it to set the hook, and whispered his usual prayer for bounty. It was a ritual he'd always had, but in the days since the visitors came — and especially since they formed their cities and the world beyond became lawless — it had found new meaning. Shen's village was tiny, nestling a valley few had reason to cross. Even as news of the crumbling world reached Shen, he'd mostly ignored it. He had little use for such knowledge; his life consisted of fishing and family and farming, with little need for anything else. Small prayers in thanks for fish seemed a fitting way to show his appreciation to that which kept his life the same, that kept his family safe while the planet changed forever.

Shen reeled in his catch. On the end of his line, somehow fused with the hook, was a metal ball the size of a large walnut.

Shen touched it, and took it from the hook into his palm. It wasn't wet or slimy, hadn't spent who-knew-how-long on the stream floor. There were no punctures to indicate where the hook had been, or how it had entered. Perhaps it had been magnetism holding it in place. He could almost feel its energy warming his skin.

He hefted it. Used one finger to roll the thing, noting the way it warmed wherever it touched him. It was a pleasant feeling that made Shen's stiff joints feel better. He moved it around more, old fingers making it roll.

"Like this," said a voice.

Shen jumped. His pole stayed in the boat, but the vessel rocked, sending a radar of ripples from its hull toward the stream's bank.

There was a man sitting in the boat behind him.

"Don't *force* it to roll," the man said, looking down. "*Let* it roll."

The man was white with a long, weathered face, but he spoke Shen's language perfectly, down to every nuance of the dialect. But his words weren't what Shen noticed most, nor was it the fact that he'd simply materialized in his boat. Shen was *most* transfixed by the similar silver balls — three of them — rolling circles against each other in the man's large right hand.

"It's like a dance, Shen. Do you see?"

The stranger set a second ball in Shen's palm.

"Who are you?"

Despite the man's Western appearance, he showed every sign of understanding. He simply said, "I am a friend."

"How did you get into my boat?"

"That is not important. What is important is that you take your family and cross the northern pass. There is a flat place there, with twin trees at the spot where the path emerges, then a series of pools beyond. Do you know it?"

Shen nodded.

"There you will find a boat much larger than this one. Take your family onto the boat. It is your new home."

It occurred to Shen that he should have a thousand questions. He should not trust this man, or have any reason to believe him. But he looked down at the silver balls in his wrinkled palm, felt their warmth, and trusted. He felt their weight and believed. He would do as the man said without question.

"Why?"

"Because rains are coming. And because a ship larger than any of the others is on its way to the north. It will move south after that. Only a few will find the boat I've told you about in time. For the people of Loulan Mu, there will be no lottery as in the grand capitals of Earth. Nobody holds its key. You will survive if you find it. That is the nature of Loulan Mu's test."

"Which test?"

"One that you and your family will pass."

The stranger raised his hand. He made the balls circle then roll along the top of his vein-strewn skin. Then he flicked his wrist, and the balls hopped into his palm, which he closed. When he opened his hand again, the balls were gone.

"If it is a test to find the boat, then are you not cheating by telling me where to find it?"

And the stranger said, "Yes."

Shen looked to the thunderheads above the mountains. There was a flash, too far for sound. Shen could smell the moisture in the air, like fermenting leaves. It wasn't just coming from the rain, born from the world itself.

"Why me? I am only a fisherman."

The man in jeans said, "Because if I did not intervene, you would die."

Again Shen found himself wondering if he should disbelieve. Again, he looked down at the balls and felt faith without question.

"Thank you. Thank you for saving my family's lives."

"I'm not saving your lives," the stranger said. "I'm saving mine."

In the Etemenanki Sprawl, at the lip of a crater the locals called Old Goat, two women stood looking down into the volcanic zone, squinting, shielding their eyes with their hands.

Over the past few days, the hotspots had returned seemingly all at once. The spring-fed pools had become so hot that nobody could go into them. The volcano coughed ash in a steady, sooty stream that was almost too subtle to be seen but that showed in the capital atop the shiny roofs of abandoned cars and Astral shuttles that parked for too long. There were hikes that the women used to take as part of their daily ritual — those who tempted open caverns where lava had once come and gone — that they could no longer take because the molten rock had returned. The ground sometimes shook. And now every time they hiked up to look down into Old Goat they were careful to watch the ways in and out. If floes crossed the wrong spots, it was possible (if unlikely) that they could find themselves surrounded. You couldn't just walk out when lava floes crossed your path. Rescue could only come from the air, and the aliens were picky when it came to humans and flight.

But with today's due diligence paid, the women had made their way to the crater's lip and were looking down, toward the magma chambers, when they spied something new.

"Is it a house?" Ina asked.

Her friend, Maj, squinted harder. Sometimes, she hiked with binoculars. But not today.

"Why would someone build a house in an active volcano?" Maj answered.

"Maybe they want hot springs," Ina said.

"It's taller than a house. And the bottom is narrow, like it's balanced and about to fall."

Maj squinted harder. She'd just turned forty, but Ina was twenty-nine. The last thing Maj wanted to admit was that she could see none of the same detail, and that to her it looked more like a fortress of metal and wood atop blue scaffolding.

"Maj ... " Ina trailed off. And when Maj looked over, her friend's eyes were wide, hand pressed to her chest.

"What?"

"I think it's ... "

"*What*, Ina?"

"I know how this sounds."

"It sounds like you being ridiculous because you won't finish a sentence."

"Don't you see it? Tell me I'm not crazy."

"Maybe if you told me what you might be crazy about?"

"The message. From the Astrals. You know how the woman talked about 'vessels'?"

Maj nodded. She'd thought of little else. It was a sticky problem. As the viceroy of Etemenanki Sprawl, her job was to protect her city, but how could she do that if her mandate said that only 1 percent would survive whatever the aliens were brewing?

"Of course."

"Well?"

"Just spit it out, Ina. I can't see that far because I'm too fucking old, okay? And if you keep reminding me, I won't let you sit in on the viceroy rendezvous. I'll kick you right the fuck out of the Cradle and you can just walk until your skin burns off."

"Wow," Ina said. "Old bitches sure do get touchy."

Maj sighed. There was no help for her friend.

"It looks like a *boat*, okay? A big, giant boat right in the goddamned middle of the crater, surrounded by rivers of lava."

Maj looked again. Now that Ina mentioned it, it *did* look sort of like a dry-docked boat. But there were no rivers or lakes, only the distant, frigid ocean riddled with icebergs this time of year. The days were already short, and would be shrinking still as winter came. Boating sounded horrible. When Maj heard that the city would be given a vessel, she'd personally been hoping for a luxury spaceship. The lucky 1 percent could tool off to Mars and live in style. That would be fine with her. If humanity had to die, she could stomach being with it but didn't wish to see its final breaths.

"You can't get to it," said a small voice. "That's what he told me."

The women turned. There was a young boy, maybe six, standing a dozen yards away. He couldn't possibly see the boat from where he was standing, and must have come up earlier to peek in.

"What who told you?" Maj said.

"The tall man in boots."

Maj's head spun around, searching. These near-outlands were patrolled and had few problems with raiders and gangs so near the city. But troublemakers occasionally broke through. A *man in boots* might be a hiker intent on seeing the outdoors no matter what, like Maj and Ina. Or he might be part of a larger problem.

"He's not here," the boy said. "He never was."

"Then how did he — "

The boy tapped his head and said, "Something has changed. I can hear them now."

Maj resisted the urge to squat to his level. There was something in the boy's strange manner of speech that told her he'd find it condescending — and would probably use that word to describe it, too.

Lightborn.

Maj and Viceroy Mara Jabari had talked extensively about their cities' Lightborn, and in particular how the Astrals had ignored them entirely. The Lightborn in Ember Flats had formed a sort of commune, whereas here they'd spread out. There were few common denominators except that they all seemed able to predict the near future and read one another's minds within a small, contained radius.

The gifted children both fascinated and frustrated Jabari — one more thing her Initiate had failed to anticipate, and Jabari didn't like loose ends in her research.

The boy came closer. "You're Viceroy Anders." It wasn't a question.

"Yes. And who are you?"

"He says it's a puzzle. That there's nothing keeping anyone from reaching the boat, except their lack of ingenuity."

"Ingenuity, huh?" Maj said.

"In Loulan Mu the test is opportunity. In Hanging Pillars it is bravery. In Ember Flats it is morality. But ours is about solving puzzles. If you can reach it in plain sight, you can board. That is what the man told me."

Maj fought the feeling of unease threatening to surround her. The boy's voice was even, unconcerned, almost prophetic. His mention of Ember Flats knocked loose a bevy of worries Maj had thought she'd shelved — but now, as the sky dimmed with what looked like distant rain, she found herself thinking of Jabari, who'd set their next virtual meeting. Jabari and her select few were supposed to flee before then, anticipating particularly strong trouble in the Astral's Capital of Capitals. And whereas Maj, Ina, and the others were supposed to wait, Jabari was the one who'd run the gauntlet to her Cradle first.

But Ember Flats, since then, had gone darker than dark.

What makes you feel you can believe this man?" Maj said.

"Because well before I could see the cloud, he told me it was coming."

Maj looked at Ina. They both looked around.

"Cloud?"

The boy pointed. The women turned to see the largest of the storm clouds in the horizon's dark heart. Maj saw nothing unusual. It was simply dusk approaching in the shortening autumn days, blurring the horizon from end to end.

Except that the horizon seemed darker and longer than usual. And the sunset seemed a bit early, even with the storms on their way.

Suddenly Ina gasped, as she'd done earlier. Hearing it, watching the horizon and its strange, overly dark shape, ice wrapped Maj's heart.

"I swear, Ina, if you make me force it out of you this time ... "

"It's not a cloud," Ina said. "It's a black ship, big as Iceland."

In a small, original construction one-bedroom house in the rundown section of Roman Sands (a place that hadn't been nice before the Astrals, when it was a South African armpit, and still wasn't nice now) a thirty-one-year old man named Carl Nairobi squeezed his enormous frame through the doorway to find an unauthorized white man sitting behind his grandma's shitty old chairs in his crappy little kitchen.

"Hello, Carl," said the man.

"The fuck are you?"

"You're looking well."

"Maybe you didn't hear me say, 'What the fuck you doing in my house?'"

Carl didn't smash one fist into the opposite palm to punctuate his question. His broad shoulders, six-four height, and thigh-sized arms did it for him. Every inch of Carl was earned muscle. You didn't have to have a job in Roman Sands. The government took care of everyone. It was part of what made the place so horrible. So Carl moved bricks. All day, every day. Sometimes he moved them for people who needed bricks moved because ever since Astral Day, Roman Sands had been the kind of place where things were always being knocked down. When nobody needed bricks moved, Carl went across the street to what had once been a park and moved the pile of bricks there from one side to the other. The next day, he'd move them back. It was mind-numbing. But books were scarce, and all but propaganda broadcasts were nonexistent. For Carl, who'd been incarcerated before the bugs and ghosts had plopped their asses on his town and changed its name, moving bricks was the equivalent of doing pushups or pacing a cell. While he worked, he played the golf course he used to work at in his head, imagining walking the links and keeping score. He'd never done it in life — wasn't right for a black kid to play golf when football made people respect him — but he'd steadily improved inside his mind. The whole thing, body and mind, kept a man sharp. It kept a man sane.

"That's *not* what you said the first time."

Carl lunged at the man. He must have blinked when he did so, because by the time he reached the chair, the guy had somehow leaped behind him.

"I'm not a vampire, if that's what you're thinking," said the man from near his right ear.

Carl spun. It was half turn, half punch. He had no qualms about killing the guy, and he'd ended one unlucky fellow with his fists before. That had felt terrible; Carl had only been a kid himself at the time, and the guy had been an asshole, undeserving of death. The cops hadn't arrived in time, and Carl had never been punished. It would have felt so much better if he had.

But this fucker? Well, he was in a man's private residence. And this was the shit end of Roman Sands after a big announcement about End Times, so what the fuck ever.

But the reach-punch missed again, and this time the guy was behind Carl's other ear.

"Admit it. You're thinking I'm a vampire."

Carl drove an elbow hard into the man's sternum. Without wasting the extra time it took to rotate, the blow landed perfectly. It folded the intruder like a deck chair, and two seconds later Carl was standing above him, watching the man squirm and gasp for air.

"So this is what pain feels like."

"Bitch, you're lucky you're not dead. I killed motherfuckers before for less." He clenched his fists and took a step.

"Sure you have," the man said, trying for breath, pressing his chest as if the feeling intrigued more than bothered him. He came up on one elbow. "But you didn't kill the man who stole food from your refrigerator. And you had all the time in the world. That was before you broke your baseball bat. And you had all the room you needed to start swinging."

Carl's fists sagged. "How'd you know about that? You been spyin' on me?"

"Yes," the white man said, scooting back to sit up, still wincing. "I've been spying on you for *eleven years. That's* how I know."

Carl felt his mouth form a frown. It had been about that long, yes. He remembered it vividly. The intruder had been unarmed, and Carl had caught him holding a loaf of bread. If it had been a ham or leftover lunchmeat, things might have ended differently. But the man that day had literally been stealing bread to feed his starving family. Carl had let him leave with the loaf.

"Now, the gang of kids who came here two months ago? Them, you handled."

"I didn't kill nobody that day."

"Not that you knew. But the tall one? The one with the cap you thought looked stupid? You cracked a rib into his lung. He didn't even try getting to a hospital, and died the next day."

"Had it coming. Those three was terrorizing this neighborhood. They wasn't just coming to take my house. They raped like three girls I know 'round here."

"Yes. Of course. So you kind of liked it when they came for you, didn't you? Saved you the trouble of finding them." The man sat up straighter. "Why did you want to go after them, Carl?"

159

"Don't know. Seemed right."

"Even in Roman Sands?"

"Maybe *especially* in Roman Sands."

"They didn't have guns. Can't get guns here anymore, or anywhere other than the outlands. Can't smuggle them into the city. But would it have made a difference if they came at you with guns instead of chains and bats — and you with nothing but fists?"

"Dunno. Who the fuck are you?"

The man stood. Incredibly, he extended his hand. Even more incredibly — probably because he felt a bit beaten himself with all the man's knowledge — Carl shook it.

"You can call me Stranger."

"Seems about right."

"Can I sit?" Stranger gestured toward one of the kitchen chairs. There were four, despite Carl having lived alone for years. Each was made of peeling, chrome-colored piping and hard cushions embroidered in a flower print, oozing out at the seams.

"Try it and find out."

Stranger sat. Pushed himself back and crossed his legs, making himself at home. Finally, unsure what else to do, Carl pulled out a seat and sat opposite him.

"How'd you know all that about me?"

"Same way I stayed out of your way the first two times you tried to hit me. Don't let it bother you that it took three tries. I doubt anyone else could have hit me at all."

"Okay. So how'd you do that, too?"

Stranger pulled a hand from his pocket. It emerged with a bright white Slazenger golf ball, marked with a 7.

"Do you know what that is?"

"It's a golf ball. You think a black man don't know what a golf ball is?"

"Aren't golf balls supposed to have dimples?"

Carl held the thing up to point out its perfect number of dimples. But what was once a golf ball was now a smooth silver sphere.

"What the fuck?"

"Bet your friends wouldn't have been supportive if you'd played golf like you wanted to."

"Wasn't *my friends* had a problem with it. *Shit.* You didn't grow up where I grew up."

"I didn't grow up at all."

Carl set the sphere in his grandmother's empty fruit bowl, center stage on the vacant kitchen table.

"Why are you here?"

Stranger sat forward. "Because *you're* here, Carl."

"Who are you? Really."

"Grit in the works. Sugar in the tank. The wooden shoe in the gears. The wrench in the big, bad machine. My nature is disruption. Chaos. If I want to keep on living, this is what I must do."

"You an alien?"

"Maybe. Sort of. Once. But I was always more human than Astral, and now I'm almost entirely like you." He eyed Carl's impressive frame. "Well. Not like *you*."

"What you want me for?"

"You're the man who'd chase down a rape gang because it needs doing. You're the man who'd watch a man steal food he can barely afford because the other person needs it more. You're the man who knows what's supposed to happen, even though you tell yourself you know nothing at all."

"I sure don't know what the fuck *you* talking about."

Stranger uncrossed his legs, recrossed them in the opposite direction.

"Carl. Serious question. You heard the announcement, right? From Divinity in Ember Flats?"

Carl suspected Stranger already knew the answer, but he nodded anyway.

Stranger leaned forward. "Can you keep a secret?"

"Try it and find out."

"They've already found the vessel for Roman Sands. It was placed in a protected government area, right where Viceroy Knight would have wanted, so nobody could see it. But they're not letting people on."

"Story of my life, man. Think I should get a suit and change my name to Gerald Huckabee the Third?"

"They *will* let people on. And say what you want about Roman Sands, but everyone will get a fair shot." Stranger leaned even farther forward. "But do you want to know more secrets?"

"Okay."

"The broadcast came from Ember Flats because that's where the Divinity that broadcast it was at the time. But it's not just their ordinary mothership, like yours, that I'm talking about here. Some smart people saw this coming, and they thought the motherships might move off and form some sort of an antenna to call their buddies to Earth. That hasn't happened. Because their buddies are already here. In a *bigger* mothership that settled over Ember Flats when ... well, when something important was unlocked."

"A bigger ship?"

"An enormous black ship as big as all the capitals put together."

"What's it doing there?"

"It's not there anymore. It moved north."

"To, what? Europe?"

"To the north pole."

"Fucking with Santa ain't smart."

"It's going to melt the ice caps, Carl. First the north. Then the south. There will be worldwide storms, and whatever doesn't flood will burn. That's why the vessels are boats. Just like Noah's Ark."

Carl tried to keep his face neutral, but it betrayed him. He quickly recovered. After all, he'd resolved to die a long time ago.

"The vessel for Ember Flats showed up right in the middle of their city, with a force field around it. The government there will be asked to mediate the process of deciding who boards. There might be a lottery. Nobody knows how it'll be decided — only that it will, by humans."

"Like with us," Carl said. "With Roman Sands."

"No. Each city has its own test. For Ember Flats, the Astrals want to see how morality and fairness play out. In Hanging Pillars, the vessel's position and the challenge to reach it tests human bravery. In Canaan Plains, the viceroy can unlock a force field like in Ember Flats, but the ship is hidden, so it's mostly about the persistence of those who seek it. And in Etemenanki Sprawl, the vessel is in the bottom of a volcano, seemingly unreachable. The Astrals won't let people fly to it. So the test is about ingenuity, working with what's there to be among the chosen few."

"What about this place, if you say Knight knows where the vessel is already?"

"Roman Sands's test is *cutthroat*. There will be an initial group put onto the boat, but then everyone will be given a choice. They can take a spot on the ship that's already held by someone else, or they can pass. Pairs will be determined in advance, and from what I can tell, they'll all be people who know one another. Friends given a chance to save themselves by dooming others to their deaths. You might be given the chance to swap places with your mother-in-law. With your childhood bully. With your spouse, even. For every trade, two things happen: you get to live, and the other person gets to die."

"There's not enough spots on the boat for that."

"It's tiered. Like a tournament. They've thought this out, Carl."

"And how do *you* know so much about it?"

"Same way I know you used to have an invisible friend named Maurice. Same way I know your mother used to chew her nails until her own mother died, and she looked down at her gnawed-down hands across her chest in the casket."

Carl shoved his surprise as low as it would go. "Okay. So why you tellin' me?"

"Because the person whose spot you'll be given the chance to take is the man who murdered your sister. And because I need you to refuse."

CHAPTER 24

When Clara blinked and realized she'd apparently been standing in the middle of the Hideout floor in some sort of a trance, her first reaction was embarrassment. She'd already put a flag on top of her head as the resident weirdo — inside a group finally weird enough to welcome her. Now she was blacking out (and losing a decent chunk of time according to her internal clock) in the middle of a conversation with Nick while both were on their way over to speak with Logan? Not good.

But Clara wasn't the only one blinking and looking around. Nor was she the only one wearing a half-confused, half-embarrassed look. She heard an out-loud fog of muttering alongside a subtler one in her mind.

Whatever that was, it hadn't only happened to her.

Whatever had knocked Clara into another place (or at least out of this one), she wasn't alone.

"Nick?"

He didn't seem to hear her. Nick was looking at his hands as if he'd never seen them before. Looking at the floor as if grateful to find it. At the ceiling as if it might have vanished.

"*Nick?*"

He'd turned away, was walking off slowly, as if just waking up. Clara, unsure what else to do, followed. She couldn't shake the not-quite-departed vision. It hadn't been like seeing someplace else. It hadn't even been like *being* someplace else. It was more like sharing space that didn't exist. It was mind to mind, soul to soul — and yet whoever had abducted her to take her there just now, Clara could barely say.

Sort of like sharing minds with Mr. Cameron, as she'd almost done in the street on the way here — despite a certainty that he'd left the world for somewhere else.

Sort of like the other whispers she'd heard, but not really. When she'd sorta-kinda overheard the Astrals muttering their plans, that had been like unintentional eavesdropping — like overhearing conversation in a public place.

But most of all, sort of like what she'd felt when the Pall had been with them. When it had first appeared outside Benjamin Bannister's Moab ranch. When it had followed Peers's battle-converted bus. When it had taken the shapes of people it pretended to be.

Nick turned and looked at her.

"Were you ... ?" He was beyond tentative — the way a boy who likes a girl asks if she likes him, too.

"Yes."

"What was it? Has that happened to you before?"

"Maybe. Sort of. But not like ... *Nick?*"

He looked beaten up. Like all of the others. They were dazed, eyeing each other while trying not to look directly. A few were leaving their hypnosis, but Clara could still feel it clinging to her like cobwebs.

"I need to talk to Logan."

"Nick, listen."

But he was walking away, back toward the group, headed to where he'd been when whatever-it-was had struck them all blind, just as Clara was saying she could hear the Astrals talking to each other: that the blood water was playing and that something much worse — heralded by static blasts and beeps — was surely coming.

"Nick!"

Clara followed, swatting at the vision's final remnants. She could still see the man in her mind, still feel the rock seat beneath her, as they'd sat on opposite sides of a mental fire. In her vision, the denim-clad man had looked comfortable, leaning back on his rock in what seemed like a dark desert night. He'd pulled something from his pocket and played with it like twiddling a pen — *No, no,* Clara thought, *it had been small silver balls.* He'd told her something that her conscious mind was already losing its grip on, though her deeper mind had clung tight.

Let's have a palaver, you and me.

And the silver balls, they'd danced in his palm and rolled across his large knuckles as he spoke, effortless, as if the man barely knew they were there.

And the man had said something. About someone. About her. About all of the Lightborn. Maybe even *to* all of the Lightborn, judging by the others' behavior. Had they been there around the fire with her and the stranger?

Did I ever tell you about my cousin Timmy?

As Clara followed Logan to the knot of Lightborn in the middle of the Hideout, she felt a familiar feeling returning. Like *déjà vu* in a way: Clara plodding slowly into a situation she'd just left, like the ring of Lightborn joining the tall man around the fire.

Clara felt herself joining something bigger than herself. Uploading her consciousness the way her grandfather was always uploading reports to the network in Heaven's Veil. Her focus stayed present in the room, and her human eyes watched the others as they assembled — but still she could feel that transfer of consciousness at the same time.

It wasn't like the telepathy she'd felt with Nick and Ella.

167

This was something immersive. Something bigger than conversation.

She was joining them. They were all joining each other.

And as each of them began to understand, paralysis shattered. Clara felt the enhanced collective thinking like a single mind. Like the Astrals.

Like the Astrals expected us to think when they showed up. Only better. Newer. Version 2.0. We're something new. Something that couldn't have existed before.

Logan stood in the group's center. They'd assembled into a small crowd. A group of children beginning to see the truth.

Logan looked at Clara. She hadn't met him yet, but now, after whatever had happened, she found she didn't need to. He knew her fully. She knew him. She knew Logan the way one arm on a body knows the other. The way a hand knows its fingers.

Her mind was still her own.

But it was theirs now, too.

"Do we stay?" Logan asked Clara. "Or do we go?"

A buzz of thoughts came from below, from all directions, every voice. And yet each struck Clara as a different version of her own.

the vessel

the lottery

the flood

Clara saw the man by the fire, in his scuffed brown boots. She saw a ship left by the Astrals — the Noah's Ark that could save only a few. She saw the giant black Deathbringer the stranger had shown them, drifting above the polar ice. She saw death. She saw the network, knew that death no longer strictly mattered.

Should we stay, clara?

Should we go?

You're the hub of the wheel.

You're the way to the source.

"Clara? It's time to decide. The man by the fire said that Viceroy Jabari will establish a lottery to decide who goes on the vessel. It's part of the test, for her and for us: how Ember Flats will handle an impossible decision about who gets to live and who must die. So we have to get there now — you know she'll choose us to live."

Clara did. Of course. In Mara's impossible challenge, she'd try saving the future by way of its children. But even among them, the Lightborn stood out. Everyone sensed their significance. But only now did Clara and the others understand *why* they were so important. Only now had the man in jeans explained what made them different, and opened communication between Lightborn around the globe.

To survive what was coming, they merely needed to reach the vessel and ask.

If they all did that, people who would otherwise have taken those spots would disembark and greet the floods. Clara and her new friends would need only to request passage so that others could die in their place. An impossible conundrum — one Clara might have seen differently before her vision of man and fire.

She imagined Sadeem's puzzles. She solved one after another, her mind flying through all those tests like a video on fast-forward. Then the puzzles opened like flowers in her internal vision, becoming real things: ships the Astrals had laid across the globe like chess pieces, the archive they'd sought since Heaven's Veil's destruction, sacrifices from Cameron, Uncle Trevor, and Grandma Heather. Each new contribution to the hive mind changed it, and the change propagated and became something more.

Not in the way the Astral mind worked.

Not in the way the modern human mind had worked before the Lightborn.

Not even in the way human minds had worked in the days of ancient Egyptians and Mayans — the ways Astrals had expected human minds to be when they'd arrived.

Their current situation was a puzzle, no different from Sadeem's.

A puzzle solved without effort.

Once Clara knew what had changed, the others realized it, too.

Outside, thunder boomed like dynamite.

And the rain began to pour.

CHAPTER 25

The children had come and gone.

Liza Knight sat in her office, looking out in the general direction of Old Johannesburg through the growing rain. The city wasn't visible from here, of course, and hadn't been even back when the buildings were still standing. But she'd never been able to look out this particular window without thinking of the city. Not since Black Monday, when the Astrals had made it one of their examples. Rome, Paris, Budapest, Shanghai, New York, Mexico City: on that day, they'd all had one unfortunate thing in common. Liza's memory of a column of black smoke that burned for weeks was only one of the many millions — lost metropolises, purged from the Earth to make way for the new cities and a new age.

She thought of what the children had said. And yes, it all made sense. Pieces were all in place, as far as appeals went. They'd come as a group, gathered throughout the city. They claimed to represent a larger collection of kids with gifts from all over the planet (some sort of global mind meld thing, Liza gathered), and surprisingly, even *that* had made sense. The notion of rigging the cutthroat election process for the Astral lifeboat? That *sort of* made sense, despite the rivers already cresting in all this rain, and the Ember Flats natives growing restless. She'd already turned her back on obeying Astral commands, sorta, and had told the other rebellious viceroys that she'd join the satellite feed if she was still able at the specified time, from her appointed place, outside the city, after she'd fled in the Cradle.

So yes. When the kids (who'd known a hell of a lot more than they should) had suggested she disobey the Astrals further, she'd found herself at least tacitly willing to do so. In for a penny, in for a pound.

Instead of letting the citizens vie for their spots on the lifeboat by yanking one of their friends or family off of it, she could do as the children suggested. The kids said it was all a game to the Astrals: that Roman Sands was being tested; it was the viceroy's and the people's reactions — not their adherence to rules — that mattered. The children said that *someone else* had told them a secret: that the Astrals didn't care if anyone obeyed the rules or not. They only cared about watching human reaction when forced to jump through various hoops. To the Astrals, the planet was an ant farm. And to Liza, *that* made the most sense of all.

She probably *could* refuse to obey the rules.

She could, perhaps, even commission quickie construction of many other lifeboats. They'd have to hurry if the ice caps were being melted and the rains continued, but if the children were right, the Astrals probably wouldn't try to stop them.

But one thing bothered her.

If Liza disobeyed the Astrals, she was likely flushing her chance to lead the New World, after the floods receded and tiny pockets of humanity remained.

There was a knock at the door. Liza called for the visitor to enter.

"Viceroy Knight?"

"I keep telling you to call me Liza."

He looked down, shuffling papers, the door ajar.

"What is it, Mick?"

"That group of kids gone?" He looked around her expansive office.

"Yes. Just a few minutes ago."

"What did they want?"

Lila lied as a knee-jerk reaction, unsure why she was doing so.

"You know peaceniks. They send kids to do their dirty work. 'Let's all get along' and all that, mindless of the realities."

"They tried to convince you to stop the vessel selection process?"

Liza nodded, again wondering why she wasn't telling Mick the truth. "What do you need?"

"The Astrals have sent the pairings. Came from Divinity just a bit ago. It's ... " He trailed off, looking vaguely ill, holding a clutch of papers. From where Liza stood, even the paper looked disheartened, sagging as if wet.

"Come in. Close the door."

Liza's aide did as instructed. Then, when she gestured for him to sit in one of the two black leather chairs across from her desk, he did that, too. Liza stayed standing. She paced when she thought, and now was a thinking time.

"What's bothering you about the selection pairings?"

Mick looked down at the papers. He was holding them hesitantly, as if they were covered in something disgusting, and didn't reply.

"You can speak plainly. We're friends here."

"Actually, I know we are," Mick said, holding up one of the pages. "Because the mothership's Divinity sent down an optional bracket as well, and we're on it: you versus me, cutthroat as any of the other pairings."

"Bracket?"

"They've arranged this in levels of elimination. Winners advance to the next round. I swear, it's like a football tourney. Like the goddamned World Cup." He held up the same page, fluttering it. "This is a bonus round if we want it, in case we want to play fair. And guess who you get to kick off the vessel?" Mick jabbed a thumb back at himself.

"They said we had a guaranteed slot. Both of us. *All* of us in the Circle, Mick."

"Oh, I know. But this ... " He was almost pale, having a hard time forcing words. "It's so ... *harsh*. So devoid of emotion. Why would they send anything optional for a horrid thing like this? It's like, 'Oh yes, Viceroy. If you'd like, you *can* play out a fun side game where you steal your number two's spot and condemn him to die. You know ... for fun?'"

"We knew it would be harsh. When the first order came down, they used the word 'cutthroat.' *That* human concept, at least, they seem to understand fine."

But Liza's mind flashed back to the children, and what she'd believed when they'd said it:

You can ignore it all if you want. You can refuse to play, and the Astrals will do nothing. You can all try to survive, and they won't stop you.

The Lightborns' message had been on her lips when Mick entered. He knew about the other Viceroys; he knew about the Cradles; he knew about all the covert assemblies and the failsafe meet-up they were scheduled to attend at noon GMT on the second day following the shit hitting humanity's collective fan. Mick was her partner in crime, her co-conspirator, her bearer of secrets. She needed a sounding board for this new information, but he seemed compromised already, too emotionally invested.

Right now, Mick looked like he'd do anything to avoid the coming tournament. If she told him what the children had said — and especially if she told him that she believed it was true — Mick would leap on the chance to end it and disobey. He'd burn Divinity's instructions and run to the cresting river, woodworking tools in hand.

Maybe she'd better *not* tell him.

Survivors meant competition. Especially for viceroys who fell out of Astral favor because they hadn't followed instructions when given the chance to lead.

Mick looked up at Liza with big eyes.

"Forget it, Mick. You said the last one was optional. Don't let it bother you."

"The whole thing bothers me."

"Of course it does. But we don't have a chance, do we? You heard Divinity. If we don't comply and officiate the cutthroat tournament to see who gets a slot on the vessel, they'll flatten Roman Sands like Heaven's Veil. You remember that, right? When Dempsey disobeyed them?"

"Yes, but — "

Liza waved him off. He was probably going to refer to the fact that not only was Dempsey still alive; he'd apparently multiplied. Or maybe he was about to repeat what the Dempseys had said before this all started: that Heaven's Veil wasn't what the world had been led to believe. It was all conflicting information. Loose ends now would only cloud an already difficult decision.

"But nothing. I understand it's repugnant. But it's this or nothing. At least we can take a pass."

Mick was leafing through pages, shaking his head.

"Okay, Mick. Get it off your chest. Just tell me what's bothering you so much."

He thought for a second then said something strange. "Do you remember Internet dating?"

"I'm good being single."

Mick laughed a little, but for the most part his mood seemed unbroken. He shook the papers.

"It's like the Astrals have a big dating site database on us. On all of us. Everyone in the city. For all we know, all over the world."

Liza nodded, even though she knew it probably wasn't that dire. The children had told her Roman Sands's method of selection was different from the others — that they were *all* different from each other. More evidence for their argument: that no one needed to obey because it was all arbitrary. As long as the Astrals could make humans squirm then observe their behavior under pressure, they were as happy as alien overlords could be.

"But it's not just 'Single White Female age 35 to 40 seeks nonsmoker for dating and marriage.' The Astrals don't just have our likes and our dislikes and our ages and attributes and what sex positions we enjoy most. It's like they've sucked out *who we are* through those mindfuck stones around the city."

"What do you mean?"

"A university friend of mine is in here," Mick said. "It'd make sense if he were pitted against his mum or something. Twisted but sensible."

"Who'd the Astrals pair him against?"

"It's this girl he had a crush on since primary school. He never even told her about it. And oh, I imagine he's over it now that he's married with three kids, but I remember my first crush, too. It never really goes away."

"Was it on me?"

Mick's eyes hardened. "This isn't funny, Liza. The shit that's in here ... it's ... *pathological*. It's the kind of tournament a serial killer would set up."

"Why are you torturing yourself by looking through it? We officiate. We make sure the rules are followed. That's all. You can't make it personal, Mick."

"Would *you* like to look through it? See who's on the list that *you* know?" He brandished the papers like a weapon.

"Not at all. Because this changes nothing. Jabari made her plan, and the Astrals basically rubber-stamped it. The timing is perfect, as if Divinity knew we were planning to leave the city and run for our Cradles. *Look at it*, Mick," she said, hardening her voice. "Not the pairings but the timetable. We conduct the contest and run right to the Cradle afterward; there's exactly enough time to make it before they presumably remove the levies and let the city flood."

"You don't know that's how it'll happen."

"Ever read the *Bible*, Mick? See the rain? I've heard there's a big ship that visited Ember Flats then headed to the north pole to melt the ice caps one at a time. The idea of a big flood? Sure sounds familiar to me."

Mick looked slapped. "When did you hear about a new ship and the ice caps? From whom?"

"I can explain later. It only matters that I believe it." Something seized Liza then: an idea for how to piggyback on what she'd said, building a better case for Mick. "Just like I believe another thing I heard from the same source: that the Astrals don't care how we survive. If not on the vessel, using the Cradle is fine with them."

"Where are you getting this?"

"Look. We're trusting Jabari's research. Meeting the other viceroys is all that matters, right? That means we need to reach the Cradle, and the rendezvous. *That* is how humanity fights back: with a meeting of minds, backed by research. The plan was always to avoid rocking the boat, then sneak out. We meet the others on the satellite and go from there. Human leadership survives under the radar. Triage was always part of it, Mick. We knew we'd need to break some eggs. I'm sorry if you're feeling guilty, but what's the alternative? Would you rather fight here and get us *all* killed? What happens to the resistance if we do that?" She shook her head. "No. Priority One is keeping the viceroys and their supporters alive to fight another day, and that includes us."

"But Liza — "

"Give me those papers." She jabbed a long arm at him. "Why?"

"So that you won't have them."

Slowly, Mick obeyed.

"Don't print new ones. Don't look at the database or the Divinity channel, either. Your job, until we leave the city, is to manage Cradle prep. Got it?"

Mick nodded.

"For what it's worth, I'm sorry," Liza said, allowing her manner to soften. "Please understand. It's not that none of this bothers me. It's that *we only have a chance if we stick to the plan.* Our only choice is getting to the Cradle and out of the city. If we don't make it, this will be the game's final play, and the Astrals will win. For whatever reason, they're letting us go." She gave Mick a tiny, knowing smirk. "But the Astrals don't know about what we have planned, do they?"

Mick gave a grim nod of agreement.

"There's no other way, Mick. If we don't make the virtual meet-up with Mara and the others, we can't make humanity's final stand. We'll lose because human leadership can't keep fighting if we're dead — and that's what may very well happen if we refuse to officiate their contest before leaving. Do you understand?"

After a long moment, Mick sighed and nodded.

"Leave the cutthroat to me. I'll keep you out of it, okay? I need you to prepare for our exit. Make all the preparations you can so that when this is over, we can reach the Cradle and meet the others. There's still hope for humanity if we play by the rules for a bit longer, as hard as it may be to stomach. It's for the greater good."

Mick waited another long moment then rubbed his face with both hands. He gave a big, desperate sigh and said, "Okay. Fine." Then: "I trust you, Liza."

He stood. With a final glance back, he left.

When the door closed behind him, Liza felt a rush of guilt. She'd been telling him too many lies, but it *was* for the best — even if it that technically meant Liza Knight's definition of "best" more than humanity's.

If the Roman Sands group didn't meet Jabari and the others at the established time, the other rogue viceroys might think the worst. They might think she was dead or incapacitated, then have no choice but to make plans without her.

And if that happened, Liza couldn't play her ace.

As far as the viceroys believed, the satellite channel that the Da Vinci Initiate had set up years ago for emergency communication was secure, under the Astral radar, using technology the wider world — and particularly the Astrals — hadn't ever seen.

But that could change, if someone introduced something the Astrals *had* seen. Something they'd extracted, extrapolated, built windows into, and inoculated themselves against.

Liza pulled a small silver cylinder from her desk drawer and slipped it into her pocket.

If she wasn't there to meet the other viceroys, who else would introduce Terrence Peal's Canned Heat virus into the feed so the Astrals could listen in?

CHAPTER 26

By the time they were two miles north of the city, by Kindred's estimation, rain was pounding upon them in a relentless deluge. It was like standing under a waterfall. There was little shelter along the way save abandoned lean-tos, and no point in standing beneath them for longer than it took to catch the group's collective breath. Either Jabari hadn't planned on driving rain when her think tank had made these plans, or she liked getting wet. Because even if they'd had umbrellas and didn't mind drawing attention, they would have been useless. Rain seemed to come from every direction at once. He was soaked through to his skin, his heavy clothing pulling at him like divers' weights.

They were back in the upper edges of the lowland Nile valley, trudging well east of their intended course to keep clear of the river's rising floodwater, when Piper took his arm.

"Where are we, Kindred?" She'd raised her voice to be heard over the pounding, like projecting in a noisy restaurant.

"North of Ember Flats."

"How long to the Cradle?"

"I don't know exactly. Jabari programmed everything into the tablet." He looked up. Rain on his face was like a high-pressure showerhead. The downpour came in fat drops. "What do you think? Should we get the tablet out right now?"

"So you're working from memory."

"Yes."

"And fortunately your memory is infallible."

He hesitated a second. Then: "Yes."

Piper's eyes went to the others. Peers and Meyer were in the lead, the soaked dog plodding in the mud beside them. Lila was a dark shape in the rain behind Peers, stalking closer than Piper liked.

"Luckily you have Meyer's mind on this, too," Piper said.

"Luckily."

Again Piper watched him. Kindred didn't like her gaze. Irritation had been stewing in him for days, but his reaction to Piper now was something else. Logical wariness, as if something deep was calculating a chance of danger.

"I can hear your thoughts, Kindred."

"Don't. My head is *my* business."

"And I notice how Meyer isn't there nearly as strongly as he used to be."

"It's more complicated than that."

Piper gave an *if you say so* sort of nod. She probably sighed, too, but Kindred couldn't hear it in the rain.

"We shouldn't pretend, you and me. We shared a life back in Heaven's Veil. When did we become such strangers?"

"Maybe when you took up with Cameron?"

Kindred regretted the jab as he said it. Piper's eyes registered a cheap shot, and Kindred was left wondering where it had come from. Once upon a time he'd been Meyer Dempsey in full, sure of himself even when unsure of what to do next. But that was no longer true. Now he was a ball of loose ends. The Ark's opening had changed something.

Piper seemed to shrug it away. The topic changed as they trudged on, looking ahead, the Nile valley overfull to their right, down a gently sloping line of land.

"I know something is different with you," she said. "I can feel it."

"Nothing has changed."

"You're angry. You're confused. It's like you're becoming a hole in the air. A cold spot."

"Jesus, Piper."

"You were always your own man. You kept to yourself, just like Meyer. He was always a tough nut to crack. And when you thought you were him, you were the same. Even after, it's like I couldn't tell you apart, once he put some meat back on his bones. If he hadn't grown his beard and you didn't wear different wedding rings, I'd never have been able to know who was who."

Kindred pointed, not liking where this seemed to be going. "I think it's up that way." But they'd have to detour around; he'd pointed toward a flood. Debris in the water showed how fast the overfull river was flowing. His eyes noted a piece of what might once have been someone's wall, its window still intact. He saw the roof of a submerged car, racing off to some underwater expressway.

"But now you're easy to tell apart," Piper continued. "You're coming apart. Like you're half a person. What is it you're looking for, Kindred?"

"Just the Cradle. Like the rest of you."

"That's not what I mean. It's like there's a magnet inside you. But I can't tell what it's attracting. Where the thing you're seeking is. I only know it's coming."

"That's ridiculous."

"The Astrals connected us," Piper went on. "Anyone within range of those big rocks is connected, but ever since the Ark opened it's like everything is magnified. I can still feel Cameron, Kindred. I can still hear him in here." She pointed to her head, looking distraught. "I can hear almost everyone now, but only on the surface. I know you're seeking something, but not what it is. I know Meyer is afraid, but not why. I know Peers is keeping a secret that's eating him up inside, and it's not just that he used to be Mullah. It's something much worse. Something he'd rather die than say out loud."

"Piper ... "

"And I can feel Lila's festering anger. At first she was worried and nervous, but those feelings have been growing darker and darker since we left. Maybe since before then. It's not like your rage, when it flares up. Lila's has direction. It's poison. I know she's mad at Peers, and that she doesn't trust him. But Kindred ... it's so much *heavier* than that."

"What do you expect me to do?"

"To tell me the truth. You and Meyer are supposed to be our compass. We lean on you as if you were the same person. You're like two halves of the same — "

"Well, we're not, okay?" Kindred blurted. "I'm me. He's him. And if that's the way things are, you'll just have to fucking deal with it."

Piper looked at Kindred sidelong. The rain between them made a partial curtain. Piper's black hair was plastered to her head, rain running in tiny rivers down to her neck, along her face and dripping from her chin.

"Maybe you should tell me what's really going on," Kindred said. "Or maybe you could talk to Meyer instead of me. If this copy of Meyer is falling apart, maybe you should leave me the fuck alone and talk to the original."

Piper watched him for another long moment. Either they were walking lower without meaning to, or the river was rising that fast, because Kindred felt his steps getting wetter. He looked down to see their feet ankle-deep.

"The man in my head says the Astrals know who we are and where we're going. That they've known it from the start."

"Good for him," Kindred muttered.

"He says that Jabari really did create a secure line of communication between all the viceroys. And he says that if we can make contact, the Astrals can't listen."

"Good for *all of us*," Kindred amended.

"So far it hasn't mattered that they can't listen because they think they know what we're going to do. He says it's what we've always done, time after time after time."

Kindred was going to ask about that, but Piper was inside his head. Her feelings flavored her words, and he found himself understanding. Throughout time, the same events happened over and over. There was always an exodus. There were always survivors. There was always a deposed King who lived, although those who traveled with him seldom did.

"Bullshit," Kindred said, feeling nerves prickle his neck.

"He tells me that we have a chance to turn the tables this time. Because of the children. And because of *him*. We have just this one way to plan without the Astrals listening. This one way to surprise them. This *single ace in the hole*, as long as we can make it to Jabari's rendezvous point."

"Why are you telling me this? Go tell Meyer." Then, with venom that came from nowhere, pulling from Piper's thoughts, he added, "Go tell the *King*."

"Who is the man in boots?" Piper asked.

Kindred walked a few more paces before realizing she was staring right at him. She wasn't asking a rhetorical question. She was asking him for real, as if she thought he might have a clue.

"What the hell makes you think I'd know?" Kindred asked.

"Because what the ,man in boots wants more than anything," Piper said, "is you."

184

CHAPTER 27

Around a copse of barren-looking trees, in a tiny inlet that was more lake than river by the time they reached it, Meyer pointed at the edge of something in the water and said, "There."

"There what?" asked Peers beside him.

"It has to be Jabari's Cradle."

"Looks like junk floating in the water to me," Peers said.

"It's a dock."

Lila came up beside him. Piper and Kindred followed, and Meyer noticed a strange glance move from one to the other.

Piper said, "What are we looking at?"

"That thing in the water there. See it?"

Piper squinted. Meyer tried to see it through her eyes rather than his memory. He'd spent fifteen minutes looking through the information on the tablet at their last stop, careful to stay in the center of the ramshackle shelter and keep both the tablet and its waterproof bag dry. The dock was temporary, shoved way back. In the photos, the thing wasn't visible. It looked like swamp — a stagnant corner of a river branch where no water circulated, where trees overhung the water and crocodiles were probably plentiful.

But the point was to hide, from both the riverbank and the sky. They'd have to cut through brush (and, again, crocodiles) to reach it. Or at least that's how it would have been, before the coming flood. Now the water had risen several feet above the normal surface, and the river appeared much broader than in the photos. The stagnant inlet was no longer stagnant, raised enough to make it part of the river proper. They wouldn't have to hack through brush at this point. But they might have to swim.

"That thing that looks like a piece of aluminum?"

"Yes."

"How is that a dock?"

"It's a floating dock. You saw the pictures."

"I forget the pictures, Meyer," Piper said.

"It's not permanent. Jabari said they planned to rotate the location if needed, if new viceroys joined or left their little group. So it's a floating aluminum dock, tethered to concrete anchors." Meyer looked again. "Tethered well, by the looks of it. We're only seeing the corner."

"You're sure?" Piper asked. "Maybe it washed away."

"Concrete anchors wouldn't keep a floating dock under like that," said Peers, shading his eyes, trying to see better.

"The air barrels might have been punctured by river debris. If a few of them filled with water ... "

"There's no way that's it," said Peers. "Where are the trees? The dock in the photos was huge."

"The trees are half-submerged, Peers. And so is the dock."

"The *entire dock?*"

Kindred's hand was between them, snapping its fingers.

"Give me the pack."

"Why?"

"Just give me the fucking pack, Meyer. You're not the only one in charge here."

Meyer gave Kindred a glance, feeling almost nothing in their shared internal space. He'd grown used to Kindred's absence, but it seemed strange now that he noticed it. There was something different about him. Some unspoken change of which Meyer was unaware. Usually, Kindred felt like a mirror. But now he struck him as an annoyed man with poor social awareness.

Meyer watched as Kindred stalked away. There was an abandoned car farther up the hill. He tugged on the door, found it unlocked, then closed himself inside. Meyer and the others watched his head as he did something: probably opened his pack to look at the tablet.

Meyer turned to Piper. She'd been watching the exchange and seemed to understand his brewing questions. He'd seen them talking — but unlike in the past, Meyer found himself unable to access the content once Kindred was alone with an unoccupied mind. Piper, on the other hand, was a one-way street, able to see into them all. But Meyer couldn't see into her. Without Kindred's pairing, he felt incomplete, blind and all too mortal.

???

And Piper's eyes and slow nod seemed to say, *Later.*

Kindred returned a few minutes later. He handed the backpack to Meyer, with an apology somehow present in the simple gesture. He seemed to be offering Meyer the pack rather than commanding him to take it. The acquiescent manner of a kid about to say, *Aw shucks, I didn't mean nothin' by it.*

"This is it," Kindred said, looking at Peers first then the others. "Meyer is right. It's a four-slip floating aluminum dock, and there are twelve flotation barrels beneath it. Jabari's specs say it's anchored to concrete with heavy chain, but only in two places. So something would have to have burst the barrels. But this is the spot, all right."

Meyer watched Kindred finish, wanting to note his many omissions. The way their minds used to work, their shared consciousness would have determined all the specs, including the likelihood that the entire dock was still submerged instead of part of it having broken away.

How many upward pounds of buoyant force does a sealed plastic barrel containing such-and-such cubic feet of air exert when submerged two feet beneath the surface? What's the tensile strength of the chain the builders used as tethers? Normally, Meyer would know it all. *Either eight of the twelve barrels were punctured, or it's broken off; those are the only two possibilities.* And they'd have calculated the odds of each.

But now there were only Kindred's words, the river, and the rain.

"How can you be sure?" Peers asked.

"GPS is still working through Jabari's protected protocol — the same one we'll join once we reach the ground repeater at the rendezvous point."

"Maybe the Astrals hacked the GPS signal," Peers said. "How do you know they don't know exactly where we are?"

"They *might* know where we are," Meyer said. "But not through the network. It's secure."

"We don't know it's secure," Peers said. And Meyer noticed how Lila stared at him. Cold, like a snake.

"It's secure," said Kindred. "I looked at those specs, too. It's a closed network, like an old company intranet. Not like the Internet."

"So?"

"So it's not accessible from the outside. There are no connections to any wider networks. It could only be hacked from the inside."

"You can't be sure that means — "

"You're awfully worried about security," Lila said, cutting him off, "for a guy whose buddies managed to shut down the palace's security when they grabbed my daughter."

"Now just wait a goddamned — "

"*Lila,*" said Piper.

"*All that matters,*" Meyer said, projecting his voice, "is that we made it here. We can worry about the rest later. "This was step one. Either those subs are still on the dock, or they're not."

Kindred nodded. "The specs say they're designed to be stored with the ballast tanks flooded, so they'd have been resting below the dock either way. If it's still here under the water, submersibles should be, too. Each holds ten people, so we can all fit in one. I'd say our odds are good. Only one needs to have survived and kept its tether."

"How do we get to it?" Piper asked. The river was dark in the evening light, under the gathering clouds. Its overflown banks had made it surging and angry-looking. The plus side was that crocodiles might have a hard time treading water long enough to eat them, but the downside was that if the crocs weren't able to swim in this, humans probably wouldn't either.

"Jabari put a startup app on the tablet," Kindred said. "I initiated it for all four subs. Instructions say it'll take a few minutes for the startup routines to run and safety-check, then blow out the tanks and surface. But she gave us a rigged version of the app because she needed to keep her own authorization while letting us have a piece, so the status indicators are less than ideal."

"In English, please," said Peers.

Kindred sighed. "I don't know if the subs are actually there and initializing or not."

"So what do we do?" Piper asked.

"We wait," Kindred answered. "Either one or more will come to the surface, or they won't."

"And if none do?" Lila said.

"Let's cross that bridge if we find it," Meyer said.

They looked out across the water. It was full of debris, as if the monster swelling the river had reached out, taken civilization by the throat, and dragged it in to drown. Vehicles moved past. Sections of roofing and drywall. A small shed, intact. Clothes, sheets, children's toys.

"Something you might want to know," Kindred said, not turning. "When I was up there on the tablet, I opened the feed to Ember Flats."

"And?" Meyer said.

"We don't have a live line to Jabari, but her man Kamal thought to leave us a message."

"Kamal?" Peers said, looking guilty. "So he's ... okay?"

"Okay enough to type. He said Divinity came for Jabari, using a human body. Walked right up to the bunker door and knocked. They told her that the flooding will come from more than the rain, that the big ship we saw moving away was going north to melt the polar ice cap. And they told her the big boat the Astrals left to save a small number of people would be filled however she wanted — her choice alone. So Jabari's combing the citizen roster, looking for ... " Kindred sighed, and Meyer thought of how much it must take for the man — never very emotional — to sigh. "For the people *most worth saving* if most of humanity is to be exterminated."

Meyer met Piper's eyes. She looked crushed, but somehow strong.

"She won't be joining us," Kindred continued. "Divinity put her on the Ember Flats Ark. She's not allowed to surrender her spot for someone else."

"How did Kamal leave the message for us?" Lila asked.

"Kamal," Kindred said, "*was* allowed to give up his."

The thought settled. A dark veil fell over the group of six — human and canine — beside the rushing and violent river.

They waited. They watched the river. Rain pounded, and even during the few minutes they all spent being soaked, the level inched higher. Much more, and the delta would flood. Egypt wouldn't be much of a desert after all.

Waiting for the submersible to surface. Waiting for their one and only way through the coming decimation — and, if Jabari's viceroy cabal really did have a surprise yet up its sleeve, humanity's final shot at salvation.

"Nothing," said Lila, watching the dock's corner. "There's nothing there. There's no way out."

There was a loud and terrible banging. Then another. And another. Even behind the sonic backdrop of rain, it was like gods banging anvils with titanic hammers.

Across the flooded Nile, the dock was jerking up, then sagging down.

"*Shit,*" said Kindred.

Peers looked at Kindred. Piper and Lila looked at Meyer.

"They're not here, are they? The subs. They all broke away."

But Meyer didn't need his Kindred connection to figure out this particular logical puzzle.

"At least one of them is still here, all right," he said, "but it's trapped under the dock."

CHAPTER 28

Sadeem Hajjar paced the all-white room, wondering exactly where he was supposed to sit — *if* he was supposed to. The walls were featureless, and the space had no furniture of any sort. Ceilings and floors blended into the walls in huge, drain pipe-sized rounded corners. If the room were to roll end for end, a child could keep sliding from wall to floor, floor to wall, wall to ceiling, over and over, laughing with boundless glee.

Sadeem, on the other hand, was not feeling joyful at all. His glee had *many* boundaries. He'd thought more than once that he was nervous enough to shit date pits, then actually laughed aloud — something that made him all the more aware of just how nervous he truly was. Nothing bad had happened, but he almost wished something would. The waiting was so much worse. He was so nervous he couldn't stand, and yet it felt wrong to sit cross-legged on the floor. This was its own water torture: put a man in a room, then let him be. Anticipation could kill him.

A door at the room's far end opened. Sadeem hadn't realized it was there. He knew there was a door in here somewhere because a Titan had ushered him through when he'd come over from the Ember Flats mothership. But he'd lost his location the moment he'd turned around. It was like being lost in the world's easiest maze.

A woman stepped through the door. Something in her manner immediately told Sadeem that she wasn't human, nor was she the Divinity who'd spoken with him earlier, before they'd brought him to the big black ship. The Ember Flats Divinity (and this assumed they didn't rotate forms, which they might) was entirely different. This one — presumably head of the fleet's biggest ship — was still a woman, but the first ship's Divinity was brunette where this one was blonde. The first wore no-nonsense human pants and a no-nonsense human blouse. This one was in a red dress, just above the knee. It made Sadeem uncomfortable to see so much skin, but it had been a long time since he'd seen his first Western woman or been truly shocked by their immodesty.

Except that she wasn't a Western woman, nor was she a woman at all.

"If you are fatigued, you may sit."

Sadeem was about to ask where exactly he was supposed to do so, but then part of the floor slid slowly upward behind him, forming an all-white stool that looked like a stump blooming from the all-white floor.

"Thank you."

"Your name is Sadeem Hajjar."

"And you are?"

"We are Eternity."

"I thought you called your command caste 'Divinity.'"

"Divinity control those under a single ship. We control Divinity."

"Where are the rest of you? The rest of Eternity?"

"Who is the Stranger?"

Sadeem blinked. It was as if she'd heard his question then decided to deliberately ignore it. To blindside him with yet another question that meant nothing.

"What stranger?"

"The one who speaks for you as we speak for us."

The use of double plurals confused Sadeem, but he recovered, still unsure what the woman was talking about.

"Nobody speaks for all of us."

"We sampled him. He browsed our repository, and when he was gone we had our imprint. But he is not what he claimed to be."

"I'm sorry; I have no idea who you're talking about." Then, sure he was being unhelpful: "Can you describe him?"

In an instant, a tall, long-faced man wearing a plain button-up shirt, jeans, and scuffed brown boots appeared before Sadeem. He blinked so quickly into existence that Sadeem staggered backward away from him, shocked. Then a shiver of interference ran through the man, and Sadeem realized he wasn't actually there. The man was merely a projection.

Sadeem stood. Examined the man.

"I don't know who this is."

"He speaks for you."

"He doesn't speak for *me*."

"He is your nexus. We see it in his trace. Do not try and fool or deceive us. Who is he?"

The woman's voice had become short, almost angry. Her shoulder-length blonde hair bounced as she spoke. She was slim but full in all the right places. Sadeem found himself inexplicably attracted, despite knowing what she was, despite knowing that even if she was human, he was probably thirty years too old for her.

"I ... I'm sorry. I have no idea."

She seemed to make an effort to contain herself. Sadeem wondered what her brief spat of anger might mean, and what it meant that the Astrals' highest class — one higher than the wisest Elders even thought to exist (commanding the Dark Rider) had so accurately and completely embodied human sex appeal.

"You are Mullah."

"Yes."

"You keep our portal. We have always communicated."

"Our eldest Elders have. I have never seen the portal."

"Who among you is senior? Who would know this stranger?"

"I don't know. We were scattered. You sent in drones. You took me away and left at least some of the others. So many of our groups have already come under attack. You probably killed our eldest. If anyone would know about us other than me, it's whoever sent drones to invade us."

"The drones were not invading. We have always respected peace with the portal-keepers."

"Is that why you flooded our chambers with flying BBs?" It was Sadeem's turn to be angry. In all the confusion and panic of abduction (and worry over Clara, who had at least blessedly seemed to stay hidden), he'd turned penitent. But Eternity was correct: The Astrals *were* supposed to respect the peace. On the human side, there had always been the Mullah, keepers of the portal. It wasn't correct to say they were allies. The way Sadeem's teacher had explained it to him had always seemed most accurate: The Mullah were mediators and mitigators. They accepted that the Astrals would eventually return, and did what they could to make sure the damage they inevitably did was as minimal — and painless — as possible.

"We were sweeping the area."

"Then why bring me to your ship? Why did you take me from that ship onto this one?"

"The drones must have detected an anomaly. Something you were hiding. Otherwise you would not have been flagged."

Clara? No, certainly not. Even as he'd been dragged away and losing consciousness, Sadeem had seen that the closet was still sealed, Clara almost for-sure knocked out by the incapacitating gas. The drones had moved on. There'd been nothing to alert them of a reason to return.

Clara was safe. He had to keep believing that. The Lightborn were this epoch's wild card. Sadeem didn't know why their puzzle-solving minds were so important or what had caused them to become as they were. He only knew that it mattered — and that the Astrals, last time he'd heard, hadn't a clue.

"I wasn't hiding anything."

The woman pointed to the hologram.

"You have never seen this man?"

"No. Never."

"He is not a leader? He does not represent humanity?"

"Not as far as I know. What makes you think he is?"

Sadeem watched the woman think, wondering distantly if she actually *was* thinking in a way he understood thought. Probably not. Divinity — and now Eternity — always referred to "we" instead of "I." The Mullah knew they thought in a collective. From an Astral perspective, humans simply didn't understand reality: that individual beings were instances of something larger, not entities in and of themselves. The *thought* he was seeing on the woman's face was probably Eternity's interpretation of modern humanity combining with Sadeem's own prejudices. The real cogitation was happening somewhere else. Maybe *everywhere* else.

"This man came to us. He requested an audience with Ember Flats's Divinity. He exhibited certain ... *unusual* mental attributes." She took a step forward, hips swaying as if with intention. "He told us that the Mullah were hiding something. Something you have not yet admitted to."

"Then he was lying." Sadeem's heart beat harder. He hoped sensors on the big black ship couldn't see or hear it.

"He had knowledge he should not have had. Knowledge he said we did not possess, but required. He made a bargain."

"What kind of a bargain?"

"We gave him limited access to an inconsequential data stream. We thought we pattern-tracked him but we did not and the match fell apart. By the time this was discovered and we realized a need to access the man's mind again, we were unable to find him."

Sadeem looked at the hologram. He'd thought it was motionless and that the small movements he could sense were merely a shimmer, but as he watched it now, the hologram reached into its pocket. The hand came out with three sliver spheres, and rolled them across its palm.

The hologram blinked away and was gone. When Sadeem turned back to the woman, her unflappable Astral countenance seemed disturbed.

"The Mullah scrolls tell us the Horsemen lack emotion. Out of academic curiosity, is that true?"

The woman's face again became wooden. "Your scrolls are accurate."

But that wasn't true. Intentionally or not, Eternity aboard the Dark Rider had presented itself as a sexually interesting human female sending out all the right signals. It had become angry when Sadeem appeared ignorant. And now, when the hologram had raised its hand, Eternity had grown flustered. Why?

"Why do you want to find this man so badly?" Sadeem asked.

"He has information we require. Information you have been brought here to provide."

"Which information?"

"The children you call the Lightborn."

Sadeem stifled his shock. And fear. She'd already mentioned that the Mullah were possibly hiding something.

Hopefully the two weren't connected: hiding the Lightborn from Astral eyes.

"What about them?"

"What are they?"

"They are children."

"But they are different."

"Many children are different."

"Do not be obtuse. Our drones have observed you in safe zones, where our treaty permits. You have displayed intense interest in them. You have proposed the solution lies in puzzles."

"You misunderstand. There is no *solution*. The children are merely precocious. They grow and develop early. They are highly intelligent and creative."

"What causes them to?"

"I do not know. Perhaps they are a symptom of being raised in Astral presence, or around your impressive repeating stones." Sadeem watched the woman, wondering if Eternity's surprising Astral emotion was immune to flattery.

"Why do they interest you?"

"They simply do. What interests you?"

"They are an aberration. Why does your interest in them center on games and puzzles?"

"Why does it matter?"

"That is not of your concern. You will be kept here until you assist us."

"Why don't you just suck the thoughts out of my head?"

The woman's face contorted slightly: another semi-emotional response, indicating that he'd inadvertently stumped her. Apparently the Astrals couldn't just suck the information out of his head, or they'd have already done it. And whoever this man with the silver spheres was, he and whatever he'd almost told Divinity about the Lightborn before vanishing mattered a hell of a lot.

"The man in question told us that the Lightborn would see through a certain ruse. We presented the bloodwater out of the archive of human expectation as we've gathered through our repeater stones, but it was only presented to gather attention. The humans took it as a plague, but it was not. As many things are not as they seem."

"What things?"

The woman seemed to decide she'd said enough. "That is not of your concern. The man told us that the Lightborn would not be fooled. It did not matter. We observed he was correct. There was a dangerous fault in his frequency, and so we corrected it as he exited his view into our stream. There was no reason to keep him. He was dropped off outside Ember Flats."

"And?"

Another uncomfortable look. "It seems this man was able to open windows we did not anticipate. Windows we used to access this planet from our own."

"Like the portal? The one in the Mullah Temple?"

"Like that window and others. There are substances that alter consciousness here and give humanity access to a connection to the collective mind that it otherwise lacks. This man can do this without those substances."

"He can get high without getting high?"

Her features sharpened. "There is pollution in *your* stream now. At each point, around your planet, we are seeing disturbances to the expected flow that seem to have no cause. We have recursively scanned our records, including those from the past epoch from our judgment archive, and the only likely conclusion was that we have simply been unable to see the Lightborn minds except in moments of extreme signaling."

Sadeem had already figured that out. It's why he'd hidden Clara.

"You mean you can't hear them unless they're emotional?"

"So you do know of them."

"Only from personal curiosity."

"Because the disturbances around the globe seem to have no traceable origin, we believe they were begun by Lightborn. But our own investigations show that although your children have stronger mental gifts than the rest of you, it has a limited range."

"So?"

"Ships that have managed to find Lightborn children since and investigate them have found that the children share something in common. *One* thing. They believe they've been contacted by someone from another place. Someone able to open windows."

"Your man in boots."

The woman nodded.

Sadeem waited, realizing it was apparently his turn to speak.

"Someone's running amok, telling the planet's Lightborn to ... cause disturbances of some sort," Sadeem said.

"In the stream," the woman clarified. "It's misdirected and unexpected. The only pattern seems to be an intention *to cause disturbance*. To initiate chaos."

"So what do you want from me? Why don't you poke your Horsemen heads into the portal and shut the windows for good? You have ships around the world. *You* hold the upper hand."

The woman said nothing.

"You can't do it, can you? Whoever this man is, he's beating you, isn't he?"

Sadeem looked up at the woman. Her fists were clenched. Her face was set. And for the fraction of a second, her eyes flashed as red as her dress.

In a blip, the floor seemed to vanish. Sadeem thought he might fall but then realized he was on something clearer than glass, looking down on an endless expanse of blank white nothingness.

He was seeing the ground, far below his feet. And judging by the horizon's curvature and the black space beyond, he knew the enormous black ship must be very high up.

A blue glow seemed to bloom from the center of the floor — from the bottom of the ship, far below.

It grew.

And it *grew*.

"Where are we?" He looked at the stark white landscape below. "What happened to Ember Flats?"

"The Deathbringer is no longer above Ember Flats."

He looked down. He saw nothing but white snow and ice, shrouded in the darkness of a six-month night.

"Let us see," the blonde woman said, "who is beating whom."

CHAPTER 29

Lila ran down the shallow embankment, heels skidding in the sandy soil. She'd left the car door open behind her. Mara's tablet was safe from the pounding rain for now, sitting on the opposite seat. But the passenger side of the wreck, where Lila had been sitting and pretending to be staying out of the way, was getting soaked. She'd need to return for the tablet, and take pains to make sure it was stowed dry and sealed.

But for now there was only the panic.

"Dad! Piper!"

They could barely hear her. The rain's intensity and the sound of its assault had tripled. Her father, Kindred, Piper, and Peers were being pelted with fat streams of water as they waded into the rising Nile, trying and failing to hold onto each other for support. Not long ago — about the time Lila decided the feeds weren't going to show Clara simply walking past — there'd been hail. The others had simply stood in the open through it. Even Nocturne was helping. He was on the shore, barking at the water.

"Dad!"

Instead of turning, leaving the water, and running to help her, he dove in headfirst.

"DAD!" Lila shrieked, watching him vanish, the fear over her news temporarily lost in a certainty that he wouldn't surface, that she'd seen the real Meyer Dempsey — former movie studio mogul, father who'd wanted to ditch Raj in New Jersey, and had maybe been right all along — for the final time.

But then the surface broke, and she saw him paddling among the flotsam. He was more treading water sideways than swimming properly; the surface wasn't as turbulent near the shores as it was in the middle. But then Meyer reached the current and changed to a forward crawl, kicking in what Lila was shocked to see were the same black dress shoes he'd worn for his State of the City what felt like a thousand years ago. They'd bog him down. He'd drown because he hadn't removed his stupid shoes.

She was in water to her ankles. To her calves. To her knees. She'd waded nearly to the point where Meyer had started swimming when Kindred's hand wrapped around her upper arm.

And he said, "Don't."

She wouldn't leap into the water. She wasn't crazy, like her father. And yet she felt Kindred gripping hard to hold her back because her muscles were fighting to go, to follow, to do something, anything.

"It's okay, Lila. He's trailing a rope."

She looked and saw it, following behind him like a river anaconda.

She wanted to say something obvious. Like how a rope wouldn't help him cross. Like how it would only snag behind and pull him under if (when) it broke, and the that other end would merely allow them to retrieve his body.

But Meyer swam on, arms pumping hard, legs kicking harder.

"There's a rip current underneath. Feel it?"

Lila looked from Kindred to her own waterlogged legs. She felt it, all right. The river was moving near her knees, while flat-out trying to knock her down at the ankles.

She looked up, watching her father — a champion collegiate swimmer in his day, he'd often boasted — swim a full 45 degrees upstream of the submerged submersible dock. He was staying flat at the top, in the slower-moving water that still didn't look all that slow, kicking and surging.

The current shoved him back toward his target. A huge sheet of torn wood and plaster, nails exposed, came rushing toward him. Lila gasped as it nearly clipped him, but he dodged, losing water to the current, struggling harder to push on. The giant piece of debris passed behind him, and for long, horrible moments Lila was positive it had missed her father only to snag his rope and drag him down to his watery grave.

But the flotsam passed, and the rain intensified. Evening gloom obscured her vision and blocked the sound until finally Kindred straightened and, apparently feeling Lila had found her senses, loosened his grip on her arm.

"*What?*" Lila asked, watching him. It came out as a hysterical demand.

"He made it," Piper said.

"I can't see him!"

"He's on the far side, Lila. It's okay."

Lila looked from Piper to Kindred, seeing relaxation she didn't feel. The situation suddenly seemed absurdly unfair: Everyone could read minds except for her. And Peers, of course.

"Okay," Kindred said. "Where's the tablet?"

Lila blinked around, heart pounding, panic not nearly abated. But it wasn't just her father she'd been afraid for when running down here. He hadn't even gone in yet as she'd been scrabbling down the shore, an announcement on her tongue. But she couldn't place it. Couldn't even find her place here and now, as a person, by a river, missing a daughter, afraid for her father. It was all so terrible. But then it slowly returned, along with the fear, and she found herself staring at Kindred, more frustrated by his impatience than moved.

"The *tablet*, Lila. Where did you put it? I need to flood the tanks so Meyer can work. I need to— " Kindred stopped, looking up at the stalled car. "Who left the door open? Where's the tablet?"

"It's in the car."

"With the door open? In the rain? Lila, what the hell is wrong with—?"

Then it was all back. The rushing horror. The sense of doom. The feeling that time had already run out, and that every second mattered. She'd just spent a hundred or so, maybe more. And the clock was already at zero. She'd seen it with her own eyes, on the backlit screen, while poking around the feeds to find her daughter.

This is a message from the Fucked Up Earth channel, broadcasting on all frequencies.

Our movie Desperate Search for Clara *will return in a moment.*

We interrupt your regularly scheduled programming to bring you the apocalypse.

"We have to hurry," Lila said, now gripping Kindred, then Piper as she came up beside him. Her eyes were wide enough to hurt. Hair, drenched by the rain, was plastered to her face. Nocturne barked behind them, as if he alone understood.

Piper was holding her by the upper arms, peering into her eyes. "We're hurrying, Lila. It'll be okay."

"*Dammit, Piper!*"

Something surged between them — an emotion, cut from its tether. Then Piper understood, too. Maybe not exactly *what* had happened, but that something horrible had.

"What is it? What did you see?"

"They did it. It was on the tablet. Like a broadcast. Like they were proud and wanted us to see."

"What, Lila? What did you see on the tablet?"

"The big ship. The one we saw leaving Ember Flats. It's melting the ice. It's flooding the planet. I saw the white disappear and the blue beneath. They showed Greenland and somewhere in Russia or something? Or the Ukraine. Like it was a goddamned news report! Like we'd want to see the waves hit the shores!"

Kindred looked at Piper.

"She's hysterical."

"For a good reason."

"What's she talking about?"

"We have to be quick, Kindred. This planet is about to get a whole lot wetter."

Something clicked. "Not the ice caps."

Lila nodded. Peers, who'd barely heard in the downpour, came over. He was close to Lila, and she fought an urge to throttle *and* smack him, in that order. She couldn't touch the Astrals who'd done this, but their buddy Peers was the next best thing.

"We have time. There's a lot of ice up there. They can't just melt it all. It'll refreeze as fast as they do it."

"See for yourself." Lila pointed. "Go look at the feed if you don't believe me. *Go and look if you don't think they can do it!*"

"Lila, calm down."

But she was done with calming down. Through pretending that everything would be fine. In the past days, she'd had her daughter stolen, abandoned all chance of finding her again, learned one of their own was an enemy *still* beside her, been showered in blood, witnessed the world's end, and was about to lose her father to drowning. That didn't even count the death she'd seen less than twenty-four hours ago, the death witnessed on the way here, the cannibal rape gangs who'd paused to gawk but could return at any time, the loss of her mother, brother, husband, friends.

Lila had been calm enough for long enough. It was time to try something different.

"Fuck you, Kindred! Go look! Go and fucking look!"

"Either way, we need to stay calm. Getting hysterical won't help us get out of — "

He stopped when Lila slapped him, hard. Kindred glared back at her, his eyes dark. His stare wasn't precisely angry, though there was rage within it. His stare was mostly disapproving — the kind a father gives his unruly daughter when she disappoints him.

She tried to hit him again. This time Kindred caught her arm, pinned it down. And when she tried from the other side, feeling herself losing control but unable to help it, his dodge made her fall. Then Kindred, Piper, and Peers were above her, and she was turning her head to the side, trying not to drown as rain filled her mouth and nose.

"I'll hold her," Kindred said. "You help Meyer. Since we can't see or hear him, you'll have to flood the ballast then give him time to swim under and hope he can — "

"It's okay, Kindred. I can hear him now." She closed her eyes: a yogi in the heart of a storm. "He's okay. He's waiting for us."

Lila was still wrenching out of Kindred's grip, but now it was protective. She wanted to roll to the side, curl into a comma, cry in the rain, and never move a muscle again. Even if her father didn't drown freeing the sub, what were they supposed to do? The world would flood — halfway now, the rest of the way when the ship presumably headed south to expose Antarctic soil. It might be storming like this around half the globe as the climate adjusted. The sub would be tossed like a toy. They'd die inside a tin can instead

EXTINCTION

of outside one. Even if they survived, what was the point? Would they live on a sub forever? Or would they find an exposed mountaintop and set up shop in a lonely paradise, lying on a fresh beach until their food ran dry?

Visions of the Greenland feed returned, followed by the Ukraine.

How long would it take for those waves to reach them? Would they get the waves at all, nestled in the gulf and bunkered to the north by land? Or would they claim the land, too, and swallow Gibraltar before burying Egypt?

Kindred let go. He stood, maybe moving by Piper. But Lila couldn't see. Didn't want to. It would be so much easier to die now and be done with it all.

Someone else sat by her, water lapping their ankles.

"There, there," said Peers, patting her side.

Nocturne licked her hand.

The water rose, faster than seemed possible.

CHAPTER 30

"Logan?"

The voice wasn't really commanding his attention. It was a hesitant word of fear — exacerbated by the video feed that had butted in and displayed itself on every tablet in the Hideout minutes ago, shocking even far-seeing Lightborn minds.

"Logan!"

The tall boy hustled over. As Clara watched him pass, she found herself feeling sorry for him. He'd somehow become the group's leader, and had stepped into his role. Based on what Clara could see/feel as her mind touched the Hideout Collective, the group held him in high esteem. They found Logan strong, fair, brave, and as wise as a sixteen-year-old could be while trapped in an adolescent's turbulent body. But what Clara saw on his face belied a secret he kept locked away, same as they all kept their secrets. Logan's was his fear, scared as the rest of them most of the time, despite his brave mask.

Clara followed the others, believing in Logan.

Her head was swimming with the recent change: this sudden ability to feel not just the Lightborn around her but those that seemed to be far away. As walls between clusters of Lightborn inexplicably became open windows, their worldwide blending was slowly unfolding, like two dogs sniffing before greeting. But there were other voices competing for space in Clara's head as well. The voice of her mother, whom she seemed to distantly feel but who, she doubted, could feel her, afraid and far more alone than Clara herself. The Astrals, still audible and plotting their worldwide plans. And most of all there was the voice of the man by the fire: the man who saw himself as a pry bar, meant to wedge between gears of a machine and break them apart.

Amid it all were the images seen by them all:

The northern ice cap melting — the planet's top hat turning from white to overflowing blue.

The shores of Greenland greeting the waves.

The people. All of them drowning, the water washing the world away.

And the big ship leaving. Headed south to do the same thing again.

Logan came to the door, where the boy who'd yelled was standing. But he wasn't peering through the peephole as Clara had assume he'd be, warning the others that Reptars had come.

Instead, everyone by the door was looking at the floor. Where a slow, even flow of water was leaking from beneath the sweep.

"It's happening," the boy said. He was a big, broad kid, maybe fourteen. He looked terrified. Inside Clara's mind she could see/feel the blip of consciousness that was slightly more *him* than the hive mind, and saw little but worry streaming, reaching out for the group's comfort.

"It's only rain," said the red-headed kid, Cheever.

"It's the floods. Like in the *Bible*. My mom kept reading the bad parts out loud before they took her. She said it was happening all over again. And now it is."

"It's only rain, Josh," Cheever repeated, rolling his eyes. "My mom said — "

"*Fuck* your *Bible*-beater mom!" Then he seemed to remember himself and said, more reasonably, "But dude, that shit just happened. There aren't tidal waves. We're not ... " He sighed then put his hands on the handles and said, "Look."

Logan reached out, grabbing for Cheever and the doors. "*Wait!*"

But he was too late. Cheever flung the left-side door wide. Water outside was three inches high and seemed to be rising fast. The flow surged inside, almost knocking Cheever flat. He waded to stay upright as filthy water doused his lower legs, spreading across the Hideout floor in seconds, setting shoes and belongings afloat. Inflowing pressure knocked the catch off the already partially open right door, and for a few long seconds there were miniature rapids at the door until the turbulence subsided, water found its level, and the Lightborn were left with soaking feet.

"It's happening, man!" Josh blubbered.

This time, Cheever could only gape back at him, his mouth open and face disbelieving, as if blaming Josh for getting everything wet.

Nick came up beside Logan. From where Clara was standing, they looked like a reluctant leader and his right-hand man.

Inside her head, she heard Nick ask the collective — Logan mostly: *What should we do?*

Logan's response came as if he hadn't a single doubt, though she knew he had plenty.

We go to the middle of town like everyone else, Logan thought/said, *and take our chances.*

CHAPTER 31

Piper was piloting the sub.

Meyer couldn't see her through the weather, and the torrent was deafening enough to drown her out entirely, but he knew it was her hand on the tablet. Meyer had shared his bond with Kindred until it had somehow soured, but beyond that he hadn't been touched by the psychic kiss so many seemed to feel around the large Astral rocks. Piper was different — especially since Cameron had opened the Ark and done ... whatever he'd done. Her mental presence wasn't passive. It was like a force, and Meyer could feel her shoving his mind at her now.

Can you hear me?

He didn't think he could respond — at least not in words. But the shifts in her thoughts as he worked told him she was getting his flavor. She knew he was alive. She knew he'd ducked below the river, his eyes stinging from the water's flow and grit, and felt the river shove him back, almost losing his grip. She knew he'd seen the sub, and the dock line snag in the rising water, when the sub's weight had fought with the submerged dock's buoyant force.

Are you okay?

And although Meyer couldn't answer, he could *feel okay*. She could sense his feelings, as the empath she'd become, and know the answer all the same.

I'm filling the tanks, her dominant thoughts told his. And that was all right because Meyer had been trying to tell her as much: to fill the ballast enough to drop the sub from the dock, so the line would go slack, so he could use the knife in his submersible rescue kit to cut it.

He held the dock's corner, stuck his head under water, and tried to see the dock line through the muck and gloom. If only the submersible rescue kit had included goggles.

And an unarticulated thought rushed through his mind, red like a hundred-foot stop sign.

!!!

Meyer surfaced, whipped his head around, and saw what Piper must have seen from the other side: a Nile crocodile, its snout long and narrow, swimming by like a log with yellow eyes. But the thing was either fighting the current or riding it like a roller coaster and didn't even pause.

Meyer's pounding heart receded, trying to feel okay so Piper would know the crocodile had let him be. He looked inward, pausing his task, to summon the serenity that came fastest when he recalled their marriage, when they had slept so soundly, side by side.

And with the image in his head, he tried to think back at Piper: *I'm okay. I'm –*

But the crocodile wasn't what Piper she'd tried to warn him about.

Meyer dove beneath the surface as a huge sheet of metal came directly at him. The current had its bulk and was tugging it downstream, turning slightly as the middle moved faster and the edges dragged nearer to shore. He heard a crunch as the thing struck the dock.

It wedged to a stop. He looked up at the thing — heart beating in earnest — and moved around it to surface for air.

Time was short. He needed to free the sub then get them all to claw their way over on the line he'd dragged and strung across the river.

But Meyer went for daylight, and came up short, somehow restrained at the waist.

The sheet metal had pinned itself against his end of the rope, resting overhead, holding him under the surface like an anchor.

CHAPTER 32

"Kamal. It's Mara."

"You don't have to introduce yourself, Mara. I can see you."

"I didn't know if you could see me. Maybe the Internet isn't working."

"The Internet stopped working a long time ago, Mara."

"The Ember Flats net. You know what I mean."

"Can you not see *me?*"

"I see you fine."

"Then please. Tell me who I am, and introduce yourself again. I think there's a chance for confusion."

Mara almost had a retort for Kamal's smart mouth but discarded it immediately. It was far too grim and far too true for words: that he sure was sarcastic for a guy about to die by drowning.

"They're probably watching this, you know."

Mara nodded. Kamal was saying to watch what she said about plans to hook up with the other viceroys on their secure channel. Mara herself wasn't going to make that rendezvous, but with luck Meyer and his group *might*. Humanity had few chances left — but this could be one, if the secret could truly be kept from the Astrals.

"I know. It's okay. I'm just checking in."

There was a long silence, her question's weight hanging between them: checking in to see how he felt, knowing the caps were melting, that titanic waves were obliterating the north as nothing refroze, and that once the vessel was full and floating, Kamal would be breathing his final breaths.

"Things are fine here, but I'm turning your room into a tanning salon if you're not coming back."

"I meant — "

"Or maybe an aquarium," Kamal interrupted.

Mara sort of shrugged: *What am I supposed to say to a joke like that?*

"It is what it is, Mara. You have a job to do, and it's important."

"I don't want it, Kamal. I'm deciding who lives or dies."

"Don't think of it as choosing who doesn't make it. Think only of the people you're saving. Have you ever heard the starfish parable?"

"Maybe."

Onscreen, Kamal situated himself as if settling in. "I'll make it quick because I know Big Muscular Brother is probably looking over your shoulder and tapping his foot. Kid is walking down the beach, and a storm washed a shit ton of starfish onto the sand. They're all slowly drying out in the sun. And the kid is picking a few up here and there, over and over, and tossing them back in to save them. So an old man walks by and sees him doing this, and he looks along the long beach with all its starfish and says, 'Hey, kid. There are a billion starfish out here. What you're doing isn't making a bit of difference.' And the kid, he picks one up. He holds it in front of the old man then wings it out into the surf. And he says, 'It made a difference to that one.'"

"Yeah, I've heard — "

"I know you're a *realist*." He said it like *booger*. "But you don't get to win this argument with me. It might be our last one."

Mara sighed, nodded, and finally said, "You know, if you'd been as sage, as immature, and as stupidly irreverent around Peers Basara and Jeanine Coffey as you are around me in private, maybe they wouldn't have beaten you up."

"I try to bury my personality and maintain a professional front. My boss is a realist."

Mara looked away, blinking. She wasn't usually emotional, but this was all so sad. Too tragic. None of it fair.

"Look, Mara, it's the fate you've been handed. Maybe it'd have been easier on you if the vessel had been open seating like you'd originally thought, and everyone had just fought and killed each other to get on and stay there. But from where I'm sitting, the Astrals made it better for everyone else while making it harder for you. They've got your back whether you want it or not. Nobody's boarding that ship without your code and permission. So, yeah, you have to conduct a lottery, and maybe that makes you feel like you're playing God. But boo-fucking-hoo for Mara Jabari. In a few hours at most, I'll be drinking gallons of water."

"Kamal, that's not — "

"I've been watching the feeds from here. It's dry and cozy. The sump pumps you installed must be top-notch. I'm good until the seals fail or water reaches the vents. This is how I get to save my own share of starfish, but in order for me to do what I must, you've got to do your part without bumming me out. So fuck you for wanting to deprive me of my duty now."

Mara nodded. "Okay."

"Now that the Astral patrols are back to assist the lottery process and have stopped shooting everyone willy-nilly, the city is more or less behaving. People seem to understand that if there's pushing and shoving they'll be shot or eaten by the nearest Reptar. The rioting and killing has stopped. If the city records they gave you to select your fellow travelers were accurate when you got them, they're probably still accurate now."

"I'll try getting them to let me stay. We can hang out together, you and me."

Kamal's face became serious. "Mara, *no.* You might know more about the Astrals than anyone alive. Your Initiate ... " He stopped, seeming to remember their conversation probably wasn't secure, then tiptoed around the viceroys' covert plans. "Knew a lot and did a lot of figuring things out. Not to sound like a cliché, but humanity needs you."

She considered protesting then decided she couldn't win and let it go.

"Just do your best to choose the best and brightest. They're going to destroy the planet, Mara. The big ship is already at the southern ice cap, so it's only a matter of time before Egypt gets flooded from both ends. Soon we'll be a big swimming pool, just like Kevin Costner predicted years ago."

"Who?"

"Didn't you ever see that old movie *Waterworld?*"

"No."

"Good. Don't. It's terrible."

Mara almost laughed. She was going to miss Kamal.

"They said all the capitals would get vessels. You told me yourself they never totally sent us into extinction before. They erase the old societies but leave a seed to try the human experiment again once the world has been washed clean. You'll live, and so will those you select. And the people on the *other* vessels will live. I guess maybe the flood will eventually recede as it did for Noah, and you can begin anew. But it's still not a lot of people, Mara. Choose carefully. You're a scientist. So I need you to promise that you won't flinch from this. Okay? It's a poor aide's dying wish."

"Kamal ... "

"The shape of humanity to come, Mara. It's up to you."

The screen went blank.

And there were footsteps behind Mara. She turned, angry to have been cut off from Kamal, presumably forever. A shout was on her lips. But it was Divinity behind her, and she'd already learned that with Divinity, shouting never did any good.

"The time to choose survivors is now," Divinity said. "The end of this epoch has come."

CHAPTER 33

"He's stuck somehow!"

Kindred watched Piper's mood flip from alarm to relief to babbling incoherence then back to alarm (bleeding into red, dripping panic) in seconds. He saw every nuance of each fascinating change.

"Go help him, Kindred!"

But the body pushing past Piper to find the rising river water was Lila's, not Kindred's. He stood there like a slack-jawed bystander as she struck his side in a run, dove headfirst, and vanished in the brown flow before surfacing with one hand barely grasping the rope Meyer had dragged behind for the rest of them to cross. He'd tied it off on his end, both to secure it and to protect himself lest something snag it in the middle and not drag Meyer away. But according to Piper he'd somehow managed to get trapped anyway, and just watching her was its own feast of emotion. She was by the Nile bank with her chest heaving, mouth open in the rain, hand on her breast, now equally terrified for Lila and Meyer.

"GO! THEY'RE BOTH GOING TO DROWN!"

Piper shoved him. Something stirred as he watched her, still fascinated. Kindred didn't precisely feel a sense of concern — more like a memory of the emotion. He remembered the moment Nathan Andreus had told him Trevor was gone. He remembered learning that Heather had gone. And he seemed to remember the time he himself had gone, shot in the chest by Raj Gupta. But that hadn't happened, had it? Because he was still right here, very much alive. So why was there a ghost of death still inside him? The ghost of loss, of regret?

He wasn't afraid for Lila, or for Meyer. It was more that he knew he should be, and wanted to be, but came up empty.

Then there was a shift. Looking into Piper's fear and worry, the same emotions rose from slumber inside him.

"Lila!"

But of course she couldn't hear him, or turn back even if she could. Nobody had seen Meyer across the river in the rain, but they'd all seen the section of sheet metal roofing and felt the crunch as it crashed into the submerged dock. If Meyer was trapped anywhere, it was either between metal and dock — or, worse: underwater. Either way didn't give him much time, and Lila knew it. If the northern ice cap had truly melted, it was only a matter of time before the rising water made its way to the planet's middle.

Kindred doffed his shoes and jacket then dove in after Lila, half swimming and half clambering hand over hand along the strung rope. It seemed to be taking forever. Lila was still several body lengths ahead, and even she hadn't entered the water until whatever had gone wrong had been happening for at least ten or fifteen seconds, followed by another twenty seconds of indecision and swimming, maybe more. How long could a man hold his breath?

"LILA!"

She held her lead easily, passion outstripping Kindred's superior strength. Kindred could practically see need radiating from the girl like heat from a coal. She'd reach him because she had to, not from duty. Not because Piper had ordered it.

The sheet metal shook in the current, straining as the river pushed it on and the dock held fast. The noise of buckling aluminum was like blasts from a shotgun.

Lila was gone. Just ... *gone.*

Kindred looked back to the shore where he'd left Piper and Peers. He could only see silhouettes. He glanced toward the dock, seeing now that there was no way to go around the huge obstruction. Lila had crossed as far as she could on the tied-off rope, but then it vanished beneath the section of roofing. She'd faced a choice: crawl hand over hand around its outer edge until she came back to the dock, or swim for it.

Swim *underwater.*

Kindred looked at the place where Lila had vanished, feeling uncertain. With the bulk of metal above, it'd be nearly impossible to see down into the already murky water. How would she find him, if he really was there — something that, now that Kindred could see the alternatives, seemed almost for sure? And how, if *he* tried, would he find Lila?

She'd have had nothing to hold, only blindly swimming, trying to find Meyer and free him. He'd been under water for almost a minute by now. Would he be unconscious? If the chances of Lila making it were slim, the odds of her making it out while dragging a 180-pound man were nil.

You're supposed to go under. This is where you save the day.

But the voice of conscience was merely a whisper. He *should*, but what was the logical point? He wouldn't be able to see them, or hold his place against the undertow with nothing to cling to. And if one or both of them were somehow hung up, he probably wouldn't be able to free them. There was a knife in the pack, but it was still in the car, where Lila had left it. Kindred had only his hands.

Going for them was stupid. It would mean trading two casualties for three. He'd die too, then Piper and Peers would be alone.

You're supposed to go under.

His mind showed him Trevor, Heather, and a dozen others lost along the way.

Maybe one minute gone. Then a minute and ten seconds.

He broke the surface, clawing for purchase under the large flap of metal. To Kindred's surprise, he found that Meyer's guideline was not only unbroken beneath it but simple to grab and hold. He kicked his feet in the current, using the line to move hand over hand along the large thing's underside. It was dark, but once Kindred's eyes were open and mostly adjusted to the water's assault, he could see enough to navigate, his own breath assiduously held.

There was the dock.

The floatation barrels, two with big gashes in the sides, flooded.

One of the submersibles, still in its slip, banging against the dock, obviously battered.

And there was —

Something hit him. Hard. Kindred's head spun, and his hand slipped from the line. Semiconscious and losing air, he scrabbled for a handhold, but beyond the rope it was all slippery metal. He dragged his fingers along it, feeling the slower, near-shore current tug him toward the dock's bent structure, beneath it.

The water became darker.

Darker.

He stopped caring about the water. Stopped caring about the fear. It was easier to let it go.

Instead of two people dead, now there'd be three.

But at least I did something.

The last of the light bled from Kindred's world. He felt the water. He felt it carry him away, like flying.

And someone or something, maybe God, maybe whatever was out there, was saying, *You did it. You did something. You* –

– 'd better not fucking give up now! *I didn't get him just to lose you!"*

And there was a slap. *Hard.* God wasn't supposed to slap people.

"Move. Give me room."

A strong hand on his wrist. The last of the flying sense became a feeling of dragging. His shirt was untucked, grit and gravel scooped into the back of his pants by the hard line of his belt.

Kindred blinked, a vision before his eyes. At first he thought he was seeing himself from above, the way those woo-woo nut jobs in Meyer's memory said you saw yourself when you died. Then he saw that the man had the start of a salt-and-pepper beard, whereas Kindred was shaven. And he wasn't looking down. Rain was still pelting his face —he was looking up at Meyer, who'd dragged him to shore.

There was a rope around Meyer's waist, its end frayed as if sawed. Lila was behind him, big brown eyes wide and wet, the backpack knife in her hand. Beyond them, only partially visible, was the popped top of what could only be a freed submersible. Just in time. The river was visibly rising, water surging as if shoved by an oncoming wave of titanic proportions.

Kindred's mind spun through the past few minutes.

How he'd reacted when Piper told him to go after Meyer. How he'd reacted when Lila had gone in. The time he'd spent ruminating on Heather and Trevor rather than acting. The recollection of his death, which hadn't actually happened. And most of all, the way he'd watched the black water, coolly deciding he'd serve them best by saving himself.

Kindred closed his eyes. Everything was spinning. Everything hurt.

"You're okay now," Meyer told him. "You'll live."

Kindred decided the second half of Meyer's statement was true.

But the first was so obviously false.

CHAPTER 34

The Ember Flats town square was less quaint than its name implied. The city had started large by the time it officially started at all, like Heaven's Veil. One day the Astrals came down, helped build the palace, then the walls that kept it safe, and called it the Capital of Capitals. It had since grown further, packing tighter and rising in height rather than expanding outward. Now the town square was a place where four roads crossed in a giant tic-tac-toe board, and instead of making the block between them fit for building, it became green space. But it was always packed, and by the time Clara arrived with the Lightborn, it was as if every citizen had come to the one block of land, pressing so close to the vessel's invisible shield that the air crackled with warning static.

But there was no pushing or shoving. The Astrals were seeing to that, patrolling the crowd with weapons Clara hadn't seen since Heaven's Veil — and plenty of Reptars in tow.

On their way across the otherwise empty city, Clara had made a mental count of Lightborn. It had been for practice navigating their shared mental space if anything. And in that common field of thought, she'd counted thirteen distinct nodes, over and over and over again. In the mental sameness, thirteen spots with their own unique sense of self — and maybe, if her experience so far was any guide, their own secrets. Just thirteen of them. Same as the bodies in their group, with Logan at its head.

In the square, water had risen to the height of an adult knee, halfway up Clara's thighs, surging as it rose. Clara kept thinking of what Josh had said about the ice caps: something she'd already seen inside her mind because the man in boots kept showing it to her.

She'd seen rising water claim Canadian shores. Same in Ireland and Scotland, in the Ukraine, in Sweden and Finland and Norway. She'd seen the waves crumble cliffs and obliterate fjords. And feeling the force tugging her legs now, it was hard to keep her mind off the idea that propagation only took so long, and that it was only a matter of time before the waves came here, too.

"How long, do you think?" Ella said beside her.

Clara didn't bother to ask what Ella was talking about. She knew. They were holding minds the way some little girls held hands.

"I don't know."

"Are we getting on the boat?"

"I don't know, Ella."

There was a surge in the water from the city's north. In seconds, it rose to Clara's waist. She and Ella gripped each other, and in the square ahead the crowd muttered then shouted. Mothers held their children tight, lifting those who could be carried out of the water, and the liquid unknown.

A few scattered screams. A few jabbering words of panic.

But the surge stopped, the rise arresting at its new level.

"If we're not getting on the boat, why are we here?"

But Clara didn't feel like opening her mind the rest of the way, or pandering to Ella's questions. She liked Ella and the others, but there was something different between Clara and the rest of them. Nick had said as much, and Ella had told her the same. Clara was *brighter*. A Lightborn among Lightborn, able to maintain balance without the collective, able to reach where the others could not, to keep those thoughts safe.

"Shh, Ella. Listen."

Logan's strong features and bold eyes were fixed on Ella. "Yes," he said. "Listen."

The Astrals' vessel lay in the heart of the square. Up close, it didn't look like Noah's Ark at all, except that it happened to be an enormous boat in the center of a flooding city. It was more like a miniature cruise ship without the amenities and logos, metal on the bottom, wood and steel sharing space at the deck and quarters.

Beside the Ark was a platform.

And on it was an Astral contingent — Titans and a woman Clara knew wasn't as human as she appeared — next to Viceroy Jabari and a handful of human assistants. There was a microphone set up, and one of the assistants kept reading names into it, seemingly directed by Mara. Each name brought a person from the crowd, who came to a long gangplank like a tongue from the vessel's side. A Titan by the gangplank nodded as the person passed, and with some activity on the platform a section of air shimmered and turned green long enough for the chosen to pass through. Then the whole thing would repeat, one by one by one.

With each person, the assistant read a profession or credential:

Civil engineer.
Microbiologist.
Civic leader.
Mother.
Mother.
And *mother*.

But Clara could hear other credentials that the viceroy and her team weren't daring to speak aloud.

With the exception of a librarian and a physician, there were no women over the age of thirty-five. And Jabari's logic said, *Humanity needs fertility.*

The ratio was skewed for gender. There were three times as many women as men. And Jabari's logic said, *Men can father as many children as there are women willing to carry them.*

And Clara heard: Eadric Khouri, obstetrician. Taavi Kalb, gynecologist.

At the surface were trends of rebuilding societies. Minds that Mara seemed to be saving for history's sake: an archivist, a storyteller, a chess master, a scholar in the study of memory. And below it all a single trend: *reproduction.*

Go forth and multiply.

Mara's logic said: *Diversity prevents the chance of quasi-inbreeding — of unfavorable recessive genes finding their matches. We can't have heart defects. We can't have cancer markers. We can't have high cholesterol. We can't have diabetes.* And within Jabari's radiating mindscape, Clara saw a cloud of internal strife. She saw the viceroy's guilt. Her hatred of eugenics. Her recognition that what she was doing wasn't different from when the Nazis tried to "purify" the world, alongside the acknowledgement that she had to do it anyway.

The only difference between me and Hitler, Clara heard on the wind, *is that the Astrals are doing the killing for me.*

Fahim Khoury, mother.

Jacki Sarkis, mother.

Raakel Naser, mother.

Paavo Bitar, nurse and mother.

Clara felt Jabari's pain in her chest like a knife. A knife that Clara, even from where she stood, knew Jabari would prefer to use on herself.

And children were called. *Many* children. Women and kids came first, this time out of necessity. If there was an extinction coming, survivors needed two things most: healthy children and the potential to multiply.

Then it hit Clara.

Why they were here.

Why she'd felt so compelled to come.

"We need to get on that boat."

Logan turned to Clara. "What?"

She didn't bother to repeat herself. Of course he'd heard her.

"Listen to who she's picking! It's all about the future of the species." Clara sent the collective all the mercenary, triage images her mind could find: hard decisions made by leaders to preserve the greater good.

"And?"

"We're the future. That's what the man in boots has been trying to tell us."

"They're calling lots of kids, Clara."

"Not kids! *Us!*" Again she flooded the collective with images, suddenly sure that time was shrinking. The collective's awareness of the world's other Lightborn seemed to have faded into the background, but in Clara's mind they were still fresh and bright. Still present. She could hear them in Bristol, in Nice, in Petrograd, in Montreal and Tokyo and Krakow and Stockholm. And the waves were coming. The waves had already come.

She showed them their own group mind, like looking in the mirror. She showed them the way they processed thoughts in parallel and the way most minds processed them linearly. She showed them other Hideouts like theirs. And she showed them the Astral eye, blinking away but unable to see.

"Don't you understand? We can teach them, Logan! We can teach the other kids how to be like us!"

"We ... *What?*" He shook his head, genuinely not understanding. Clara felt frustration rise and bubble. She wanted to shake him. Wasn't he supposed to be the leader? Weren't they all supposed to share a consciousness? How could they not see the puzzle fitting together?

Water surged. More people screamed. Clara found it at her waist, now wearing the waterline like a belt.

"Come on," Clara said, not waiting for the others before pushing forward, past a line of Titans who paid them no mind. "I have an idea."

CHAPTER 35

In the Etemenanki Sprawl, terrified locals stared as the sea to the north rose in a wall of water with no ceiling. It towered above them, seemingly as tall as many of their tallest buildings stacked atop one another like building blocks. Their minds told them to run and hide. But a more practical and primal part admitted that there was nowhere to go. The entire island was either lowlands or a risen middle. The wall looked taller than all but the highest mountains, and there was no time left.

Waves swallowed the shoreline. There was little gap between the first surges driven by the waves and the waves themselves. For a brief time waterlines on the beaches and cliffs rose, sometimes kissing the foundations of far-back houses, sometimes leaking down streets and overflowing storm sewers. Then for a briefer time, water receded, and those unable to flee and only seeing the approaching wall in the silhouette of the north's short days allowed themselves to believe it might not happen, though every one of them knew it was a lie. Water moved back on the undertow preceding the assault. Beaches became long and dry, cliff basins seeing more of their bottoms. Then the entire island seemed to inhale and hold it, knowing what the broadcasts had made sure they saw. The glaciers were gone, along with the ice shelves. The north pole was nothing but ocean.

Water came in its first wave, still rising, rolling forward with a continent's force. Lowlands were leveled first, washed clean second. On the new ocean's floor, once the people had either died immediately or floated up to perish later, humanity's artifacts lifted away from the old surface and stirred in the currents like sugar dissolving in water. Today's buildings now tomorrow's relics.

Atop the Old Goat crater, Viceroy Maj Anders stood and watched it come. The distant ocean became the sea at her feet. Old Goat was tall, but the water would soon grow taller. It wasn't yet over, and the seas were still rising.

The foolhardy had tried to reach the Astrals' vessel since its location had been reported. The aliens had shot anything with wings or propellers or that glided or floated out of the sky. Lava had handled all the rest who'd attempted bravery and failed.

There was a tall mountain beside the Old Goat crater, and as Maj looked up she saw the heartiest of her capital's people at its top. They'd known the water would rise, and they'd tried to rise above it. Maybe they'd survive. Maybe, on those few square miles of barren rock without food, fresh water, or shelter, they'd manage to survive what was coming until they finally couldn't anymore, and expired in the last of humanity's unprotected remnants.

But lower down, near Old Goat's rim with Maj and the others, hundreds of people wore grim expressions. She'd heard not a word whispered between them, but they all seemed to have reached the same conclusion as the Astrals had given her — as they'd commanded Maj to follow and obey, as viceroy of her people.

The water rose and seeped into the crater, quenching the lava in a deafening dragon's hiss. The people backed away as the scalding steam rose skyward.

Water rose. Waves came. And when the ocean was too high to stand, those who'd come to the lip of Old Goat swam away until the vessel broke free and the water cooled to merely tepid.

Then they swam back to the great boat and climbed aboard, the lava's challenge irrelevant.

In Hanging Pillars, the archipelago trailing from Old Greece went first, those who'd made outland homes climbing into both small and large boats that, in the teeth of the surge, all became tiny. Water towered dozens of feet, to hundreds of feet, and then kept coming. Inland surge on the mainland, away from Hanging Pillars proper, increased its volume and fury as citizens stormed for higher ground. It hadn't been raining in Hanging Pillars just as it hadn't rained much at Etemenanki, but once waves swallowed the beaches, humidity rose in the Mediterranean sun, and a low fog boiled from nowhere.

The rise came more slowly to Hanging Pillars than it had to the northern countries, who'd been first in line for the melted water's assault. Boaters felt confident at first, many men and women in swimsuits with bronzed skin, daring the apocalypse to take them. They'd live it out in style, they boasted. They'd prepped. They knew how to survive. And in Greece, the sun — once the fog dispersed — would still be warm.

But as the water rose, currents formed as the ocean found its new level, as water wicked into the land's hidden spots and dragged eddies with it, as fresh water from the north made its slow way down to the middle latitudes, as fresh water from the south percolated upward when the south was melted. And as the salinity changed along with the water's temperature — as the fog rolled in and out, as the jet stream shifted in response, moving from high pressure to low — invisible rivers within the water made it turbulent. Boats moved independent of their motors, and whirlpools beckoned. New waves formed as the water tried to equilibrate and find its balance.

One large boat — a cruise ship commandeered by its former captain and staffed by a willing crew — swayed as a cross-current struck its underside, then listed in earnest as its hull dragged along what had previously been a summit of one of Hanging Pillars's highest hills. The hull punctured like a modern-day Titanic then was driven toward a large swirling vortex caused by water filling the city's sewers, tunnels, and subways. The ship sank slowly, its survivors swimming on borrowed time.

Cool, fresh water coming from the north drove the tropical fish toward the warm mass of what had recently been hot, urban rock, and as the fish came predators followed. A man named Spiros, who had prepared his fishing boat with a cooler and hoped for the best after realizing he was nowhere near brave enough to reach the Astral vessel, found himself temporarily superior to many braver men who hadn't been quite so courageous (or at least fast) enough to reach the vessel in time. He watched as his friends and neighbors swam above what had recently been his neighborhood, then turned away in horror when sharks came in the hundreds.

In Canaan Plains, Viceroy Jayesh Sai stood hand in hand with his granddaughter, Nitya, aboard the vessel as it broke its own Astral-fabricated moorings and rose with the ocean, simultaneously guilty and glad for the white stranger's intervention. The stranger had told Jayesh where the ark was located — a good thing because although Jayesh might have made it on his own, Nitya and her mother never would have. The way was too rough, the terrain too rocky.

The Astrals' challenge, the man had told him, was supposed to test human persistence. Then he'd waved his hand dismissively and said that even pre-Astral video games had offered cheat codes and shortcuts. It wasn't unfair to exploit them. It took as much persistence to find those shortcuts, and much more courage — for the unknown — to use them.

A very long tunnel, traversable on Jayesh's electric golf cart. A short climb up a ladder. Then the inaccessible ship had become instantly accessible for anyone to whom Jayesh revealed the stranger's secret.

If all board the ship, there will not be room for those who must *board. It is not right that I should survive while they do not.*

But you already survived, the man had told him. *This is what the Astrals intended. You have the code, and only you can deactivate the shield around their vessel.*

But I was meant to take the hard way, Jayesh had said. *I was meant to take the same test and prove myself worthy same as anyone not blessed to be the viceroy.*

But what of Nitya?

What of her?

You would not have gone without her. Not without Nitya, not without Suri, not without your friends Eshan and Keya. Don't you see, Jayesh? I haven't shown you a cheat. You would not have gone without my intervention. And because you are the one with the code, nobody would have reached it and all would have died.

Jayesh had looked at the strange man in his Western garb — blue jeans, scuffed and dirty boots, hands that were large and worn like leather. And he'd said, *You are telling me only what I wish to hear, not what is true or fair.*

Balls had reappeared from the man's pocket. He'd rolled them around for a few seconds then made them disappear. One remained, and he'd handed it to Jayesh.

Just because it's what you want to hear doesn't mean it's not fair or true.

It's not as the Astrals wanted this to happen, Jayesh had protested.

At this, the man smiled. *That's why it's fair and true.*

Now, with the ocean rising and the land almost gone, Jayesh looked across his former kingdom. He'd told no one how he'd reached the ark. Only those he'd taken knew. They were all as reticent to give themselves away.

He reached into his pocket, removed the stranger's silver sphere, and tried to roll it across the back of his palm. It seemed to fall away, and because he was at the vessel's railing, Jayesh was sure that the ball would drop to endless ocean's floor. But then the thing seemed to pause its fall long enough for Jayesh to snag it. He slipped it back into his pocket, wondering what it was. He had a strange impulse to get rid of it but kept changing his mind. He was curious, now, why it hadn't dropped away. Maybe it wanted to be held, and staying in the possession of Jayesh Sai had become its purpose.

There was a storm in the distance.

This was far from over.

In Loulan Mu, Lee Sln stood by the gangplank of the vessel nestled high in the mountains. All was quiet. Plenty of people had already boarded, but only a slow stream of newcomers had shown themselves.

She stood, touching her pocket, feeling the silver sphere in its hiding place as she considered, yet again, going for her tablet. The pull was strong but compulsive; she definitely didn't need to know more than she already did. She'd heard reports that the water was rising fast, closer to the ocean. But despite all the fear in those reports, it was getting hard, now that she'd met the man who called himself Stranger, to separate Astral fact from propaganda. The blood? That had been designed for reaction. The melting ice caps? That, judging by the reports of rising oceans, was fact. But was it *really?* Stranger made her wonder.

Do you really think the Astrals didn't know about your plan to rendezvous with the other viceroys? Do you really think they haven't known all along that you're all rogue? Do you truly believe that you and the others were chosen as humanity's best representatives ... rather than because you were the most unwilling to do as others said?

Do you really believe that all of this isn't propaganda – done specifically to provoke a reaction, same as Heaven's Veil's destruction?

Sln didn't buy the insinuation. She didn't *want* to. It was too bleak. She could stomach anything as long as there was hope, but Stranger's implanted idea left little room for faith. If any humans were alive now, it was only because the Astrals meant to keep toying with them, and any plans Sln made to extricate humanity, the Astrals were already well aware of, giving them the green light to see what might happen. Forget about any genuine odds of survival.

She pulled the ball from her pocket and looked at her reflection in its shiny surface.

Don't worry, Stranger had told her. *They might know about your intention to meet with the other viceroys, but not what you would say. Just like they know I'm here, but not what I mean to do. Not the ways I've made some changes of my own.*

But the words seemed hollow to Sln now that she watched her vessel fill. The flow was smooth and orderly because only people who stumbled across the thing could board it. Stranger had told her that in other cities, vessel occupants had been decided in other ways — and yes, there had been rioting and bloodshed as citizens jockeyed for their places. The same wasn't true of Loulan Mu. In Sln's city, the vessel's existence hadn't been announced. No one was looking, so it was only discovered by the lucky few who wandered far. A crew of hearty, healthy loners. People who hiked enough to discover something so hidden by chance.

The ball dropped from Sⁱn's hand, striking the rocks underfoot and rolling away, before stopping quite suddenly at the feet of a man in worn sandals, surrounded by his family, holding several fishing rods and a box of lures and hooks.

He retrieved the ball at his feet.

Then he limped forward.

He handed the ball to Sⁱn and made a small, polite bow before limping up the gangway with his wife and children behind him.

Sⁱn watched the man. He didn't fit the profile. A fisherman who'd come as if prepared, with rods and tackle and packs on his family's backs — a fisherman with a pronounced limp who'd have trouble hiking for a few hours at most?

She gripped the small silver sphere. And as she did, Sⁱn heard Stranger's voice as clearly as if he were whispering in her ear.

They know more than humanity realizes, but they don't know everything.

CHAPTER 36

"Liza?"

"I know."

"*Liza!*"

"I know, Mick! I know, okay!"

Mick held up the tablet. "No, this is from our man Tad. You know, the oceanographer? He says — "

Mick's voice was rushed, urgent, jamming in words before Liza could cut him off. But she was just as rushed, equally urgent, feeling like she barely had the seconds required to rebuke her right-hand man. He was supposed to be helping her finish what needed finishing. The world had enough alarmist assholes, and had since well before Astral Day.

"That there's a huge wave coming at us from Antarctica? Because their big ship just melted the goddamned ice cap? Yes, Mick, I know! Okay? Now *get the fuck over here, and help me with this!*"

Mick walked obediently toward the desk in their makeshift operations center. The place had the feel of a construction office: a converted trailer floored with cheap carpeting, possibly with company calendars on the walls showing heavy machinery moving dirt, cranes lifting girders. This command center was a bit simpler and starker, but that was mainly because Liza and her staff didn't need much. Charlize was out front calling cutthroat pairs into a microphone. Jason and Lucy were entering results into the vessel's passenger manifest just because it seemed right to have one. But really, Liza could have handled this by tossing weapons into a pile and announcing a *battle royale*. And really, now that the clock was ticking, that's exactly what she wanted to do.

"How long, Mick?" Liza asked. "How long did Tad say we have before the waves hit?"

"Depending on the melt rate and — "

"Just give me a number. Make a guess."

"Hell. Thirty minutes?"

"Thirty minutes?"

"We're at the cape of Africa. It's *right there*. He says it'll hit us before the water from the north cap makes its way down here."

"I just heard from Jabari, and — "

"I thought we were cut off?"

"Just a message. She —"

"But once we get to the satellite hookup, all the viceroys can talk for real, right?"

"I don't think the meeting will happen. Did you see the feed from Etemenanki and Hanging Pillars? Anders and Cocoves are already on their vessels. I'm not sure about the rest. The Da Vinci Initiate never counted on a fucking Noah's Ark situation. The dishes are either already underwater or will be soon, and I don't see how we'll hook up without them. It's not like a solar sat-phone is the kind of thing that would fly under the Astral radar."

"But you said — "

"I know what I said!" Liza held up a hand, palm out, as if to halt her own panic. She'd been deluding herself, and the only way to keep calm in the face of a killer tsunami's arrival

a half hour from now was to keep on deluding herself at least a little longer. Liza's rational mind understood that Jabari's plan had probably fallen apart hours ago, when they'd learned the black ship was hovering above the northern pole. But she still had the Canned Heat cylinder in her pocket even now as if she might be able to open the covert frequency. Even as she yelled at Mick for his stupidity in wanting to believe the same.

"We thought they might just blow us to bits. Maybe there'd be some flooding. Either way, there'd always be a way to reach the communication points. That's off now, and I don't know about you, but I don't want to try my survival odds in a Cradle submersible. I'd be much happier in the big ship the Astrals gave us for that exact purpose."

"Which reminds me, Liza. The shipyards ... "

"Forget it, Mick."

"But there are hundreds of ships there. Some of them giant. I don't exactly know how hard it is to drive one of those things, but they must have manuals, right?"

"I said forget it."

"But Liza, half the city or more could probably survive on — "

"Mick! Focus. We only have a half hour. You know the Astrals are guarding the shipyards. You know we can't just run over there and throw everyone onto freighters."

"If we just — "

Liza grabbed Mick by the shoulders.

"You know I love you. You're a great person, and you've always been a great help to me, and I really appreciate it and always will. You know that, right?"

"Of ... of course, Liza."

"Then don't take it personally when I say this. But if you don't let it go, I'm going to become a lot more interested in the bonus brackets. Me versus you. Just toss your ass out while I take your spot on the ship. I'll be drinking Mai Tais on the Lido deck, and you'll be swimming. You hear me?"

She'd meant it as a joke and a smile had made its way onto her face, but the smile was too toothy, an inch from earnest. The ticking clock was in her veins, in her blood. Maybe she *would* toss Mick to the wolves – or sharks – to get this done. She hoped he wouldn't make her find out.

"All right, Liza."

"They're guarding the shipping yard. And the docks. That big boat there?" She pointed through the command center window. "That's the only ride out of town. Now are you with me in getting it filled, or do you want to bang our heads against the wall and end up not finishing our business, leaving even more people to die?"

"I'm just – "

"Triage, Mick. Like I said. None of this is easy. It's not like we can

(*walk right past them*)

fight the Astrals on this."

Liza blinked at the intrusive thought, returning her attention to the cutthroat brackets. It's what the Lightborn children had told her when they'd come to her office. It's what Liza believed. But even if it was all pomp and circumstance on the Astrals' part – even if she could disobey, knowing the guards wouldn't stop her – she wasn't ready to throw the baby away with the bathwater yet. Maybe the viceroys couldn't meet on satellite like Jabari planned from the start, and maybe Liza's plan to expose those chats to the Astrals wouldn't work out. But there were other ways to show the aliens her loyalty. The end was here, and at least some of humanity was going to survive. There were other ways, if she toed the line, to be their new queen.

"Of course, Liza. What do you need from me?"

The door to the half office banged open. Charlize stood there, her pretty face puzzled.

"Viceroy Knight?"

"Yes?"

"The brackets you gave me. They're supposed to be live and real time, right?"

"Correct."

"So if someone is on here ... " She held up her tablet. "It should mean they're alive right now, not caught up in one of the flash floods or something, that they passed the checkpoint on the way into the square, all that?"

"That's what Divinity told me. Why? What's up?"

"One of the pairs isn't responding. We keep calling his name over and over, and there's nothing. Do we assume he forfeits, and the guy he's up against gets to stay aboard?"

Liza's eyes ticked toward the clock. It was 4:21. Seven full minutes had passed since Mick had guessed Roman Sands might only have a half hour left. Her pulse made itself known in the hollow of her throat, and it felt impossible to swallow. But she pushed on, forcing her focus. There was only one way they'd all get through this, and it was one choice at a time.

"Is it a high-profile pairing?" Liza asked.

Charlize shook her head and looked at her tablet. "Random guy. Carl Nairobi.'"

"Then move on. If he doesn't show up to challenge his pairing, he loses the slot."

"Yes, ma'am."

Charlize moved to close the door, but Liza stopped her. "Charlize?"

"Yes, ma'am?"

"How many more?"

She looked down. "Fifty?"

"And how many people are calling pairs?"

"Ten, ma'am."

Ten callers. Ten pairs being decided at a time. That was five or more rounds remaining, and people always hemmed and hawed, soul searched on the whole *condemning someone to death while saving themselves* issue, walked to the gangway slowly, and generally acted like they didn't know they were all about to be washed away any minute. Probably because they *didn't*, and Liza had no plan to tell them.

"Get Jason calling pairs too. And Tanya. Anyone out there who's not doing something indispensable. Anyone *at all*."

Surprise — or perhaps alarm — crossed her face. But Charlize simply nodded and closed the door.

When Liza turned back into the room, she saw Mick at the window, looking south.

"It's hard to believe that in twenty minutes this town will be underwater, and everyone will be dead."

"Come on and help me with this," Liza said, grabbing his arm. "Carl Nairobi might want to die, but I don't plan to."

CHAPTER 37

Carl Nairobi did not want to die.

At 4:41 p.m. South Africa Standard Time, Carl's shitburg rundown sonofabitch Chrysler with the rusted-out front grill and the duct tape half peeling from the crack across the windshield struck the shipyard entrance fence. His eyes trained on the heavy chain and padlock strung through it as his big hands gripped the steering wheel. There was a bobblehead Jesus on the dashboard, and Carl often thought while driving that Jesus was nodding along with his music. This time his shaking made Jesus seem scared enough to hop off the dash and run away. That sounded about right to Carl because he wanted to do the same. Fuck bravery. Fuck being the hero the white man had said Carl tended to be. Right now he wanted to be a coward, get the hell out of Dodge, and hole up with some beers and a good woman.

Carl hit the fence at exactly 60km per hour, the chain and the fence's center point squarely lined up in the rearview. But Hollywood seemed to have lied because the chain didn't break, and the fence didn't neatly pop open. Instead the big car hit the fence and dragged its gate five or six feet forward, bending it to shit, as the car wrenched to a stop. Luckily, Carl was spared the airbag's assault. Someone had broken into the Chrysler and stolen them a decade ago.

"Dammit!" Carl told the empty car, pulling back from the seatbelt's sting.

But there were people in the rearview, running straight at his marooned ass.

Carl climbed out of the car and grabbed his thug bat, nicknamed Motherfucker, from the back. The oncomers — a dozen or so people who didn't look used to seeing a big black man brandishing a bat like he couldn't afford a single fuck — skidded to a stop. A few had bats and boards as well, but Carl was pleased to see that the Astrals' ban had worked on at least these former law abiders. There wasn't a firearm visible among them.

"Come on. Step up to the bat, and let's see what happens."

"You a captain?" shouted one of the men.

"The fuck you talkin' bout?"

"The shipyard." The man pointed, keeping his distance. "You going for a ship?"

"The fuck else you think I'd be here for?" Carl swung the bat in tiny circles, like a pendulum made in Louisville. His arms were tensed, legs positioned to hit a home run. Just let this white man try to throw him back in a box. The days of racism were over in these parts, and Carl had won.

"Can ... can we go with you?"

Carl's arms relaxed, a little. The bat lowered a hair. His eyes scanned the group. They were a mixed batch, enough that it seemed someone had reached into a big bag of the world's people and grabbed a handful at random. Beside the man who'd spoken was an unarmed blonde who hadn't yet moved the hand from her stomach. She was pregnant, and now that Carl looked closer, there was a kid hiding behind her.

Before Carl could answer, there was a low hum that set his neck hair on end. He'd heard it before, over and over, and it was never a good thing.

A silver Astral shuttle came around one side of the shipyard fence. Then another circled from the other side. Walking beside the shuttles, as if escorting them, were Titans — two on Carl's right, three on his left. There were no Reptars, but the Titans had those giant weapons they only carried when they meant business. That and the shuttles did nothing to relax Carl's tension. Used to be, Titans wouldn't touch you. That changed a few years back. Now — at least in Carl's experience, in Roman Sands — they tended to shoot first and ask questions later, just like human police.

This was the sort of situation where Carl figured he was supposed to raise his hands. But then again, fuck that. He'd driven here because although he was willing to do as Stranger asked and not participate in the cutthroat competition for passage on the vessel, he sure as hell didn't plan to sit home and drown. All boats floated, and the shipyard had plenty under lock and key. He'd come here intending to break through the locks and steal the keys necessary to keep his ass above water, and he wasn't about to surrender now.

Let them shoot him if they wanted. He'd driven through several flooded areas on the way over, and if what he'd heard about the aliens melting Santa's crib were true, it was about to get a lot wetter real soon. He could die now or take a chance of dying later. Desperate times, as the expression went, called for a man to stop giving a shit.

"You wanna shoot me, just do it in the chest. My mamma gonna want an open casket."

The Titans didn't raise their weapons. They marched slowly forward, shuttles hovering and humming along between them.

"I ain't going with you. Don't even try."

The group of people hadn't retreated. Carl could see nervous glances from several members, trading time between looking in Carl's direction and looking back, behind a rise where Carl couldn't see. There must be more Astrals behind, coming to surround them.

The aliens didn't advance, or level their weapons. Instead the Titans acted as they used to: staring mildly as if politely amused. The shuttles didn't open or shift in any way Carl could see.

He lowered the bat. Let it hang near his side, ready if needed. His eyes moved to the fence. His Chrysler had wedged it up enough to crawl under — something he'd already have done if the ET patrol hadn't shown up first.

"You ain't gonna stop me from going in there."

The nearest Titan smiled.

"I ain't gonna do your stupid contest. Ain't nothing worth that."

The first Titan looked at the next; both of them nodded like idiots.

Carl kept his eye on the Titans. Approached the fence. And when the Titans and shuttles still didn't move, he got to his knees, ready to spring if given a reason.

The man who'd spoken earlier was staring at Carl, a question in his eyes. Carl nodded, flicking his attention to the flanking aliens. Then the group came forward, and as they moved down the ramp toward the gate, the invisible third Astral contingent followed at a distance.

The man reached Carl.

"My name is Lawrence."

"Fuck if I care!"

"Why aren't they stopping us?"

"Who cares? Get in there if you wanna get."

So the group made its way under the wedged-up fence while Carl waited with a wary eye on the Astrals. When they were all through, he ducked under, moving backward, and pushed the group back, retreating.

There was a sound from Carl's rear. He turned and saw something that definitely would have made Dashboard Jesus jump and jive: The line of the ocean was much higher than it should be — much closer to the sun.

"We gotta hurry," he said.

Lawrence looked where Carl had been looking, then several others in the group did the same. There were gasps as they realized what they were seeing: an ocean swell tall enough to swallow half the country.

Lawrence pointed. There was a small, apparently noncommercial slip off to the right. Docked there were several pleasure cruisers and fishing boats, none of which should be much harder to operate than a car.

Carl looked away then ran toward the commercial — behemoths that were like small towns more than vehicles.

"Hey! *Hey!*" Lawrence shouted from behind him. For a second Carl thought he might be on his own again, then the man decided he'd rather not go it alone and gave chase. The woman, the kid, and the rest of the group followed.

"*This?*" Lawrence looked up at the ship Carl was crossing a gangway to board. The *huge* ship. He was looking at it as if only seeing the thing's unwieldiness, but to Carl — who'd never been on open water and wasn't looking forward to doing it now — saw only practicality. They could try a yacht and live in luxury, or board something meant to survive the open ocean — maybe something that, if they were lucky, came standard with stocked cabinets and freezers, made to serve hundreds of people for weeks.

Carl didn't answer, uncaring if they came or not.

"Can you drive a boat?" Lawrence asked, scampering along behind him.

Carl didn't answer until the entire group was aboard and the door was closed behind them, the watertight wheel already spun.

"I guess we'll find out," he said.

CHAPTER 38

The river surged upward. Piper, with one foot in the sub, faltered. She almost fell, but Meyer caught her. She gave him a thankful look and was about to say the same, but a loud shout from the south grabbed her attention. Piper turned to see something that, at first, knocked her sense of equilibrium out of kilter: They were all soaking wet, climbing into tiny submarines they didn't know how to use, without yet knowing where they were going. And now there were rows and rows of people on the opposite bank, painted blue and red and black and purple. Someone had shouted, audible even over the downpour. Even as hard as it was to see them (only the slightly abated rain and their colors made it possible), every one seemed ready to spring forth, bellowing, coming hard.

Menace, in multiple human forms.

"Get inside," Meyer said, looking back.

"The cannibals," Piper said.

"Get inside. Leave me if you have to."

Piper was about to protest, but Meyer shoved her roughly downward, through the hatch. The interior space wasn't as cramped as she'd feared — utilitarian but well lit as Peers managed to spin up the power from the front, surfaces padded in what almost looked like tan-colored acoustic paneling. There was a bench along each side and a circular hole in the floor that looked like it might be home to the supporting post of an easy to stow, temporary table. There were strapped-down cabinets along the top like airplane overhead compartments that Piper assumed (and dearly hoped) were full of food.

There were portholes along the outside. She pressed her face to one, noting the glass's thickness. The thing, as Piper understood it, wasn't a true submarine designed for depth. It was more like a boat meant to skim just under the water as much as on top of it — and, if she'd read things right, could float topside where the river got shallow. But the portholes still meant business, and seeing how thick they were gave her a creeping sense of claustrophobia.

Meyer and Kindred were still outside. Peers was in the nose, monkeying with controls, oblivious to the newcomers' arrival. Lila was beside Piper at the next porthole, her presence more felt than seen.

"Are those ... ?" Lila trailed off.

"I guess they followed us. Got tired of staring at the big ship."

"Or maybe they saw the broadcasts, too. Maybe they know what's coming."

And although Piper didn't want to say so, she tended to agree. When they'd approached Ember Flats the first time, the cannibal crews had chased them almost like sport. This time, she could see method to their colorful madness. They seemed to be lined up almost like allies: hundreds of warriors meaning to pull the sub's occupants into the open first then turn to the task of deciding who'd replace them in the lifeboats after.

The cannibals knew the flood was coming, all right. Many of the other capitals had already been hit, and Ember Flats was living its final hours on borrowed time.

Meyer and Kindred stood in front of the sub, hands defensively raised. The clans were moving in an orderly fashion toward the line Meyer had pulled across the river, already grabbing at the big piece of sheet metal to climb aboard as a pull-along ferry.

"Close the hatch, Piper." She heard Meyer's words as if through a pipe, coming down from above.

She moved away from the porthole and poked her head topside. Something shot past her and struck the metal, making her duck. The sub lurched upward again, harder than it had moments before. Piper, feeling dizzied, poked her head back up and looked north, toward the surge, and saw a torrent of water coming from the Nile's gaping mouth.

"Close the hatch!"

"The flood is coming, Meyer! Get inside!"

Something else flew past Piper's head, milliseconds after barely missing Kindred. It was a spear. Some of the clans had fashioned them, just as others brandished knives. More were poised to throw, their arms back like tensed slingshots. Their clan vehicles were just behind, and only the river held them in check.

"Meyer! Kindred!"

Sounds from behind. From the other bank.

Piper turned and saw more of them behind her, engines idling, shouts and motors beaten down by the rain.

"Get inside, and close the fucking hatch, Piper! Go without us!"

The cannibals began to cheer and shout.

The onslaught came.

CHAPTER 39

Clara's idea crumbled the instant she had it, and the panic began.

Just as she and the others were moving forward, something seemed to crash on the outskirts of town. Rain slowed, and a new surge entered the square, carrying debris — and bodies. Several people screamed, but most didn't even see the dead people floating in. Their attention was on a big screen at one end of the square that the Astrals and viceroy used to project news or magnify the faces of speakers on the platform, and as the town watched, it changed to show cities Clara had never seen and now knew only from the banners at the bottom.

El Dorado Lea, Peru. Underwater, civilization's remains turned to floating detritus, humans clinging to whatever they could, screaming for help that would never come.

Etemenanki Sprawl, Iceland. There was literally nothing visible above water during the brief clip other than a single mountain peak: just wave after wave battering its shores as people shuffled worriedly about at its top, water eroding rock at its enormous base, trying its best to knock away the last of what remained.

Avalon Downs, Iraq. This one was equally flooded, with one macabre addition: Astral shuttles flying above, shooting lifeboats from the water. The Lightborn watched, feeling a sickening drop inside as beams struck and each ship exploded in splinters and blood, as each death seemed to erase someone from their internal equations — gone, as Clara nearly met their eyes onscreen, from the collective unconsciousness.

"Wait," said one of the adults near the group of children. "If that's Iraq and it's already underwater, isn't that about the same latitude as — "

A horrible wrenching of rending metal screeched through the square like a living thing in pain. There was a distant explosion, possibly an implosion. And in the abating rain, a lesser but much more frightening sound grew dominant: the immense rush of oncoming water.

"*Hurry!*" Clara shouted to the Lightborn.

And as she led the group, only half caring if they followed, Clara thought: So much for the plan. So much for Mara's lottery and ensuring that only the best and brightest made the vessel's manifest. So much for subtlety and the need to find a way onto the ships in the name of the greatest good.

They rushed forward, stopped short by a human wall made of muscle and fat and bone and unyielding backs. Nobody in Ember Flats seemed to care about decorum, or about the children prying and pressing at their backs. There was only their own survival and those of their children, clamped fast at their fronts like belongings. The Lightborn had homes and mothers and fathers, of course, but based on what Clara had seen inside their minds, those old ties were so far abandoned that they might not have existed. Logan and Nick and Ella and Cheever and the others might have once had parents in the crowd to protect them, but they would never find them now.

Josh, the big kid who'd been so near panic, was ripping and clawing at the people in front of him, his fear a red-hot presence in Clara's mind. Others were doing the same. There was the hive, and then the individual.

Clara forced herself to breathe. To press something cool and quiet into the Lightborn mind. In her internal vision it was blue-green and viscous, like aloe smeared atop a burn.

In the chaos, minds turned to her. Panic eased.

Around the back.

Water came fast. Clara chanced a look behind her as she led others to the side, away from the gangplank and Mara's gatekeepers — away from the shoving throngs reduced to the monkey brain's animal needs — and saw it come as rounded surges like the waves in a water park pool. It squeezed between Ember Flats's curious old-new buildings, stone, glass, and wood finding harmony in the city that was so recently desert. Astral glass didn't crack, but wood did, and stone beneath crumbled as debris struck it. Even as far forward as Clara and the others were, the mostly-filtered water struck and shoved them into each other, jostling like bobbing corks. The wave passed, and Clara found it had reached her armpits. It was no longer walk and wade. Now it was push or swim.

Inside her mind, the cool aloe pacifier bubbled as the panic beneath threatened to boil.

There's a cargo hold. Around the back. Just keep moving.

And someone thought, *How do you know? We're moving away from the entrance!*

But they'd never make it through the entrance, properly, up the gangplank. Water was coming *hard*, but there were still minutes on the clock, and Mara's people were still in front, holding hurried court, seemingly intent on properly loading the vessel before it was forced from its moorings. Many of the Astrals had lifted off in their shuttles, buzzing over the water in the square. Clara watched, rationally understanding they still meant only to assist the orderly loading of the boat, irrationally certain at the same time that they'd turn on the citizens and blast them to ash. Visions from the screen were on her mind, of Avalon Downs and the target practice there.

What's the difference between there and here? she wondered. And the difference, she decided, was time. In ten minutes, Ember Flats might be like Avalon — if too many people took to unsanctioned rescue vessels, insistent on saving themselves in unapproved ways.

They're going to kill us all, someone said.

Just keep moving.

Clara could feel them behind her. She felt their hesitancy, wanted to leave without them if they chose to stay and drown. But this wasn't about saving their lives. She understood that now. The man in boots wasn't here, but she could hear him as though he was. And in that way, his ghost kept whispering in her ear:

The children are the tinder. But you are the spark.

Soon there would only be a few humans left — millions still, but a handful for an empty and flooded globe.

Those who remained would be disproportionately children because they were the future.

And if the Lightborn weren't around to light them up, the future's children would remain ... only that.

Around the vessel's back, away from the crowds, not at all away from the rising water.

Clara moved to her tiptoes. Some of the smaller children were swimming, fighting the current. Bigger kids had taken those who couldn't swim — some tottering on unstable backs, some merely clinging, treading water as they held tight with one arm. They pushed forward, into a protected pool behind a stack of crates beginning to lift up and float away. Once at the rear, the shouting grew hushed. The water's surge waned, and they found themselves in a still pool that had become a flood's version of stagnant: cluttered with everything floatable that had previously lined the streets. It was filthy, clotted with garbage, topped in places with the rainbow slicks of unknown oils.

"Gross," said Ella, treading along at Clara's side, dodging something that looked like a sock.

Beyond the great vessel, there was a long, low crumbling. Screams chased the sound like an aftertaste.

"There's nothing back here, Clara," Logan said. "Maybe we should ... you know ... try to find our own boat."

But inside his mind, she saw only death. Logan wasn't a fool. They wouldn't allow any boats to survive, even if the Lightborn could find one. Which they couldn't because water kept surging, bringing the level nearly to Clara's chin, lifting her like a tall slat of balsa wood on her scrabbling toes.

"We have to get on. We have to!"

"That's what everyone feels, Clara. Maybe it's not meant to happen. Maybe we should just accept that ... "

He sighed, half shrugged, and gave Clara a frown that looked like the one Cameron used to give when he said, *Shit happens.*

He didn't understand. She wanted to shout at his idiocy, but that was only frustration. Logan meant the best but didn't see that his best wasn't good enough, and that if they stayed behind to let others have room on the boat, they were merely condemning them.

There was a loud commotion from the boat's far side. Clara heard bodies shuffle and strikes clang on wood or metal. There was a gunshot: Someone had kept an illegal firearm and was now using it as an ace. Then there were screams, more clangs, and a heavier shuffle. Finally there was the brief, businesslike *pfft* sound of an Astral weapon discharging.

More screams.

Then mutters and the soft sounds of sobbing, the trudging of feet.

"We can get in through the cargo hatch."

"What hatch, Clara!" It came out as an exasperated sigh rather than a question.

Something broke in the distance. Something fell. There was another bang, but this one more like an explosion than a shot. Water surged, making the junk behind the vessel rise, sickening Clara with its filthy presence so near her face.

Clara's eyes scanned the vessel's smooth, metallic hull. Nothing else would get loaded. But Logan was right: there was no hatch to the rear. She'd been so certain. This was the only way to do as the man in boots had told her. Had told them *all*, Clara thought in frustration, if the other Lightborn would only look back to their shared vision and listen.

Not just the Lightborn in Ember Flats.

Every Lightborn child, everywhere.

A great surge tore through the square. Clara sensed it before she felt it, then experienced it before she saw it. The vessel creaked on its big base, the scaffolding holding it upright creaking like a tree in high wind. Her feet left the ground for the last time, and they all found themselves swimming as the waves rose and fell, fighting the current, gasping to stay above the surface.

With a mighty groan, something snapped like a twig, and the vessel drifted toward them, its enormous side leaning over as the thing's supports broke, the water not yet quite high enough to support it. But that lasted only seconds, then another wave came. This time Clara could see buildings in Ember Flats succumb and fall as the water lifted her higher. The ship settled in, now a giant bobber, its smooth sides offering no purchase. On the far side, people screamed and shouted and splashed — Clara heard a long and low grating that must be the gangplank being retracted.

To the north, water came. The next swell toppled the church tower and the library's western spire, red bricks hitting the waves and vanishing. Then water took the gymnasium dome and the white stone buildings where the government had made its home.

She looked up at the vessel's side, *couldn't* look at the children behind her, whom she'd led around to the back, away from the entrance, to drown.

They were going to die.

But then an aperture opened in the vessel's side, just above the waterline. No hatch, only a hole, born from nowhere.

One by one, they swam over, clambered up, and climbed in. Within minutes all the Lightborn found themselves inside the big ship's guts, wedging feet against down-arcing support members to keep from sliding to the pinched space at the bottom of the thing's long keel, below the cargo hold.

The hole closed.

The dark that came next, made worse by the ship's sickening sway in the rising water, nearly stopped her heart. She felt around blindly, groping for the hatch, unsure why. Was it so terrifying in this rocking, lightless space that she meant to open the door and jump back out into the flood?

But she couldn't find the door's edges because the door wasn't there.

A hand somehow found Clara's in the darkness.

I'm scared, said Ella.

Said — in feelings if not in words — every member of the collective.

Clara realized that they were no longer looking to Logan as their leader. She had somehow led them here. And it was Clara, if anyone, who'd know what to do next.

But Clara was scared, too.

Something hopped into her other hand. Small. Heavy. Warm. It had the feeling of a small animal climbing into her palm, but for some reason Clara didn't flinch. It was already giving her the comfort that Ella wanted from Clara. A comforting presence. Something she didn't try to understand, because confused comfort was better than raw-edged terror.

Clara closed her hand on the thing.

It felt like a small, smooth sphere, about the size of a golf ball.

CHAPTER 40

Meyer was about to climb up and slam the submersible door — knocking Piper out to keep her from preventing it, if he had to — when he heard the sounds.

The cannibals seemed to hear it, too, even over their shouting and deafening engines. A one-two punch, two events in seconds. They shouted; they drove forward and they ran; they threw their spears and brandished their blades. But almost immediately afterward there came the cacophonous riot of a levy breaking, like the roar of an oncoming train.

They all looked up, assaulted and assaulters alike. And when they saw it, the chase stopped mattering. Reaching the sub was all that mattered in the world.

"*Meyer!*" Piper shouted.

His paralysis wouldn't have broken in time. It happened too fast. But then Kindred was against him, shoving Meyer like stubborn luggage, pushing him against the submersible's side, up the short length of ladder. Only a few seconds had passed, but no human seeing what they saw could have moved before the shock became fear became flight because fight wasn't possible.

But Kindred wasn't human.

"*Move!*"

No hesitation. No pause. No shock, just logical recognition. The space between Kindred and Meyer's decision to board the sub after all (the others soon wouldn't need defending) and the cannibals' decision to give chase was only a second or two at most, but it was enough.

Piper grabbed Meyer at the shoulders and pulled hard, inverting him as he made his way inside, dropping him headfirst to the deck. Kindred followed, trying to climb in properly, finding himself unable as the clans turned and came at them. They almost had him; Kindred tried to kick one in the face, and the green-painted man grabbed it. But then Piper had his other leg, dragging him down, almost racking his head. Kindred got his leg free and kicked *hard*, the man's nose splintering underfoot like the crunch of a smashed cockroach.

Peers was at one of the portholes, gaping out. And he said, "*Oh, fuuuu –* "

Water hit them, and the submersible, meant for calm exploration, took off like a rocket. In an instant their pursuers were gone and had become their own problem while Meyer, Kindred, Peers, Piper, Lila, and even the big obedient dog faced a new one.

They were weightless, turning end for end in the water. Meyer felt the sub hitch and jerk sideways as they struck something, hearing a crack that he hoped wasn't vital. But it could have been anything. There was — or there *had been* — an array of delicate-looking instruments to the sub's stern. They could be for communication; they could be for navigation; they could be for their goddamned *air* for all anyone in the sub knew. Whatever they were, Meyer hoped they weren't essential to survival. Because Piper had already shouted that they had a bevy of supplies including food, but he doubted even a bonus cache of phones would let them talk to anyone if an antenna was supposed to be necessary.

He couldn't get his bearings enough to be sick. For a long time, the world was just limbs and equipment and the sub's padding-wrapped surfaces. And thank God for those; Meyer was only dimly aware as they rolled of striking one and then another like balls in a hopper. He felt a sharp but not particularly painful bang to his temple; it felt like pressure and confusion. One leg was caught in something he thought might be a bunk, and in the space of a long second he had time to wonder if it'd stay trapped and break as the sub whipped around.

An endless time later the chaos stopped, and Meyer found himself on the floor, staring into a pool of vomit that was probably his own. He wasn't alone; Piper and Peers were both retching in the corner. The air inside was hot; it smelled like acid and burning and adrenaline. He hadn't yet found his equilibrium; he nearly fell as he stood. His head hurt. He seemed to recall smashing it on something. Although he didn't have it as bad as Peers — the man was bleeding from both mouth and nose. Piper was shaking out one arm, bending it, seeming to wonder if it was broken. Lila was caked with blood.

"Is everyone okay?" Piper asked.

Mumbles filled the sub.

"Answer me!" She exhaled, seeming to gather herself. "Lila."

"I feel sick."

"Anything broken?"

"I don't know."

"Meyer?"

"I hit my head. But I think I'm okay."

"Peers? Are you ... ?" She looked him over, watching his face smear with blood as he tried to wipe it away, the flow not stopping.

"I bit my tug," he mumbled, barely comprehensible. "And I hit my node." He nodded as if trying to convince himself. "I'd be okay," he flubbed.

"Kindred?"

"I think we're all okay, Piper," Meyer said.

Nocturne barked as if in support. He looked unharmed, and Meyer noticed he'd somehow become tangled in blankets. Built-in doggie bed and shock-absorption system all in one.

"*Kindred?*"

"He's okay, Piper. We're all okay."

Piper turned to Meyer.

"You sure you're fine?"

"Yes."

"*Absolutely* certain?"

"Yes."

Piper slapped him very hard. His skin stung.

"I told you to get on the sub. I told you."

Meyer rubbed the spot, meeting her glare. "Someone had to keep them from getting to you before you could launch."

"How did that work out?"

"I don't know. Have you been eaten?"

"Fuck you, Meyer. You don't always know best. You don't always need to think of yourself!"

"I was trying to help *you!*"

"We couldn't leave without you! Don't you get that?"

"If you weren't so goddamn stubborn, you sure *should* have. You'd have been screwed if that wave hadn't come. It was supposed to be the difference between three of you surviving instead of none of us." That made Meyer wonder, and his eyes went to the porthole to see what the surface looked like and where they'd ended up.

"No, I mean ... " She sighed. "Tell him, Peers."

Peers turned around, said nothing, and threw up in the corner.

"You survive," Piper said.

"Thank you."

"No. You don't understand. *You survive*. At least one of you, anyway." She looked at Kindred, rubbing his arm. "Peers was telling us. The Mullah know all about this. It's happened over and over."

"Good for the Mullah."

Piper looked like she might hit him again. She was that furious, and Meyer didn't understand why.

"*You survive*. No matter what, Meyer Dempsey makes it. Do you understand? If you want to protect us, stay with us. Then maybe *we'll* survive, too."

Meyer didn't understand. *He survived?* What kind of nonsense proclamation was that? What loose balls in his usually kooky wife had recent events finally knocked loose?

He opened his mouth but had no idea what to say. Should he apologize for some weird metaphysical discourtesy? Should he ask questions? She was speaking about it all as if it should be obvious, but she'd been doing the same since Cameron died. Maybe she'd finally tipped. Or maybe — and this, he didn't like to consider — she was right, and he'd almost done something terribly wrong and nearly killed them all.

Except for himself and possibly Kindred, of course. Because *he survived*.

"Piper ... "

"Hody sit," Peers said, speaking around his wounded tongue. "Look ad dis."

Piper gave him a final glance then moved to the portal.

Meyer put his face to the thick glass. They were bobbing along the surface of what looked like an endless ocean. He couldn't see the dock or inlet. Only water, as far as the eye could see.

"Bad news," said Kindred from behind them. "We've got no power. None at all." Meyer turned. Kindred flicked the caged light ahead, somehow intact, lit up like a contradiction. "These seem to be solar. But that's all we have."

Meyer moved to the sub's center, tested its stability by rocking back and forth while grasping the ladder, and then, satisfied that he wouldn't tip them, reached up to open the hatch. Once up, Meyer realized he could see some features invisible from below: one of the other subs, presumably vacant, off in one of the otherwise featureless directions. In the other, a distant mountain that remained above water. And worlds of debris.

On the sub's rear was a sheared-away stub of metal: the communications/navigation/whatever array, broken off as anticipated.

"Bad news, Piper," he said, surveying the open water. "I think Plan A to hook up with the other viceroys is off the table."

Nobody answered.

"Piper?"

Then her voice came up, quiet and tentative.

"Meyer? What's this?"

CHAPTER 41

The wave hit without mercy.

Carl watched it bombard the bridge's right side window. The ship was titanic, meant for hauling something — Carl had no idea what — across the open sea. He barely had a clue how to enter the thing, let alone find the steering wheel, or have any clue what it did beyond moving left and right. Carl couldn't swim, had never been on a boat, and was frankly more terrified of open water than aliens eating his brain. That's why facing the Titans and shuttles at the gate had felt so easy. If they killed him and all the folks who'd run along behind him, so what?

But now Carl was reminded of why this had been such a terrible idea.

The system of docks at the port was long and complex. Here, where the oceangoing vessels were harbored, docks were sprawling concrete piers. But out on a jut were smaller concrete piers, wooden piers, and a spider's web of dinky slips for rich people's pleasure craft and indigents' fishing skiffs.

Carl watched the wave as it propagated toward them, seeing it crest, ripping the everyman's piers from the bottom like tearing carpet from the floor. Wood broke apart like a house of matchsticks. Time froze as Carl watched in horror, as Lawrence and the lady that might be his wife stood just behind as if they thought he could protect them. He watched the water rise from flooded but mostly flat to a ski slope, pulling pillars from the inlet's bed like rotten teeth. The boats came with it. They looked like a giant's bathtub toys, then the wave rolled and crashed, its sound like a bomb.

"*Jeeeeezuuus ...* " said someone behind him.

Carl gripped a chrome handle on the control panel. He hadn't commandeered this freighter because he planned to explore the world's wet corners. He'd taken it because it could float. And sure, plenty of shit could stay buoyant, but this toy might be big enough to come up top after a wave that size ripped the —

"Oh, *motherfucker!*" Carl blurted.

The thought struck him like a punch to the face. He let go of the dash and took a half step toward the bridge door before realizing it was too late to de-dock the ship or whatever the shit captains called it when they untied the big ropes and prepared to hit the open sea for a few months of scurvy and sodomy. They'd passed the lines on their mad dash up the ramp to the first of the sealable doors, and those lines had looked as thick as Carl's upper arms, fastened to cleats the size of small automobiles, bolted to the concrete. He hadn't a clue what they were tied to on the ship's side, but the time to analyze and care was long gone. They were about to find out what happened when an unstoppable force hit an immovable object.

Lawrence looked over.

"What? What is it?"

The wave killed the need to answer. It rolled the moored ship hard, the impact that might have shattered the bridge windows thankfully dispersed as the wave's angle flattened. Carl and his prisoners of misfortune slid halfway down the floor toward the left (*port*, his mind corrected, unsure how he even knew) of the high-up room before the big dock lines caught with the feel of an enormous dog running into the end of his leash. The ship shuddered, unknown tons of floating metal waging war with the bolts or ropes or whatever else held them in place. Carl lost his footing and crashed to the deck, finding himself suddenly tangled in some white guy's bare lower legs and running shoes. The pregnant woman landed on her back and, sliding, half crotch-planted against the support pole of a high stool. Carl cringed in spite of the chaos. Good thing that kid inside her hadn't stuck his head out to see what the fuck was happening in the crazy outside world.

Then the leash snapped them back to more or less upright, the first wave passing, everything apparently still in place. Carl heard a tremendous groan. He imagined a massive section of metal shearing away from their ark's side as water fought bolts, dooming them.

"It's okay," said an older man in jeans, maybe fifty-five, with a midnight-black beard. "It's okay, we're still — "

As the ship rolled back to center, they leered back in the other direction, now on the secondary wave's downside, the metal sides of the freighter sounding like they were raking lines in the concrete. *Weren't there bumpers out there?* Carl thought it crazily as the man with the beard quit yammering, his eyes like saucers of milk with chocolate drops in the middle.

The second wave hit, this one cresting instead of rising. It caught them in its surfer's sweet spot, and for long moments as women screamed and men screamed like women, Carl was certain they'd somehow ended up underwater. This was it. This was the flood, and it had happened in half a minute. The water had risen two hundred feet, and here they were, lassoed to the bottom in an undersea prison.

But then the water rolled over the top and the ship swayed and jerked just as hard, toppling the few people fool enough to try and stand between volleys. They were still on the surface.

But a quick glimpse — all Carl could manage as the horizon dipped and dove, as his footing and stomach lurched in tandem — proved the other docks gone, like the marina they'd seen farther down, and all of the land, everywhere.

The freighter was leaning into the next wave, no longer upright between swells. The ropes were still in place, holding them taut to a pier that was now underwater. They were on their side, about to be swamped.

The people around him were skidding on the slanted wet floor, clinging to whatever they could as the ship struggled to right itself, fighting its moorings.

"We need to get lower," Lawrence said. "We're still — "

The long, low, tortured sound of bending metal grew from the ship's side like a machine winding up. Lawrence stopped his lips, looking at Carl. Carl wanted to shout at him but saw the next wave coming and gestured in a way that was supposed to mean *Hang the fuck on or die*. He opened his mouth to shout in case none of them saw the approaching wall of water, as they *leaned right into it*, but then it came and the sound of metal crested and popped like a thousand shotguns blasting in tandem. A fresh shudder ran through the floor and walls and the handles under Carl's fist, then the ship lurched in one violent arc to the opposite side, now rolling with the water. Then the roll arrested, and Carl realized that only one of the lines or cleats must have busted and the other was still there. The wave, instead of rolling, swung them hard, wrenching and grating as the ship's bottom struck God knew what underwater that had so recently been above it, the whole works canting, stuttering and digging for purchase.

As they settled with the bow 30 degrees into the wave, with the horizon 30 degrees from normal ahead, water came like a dam breaking, and the front windows finally *did* crack and shatter from their seals at the sides and corners. Water flowed in like a fire hose, and the floor became a skating rink, filling from the bottom, flooding trapped in by the watertight doors, the whole thing like unfunny slapstick as they fell and half swam and coughed and gagged and fought for air as it filled with spray.

With a lurch, the final mooring gave way. There was another tremendous racket, and after freeing its bonds the freighter bobbed upward like a cork held underwater, overcorrecting and tossing them all from their feet and scrambling knees in a half second of weightlessness.

Another great splash of water.

Another great lurch, and then another. Carl found his feet between them and was tossed down hard, on the meaty side of his right leg, muscle striking something on the deck, mashing between floor and meat with the force of a bullet.

More water. More bobbing. More tossed horizon, and in the chaos Carl heard someone vomiting.

Then another wave, smaller this time.

Another lurch.

But the worst was over, and the rest was ending. If their violent departure from the pier had put a hole in their side, it was a slow one. They seemed not upright and level, the chaotic rising sea now more like the surf in a small storm.

After a few more minutes of tossing, the world seemed to still, and Carl lifted his head from crossed arms, his face wet and dripping, clothes soaked. He found his feet, smarting at whatever blunt protrusion had slammed into his thigh. He looked down, found his pants still in one piece, no blood apparent. But it hurt like a beaten whore, and he was going to have a motherfucker of a bruise.

But to be alive? That was something.

Carl stood. Slowly, the others around him — battered and shocked, but seemingly unhurt — stood to join him.

They looked toward what used to be the shore.

But as far as Carl could see on what he thought must be the northern horizon, South Africa was gone. Floating debris was the only thing left. Other freighters had come untethered and floated around them like a child's game of Battleship.

The man who'd shouted when it started pointed through the window and yelled, *"Look!"*

Carl did, along with the others. They saw battered-but-alive people on the nearest ship, and the one a bit farther on. There were many boats between their freighter and the large thing in the far distance that had to be the Astral vessel, safely off and upright, and on each, Carl saw survivors who'd thought ahead. Or who'd got lucky.

Then he heard a buzzing.

A crackle of electricity.

And a small explosion, followed by screams.

They ran to the far side of the bridge, toward the sounds, and again Carl struck a console and felt that same blunt pain wallop his bruising thigh. He winced but didn't feel it for long; his attention was stolen as they all watched a shuttle settle over another of the surviving ships.

An energy blast.

A rain of twisted metal.

And then the shuttle moved on to pick off its next target.

They watched as one by one, shuttles cleared the world of unauthorized survivors.

Carl couldn't speak, could only watch it happen. His hand rubbed his chin. His fingers clutched unknown controls on the unpowered freighter's panel. He touched his leg where it hurt.

There was something in his loose pants pocket. Something big that explained why it had hurt so much when he'd hit the deck. Whatever was in there had slammed hard into his leg.

The shuttles, now moving systematically across the lawn of survivors in a coordinated group, picked off more. And more. And more.

Then two of them turned to the freighter. Came closer. And closer. The shuttle's humming engines set Carl's neck hairs on end. They all watched as the things came to them broadside, hovering, electricity in the air, charging their weapons.

Carl's hand touched the object in his pocket. It was like a ping-pong ball but harder — smooth and almost powdery, like fine brushed aluminum. He pulled it out and saw it was the ball the man had given him — the strange magician who'd told Carl not to try the cutthroat, but to survive another way.

Carl looked at the shuttles. Felt the gathering charge. Waited for death.

The ball warmed in his hand.

The shuttles seemed to power down, then made small, searching circles in the air.

The shuttles moved away.

And went about clearing the rest of the surviving ships, leaving their freighter alone.

CHAPTER 42

Between the blonde and Sadeem was a sort of projection he'd never seen. The closest was something one of the Mullah Elders had shown him after too much wine: an artifact said to have been left behind by the Horsemen — something that would, if you touched it, pull you into a sensory-immersive memory. This effect was similar but more distant. Sadeem, watching the scenes, didn't just see the world rendered in three dimensions like a hologram. It was more like he'd been there.

Or maybe that was simple human empathy. Watching the ships capsize in Hanging Pillars and then seeing the sharks take the swimmers had sickened his stomach as accurately as if he'd witnessed the blood firsthand. And that fit because he'd see it firsthand forever, in his dreams.

The projection ended. A soft blue circle of light appeared in the center of the all-white floor. It faded slowly, then the room was again featureless, disorienting as a stroll through nothing.

Eternity turned toward Sadeem. "It is done."

"How long will the flooding last?"

"In the past the cleansing phase has lasted forty days."

"And forty nights?"

Eternity looked at him as if he were an idiot.

"And then you will leave."

The woman nodded.

"Why?"

"Because it is not our purpose to be humanity's stewards. You will be granted another epoch, and when you feel you are ready, we shall return."

Sadeem wanted to press on and ask more but got the impression that there would be time for that before the Astrals left Earth alone to try again — apparently forty days and nights to ask Eternity questions. Seemed that some facts and figures could indeed survive a few thousand years of telephone without distortion.

"So now we wait."

"The cleansing will continue. But yes. You will wait."

"*Continue?*"

Sadeem waited for the woman's curious gaze to depart. She knew he was Mullah and might be able to read his mind, but Sadeem wasn't a Temple Elder. Perhaps the scrolls had survived somewhere — hell, maybe the Astrals even had their own copy from the last intergalactic contract-signing. But Sadeem wasn't senior enough to have read them. He didn't know all she was assuming, and wasn't entirely sure he wanted to.

"The human population remains excessive. We estimate your race still numbers in the hundreds of millions."

"It used to be in the billions."

Eternity was unfazed. "The cleansing is not complete until the proper seed number has been achieved. Your species requires a diverse gene pool for a new epoch, but not one so broad-branching that it introduces variables we cannot control for."

Sadeem wasn't entirely sure what that meant.

"Optimal target population is an order of magnitude less than is current."

"You're going to reduce us to *tens of millions?* You're going to kill *another 90 percent?*"

The woman ignored him. It wasn't an air of blatant snubbing — more that she seemed to feel this was unworthy of discussion. A bit of 101-level information obvious to even the dumbest person accustomed to apocalyptic resets.

"The Mullah will remain our contacts. You will be the first Elder."

"I'm not an Elder."

"You are now. The location of your previous portal is submerged, and the connection to the old portal has been severed. There has been no contact from those whose energy we have experienced before. We believe they have perished. We will help you establish a new portal once the waters recede and will shuttle your tribe's remainders to the new location, for you to lead."

"You *killed off the other Elders?*" The thought was chilling. Sadeem was a respected man in the Mullah order — knowledgeable for sure, a thought-leader without question. It was Sadeem who'd argued most vehemently that the Lightborn were worthy of exploration; Sadeem who, when an unexpected opportunity had presented itself to study one, had jumped at the chance. Clara's visit to the Mullah and all he'd learned about the children's unique position in the mental order had happened almost as if by divine providence, and Sadeem had been looking forward to reporting his findings to the Elders. There were many to tell. He was three broad levels from the top as far as he knew, and it was possible there were levels above about which he knew nothing.

But now Eternity was saying they were all gone? *All* of the Elders — enough to leave *Sadeem* at the top? Was this how the Astrals treated those who they'd tapped as partners?

"It was unavoidable," Eternity said. "Any intercession to guide your senior individuals to safety would have compromised the larger plan. Your order did not feel the call to reach a capital, or chose not to heed it. Yet one more example of the failure of this epoch's interconnectedness."

"There is supposed to be a truce between us! Between Mullah and Astral! We had an agreement! We do not interfere with you, and *you do not interfere with us!*"

"We did not interfere," Eternity said.

"You killed them!"

"They failed to extricate themselves from circumstances past epochs and your own scrolls foretold. But we honored our agreement. We have not harmed the Mullah."

Sadeem's mouth hung open — an incredulous look that would have had an obvious meaning for any human, but Eternity simply waited for him to speak again.

"You killed them," he repeated.

"Only individuals perished. The Mullah remain." She nodded toward Sadeem.

He still didn't know what to say. She wasn't being obstinate, if Astrals could even be such a thing. She was stating fact as she saw it.

"You may choose the new portal's location," she said after Sadeem failed to speak. "You may choose those who will go with you to build your new society of guardians."

"So that you can betray and kill them off the next time around?"

"The individuals you choose will not be alive at the end of the next epoch." Again the woman looked at Sadeem, seeming to wonder if he was a fool. How could the Astrals possibly betray the new Mullah's founders thousands of years in the future? They'd betray those founders' *ancestors*. Why wasn't Sadeem getting this?

"What if I refuse?"

"Then you are of no use to us."

"Why me? Why should I be their leader?"

"Because you are here."

"Why am I here?"

Now the woman faltered, and Sadeem found his mind falling back to what they'd almost discussed: the reason he *was* on the ship, having nothing to do with a new generation of portal-keepers. That was just before something that looked a lot like human anger had prompted the massive ship to melt the ice caps, inviting what was apparently only the middle phase of the human apocalypse.

Eternity had mentioned both Stranger and Lightborn: two wild cards that prompted a rapid shuffling of the human deck. And when Sadeem had none of the answers she'd wanted, the woman became vengeful like a human scorned.

Obeying an instinct, Sadeem spoke again before she could reply.

"How is it going for you? This *reset* of yours?"

"It proceeds as expected."

"*Exactly* as expected?"

"You have seen the process. It is something your order must understand, and record in its new scrolls."

"Why?"

"Because the old race memories must be expunged. It is the only way for a fresh start. But one group must keep the secrets. One must harbor past knowledge so as to facilitate the next cycle and prompt those who remain to avoid its immediate mistakes. That is the Mullah's burden, and yours to recall and record."

"So you kill us off, down to a few million survivors. You somehow erase our memories. And then you leave and let us do it all over."

"As was in the last epoch's Elder scrolls."

"And that includes the Archetypes mentioned in the scrolls: the King, the Innocent, the Fool ... "

Eternity's head cocked — another all-too-human expression. She didn't know this part of what he was saying, and it was written all over the face she'd either fabricated or commandeered. Apparently the Archetypes, like other aces in the-hole, were something the Mullah had discovered or created while the overlords were away.

"Never mind," Sadeem said.

Eternity paced the room. If Sadeem didn't know better — if he didn't know her to represent the supreme Astral intelligence and instead accepted the illusion that she was a stern human woman in a red dress — he'd have thought her preoccupied. As if she was uneasy about something despite the complete and total Astral obliteration of the planet, and couldn't help wondering at unseen grit in the works of their supposedly flawless machine.

"Something wrong?" The moment it rose to his lips, Sadeem knew it was the wrong thing to say. Speaking to Eternity as if it were the human it pretended to be wasn't just ridiculous; it felt dangerous. Like poking a venomous snake with a branch, daring it to strike.

Eternity glared at him.

Then the projection snapped back into the room's center, its sensory radiation already fogging Sadeem's sense of place.

The scene showed a large group of survivors at the top of a very tall hill, safe from the floodwaters, making camp. Sadeem heard a minute cracking sound like shards of broken glass crunched underfoot. A few of the campers' heads turned, and their breath puffed out like cotton in the suddenly cool air. At first Sadeem didn't understand what he was seeing, until he realized the crackling was the sound of ice forming at the edge of what had previously seemed a tropical sea. A vortex formed overhead, bringing an intense chill down from above. The people ran about, shouting, clutching themselves as they shivered. Ice crystals spread and raced out from the shallows like messengers in a hurry to deliver horrid news.

"Watch carefully," Eternity said, her blue eyes as cool as the forming ice in the projection. "There is *so much left* of the cleansing for your scrolls to record."

CHAPTER 43

Stranger reached out, felt the mind complementary to his own, and borrowed its computational power the way the humans once called on their great computer network to do the same thing. It wasn't much of a trick once you knew what you were looking for — once you understood how this epoch's people were different and unexpected. That's what Meyer Dempsey had subconsciously realized long ago, before his mind had birthed one Astral copy and then another, before the Astral hive had forced a part of Meyer's essence out to become the Pall. Before the Pall had, in turn, been changed by the addition of another human mind to become Stranger, as he was now.

Meyer had taken mind-altering substances to feel the shared connection.

But Stranger could open those same connections with a thought.

His mind spread out, became not quite itself. Machinery turned. And he saw the changes, the critical mass forming within the collective unconsciousness that was (Astral opinions notwithstanding) very much in existence. There weren't many humans left, relatively speaking, but those remainders *belonged* — not by the Astrals' definitions, exactly, and not quite by the intentions of the viceroys forced to choose. But by another definition, superior to them all.

Even now, inside the foreign mind, Stranger could feel the energy.

Puzzle pieces slotting together, as if solved by a Lightborn.

Like Clara Gupta, even now, grappled with the same puzzles as she discovered her silver orb, terrified in the dark with her friends. Even now her mind was turning, fitting the subtlest pieces together. If he focused, Stranger could almost see it happening: a corner of the mess slowly resolving.

Yes, Stranger thought, borrowing his counterpart's brainpower, *things were coming along just fine.*

He pulled a trio of silver balls from his pocket. He let them lie in the expanse of his big right hand. They turned, and as they did he let their hypnotic rhythms show him his work across the world.

Ice formed across the tropics. Not everywhere; only under the motherships ushering change. Stranger wasn't an archaeologist and even now found no true interest, but he could imagine the bafflement of future archaeologists when seeing the evidence: apparent glacial grooves along the western shores of Africa; fossils of frost-stunted plants buried in time at the Earth's hottest spot. The great ships' engines siphoned molecular inertia into themselves by a mechanism Stranger didn't understand, and as they did the water's tiniest pieces slowed, stopping, coming to rest in a crystal lattice. Within hours the equatorial waters where survivors thronged, despite the sun's assault, were frozen twenty feet deep. Those who'd thought themselves survivors discovered otherwise, and another percentage of the population perished.

In the tiny sub, Stranger watched as Piper Dempsey found the silver sphere in the backpack beside Mara Jabari's tablet from what must feel like forever ago. He watched as she summoned the others to see then saw her hide it when they turned to look. *I meant this*, Piper told Meyer. *What is this?* Showing him the first thing she could find after changing her mind, which turned out to be a cache of medical supplies. Wounds were patched. Bruises were treated. And only later did Piper pull the small sphere back from her hasty hiding place and stare into its polished surface: a face that Stranger, by looking into one of the spheres on his own palm, could see looking back out at him.

Stranger watched as Piper noticed its warmth and vibration, as she noticed the Cradle's instruments warm from dormancy as she held the sphere close, as she tucked it into a compartment near the steering fork and announced, without explanation, that the sub's electronics were working again ... and that the GPS, which had no signal, was nonetheless steering them somewhere she believed they should go.

Stranger watched Etemenanki Sprawl as the city's vessel left its former shores, full of those ingenious enough to board it. He watched Viceroy Anders set aside the sphere he'd sent, obeying an internal compass she felt was truer than his as she commanded the vessel to turn and rescue the stranded. But then the last of the crust holding Old Goat's true bounty at bay sheared apart under the water at the urging of the nearby Astral mothership, lava frothed forth, and before it could be quenched the waters around the former Iceland boiled. There were no magma ducts leading to the higher peak where Etemenanki's survivors, near but not atop Old Goat, had made their marooned new home. Still the magma found its way upward as the

Astral mothership cut its way, and the tip broke loose before Anders could reach the stranded. An ordinary mountain birthed a new volcano, and the people burned.

Stranger watched as, in both Hanging Pillars and Roman Sands, late waves settled and those who'd found vessels were overtaken by motherships and shuttles. Unlike Viceroy Anders, Liza Knight of Roman Sands was more practical. She did not command that the already-overfull vessel turn back as shuttles worked.

The raking did not take long, and mere hours later Stranger could tune into both cities and see almost nothing — except for a single ship that the Astrals had for some reason failed to jettison: a freighter with a captain that could not fire her engines or steer her, and yet found himself both knowledgeable and able once he set the sphere from his pocket onto the great ship's dashboard. And after that, Stranger watched the big ship make slow loops, its movements curiously agile for something so large, its engines burning no fuel. He watched as, one by one, the small group in the bridge found boats and land the Astrals had missed, stopped beside them in ways such a large ship should not have been able to manage, and dropped ladders that they had no trouble finding or knowing how to use.

When the local sea was bare and the freighter was more occupied, Stranger watched as the captain — a Warrior of sorts more than a captain — turned the ship on a bearing that avoided obvious land, toward the seemingly endless water, inspired by his spherical lucky charm.

The vessels of both Canaan Plains and Loulan Mu were only partially filled, but as Stranger looked at both places he saw a sea overfilled with all the world's nightmare creatures, overtaking lesser vessels one by one and leaving the large ship untouched. He saw sharks, all of which had developed an intense interest in human flesh. He saw fish with teeth — knowing that despite their reputations they seldom attacked people — swarm and leap. He saw those too near the water get snatched like something from a bad movie, dragged sideways, tipping their boats into the water. He watched water snakes and fish with deadly barbs clog the surface like flotsam, turned inexplicably savage. There were aggressive whales and unkind dolphins. Smaller craft were capsized, while larger ships were bombarded with wave after wave of kamikaze sea life, rushing the spinning engine blades until they were jammed, overheated, and stilled. Then the few clouds parted, and the marooned ships baked in the sun, decks covered with ravens who'd developed curious eye-jabbing habits, with goliath hornets displaced by the flood, intent to vent their aggression on any humans who chose to stay on deck.

Onboard the vessel previously of Ember Flats, the old order's Capital of Capitals, Stranger watched Viceroy Mara Jabari stare into her own silver sphere, wishing irrationally that the time was right to reach out and speak to her. But the dominoes had been laid, and this was a delicate time, as the Astrals plunged powder-white fingers into the soft flesh of humanity's psyche, believing it to be disconnected. Now was not the time to reveal the truth: that humanity had not grown without a developed collective consciousness, but that it had simply grown one the Astrals had never seen. Stranger, being mostly human himself, could see the connections, feel them forming as the Astrals did their work, reducing the human population to only those who, thanks to some wrenches in the works, contained enough seeds to germinate.

But Jabari looked into her sphere and rolled it across an old map of the former globe that someone of wit had included in the vessel's onboard supplies. And if Stranger focused, he could catch the tone of her thoughts: guilt, regret, and resentment. Jabari wondered at what might happen next, more fearing that she'd remain a leader than hoping to be one.

I've failed them, she thought. *The viceroys cannot meet. There are no hookups remaining, and the Astrals control the satellites.*

Meyer, and all that made him special by the Da Vinci Initiate's reckoning, would die along with everyone else. Even if he and Kindred made the Cradle, they'd starve like the rest of them, with nowhere to be and nowhere to go.

They might all be dead, her mind twisted the knife. *ALL of the viceroys. I might be the only one left. This single ship might be all that's left of mankind.*

It wasn't true, but Stranger couldn't tell her.

More would perish. *Many, many* more.

The viceroys would not meet as planned.

But below the surface, something new was growing.

Stranger, as he sat top the big hill, looked down into the spheres. He wondered if this — all the work he'd done — made him selfish. He wanted very much to live, and it was only his own arrogant need that served the rest, purely by chance.

In the end he decided that there were many things that even he didn't know or understand, and that all plans had their masters, and that the only thing more selfish than what he'd done so far would be to ignore the commands of his own plan's master.

Then the first thing happened that Stranger hadn't anticipated. The first of many things he hadn't — and wouldn't — see coming.

The first connection lit.
And then the next.

CHAPTER 44

"Did you say something?" a girl asked.

Clara looked over. They were in the lowest level of the Ember Flats vessel, half the ship's kids tossed into one giant pile with only minimalist wooden bunks to tease their comfort. Clara didn't understand any of it. If the Astrals were such magicians, how about a few mattresses? Heck, how about some *TV*? Anything to pass the time in this dank ship, so much like something from hundreds of years ago.

But, she thought, at least it was better than the belowdecks space they'd been in before finding a hatch leading up here. That had felt like pure luck, and thank God for it. Clara didn't know how it had happened. She'd had this feeling that the hatch was to one side so she'd crawled there, even as other Lightborn protested in the dark.

"Sorry?"

"I said, 'Did you say something?'" The girl stopped, realizing the absurdity of telling Clara what *she'd* said when she'd asked if *Clara* had spoken. Then she laughed. She looked maybe seven, like Clara. But this girl wasn't Lightborn, and felt much younger.

"I didn't say anything." Clara let herself smile. She knew this wasn't the only ship of survivors; she could still sense the other Lightborn who'd managed similarly miraculous stowaways on other ships. But Clara felt mostly alone — the simple, quiet solitude of the surviving few. Talking to anyone felt nice. To see even a ghost of humor.

"I thought you said something about boots," the girl told her.

"I didn't."

"I don't have any boots."

"That's okay," Clara said, "because I didn't ask for them."

"And I especially don't have *man's* boots."

Clara looked at the girl again, this time taking her in from head to toe. She was wearing a fine blue dress — the kind of thing Clara's mother used to make her wear for fancy balls, back in Heaven's Veil. A strange thing for a ride in an apocalyptic ark. Clara fought an urge to take their conversation sideways, to ask where the girl had been when the water started rising.

She was watching Clara right back, as if in expectation. Her skin was almost as dark as Ella's, but her eyes were emerald green. It was a curious look, and Clara found herself spellbound.

"You heard me say something about men's boots?"

"Or a man in boots," the girl answered.

Clara turned in the opposite direction, finding the area behind her still empty. Some of the Lightborn, once they'd found their way out of the ship's pitch-black underbelly, had been antsy. Logan had nodded to Clara knowingly (deferring to her as the group's new leader, perhaps) and risen to take them away, leading them like a chaperone. Clara had felt the group's anxiety but didn't want to go along. And now, looking at the green-eyed girl, she wondered if there'd been a reason. Maybe she'd heard her the way the girl seemed to have heard Clara's thoughts about the stranger with his scuffed brown boots, and she'd stuck around to have this very discussion.

"I might have been mumbling," Clara lied. She'd been silent, but her mind had been active — yawning back to a vision of the man by the campfire, wondering if what he'd seemed to be telling them all was true. "What else did I say?"

"Dunno." The girl wrinkled her nose. "Did you say you went camping or something?"

"You don't know if I said it or not?"

Again the girl shrugged. Perhaps the oddity was dawning on her. Clara tried to sympathize but couldn't. Ever since she'd been inside her mother, she'd heard the thoughts and feelings of others. She didn't know what it was like to suddenly waken to a latent ability.

Or more accurately, *being woken* to one. By Clara's mere presence, if she had to guess.

The girl seemed uncomfortable, probably trying to decide how she could think Clara had spoken without any details about what she'd said. But mental and spoken communication weren't the same. When speaking mind to mind, answers occasionally came before the questions. You sometimes smelled aromas before knowing their source.

Clara turned herself around, rotating without standing. Once fully facing the girl — the two of them nearly knee to knee on shoddy wooden benches as if preparing for a game of patty-cake — Clara smiled. "What's your name?"

"Zoe."

"And of course you already know mine."

"Clara." The girl's face wrinkled again as she tried to recall if Clara's name had been said aloud before her friends had left to go exploring.

"That's right. Do you want to play a game?"

"My brother has Go Fish," Zoe said.

"Not like this. It's a pretend game."

"Okay."

"We close our eyes and pretend we're somewhere else."

"Where?"

"Anywhere. This ship is smelly."

Zoe laughed. "Okay."

"What kind of a place do you want to imagine?"

"I don't know."

"How about if we pretend we're camping? You said camping."

"Okay." Zoe reached for a pair of long metal rods lying along one wall, apparently as leftovers from construction that never existed. "These can be our hot dog sticks."

"No, we don't do it like that."

Zoe held the rods then set them slowly back down. "Then how?"

"We close our eyes." Clara closed hers, to demonstrate.

"Okay. Now what?"

"Now we take turns filling it up."

Clara looked around inside her mind, watching the scene come into being like a 3-D model rendered. It was the same campsite she and the Lightborn had visited with the man in boots, but this time he hadn't created the space. This time, Zoe was doing it.

"How do we fill it up?"

"Just put something there. In your imagination."

A pink dinosaur, human sized and standing on two legs, more cute than menacing, popped into existence in a small green hat.

"Nice. I like his hat," Clara said.

When Zoe said nothing, Clara opened her eyes. Zoe was staring at her.

"Whose hat?"

"Close your eyes," Clara said.

After a second, Zoe did. Then Clara did the same.

"My turn."

Clara pictured a dwarf with a nose so big he could barely hold it up. The nose was bright red and dripping.

Zoe laughed.

"What?"

"I just imagined something else. A little guy with a big nose."

"Hey! It's supposed to be my turn."

"Sorry," Zoe said.

Clara turned the imaginary dwarf into a troll. It growled, and leaped. Zoe gave a tiny shriek, and when Clara opened her eyes this time, Zoe gave a tiny embarrassed laugh.

"Something just kind of freaked me out."

"In your own imagination?"

Zoe looked slightly away, frowning. The answer, from Zoe's perspective, was probably *Sort of*. Other people's thoughts always struck Clara as obviously foreign no matter how well they meshed with her own. Each thought had an accent, and a discerning mental ear couldn't help but gather the accents of others. She knew something was strange but had no frame of reference.

But children, unlike adults, had malleable perspective. That's the whole reason Clara had been sure, once they were aboard the ships, that this was possible.

Adults had to be convinced. Their minds, through the passage of years, set like concrete.

But not children. Children could still convince themselves to believe.

"It was the troll, wasn't it?" Clara asked.

Zoe nodded without thinking then stopped to wonder why she was nodding.

"Close your eyes, Zoe. I want to show you something." Clara focused.

"What just popped up around the campsite, Zoe?"

"Dunno."

"I think you know. Look behind the pile of logs."

Zoe laughed again. "What are *you* doing here?" she said to something that didn't exist.

"What do you see, Zoe?"

"It's a pig. Why did I think of a *pig* around a campfire?"

Clara inserted a clown.

"Probably the same reason you'd think of a clown." Then Clara added two elephants, a spotted leopard, and a banana tree. "Or those elephants. Or the leopard. Or even that banana tree over by the pond."

When Zoe looked over, she seemed almost ready to run. This playmate was no fun after all. This playmate, Zoe seemed to have decided, could do black magic.

So Clara sent her emotional mind toward the girl's, cupping it in a nonphysical palm. Her mind touched Zoe's, and second by second the girl began to relax. It was like hypnosis. It wasn't easy, coming psychically alive for the first time.

"What's my mom's name, Zoe?"

"L ... Lila."

"What about my dad?"

"R ... " But then rather than finishing the name, Zoe's hand went over her mouth and she said, "Sorry."

"For what?"

"He ... "

Clara slowly opened her mind, sending out only what Zoe needed to know. She'd picked up on the fact that Clara's dad was dead and that had been expected, but Clara hadn't realized Zoe would know her father's misdeeds as well — knowledge that Clara could see on Zoe's face even now, as the girl groped for proper expression.

Clara took Zoe's hands in hers, feeling rattled. She'd had the feeling that the Lightborn would be able to rouse the dormant minds of non-Lightborn children since before the big waves — that they'd be able to "light up the connections," to use the cowboy's expression. But she hadn't realized how smoothly it would happen. Zoe's mind, as Clara peered inside, was wide open. And through that mind, Clara could see Zoe's brother's. And her brother's friend. And the kids that friend had met on the vessel, all of whom were a level up, above them now.

In Clara's mind, connections lit like Christmas bulbs coming alive.

"What's happening?" Zoe asked.

And behind that first question, Clara heard a hundred others.

Clara wasn't entirely sure. So she gave the only answer she had.

"What no one expected."

CHAPTER 45

For the first few days, as the food held out — shrink-wrapped dry goods like crackers and preserved meat sticks, plus bottled water and juices — Lila occupied herself by watching the tablet, staying amused with its stored media, taking a strange and savage pleasure in knowing they had no connection to get *more* media, and that for all they knew, they were the planet's only survivors and that no media would *ever* be made by humans again.

She watched reruns of Piper's favorite old show, which just so happened to be her late mother's favorite old show. *Friends.* It had been old when the world ended the first time, when humanity learned it wasn't alone. And it seemed ancient now — memories of a day gone by when people had no more pressing concern than getting to the coffee shop to sit around on an orange couch, worrying about their ongoing relationship issues.

Lila watched the show, numb, playing the tablet too loud, without using the headphones she'd found in one of the compartments. Hours passed.

For the next few days, after the dying satisfaction of watching mindless entertainment had lost its edge, Lila watched the waterline, occasionally popping the sub's top to scan the horizon. Kindred told her to be careful, but that was a laugh; if there were humans left, they'd have better things to do than concern themselves with one and a half rebellious viceroys. And if there were still Astrals? Well, there would be worse things, after days in an endless ocean, than getting shot to bits.

Lila's father told her to watch for land if she had to go topside. But that was a laugh.

Piper said nothing. She'd kept to herself since the electrical equipment had come inexplicably back online — divorced, it seemed, from the power that should have come from the engines. None of them were mechanics or engineers, but Lila knew that something was fishy with the sub and that they were all pretending it wasn't so they wouldn't break the spell, causing ruin. And since that time — since that little bit of sub-related magic — Piper had been strange. Almost secretive. She woke some nights screaming, clutching a small purse she'd found — a purse she wouldn't let anyone else touch. And Piper would say that she remembered nothing of the dreams. And she'd look at Lila with wide eyes and repeat the same: *It's nothing. I don't remember why I was scared, only that I had a bad dream.*

But Piper looked at Lila as if she thought Lila knew something. As if whatever she knew, Piper didn't want her to know. So she kept to herself more and more, clutching her purse, peering inside it, obsessing over the sub's broken navigation, seeming to pretend that she knew a way to go even if there was no way she could. There was no GPS. Only a nonsense heading. A place toward which Piper kept them pointed, without notes or calculations.

After five days, the food ran out.

After seven, Lila remembered that Peers was an enemy. But she forgot *why*, exactly. There'd been a time in which she'd had all sorts of problems with the man. She'd considered stabbing him once she found something sharp

— *that* thought had come on day two. But she hadn't killed him and couldn't remember why. There was something between them, so for the sixth and seventh days she sat across the sub and stared until he looked away, over and over again. And when he went topside to look futilely for land as Piper tweaked the controls, mumbling to herself, Lila considered following him up and shoving him overboard. There must still be sharks in the ocean. She could cut him before knocking him into the water. Let Peers bleed and the predators come.

On the ninth day, Lila found herself forgetting her own daughter. Worse: She remembered that daughter suddenly one day and realized that not only had she forgotten Cora but that she'd *been forgetting* her for days now. But Cora might still be alive. Cora might not have been killed by ...

??

Or she might not have perished in the ...

??

Except that her daughter's name wasn't Cora, it was Clara. *Clara. Clara. Clara.* Lila repeated it over and over like a chant.

"Lila. You look like shit."

Lila's father, talking to her, looking a whole lot like shit himself. It took her a long time to remember why there were two of him, and once she remembered that, she couldn't recall the circumstances that had created the second. Were they twins? Was the other her uncle?

"Are you okay? How's your ... your head?"

Lila was annoyed by the question. She hadn't hit her head. But then she realized why her father was asking, and it wasn't about Lila at all. *His* head wasn't all that well, and he seemed to be seeking company in some sort of mental misery.

"Why?" she asked him.

"Have you been having dreams?"

"Why?"

"I've been thinking about when you were a kid. Do you remember that?"

Of course she didn't. What a stupid question.

"Do you remember that, Lila?"

And he, the great Meyer Dempsey, who might be a twin, didn't remember either. At least that's what Lila thought.

"Do you remember what it was like, growing up in Colorado?"

Had Lila grown up in Colorado? She thought it had been somewhere else.

The questions were too hard. Lila went to lie in her bunk. She fell asleep, and dreamed of eight people, crossing the desert.

CHAPTER 46

Carl's arm snapped out as if it were spring loaded. Without opening his eyes, he wrapped his hand around the wrist of someone much smaller than him. Someone whose arm — if they were doing what he thought they might be — he could break like a twig.

"Carl! Jesus! You scared me!"

Only then did Carl open his eyes. Lawrence fell a half step back but came up tight in Carl's grip and stopped.

"What you doing, Lawrence?"

"I just wanted to check the maps."

Carl felt fully awake. For the past two weeks, he'd been sleeping right where he was, below the wheel on the big ship's bridge. He'd never figured out how to operate the freighter, but that was okay. The engines had come on without him touching a goddamned thing, and now turning the wheel seemed to be the only thing required. Any fool could turn a wheel. Never mind all the other things that *should* go into navigating an ocean vessel.

"Ain't no point," Carl said, "unless you figured out how to read the stars."

"I was just curious where we were."

"Don't matter where we are." Carl's upper back was still slouched against the console where he'd been dozing when Lawrence made the mistake of trying to steer. "We're in water."

"I think we've been going north," Lawrence said.

"Yeah. To more water."

"I can only guess at how fast the engines are turning." He looked around, then said in a half whisper. *"Carl, nobody's watching them."*

Carl let go of Lawrence's wrist. "Guess the gas tank is still full. Don't need watching."

This had come up before. But Carl was a practical man, and it was Carl — not these others — who'd decided to try and steal a big ship. It was also Carl who'd decided to pull all the other poor suckers from their shitty little shuttle-target boats. If the engine situation wasn't broke, Carl felt no pressure to fix it.

Lawrence's eyes flitted around as if the man felt guilty. Then, seeing that they were alone, he sat. Carl slowly stood, shaking his head clean of cobwebs (couldn't get them all; shit was foggier all the time) and sat as well. He put one hand on the wheel — guiding their ship on its trip to nowhere made him feel better.

"Everyone is worried," Lawrence said.

"'Bout what? There's food enough. And it's raining plenty."

"The food is fine."

"What, then?"

"You, frankly."

Carl turned another hard stare on Lawrence. The man didn't flinch, and finally Carl said, "I'm fine."

"My wife keeps dreaming about you."

"That's your problem."

"Billy, too. And Wendy. It's the same dream, Carl."

"Good the fuck for them."

"You're in the desert."

Carl looked out across the endless water. "Wouldn't that be nice."

"And you're with other people. Seven others. One is a kid. And one of them ... " His face twisted, trying to articulate. "It's like two of them are kind of one person."

"Fascinating."

"None of this sounds familiar to you?"

Carl turned back to the water. The answer was that, yes, it sounded crazy familiar. But these were crazy times, and the last thing this little floating commune needed after two weeks with no hope of an end was rumor or superstition. Those kinds of things, given the way they'd all been lately, could lead to panic. Or worse.

"No."

"But there's more. Roman Sands. Do you remember Roman Sands?"

"'Course."

"Where was St. Augustine's? Can you tell me?"

Carl's lip curled. He should know, but didn't.

"Fuck if I know."

"Carl, that's where my son was christened. Before the Astrals came, it's where I was married. People came from all over the world to see us there, and now *I can't remember where it was or what it looked like.*"

"You just tired."

"I can't remember the street I lived on. Or the name of my high school. Half the time I have to think a while before I can remember *my parents'* names! And look at this!"

Carl turned. Lawrence had a small bag by the foot of his stool, and as Carl watched, he picked up the bag, opened its top, and removed a small black device that seemed to be made of metal and glass.

"What is this, Carl? Do you know?"

"Some Astral shit."

"It's *mine!* Look!" An image filled the screen: Lawrence and his wife standing in front of a waterfall. "It's mine, and I don't remember it!" He tapped on the glass. "Look! All this music in here. The ship's outlets are all working so I can plug it in to keep it charged. And I've been playing the music. I kind of remember it, but like from a long, long time ago. You know how you'll hear music in the background and strain to recognize it? It's like that. But as far as specifics? I've looked at the name of every singer, every damned song. There I know like ten out of a thousand."

"It's nothin', Lawrence," Carl said, unsettled, trying to recall the house he'd lived in just two weeks ago and coming up blank. His mother's name was Sondra, but she'd died ... sometime.

"All of this!" Lawrence said, fishing device after device out of the bag. "I packed this. At least I *think* I did. And I don't recognize any of it. What is this?" A long, silver device studded with square keys. "Or this?" Kind of like a tablet, but maybe not. Carl knew tablets because they used them on the ship most days, but then again, maybe not. "Or *this?*"

Lawrence threw the bag to the floor. Something heavy broke.

"I've asked around. It's happening to all of us, Carl. Everyone down there's got bags of stuff, and they have no idea what half of it is. Terry has a shirt from a race, dated last year, that he swears he didn't run in. LaShawn has that tablet, with TV shows on it, and yesterday she looked at me and said, "Why am I watching this? I've never seen this show before." So we passed it around. Nobody remembered the show, Carl. And yet I'm sure we were all watching that tablet a few days ago, laughing. I remember how good it felt to laugh for a while ... but now, nothing!"

Carl looked down at the bag, and whatever had broken. He felt unhinged, even uneasier than he'd been when Lawrence had broken his sleep. But ...

But *what?*

"I don't know what to say, brother. I still remember *you.*"

"But what if you forget?"

"I ain't gonna forget."

Carl sighed, his face suddenly defeated. His shoulders slumped. His head hung.

"Something is happening. I can feel it."

"End of the world, is all."

"And you just sit up here every hour of every day, watching the wheel."

"Just coping the only way I know. You do your thing, and I'll do mine."

Lawrence looked at the big wheel. At the maps he'd almost touched before Carl had woken and grabbed him.

"Where are we going, Carl?"

"I don't know."

"What are you steering us toward?"

"Nothin'."

"Then why does it matter? Why do you guard the fucking thing like it's your ... your ... " And then he gave up, unable to finish the thought.

"I ain't guarding it. But man, if we ever want to see land again, someone's gotta do this."

"Then let someone swap you out. Take shifts."

"No."

"Why not?"

"I ain't gotta explain that to you." Then Carl stood, to remind Lawrence how much smaller he was.

"Just tell me where we're going. Give me that, and I'll be happy."

And Carl told him, "I don't know."

CHAPTER 47

According to the black hashmarks Clara had been making beside her bunk, the storms came on the fifteenth day.

They saw them on the horizon, coming from the left and right, on the line where sky met water off the ship's bow. They didn't move in tandem the way weather was supposed to: in one direction, obeying the jet stream. These came together, like two cars meaning to smash a third between them.

They'd been motoring for hours before the skies darkened ahead. Somewhere up front, Viceroy Jabari or today's appointed captain had been calling arbitrary shots as always, steering them in big circles through the world's largest pool, pretending this little pleasure cruise had a destination. They'd been moving in roughly the same direction as they did on most days — what everyone seemed to think was mostly west. Then the ship turned, and the children all ran topside, knowing that a sudden change in the big boat's direction usually meant *land ahoy*. It was hit or miss out here: an enormous game of Battleship, played blind. Only land was worthy of changing direction, though so far they'd only seen the swamped tops of tall island mountains or volcanoes, devoid of life or space to thrive.

When Clara and the others reached the deck, they saw what the person behind the wheel must have seen: not land but other ships.

Many other ships.

To Clara's eye, it looked like a floating city. She sent her mind to Ella and the others, and to the non-Lightborn children who, by now, were nearly as lit up as only the Lightborn used to be. Clara and the others were powering their minds as the man in the boots had predicted, and now even some of the adults had shown a glimmer. The powerful circuit gave them an antenna, and they collectively sent their attention forward: to passengers on the other ships, who'd found each other. An armada out of nowhere. Thousands — maybe hundreds of thousands — of survivors.

Clara felt her mind touch them, magnified by the network on their own ship. She felt her shipmates' hope and elation. But she could tell, just by listening, that the floating city of people ahead hadn't grown as interconnected as they had — possibly because they didn't have Lightborn for kindling, possibly because their own situation had a special ingredient that made it unique. But regardless Clara could feel them. She knew they probably couldn't feel her, and that made what bled through so much more helpless.

Fear.

At first Clara didn't understand. None in their mind-net understood. What was there to fear? If anyone should be afraid, it was them, on the single ship, previously wondering if maybe they'd ended up alone. But these others? There were dozens — *hundreds* – of ships.

This was civilization. A new kind of home, where all would be as well as it could be.

Then she saw the storms through their eyes. Two, approaching from both directions.

Even if the Ember Flats vessel could have halted the planet's rage, they were too late.

Possibly hundreds of thousands had been on those ships.

But when they reached the pool of debris, storms now departed as if they'd never been, they found no survivors.

And inside, Clara heard a mental voice she'd been hearing since this began: the overheard Astral intelligence, going about its business.

First they turned water into blood.

Then they flooded the world.

Now, storms.

Clara didn't think it mattered so much that the Lightborn could hear them, even if the Astrals seemed ignorant. What was left to pull over on the aliens? They'd already won; now they were only twisting the knife.

The voice seemed to say, *Fifty-five million remaining.*

And behind it, Clara thought she saw the Astrals planning.

More storms.

Ice.

Fire, for those who'd found land.

Disease. Dehydration. Contagion.

Clara climbed the metal gangplank. There was a guard at the door to the ark's bridge, but he barely gave Clara a glance. They'd been through this several times before. They might live at sea forever, until they all died. There was little need for formality.

Clara found Mara in a rolling chair, bedraggled, face in her hands, jet-black hair knotted and frayed, breathing deep and slow, seemingly close to tears.

"Viceroy Jabari?"

Mara looked up. For a long moment, there was no recognition. Then she said, "Lizzie."

"*Clara*, Viceroy."

"I'm sorry. Of course. Clara."

Still she seemed out of sorts and confused. Clara broke the invisible barrier and moved into the customary greeting they'd shared since making her presence on the ship known: a hug, as the closest thing each other had to family.

"I had a niece named Lizzie. I'm pretty sure." Mara held up her left hand. She used her right index finger to point at a small diamond ring on her left hand. "This, however, has me stumped. Was I married, do you know?"

"I'm sorry," Clara said. "I don't."

"Oh." Then: "How long have we known each other? Since you were ... three?" The viceroy might as well have been throwing darts behind a blindfold.

"Just a few weeks," Clara said patiently. "We came to the city before the flood."

"How long ago did the flood begin?"

"How long does it feel like?"

Jabari's mouth opened. Then closed. Then opened again. Then she sighed.

"I don't know."

"It's been fifteen days."

"Oh."

Without warning, Jabari's head dropped back into her hands. Tears came, and Clara let them, casting *I've got this* looks around the bridge at the others. It was hardly necessary. An hour from now, no one would remember this moment. Or the countless lives lost.

When she was done, Mara lifted her head. She wiped her eyes, and only redness remained to echo her breakdown. She no longer wore makeup to smear.

"I remember a big house. And a chandelier with crystal baubles shaped like moons. I remember a room with ... *leather?* ... chairs. Where I'd use some sort of a thing to make sure people couldn't overhear me and whoever I talked to. Was that real? Or was it a dream?"

"It was real. I remember the room. I even remember the chandelier."

"Why don't *I* remember?"

Clara sighed. She thought she knew the simple answer but not the complication behind it. Mara didn't remember because she wasn't like Clara. The Lightborn had mostly kept their memories, but everyone else — even the children who now shared the collective mind — was forgetting. Behind that loss, Clara could still feel something expanding, not contracting. But that was deep down, while at the surface everything rotted like old fruit. *Why* was anyone's guess.

Clara met the viceroy's eye. She'd come up to tell her what she was still overhearing from the Astrals, but what was the point? There was nothing anyone could do. And Jabari would forget most of what Clara told her in no time at all.

"Do you dream, Viceroy Jabari?"

"Yes." The reply, at least, came without hesitation. One thing she could remember.

"Do you dream about my grandfather? Sometimes I dream about him."

"Who is your grandfather? Not the black man. And not the Arab."

It wasn't the response she'd expected. It bristled the hairs on her neck.

"Meyer Dempsey. Viceroy Meyer Dempsey."

A light flickered — the former Mara Jabari surfacing from the mental sludge. "I know something about that name."

"You sent him off. Him and some others. To lifeboats you'd set up ahead of time. You told me about it when the floods came."

"Yes." Concentrating, holding a mental finger in a book to keep her place. "Yes, I remember that."

"You sent them to some sort of a meet-up. With leaders of the other capitals."

"Where?" Jabari asked.

"They weren't going to meet in person. You said it was a satellite connection. But I didn't think to get all the details before you … " She paused then regrouped to give Mara some dignity. "I just didn't think to ask any more about it at first."

"Oh."

"But then you said they couldn't make it to wherever they were supposed to go. Not after the flood."

"Oh."

"But in my dreams, I see him all the time. He's in a little boat, sealed with a top that opens, kind of like a submarine. And I get this feeling that he's alive." Clara swallowed. "Him and the others, including my mom."

"Oh." Mara shook her head. "I'm sorry. I don't know."

"But you said you dream."

"Those are dreams. This is reality."

"But that's just the thing. We're all having the same dreams, Viceroy. Everyone I've talked to. In the dreams there are eight people. But I get the feeling that somehow, they're really just seven. And I … " She wasn't sure how to articulate the last bit. Really — and this seemed unique to Clara's dreams — it felt more like there were *six*, not the seven (or kinda eight) that everyone else described. But when Clara tried to understand why, the answer that came was confusing. It wasn't like one of the seven vanished. It was more like Clara's presence in the dream came forward and knocked it out like one billiard ball striking another.

"Do you think it means something?"

Clara had mulled that topic many times. She'd always had a mental bond to someone — often her mother, once Cameron, occasionally Piper, and now the Lightborn. But most people had lived isolated mental lives before the Astrals came. It was strange for them to hear the thoughts of others, but Clara knew for a fact that it happened — especially in the cities, and around those big rocks. If everyone was having the same dream, it might mean something indeed. But *what?* Was it a real thing? Or another of the Astrals' games?

Clara looked through the glass of the vessel's enclosed bridge. Her mother had always said she was seven going on forty, and right now Clara felt like an old woman, several long lives into an eternity of existence.

"If you look deep inside yourself," Clara said, "do you see anything you don't recognize? Anything that surprises you?"

Mara looked confused. "Like what?"

"Everyone is forgetting things they used to know. The Astrals know it's happening. It's what they want. It's what has to happen, I think, before they can leave."

"They're going to leave? Is that something you can hear them saying?"

Clara sighed. They'd had this discussion many times.

"Yes, but it's also been broadcast to the world. On the tablets. You don't remember?"

Mara shook her head.

"They're not done with us. I think they need to get us down to a certain number before they leave and let us start over. But I think there's something else that has to happen before they can go. I think they need to wipe us clean. They don't want us to remember what happened when they were here or what came before, so we can restart with a blank slate."

"Oh."

"But at the same time, when I close my eyes and look deep inside, it's like I see lights. Same for a lot of the kids, and not even the ones like me. Something is growing while something else is going away. Do you know what I mean?"

Mara took a long second to think then shook her head with what looked like resignation.

"Try it. Now, please."

Mara shut her eyes.

"Just look deep. Breathe slowly. Shut everything out, and look into the darkness. Let me know if you see anything there, or feel it."

"What would I see or feel?"

"Anything."

Mara sat and closed her eyes, inhaled and exhaled, then finally opened her eyes. "I'm sorry."

Clara put her hand atop Mara's, which was resting on her knee, and gave the viceroy a grim little smile — and then, on instinct, a spontaneous hug. She finished, stood, and looked down at the viceroy. Clara felt as if she were the adult and Mara a child, waiting for whatever came next.

"It'll be over soon," Clara said. "One way or another."

Clara left the bridge, returning to her bunk.

When she was gone, Mara touched the sleeve of a tall and authoritative woman passing by and said, "Do you know who that little girl was?"

CHAPTER 48

A hand on Liza's shoulder suddenly woke her. She bolted upright from what seemed to have been a slouched position, remembering all at once that she wasn't in her quarters. She was right on the bridge, napping in a chair in front of everyone. But as far as Liza saw, nobody cared that the viceroy was asleep (literally) at the switch. None of the people milling purposelessly through the room was paying her any mind. And why would they? A ship without a destination was like a person without a reason to live. Every day was the same: water, meager food, and the reek of confined human bodies.

Liza followed the arm, still on her shoulder, to its source. She saw a man with stubble thick and dark enough to merit werewolf jokes. Mick. He looked as exhausted as she felt. His eyes were baggier than his age, slightly red. His bearing was mostly the same as always, but to Liza it seemed more effort was being expended to maintain — lack of shaving notwithstanding.

"Bad dream, Liza?" he asked, watching her settle from the surprise he'd given her.

"No. I don't dream."

"I almost wish I didn't. I don't suppose you remember an old comedian named Mitch Hedberg?"

Liza shook her head.

"He had this bit about how he didn't like dreaming because dreaming is work. 'I'm in my soft bed, relaxing, and now all of a sudden I have to build a go-kart with my ex-landlord.'"

Liza laughed. Mick laughed for a few beats, then his face withered.

"It's funny. I don't remember where I lived three weeks ago, but I remembered *that*. I could give you more if you want. Strange how it's all happening. When I'm not horrified at what's happening, I'm fascinated. It's like standing beside a grand old building, watching the walls fall in."

"You remembered my name," Liza said, knowing how pathetic it must sound. "You said it just now, when you woke me up."

Mick gave her a grim little smile. Then he held out his arm and rolled it so she could see the pale underside. In ballpoint pen he'd written himself a reminder: VICEROY LIZA KNIGHT.

"If I decide to take a shower and don't remember you afterward, you can't take it personally."

"Maybe you'll forget to take showers." Liza wished she could call the words back as they left her mouth. She'd been trying to play along, but that was too harsh.

"What do you need, Mick?"

He stood for moments. Then sat.

"Shit. I don't know."

"I asked you for a population report. Was that it?"

"Yes. That's it." He reached into his pocket and retrieved a scrap of crumpled paper. "We have to take the Astrals' word for it because they're the only ones broadcasting, but apparently there was a massive plague in a colony of North

African survivors. And a group in Switzerland, up in the Alps. On the Jungfrau. They came up from — "

"You already told me who they are. Did something happen to them?"

"They're all dead."

"How?"

"Locusts, if you can believe it."

"Were they farming?"

Mick glanced at his cheat sheet, which made crinkling sounds as he ran his thumbs and fingers along it. "According to what I saw, the locusts didn't eat their crops. They ... " He stopped, apparently appalled by something he himself had written five minutes earlier.

"They what?"

"I guess the locusts swarmed *them*. The people."

"How do *locusts* kill people?"

"I'm not sure I want to know." Mick folded the paper and returned it to his pocket, looking disturbed.

"Where did they come from, anyway? We've seen this story before, right?" She gestured around the bridge, indicating "this story" to mean the entirety of their current existence, the flood, everything. "Noah loaded up with two of every animal. We have a few dogs and possibly some lice. So what happens with the world's animals? Did the Astrals take care of it somehow, or are we going to be alone this time, then die off because there's zero biodiversity?"

Mick was looking at her, not really hearing the question. "What?"

"Is Noah a story?"

"Noah's Ark," Liza said.

"How do you remember it?"

"You remembered Mitch Humbug."

"Hedberg."

"See?"

"It's hardly the same. You don't forget my name. You don't have it written on your arm. You keep referring to the way things were, casually mentioning things I get the feeling I'm supposed to remember but don't. And you know stuff like Noah and his animals."

"But I don't dream."

She said it offhandedly, but Mick seemed to think it over, his head bobbing in thought.

"I get the feeling something fucked up is happening, Liza. I don't like it."

"It's hard to get much more fucked up than global elimination. I think your feelings are normal."

"It's more than that. The guys in my bunk room say they're having the same dream. Every night, like a premonition."

"What's it about?"

"A group of people in the desert." His lips pursed. "I think one of them is you."

"*Me?*"

"You and six others. Or maybe seven."

"Are they all people you work intimately with and have an excuse for being in your subconscious?"

"I don't recognize the others. At least, I don't think I do. They're all men except for you. Plus a girl."

"Maybe it's not a girl. Maybe it's just a really, really short person."

Mick gave her a look. "I'm serious about this, Liza. I've been meaning to say something about it to you for a while."

"Why? It's just a dream, Mick."

"It feels like more than that. And there's ... an *importance* that goes with it. Like, I feel that this matters a lot. Or like I've been waiting for it."

"So it's in the future. Your prophetic dream."

"I don't know. Maybe."

"Like you're a wizard."

"I know how it sounds."

"Well," Liza said, not contradicting the notion though it sounded plenty ridiculous, "at least we know we'll find land again. Me and my buddies."

"Did we discuss that already? I feel like we talked about land."

"Promises, promises. Yes, we talked about it. I've had bulletins, presumably from Divinity, same as the population reports."

"Funny thing about that," Mick said, pulling the paper back from his pocket as if trying to recall something. "I don't actually think those are broadcast reports. The geeks think they're reports coming directly to us from one of the motherships, out of sight, maybe bounced off a satellite or something. Maybe being sent *only* to us."

"So what?"

"So maybe they're fucking with us. *Still.*"

"I guess we'll find out in ... " Liza leaned forward, flipped a calendar's pages. It was ten years old; she'd found it in a pile. The date didn't matter. Only the number of boxes passed. "Nineteen days," she finished.

"What happens in nineteen days?"

"Supposedly, the oceans retreat. That's when the Astrals say we'll find land. Real land, not a mountain peak. So I guess we'll see if your Nostradamus dreams were right." She leaned back. "Then all I'll need is a desert, a little girl, and a bunch of men."

Mick looked like he might chastise her again for not taking him seriously. Liza felt annoyed by it all. She was still the fucking viceroy and he was still her employee, underling, go-fer, whatever. The entire ship was stir-crazy. Only Liza was holding her marbles. They'd be lucky to survive nineteen more days without a killing, cannibalism, or both.

"Relax, Mick. This is all just ... " She waved her hands, trying to convey a general sense of undefined fuckery. "You know. But we have to hang in there for another three weeks. *Less* than that, unless I'm being lied to. Then they'll be done with us. They'll pull the floods back, maybe plop the animals down from wherever, then do you know what they'll do?"

"What?"

"They'll *leave*, Mick. The Astrals will pack up their ships and go the fuck home. And the few of us left will have the planet to ourselves. And that's not just me believing what they tell me. That's what Jabari's think tank said, too. Each time around, the aliens have advanced our societies, killed us off, then left. Anything else is Future Earth's problem."

Mick looked unsure. But she could tell the idea of an Astral departure was extremely appealing. Light at the end of an endless tunnel. They'd talked about this already, of course, but Mick's mind was a sieve. Too much confinement. Too much fear and upheaval. The brain could only take so much, and not everyone had the mental strength that Liza herself had, to weather it all intact.

"Look," she said. "Everyone's nerves are thin. You're all feeding on each other's paranoia. You want to feel better? You want to think better? You want to *sleep* better? Maybe get out of that bunk room. Sleep up here if you want. I have plenty of space."

"Maybe things should go the other way. Maybe it'd be better if *you* left this place every once in a while. People are starting to talk. They wonder about you. You're up here all the time, never interacting, never leaving your hole. You've got your guards. I've even seen things. Like how you get paranoid whenever you're near the controls. You won't let me come close."

"Hmm. Let's compare tactics, shall we? I'd say I'm doing just fine in my Howard Hughes existence. I could draw you a detailed map of Roman Sands. But you? You're all going batshit crazy."

It was cruel, and for a second Liza thought he might call her on it. Instead he fixed her with a dumb, animal stare. "Howard *who?*"

"Never mind. Was there anything else, Mick?"

His eyes moved upward, brain fruitlessly searching for recall.

"Guess not. There's that superior 'interaction paradigm' at work again."

Mick glared for a moment, then left. Fine with Liza; she'd had more than enough of Mick. Just like she'd had more than enough of the others on the bridge, who wandered around like lost assholes, pestered her for empty reassurance, and generally looked at her when she checked on the navigation like she — not they — was the crazy one.

Liza picked up the small bag she kept tucked under her chair, its long strap always securely around her arm. She removed the silver ball, looked at her reflection in its mirrored surface, then set it aside.

The small metal canister was still in the bag's bottom. She sighed, looking at it. So much for Canned Heat. So much for cracking open the rebel viceroy's secret little club, letting the Astrals listen in on their whispers, paving the path for her competition's elimination and ensuring Liza's place at the head of the post-apocalypse pack.

If the viceroys couldn't meet, that chance to find Astral grace was out the window.

She set the canister aside and again held the ball.

If she did what it told her, there were many more chances to come.

Liza closed her eyes. Tried to imagine the dream the others were having, wondering if she could force herself to join. But instead of seeing people in a desert like Mick described, she saw a stark white room. She saw a woman with a backbone as rigid as a steel rod. She remembered distant, unarticulated pain. She remembered a far-off, vaguely troubling sense of isolation.

Liza's eyes opened. She went to the vessel's navigation system, glancing over her shoulder for watchers as she went, then made a tiny adjustment.

She didn't know where the ship was going any more than the others did.

Liza gripped the ball, feeling its intelligence, knowing only that no matter what, they had to get there.

CHAPTER 49

There was no way to track time in the mammoth ship's all-white room, so Sadeem metered moments by the cycles that seemed part of his routine, then used a sharp edge on his zipper to score a line into a discrete spot on his arm. By this count, twenty-five days had passed since the flood.

There was a meal of human breakfast food, a meal of human lunch food, and a meal of human dinner-type food. Eternity came in to speak with him several times each day, at roughly the same intervals. Sometime after the dinner meal, there was a long period during which Sadeem assumed he was supposed to sleep, and did, on a large pillow left on the floor like a dog's bed. Days passed, and he he grew increasingly used to it all.

Each day, Eternity would show him sights of the world below. It was never clear if the ship had hovered above the spots she showed or if they'd been broadcast, but a total lack of motion meant it could be either.

Sadeem saw fires, floods, and manual destruction, when the Astrals discovered a pocket of humans in one place and had a mothership handy.

Big waves, stirred from an otherwise calm ocean, sent to drown settlements.

Where there were still volcanoes above water, he saw eruptions. Dust clouds. Burnings.

There were many storms of all types. Eternity showed Sadeem visions of people swallowed by tornadoes, flattened by debris in hurricanes, drowned in flash floods in the few areas of remaining high land, even people struck by curiously abundant lightning. In areas frozen by the Astrals, blizzards froze people to death. Subzero winds suffocated the marooned, usually in warm-weather clothes.

Ice ages were localized, as if created by an enormous focused freeze ray.

Pestilence. Disease. There were illnesses on Eternity's Death Of Humanity program that Sadeem had never seen. Which diseases made people bleed from the eyes? Made them *shit* blood as if from a faucet? It was a macabre playground where masochistic alien scientists could invent beautiful horrors that, in the pre-apocalypse world, wouldn't even have made logical sense.

And each day, Eternity gave Sadeem a number.

Fifty million.

Forty-two million.

Thirty-seven million.

Each day, the number fell. Some days by a lot. On the third week Sadeem realized she'd never told him what the number was. But from context, its meaning was clear. The number never rose. That would be for after the Astrals finished their pruning and finally left the planet alone, when the time came for humans to become fruitful and multiply.

Each day, Eternity asked Sadeem about the man in boots, the man who called himself Stranger. It had become perfunctory. Sadeem had told her dozens of times that he knew nothing of the man, and it's not like he ever left to discover more. But whoever the man was, he seemed to have stayed hidden from the Astrals, his dangerous secrets still unrevealed.

So afterward, Eternity would turn to ask Sadeem about the Lightborn children.

What are their abilities?

What caused them to form?

Why do you present them with puzzles?

How are their brains different from yours?

Sadeem answered for as long as he could then finally turned it back on Eternity.

You want to know so damn bad, why don't you go down and grab one?

Then Eternity would ask more about puzzles. Make plans for the new Temple's location. And she'd teach Sadeem more, and more, and more of what he'd need to know if he was to be the first new Mullah Elder.

His mind turned inward. Comparing new information with old. Sprinkling in what he'd learned from Clara Gupta.

Eternity was supposed to know everything. And yet for some reason, judging by her actions, he was the sage.

A scant few days following the big storms, Mara Jabari forgot they'd ever happened. Clara considered telling her, along with anyone who'd listen. It seemed wrong that all of those people — maybe a half million, she sometimes thought — should be blinked out of existence without anyone knowing. But it was like fighting the tide. No matter what she told Mara, the woman always lost it.

Ella understood.

Nick understood.

Logan and the rest of the Lightborn understood.

And what's more, while the rest of the Ember Flats Ark was losing its sense of place and history, the Lightborn's connection to other Lightborn on other ships was increasing.

Clara found she could dip into the collective and speak with a boy from Hanging Pillars as easily as she could speak to Logan beside her. Maybe it was the lack of interference, as the rest of the world's minds went dim. As the rest of humanity became the blank slates preferred by the Astrals.

Sometimes, Clara envied them. The collective remembered every bit of their shared past. Clara knew how to play video games she'd never experienced, enjoyed by teenagers before the fall. Clara knew the best place to buy a taco in New York, though she'd only been there as an embryo. She had lived the invasion and occupation from every possible angle. She'd seen them come to Iraq. The Northern Territory. She'd seen them above London and Budapest and Warsaw and Chang Mai. She'd seen Moscow destroyed from the inside, through the memories of a child who'd been there. She'd seen Black Monday's decimation hundreds of times, when the Astrals had made their first round of human cuts, knocking the planet's population from nearly eight billion to three. And of course she still saw Heaven's Veil in her dreams.

Her father's death.

Her grandmother's death.

The deaths of hundreds of other kids' fathers, other kids' grandmothers.

What would it be like to forget like the others? To arrive one day on dry land, and start over without history's agony? Without all the baggage?

At night, Clara let her mind drift into the collective. Into the place that seemed unable to forget. And in that space, she watched connections form — fresh meat forming beneath a diseased skin. Too late, something was happening. They were waking the other young minds, but in time it only happened below the level of consciousness. The girl she'd talked to her first day on the vessel, Zoe, could barely remember Clara's name. But she was there in the collective, like one more node in an outward-spreading network.

Nodes here and there. All over the globe. The brightest were Lightborn, and the second-brightest were the non-Lightborn children they touched. But there were dimmer nodes too — more precisely wired and not as flexible or bright. To Clara, they felt like adults. With her eyes closed, the network was a thing of beauty. Ideal pieces in perfect slots in the big puzzle, each placed as if by design. The growing hive couldn't have existed before humanity's garbled noise had been pruned. There'd been too much distraction. Too many flimsy connections. Only now could she connect to an Indian man she felt staring out at the ocean. Only now could she hear the thoughts of an Asian fisherman, whose mind was a curious puzzle box that acted like a key the man had never known was there.

Usually it was too much to think about. The network — forged from genocide, invisible except to the Lightborn as the race memory of humanity melted to mush — was pointless. It helped nobody.

Days ticked off.

Clara found a node in the network that felt familiar as if from long ago. Just an ordinary mind, nothing special.

With her eyes closed, she nuzzled her mind close to the unremarkable node, wishing it could sing her to sleep like it used to.

On the thirty-fourth day at sea by Peers's count, Lila spotted land and shouted down to Piper, telling her to steer toward it. But Piper didn't hear because she was huddled over the controls, in her own little world as usual.

Peers caught Piper's attention. She glared at him. Then he took the controls and tried to steer toward the land, but the ship's rudder wouldn't turn. Or it would, but the boat wouldn't follow. The sub moved in the same direction it had been, and in that moment something in Peers finally broke, and he pounded on the instruments while Lila shouted from above. When she finally came down, Lila shouted at him for his obstinance. And shouted. And shouted. But this time Peers shouted back, and the fight became about something else entirely, and Lila threw a stainless steel cup at him, bouncing off his elbow. By the time the fight was behind them, so was the land.

Another day.

Another day.

Peers pulled out a roll of nautical maps stowed in the sub's nose, mostly useless without land above water to use for comparison. Peers had tried to guess their position at night and came away frustrated, unable to tell anything more than that familiar constellations meant they were still in the northern hemisphere. The total lack of information was unsettling. Weather had changed, and there were no landmarks. Hot days followed frigid ones. They gutted the few fish they managed to catch and often ate them raw. They constructed rain traps on the sub's top and caught rainwater to drink. But there was no end in sight. No place to go. Only Piper seemed to have any thoughts on their direction, but she never shared her reasoning, or used GPS to navigate. He had no idea *what* Piper was using — only that the instruments bowed to her fingers alone.

The little boat powered on, somehow avoiding swells and storms and ice, the engines forever spinning on tanks that never needed fuel.

Carl woke with a start when the world jarred on the thirty-eighth day, tossing its contents hither and yon. It took him a while to realize that the disturbance had been caused by the freighter grinding to a halt. He ran to the deck, looked around, and saw nothing.

He didn't know how to fire the engines, because they'd come alight without human intervention. He didn't know how to figure out where they'd become inexplicably marooned because he knew only that they'd started south and steamed north. But in the intervening five weeks, they'd taken one detour after another, filling the big ship to what had to be quarter capacity or more, moving east and west, then south again, obeying the weather and the silver ball's whims. But now Carl was worse than lost, and there was no way to fix it.

Still he lowered one of the small boats stowed on deck from their massive boom arms, the motor operating as inexplicably well as the rest of the ship's systems. While in the water, he steered the boat around and away, searching for the problem. And after much peering and staring down, he found it. Or rather, Lawrence did. The ship had run aground. On what, nobody knew.

They slept. And in the morning, the underwater obstruction was just visible from the freighter's deck where it hadn't been before.

Carl went to sleep that night wondering if what he suspected might be true.

And the next morning, the fortieth day, he felt the ship tilt as its weight betrayed it, coming to rest at a few degrees of lee.

Below the bow was a low rise covered in long and bedraggled green grass, now visible above the water.

They'd come aground two days ago. And now, as water receded, the ground was finally making its way to them.

The next time they saw land, it was Meyer, not Peers, who took control. He was prepared to cut the ship's hydraulic and electrical lines to stop and change its course, ready to jump into the water and push. He'd make them *all* get out and kick, if it came to that.

But the controls obeyed his touch, turning them toward land. Toward, he saw, a large something near the land's edge that had to be man-made.

Piper didn't stand in his way as she had before. She sort of blinked and looked at him with curiosity, as if this were a party she was just now entering. When Meyer ignored her, she turned to Kindred. But he'd weathered the trip worse than the rest of them. Which was to say he'd weathered it better. Lila had complained; Peers had exacerbated his own obnoxious, compulsive habits; Meyer had stewed, and Piper had been in a fugue. But Kindred had been none of the above. Most days he'd sat in one place, staring out at nothing.

Meyer called to his double for help when they got closer. He'd need the help to shore them up, and no one trusted Peers. When Kindred came up, Meyer tried to see into him, the way they once shared a mental office. But there was nothing there. Kindred was an empty vessel, still half of Meyer, but touching his mind was like touching nothing at all.

"What's wrong with you?" Meyer asked, not bothering to blunt the point.

"I can tell he's close," Kindred replied.

"Who?"

But Kindred had already finished his work with the dock line, tying it to a dead tree just breaking the water's surface. He'd waded to the new shore and was making his way, alone, toward the man-made thing Meyer had seen from open water.

Meyer recognized it immediately. He'd seen it — or one of several just like it — over and over on Jabari's tablet, on the Astral broadcasts.

One of the big vessels the aliens had left behind as human lifeboats, sent from a distant capital.

Liza Knight stood on her vessel deck as a dozen people with sponge brain attempted to figure out how to extend the gangplank and disembark. She had no idea where they were, but she'd been circling this place for days and had been watching spots of land appear — here and there, then suddenly everywhere. Based on the underwater obstacles they'd encountered just trying to get close and tie the thing off, they'd come upon a relatively flat, definitely large area. By tomorrow or the next day, their Noah's Ark would probably be permanently beached, fallen over on its hulking side in the middle of a gently rolling meadow.

"Um … " said a voice at her side.

"*Liza,*" Liza growled, seeing Mick's perplexed expression. In the past two weeks, she'd gone from sympathetic about his mental issues to irritated to flat-out angry. She didn't like spending more than a month on a boat to nowhere more than anyone else, and yet everyone came to her expecting things, trying to tell her what to do. But wasn't she the one with the little metal ball that told the ship where to go? Not that she'd shared that tidbit with anyone.

"Liza?"

"Do you have any idea who I am?" She should be more elated at finding land, but found herself nonetheless unable to enjoy it while surrounded by monkeys.

"You're Liza."

"I'm in charge here. I'm the fucking *viceroy*, Mick."

He watched her vacant, as if waiting for her to finish.

"What do you want? If you can even fucking remember."

"I left myself a note to ask you to try a GPS bearing."

Some of Liza's annoyance departed. She'd forgotten. But at least it was garden-variety forgetting, not the amnesia they all seemed to have caught like a cold. Or so she hoped.

She pulled the mobile phone from her pocket. Mick looked at it as if he'd never seen something so fascinating. Like showing fire to a caveman.

"Nothing." She put it back in her pocket.

Mick nodded. She realized he had no idea what a 'GPS bearing' was despite having made the suggestion. Mick's new systems were more efficient than sensible. He left himself reminders but seldom knew what they meant.

"I guess it doesn't matter where we are as long as there's land. Make yourself another note, Mick. Check all of the communication devices in there to see if anyone else has popped up, if there are any broadcasts, anything."

"Um ... Liza?"

"You don't know how to work any of the equipment, do you?"

Mick shrugged.

"Fine. I'll do it. But I sure hope you like the people on this boat. Because if the Astrals are leaving soon and communications stay down like I think they will, like forever, this is your life."

Mick waited for her to finish. Liza realized that if what she'd just said was true, she was going to be supremely unhappy. But what had she expected? The capitals had been spread across the globe. If Jabari's plan had worked out and the viceroys had managed to reach their virtual meet-up and make their plans, maybe there could have been a New World Order. But now she was destined to be a queen among idiots. The other ships could be anywhere, if they'd survived.

"You can go," Liza said.

Stewing, she moved around the big boat, inspecting her soggy new home, for better or for worse.

But it seemed that Liza wasn't alone after all.

There was a small watercraft in the distance, aground not far off. It wasn't big like the ark, or small and flat like a normal boat. It was almost rounded, like a mini-sub.

A man was walking toward her.

And far behind him, Liza saw another man who looked an awful lot like him.

Stranger hid behind the big rock, watching Kindred cross the new land toward the Roman Sands vessel. He watched as the leaders stood face to face, unable to see their expressions, knowing they'd be good. He watched as Liza Knight extended her hand, as Kindred took it, as they shook. And then he watched the two larger parties move toward each other, local pools of thought already beginning to intermingle.

The next day, the water had moved more than ten feet farther down, and Stranger knew without looking inside that the big Astral ship had moved back to one of the poles and would soon go to the other, siphoning the global flood back into mountains of freshwater ice. The ice didn't return to the north and south as glaciers. It returned as liquid, then obeyed the ship's whims and went to freeze where the Astral machinery told it to. If human scientists were to bore into the new ice, they wouldn't know what to make of their discovery. But the world's population was down to the seed number the Astrals had wanted, and the Forgetting had already peaked.

There would be no more scientists on Earth. Not for a very long time.

A few days on, Stranger moved to where Carl Nairobi had run his big ship aground. He stayed out of sight — more because he was curious than out of need. Carl had seen enough wonders that he might not even be surprised to see

Stranger. The man might even expect it. And by the time Carl crested a particular hill not far on from his group's position, he wouldn't have much surprise left in him, anyway. Carl, like the others, had no idea where they were or where they'd been headed throughout the past month and a half. And yet over that hill, he'd find Jayesh Sai and Maj Anders, who'd already made each other's curious acquaintance. But, Stranger thought, was it really so shocking that they'd been drawn together? Life *always* began in this place, every single time.

Stranger watched the disparate groups assemble, keeping his distance. He felt the click each time a new piece was added to the whole, as new humans found the swelling collective. As the Roman Sands survivors and Meyer Dempsey's small group met with Spiros Cocoves of Hanging Pillars and his group, as both watched Lee Sin's group, summoned by her small silver ball, enter the plain to join them.

With proximity, mentality grew. And the Forgetting, its work done, allowed their minds to function again. Friends could soon easily remember friends and new shared histories, but the old past — and its mistakes — were gone forever.

Stranger watched for two weeks, staying apart, letting the new city form in the drying land. The sun came out as the continents returned to the surface, and the land became arid, and the survivors marched until they found fresh water again in a fertile valley not far from the desert, where they discovered other viceroys who'd already made temporary homes.

Last to arrive was the Ember Flats group, who found ground late and stayed far off until they began to run out of drinking water. Then they followed Clara's ball, and Stranger watched the final thing he'd wanted to see before joining the group, finally a participant instead of a puppeteer.

And that thing, he watched close: Clara finding Lila. The two reconciling and Lila's heart breaking with joy, two halves made whole after a drought.

Stranger watched. And waited. Then he entered the new city as the mental grid flickered.

His work as maestro was done.

Now it was another's turn to guide them.

CHAPTER 50

"All that remains," Eternity told Sadeem, "is the matter of your Legend Scroll."

Sadeem looked up. Having essentially been abducted, he'd brought no belongings onto the first mothership, then onto the larger Deathbringer. So he wasn't precisely packed to leave, but it was a similar vibe. He was in the same white room as always, fed and healthy but phenomenally bored after nearly two months in captivity, now standing with no bags by his side and the unmistakable air of a man about to pick up and shove off. And yet here was Eternity, saying something that could change everything. His insides longed to scream.

"I've shown you all our scrolls. All my key can access."

"And we've sent all that was previously paired to the old Mullah Temple to the new one," Eternity agreed, nodding slightly as if finally comfortable acting human. "Your key will now access all of what your Elders were granted at the prior Temple. Your portal links to ours, and the knowledge has been sent there, from our side, for any new Elders you groom and train."

"So nothing remains. And I can go home." Sadeem thought to correct himself — wherever he was headed, it wasn't *home*. Floodwaters had receded and the ice caps had been restored, but the planet was cleansed, with most of what humans had built upon it now shrapnel, half-buried in silt or washed away.

"The Legend Scroll," Eternity persisted.

"I know of nothing by that name."

"We scanned you during your sleep last night, using the same process used to create progenitors and progeny."

Sadeem had heard those words. He didn't like where this might be going.

"Are you saying you're going to duplicate me like you duplicated Meyer Dempsey? You extracted my mind the way you did with him, and now you're going to bring a Titan in here and ... and ... "

"It is merely the same process." Betraying what Sadeem had watched bloom in the Astrals over the past months, Eternity's face wore an expression that seemed to add, *So fucking relax already.* "The human conscious mind is only so aware of itself. As we created the new portal, we needed to be certain that information obtained by the Mullah and elaborated on in our absence — not just from your perspective but from your admittedly weak attachment to a species collective — was accurate. The scan went as anticipated, and gaps on the human side have been filled. Information required for the new Temple and Mullah knowledge base is complete. And yes, you can ... 'go home.' But first there is one unexpected discovery, hidden within your mind. Of the Legend Scroll."

Sadeem felt his skin starting to creep. Eternity, as the human woman she wasn't, was beautiful. But when she stared — especially now, with a secret unexpectedly revealed — she was more terrifying than attractive.

"I don't know about a *Legend Scroll.*"

"There is no point in deception. Your intent to conceal knowledge of this matter from us was as obvious in the scan as the matter itself."

"I ... "

"Tell us about the Seven Archetypes."

"I thought you knew it all? Plucked right from my brain while I slept?"

"Knowledge is different from context."

"Same as for your lost man in boots?"

"That issue is at least partly resolved. In your mind, you call the man you claimed not to know *the Magician*."

"I don't know that. It's just a guess."

"Tell us."

Sadeem sighed. He only knew middle-tier information anyway. Perhaps the Elders knew why the Archetypes mattered, but Sadeem could only tell her the facts (or legends) as the Mullah saw them. It was probably a useless secret — like confessing to knowledge of the boogeyman, but not of where it was hiding.

"It's just a story we tell. In a book of prophecies. The Elders knew more, I'm sure, but to the rest of us it was one more thing we heard — alongside legends of the Horsemen returning to the planet, and bringing the end."

"Who are they?"

"Some in my group thought Meyer Dempsey might be the King. And that's one of only a few things rumors of the Scroll agree on: that the King survives. It made us curious to follow him, knowing that if we were right, he'd make it to the new Mecca. Or Jerusalem. Or whatever. So were we right? Did Dempsey survive?"

"He is in the new capital. The new Cradle of Civilization."

"What about his group?"

"Do you mean Clara?"

Sadeem stopped, mouth open.

"Who is Clara?"

"The girl you were hiding from us. The Lightborn."

Sadeem said nothing.

"We cannot see the girl your mind recalls in the new city, no," Eternity answered.

Sadeem's head hung. A slow exhale escaped.

"Why were you hiding the girl? Did you think she was one of the Archetypes?"

"No, she ... "

Eternity waited.

"Okay. Fine. She was Lightborn. We didn't know what they meant. Only that they were different. Something about the way their minds process things. They were unusually skilled at telepathy, beyond what we saw happened in most people around your broadcast stones. They sometimes seemed to be prescient, definitely precocious. Clara was a child in many ways, but in most ways her mind was adult. Or beyond."

"Why did you hide her from us?"

"It was just a matter of the unknown. The Astrals didn't seem to know much about the Lightborn, and that made us more interested in them. When Clara came to us, we took the opportunity. I gave her puzzles and watched her play. I discovered only that her mind was extraordinary. Nothing beyond that in any way that should bother you. If you've scanned my brain, you know there's nothing more. There wasn't enough time to learn about her before your Dark Rider came and it all fell apart."

Eternity seemed to think. Finally she nodded, apparently satisfied.

"And the Archetypes?"

"From where I stood, they were exactly that: *Archetypes.* Personifications of the types of people who'd be needed when a new epoch began. Even those below the level of Elder knew the basics of what was supposed to happen when the Horsemen returned: You'd judge us with your archive; you'd cause ruin and destruction if we failed, as we always have. When it was over, the population would shrink, though I hadn't realized *how* much. But when you left, the new humanity would require certain attributes to be strong in its bloodline. It would need leadership, so there would be a King, if not a literal king. They'd need wisdom, so there'd be a Sage. But to counterpoint wisdom there'd be an Innocent, which some feel is where the Christian story of Eden comes from."

"In all the past epochs, humanity has never been 'innocent.' There has always been evil."

"And that's why one of the Archetypes is *the Villain*," Sadeem said.

"It is merely a construct. A way for the Mullah to imagine each epoch's beginning."

Sadeem nodded.

"This is consistent with our scan. But if it was a framework for your society, why did you keep it secret?"

If she was asking, the scan hadn't been deductive enough to provide Sadeem's real answer: *That I never learned the details of the Legend Scroll and kept hoping they might be a kind of resistance against you.* But even that had been absurd from the start. The Scroll was replete with words like "always" and "each time." That alone meant that if the Archetypes had formed a resistance in past epochs, it hadn't been especially effective.

So Sadeem gave an answer that was still true, even if not all the way: "I couldn't just give you everything. Humans fight."

He thought Eternity might balk — might say "irrelevant" a few more times. But instead she nodded in apparent acceptance.

"This does explain another anomaly we've discovered. It may even explain the Stranger we've discussed during your time here."

"So you *don't* know everything?"

"In each epoch, there has been an element of uncertainty. The Founders seeded it as an essential part of your species' existence, but it has always been foreign to us. The intention was to create a variety of experience for our Watchers to study, beyond what happens in our purer consciousness.

But doing so meant working with a tool that was useful on one hand, but dangerous on the other."

"What element?"

"Your mind calls it *chaos*."

"So what's the anomaly?"

"Our intention was to recall all Astrals from the surface. But there's one entity within our collective that we have been unable to recall. A soldier, in your words, who spent enough time with humanity to become infected. That one has not returned."

Sadeem pondered Eternity's words, feeling a strange kinship with this woman-who-wasn't-a-woman — this force that had killed off all but a few tenths of a percent of his world's people. In the moment, she was almost a person, like him. A being who'd faced a human sense of defeat, even if tiny. Something she didn't understand, despite her best efforts.

"A Titan?" Sadeem said. "Or a Reptar?"

"A Transformed."

"A ... ?" The word clicked. "Wait. Are you talking about the second Meyer Dempsey? The one Clara called Kindred?"

She seemed distracted, head down: a parody of human pensiveness as if there was one brain in her one head. "But now, with your story of Archetypes, there is context. Because we can still feel our Transformed the way you can feel one of your fingers, and what's there isn't worse than defiant. It is black with infection. Perhaps it is right to stay behind. Not just to protect our collective but to seed your new humanity with evil, as your Villain."

Sadeem found himself about to respond — perhaps to protest the idea of Astrals discarding their garbage with humanity — but she was right; it almost made sense. In the Eden myth, it wasn't Adam or Eve who brought Original Sin — or its potential — to the Garden. It was the serpent.

Eternity looked up, and for perhaps the final time, Sadeem was struck with just how good at imitating humanity this inhuman thing had become.

"Then the issue is closed. Humanity has reached our intended seed number, and the land masses have been restored. The Forgetting is complete, and that seed shall start fresh."

"They've forgotten everything?"

"Now that we've retracted our influence, their minds will stabilize. Only factual memory of the past has been erased. They will not remember their past wonders. They will not remember their old civilization or old cities or old ways. Once we have returned you to the surface and verified the Forgetting is complete from within our stream, our ships will leave your planet, and they will not remember us. But they will know each other. They will know how to build fires and shelters, how to hunt and work together, how to begin the next attempt at evolving their consciousness into one like ours. Perhaps humanity will be what it has the potential to become the next time we return."

"And by 'potential,' you mean like you."

"Humanity can evolve a collective like ours. It has nearly happened before."

"Maybe we're not supposed to be like you. Maybe, since you intentionally made us different, our 'collective' is supposed to be something else."

"Perhaps."

"When you send me back home, before you leave," Sadeem said after a moment of silence, "will you make me forget, too?"

"Oh no," Eternity replied. "Someone has to be the Sage."

CHAPTER 51

Piper entered the small shelter, feeling an increasingly common sense of dislocation. It was almost like seeing something move in the corner of her eye then looking properly to discover that whatever she'd almost seen had jumped back into place after turning her head. Something wasn't quite right, but she didn't know what. Piper had the sense of her mind as a bathtub, plug pulled from the bottom and thoughts draining faster than she could turn on taps to refill it. A helpless situation — and even more, it felt inevitable. Maybe something was going very wrong, but it wasn't anything she could stop. And it would be over soon.

She sat beside Lila, who had Clara on her lap. She was too big, but Lila had barely let the kid leave her grip — let alone her sight — since their reunion. Lila didn't seem exactly eager to go through ...

To go through ...

Well, whatever peril they'd recently left behind them.

"Feeling okay?" Lila asked her, looking up. She was sitting in a chair made of metal and canvas. Not the kind of thing that could be easily made, the way cobblers in the square made things. So where had it come from? Piper couldn't recall.

342

"Just kind of uneasy. I keep getting these weird ... visions."

Lila almost asked one question then obviously diverted to another. Piper wasn't the only one having trouble articulating herself these days, and looking at Lila she seemed to remember a sense of *visions* meaning more than they did now. As if one of them had been a psychic or a fortune teller, seeing visions and reading other people's thoughts on a regular basis.

"Visions of what?" Lila asked.

Piper looked down at Clara. "Clara, honey? Do you mind helping your grandpa with some stuff he's doing outside?"

Lila's grip on Clara's arm tightened enough that the girl flinched. Then she let go a little, but Clara looked up at her, wincing.

"He's right outside, Lila. It's bright daylight, and you can see for miles."

Lila still held Clara's arm, reticent. But Piper was right. Nobody could snatch Clara without someone seeing or stopping it — especially not with Meyer and his brother watching her in the dooryard.

Lila turned to Clara, urged the girl out of her lap, and said, "Go ahead. Just be sure to stay with Grandpa and Kindred. Don't go wandering off, okay?"

Clara rolled her eyes, but only a little. Then her mother beckoned for a hug, and Clara complied without comment. A moment later she was out the door, and Piper heard the strike of Meyer's axe, the small clicking sounds as Clara stacked wood.

"What's going on?" Lila asked.

"You'll think I'm crazy."

"I promise I won't."

"This is going to sound so stupid."

"Just say it. I won't laugh." She smiled. "Or send you to the medic."

Piper's eyes darted around, her mind trying to cobble the interior mess into a cohesive whole. "Look. I feel like an idiot, but I keep thinking I see ... " She sighed. "Visitors?"

"From up the delta? From the desert?"

"From the sky."

Lila laughed. "The Astrals."

"So I'm not crazy?"

"Not about this, no," Lila said, still smiling. "Have you talked to Stranger?"

Piper shook her head. "He's so busy. Everyone is planting soon. Everything needs a blessing."

"I did, not long ago. He said, 'Thoughts of the Astrals are slippery.'"

"So he knows about them?"

Lila nodded. "He says they created us. They're from the heavens, like the gods. But then he said they're preparing to leave, as they have in the past. And that until they do, we'll remember them a little ... but once they're gone, we won't remember them at all. And for now, it's like clinging to a dream."

Piper tried to focus. She remembered personal details fine: She was Piper Dempsey; she lived in the fourth house to the far side of the square with her husband, his twin brother, their daughter, Lila, and her daughter, Clara. They spent most nights with their neighbor Peers and his dog, just sitting and talking. She knew she liked Peers but hadn't always, though she now couldn't remember what he'd done to offend her.

But when her thoughts turned to the alien ships in the sky — Peers called them chariots of the gods — it was like trying to recall something from her earliest years. Much of her history was similarly foggy, as if in flux. How had she and Meyer met? What had her pregnancy been like, and what of Lila's first years? All those things might as well have been from a hundred years ago, from another life, from a whole other world. And the Astrals, as Lila called them, seemed to be tied up in all of it.

"How has Clara been?" Piper asked, deciding the topic was exhausted at best, frustratingly deadlocked at least.

"Good. But she's strange, Piper."

"Strange how?"

"She doesn't talk much. She's not as lively as she used to be."

"It's only been a week since she came home, Lila. Give her time."

Lila's mouth opened. Her head cocked.

"It's been more than a week."

"No, a week. I've been washing her shirts. One a day. Seven shirts."

"I thought she came back months ago. Are you sure?"

"I'm sure, Lila," Piper laughed. "Maybe *you* should go to the medic."

But Lila was shaking her head. "She came back with Mara Jabari. The same time that Gatekeeper Carl and his clan joined the village."

"Lila, I'm positive. *One week.*"

"But Carl, Mara, the others ... the village wasn't even *built* when they came!"

"I don't know what to tell you, Lila. Maybe you're right. Maybe we built the village in a single week and don't remember."

This time, Lila laughed.

"She'll be okay. She's a kid. Kids are resilient. Just let it pass. If she wants to talk about where they took her, let her. But if she doesn't, don't pry. She needs to move on, and so do you."

Lila nodded.

But that night, Lila also brought a rock into her bedroom. She began to make marks on it, to count the days with a stick of chalk.

CHAPTER 52

And so life in the village continued.

The river gave them a ready supply of clean water, so they hauled buckets and used the water to drink and to bathe and to cook their meals over fires using pots that none of the citizens precisely remembered fabricating, purchasing, or trading for. They sat inside their homes (which, similarly, nobody really remembered building or even moving into) at dark, for protection, and wandered about during the day.

Sometimes wolves and coyotes came in the night, so villagers kept their food contained and their children inside and their small animals penned. Sometimes snakes made homes under their houses so they had to fish them out. The sun had a tendency to crisp the skin so they wore loose clothing or stayed in the shade when the sun was high. The land was fertile. And crops grew.

By the time the corn was knee-high, lapping up water from the river and laughing at the desolation of dry desert beyond the village, almost everyone had completely forgotten the strange visitors who'd come from the sky. There were nightmares, with black things that scuttled like bugs, purring with blue sparks in their throats. And sometimes, when a man as large as Carl came from the sun with his white covers on, those who saw his big, muscle-bound form would flinch until seeing that his skin was black, not powder white like the phantoms they remembered without recollection.

But for the most part nobody knew anything of the ships by then, or the catastrophe that had befallen them, or the old, distant cities, or the function of any of the strange relics people occasionally found in their belongings. When the villagers found such objects, they took them to Stranger, who pronounced them witchcraft, or to the strange desert-dwelling sage named Sadeem who made his home far away, in the hills, with a small tribe of disciples he called Mullah. Sometimes Stranger would make pronouncements about the relics, and often Sadeem told tales of a magic that once permeated the world like the very aether of existence, and how the shiny things — many of which came alive if you touched them — talked to that magic.

By the time two months had passed, the village was at peace. There were squabbles among the villagers, and the constant feud between Governor Dempsey and Liza Knight, who ran the rectory and seemed to know everything about everyone whether it was her business or not. But there were no outside enemies other than the wolves and coyotes and snakes, so life went on as well as it could.

The Dempsey family, which held esteem as the family of their fearless leader, was a mixed bunch, underpinning so much of the tribe's day-to-day existence. There was Meyer, of course, who ran things when not bickering with Liza. There was his twin brother, Kindred, who was strange and distant and dark — a brooding, troubling figure who most knew to avoid. There was Piper, who acted as the First Lady and made clothing as her profession. There was Lila, who taught at the school. And lastly there was young Clara Dempsey, who spent much of her time with Stranger in his magician's hut. It made Lila uneasy, but she permitted the friendship. Clara was *different*, and although Stranger was odd, he was trusted by the village and seemed to understand Clara — something Lila herself had given up on.

In Stranger's hut, he and Clara discussed things they shouldn't know but both did. Long after the Astrals were gone, Clara asked about them. Long after the ships had last graced the others' memories, Clara and Stranger still whispered. And they spoke in hushed voices about Stranger himself, who struck Clara as instantly familiar in a way she didn't entirely understand — and most often about Kindred, whom Stranger avoided like a plague. Many avoided Kindred, but with Stranger it was intentional — each steering clear of the other despite what both called "an intensely strong mutual attraction." Whenever Clara spoke with Stranger or her grand uncle, the other man surfaced in conversation. Kindred wanted nothing more, it seemed, than to sit opposite Stranger for a meal. And Stranger, likewise, wanted nothing more than to visit with Kindred. Clara could feel their mutual pull, but for a reason neither would divulge they refused to meet — as if doing so was dangerous.

Stranger would say, "We all have our burdens to bear, Clara, just as you have the burden of knowledge and insight." And Kindred, who knew less of Clara's unique "insight," would say the same. Kindred spoke of little but Stranger, using drink to still unknowable demons. Except that when he drank enough, another subject would surface. Lila heard this topic often, as the one tasked with shuttling Kindred to bed when his intoxication became too great and filled him with menace. He spoke of a woman named Heather, who seemed to haunt his past, but that Lila had never heard of.

In the mornings, Clara would often tell her mother that she was going to Stranger's place then walk past it, headed to a place far in the hills — too far for anyone to walk alone. She could make it in two hours, most of that time spent crossing barren desert with no landmarks to guide her. Clara never got lost. She tuned inward to another kind of guidance, listening to whispers from her friends: a group sometimes called the Unforgotten, but which called themselves Lightborn. Clara could hear them any time she chose to tune in, same as she could still see the strange network with all its nodes with her mind's eye. When she walked, she called on the Lightborn to guide her, to the cave where she'd find Sadeem and the Mullah. But when she realized it wasn't just the Lightborn offering directions from afar, she chose to ask the Sage, knowing he'd have answers to questions nobody else had — that nobody else could even understand.

"All the time I was on the vessel," Clara told him, "I could see this network in my head expanding. And I could mentally tap each of the bright spots, which I kind of thought of as nodes. And when I did, I'd get a sense of what that node was: not just a spot in a grid but as a person. You were one. So was Piper. All of my Lightborn friends were in there, each appearing as a node in this big, expanding grid of people. At first I thought we were connecting, the way my mind plugs into the Lightborn. But it's still there, even after everything! I think that's how I can see my way through the desert: Millions of people saw this piece of land before the flood. Even with all the landmarks washed away, what they know — or *knew* — seems to have made me a map."

Sadeem nodded, thinking. "It makes sense. Many tiny inputs from nodes on the grid, and your mind assembles them into a picture of the whole."

"But they've forgotten, Sadeem! Nobody remembers the old world! Nobody even remembers the flood, the Astrals, none of it! My own mom doesn't even remember *her* mom — she thinks Piper had her!"

"And?"

Clara looked at Sadeem with disbelief. He was sitting in front of her cross-legged, peaceful like a meditating yogi.

"And?" she repeated.

"Why would you expect it to be different? Just because they've forgotten doesn't mean they don't remember."

"Stop speaking in riddles!"

Sadeem's composure broke. He laughed.

"I suspect we've always been connected a little, Clara. That's what you're able to see. You've kept an eye on what humanity lost. It changes nothing, but at least offsets the burden of being how you are."

"So I can remember things that everyone else has let go? How is that a benefit? I wish I'd forgotten, too!"

"They told me everyone would forget, Clara. But they've never been able to see the Lightborn. It's one tiny piece of victory. They knocked down the buildings but left the foundation, in you."

"And what good does it do me?"

"You won't get lost, for one. And at least until you die, a small piece of the old world won't be gone forever."

"The same is true of you. Big whoop for being special. Even if we told people how it used to be, nobody would believe us."

"Part of their plan, I suppose. The Astrals wanted us to start over, and that could only happen if we were blank slates. It had to happen before they left. But it's good because we needed them to go. The healing had to begin, and if memory was the price, so be it. The network you see won't last forever, Clara. It'll wither and die. Enjoy it while you can. Your mind, my mind, the minds of other Lightborn and perhaps the one you call Stranger? That might be all that's left of the world we knew. But like all things, it's only for a time. I'm already forgetting things — naturally, at least. Just as your subconscious network is fading. Don't resent it, Clara. Pity it. Don't push those people's remains away. Embrace and celebrate them while they're still here."

Something sighed inside her. Sadeem was speaking as if the world wasn't dead, but dying. As if the people she already knew and loved, in the small village and the others pocked across the planet, were dying.

She closed her eyes, feeling exhausted. She saw the network almost immediately. And it was as he said: a still-vibrant core of bright nodes surrounded by endless acres of slaughtered chattel. Subconscious minds of the more than seven billion humans who'd died during the occupation were now husks. But the rest of what Sadeem had said wasn't as obviously true: As those old minds shed, leaving the living to burn inside Clara's mental network, the remaining nodes weren't dimming. Each mind still in the grid fit perfectly — *more* perfectly than they ever could have during humanity's populous but scattered heyday.

Clara opened her eyes.

"Sadeem?"

"Yes, Clara?"

"You say the nodes — this *collective network* — I see inside me ... you say those are the *roots* of people before they forgot everything? So the Peers Basara node inside my head, for instance — that's Peers as he *used to be*, not as he is now?"

"It's his entry into the collective unconscious. So yes."

"And because everyone *has* forgotten, that's why the whole thing should be shutting down? Because all those old memories and thoughts are *erased*?"

"That's right."

"But Sadeem?"

"Yes, Clara?"

"It's not shutting down. The network keeps growing brighter and brighter. It's not dying. It's almost like it's coming alive."

"I think you're imagining things."

"No, Sadeem, I'm *not*," Clara insisted. "It's been getting brighter since we boarded the vessel. Since those other, non-

Lightborn kids started to light up, and even some of the adults."

Sadeem looked puzzled. "But they forgot. All of them. The kids. The adults. Everyone."

Clara closed her eyes. Watched a small blip of internal light move from a live node to a darker one. The new node brightened a hair, then passed the light on.

She was about to try and describe it when the walls began to shake. Dust sifted, and Mullah began to shout. Then Clara saw it, all at once — inside her mind before she saw it with her eyes, as the people of the distant village saw it first, and uploaded the knowledge directly to her screaming cortex.

"It's a quake," Sadeem said.

"No. It's not."

They walked up the tunnels, reached the cave's mouth, and emerged into the open air. There they saw it together: overhead, covering half the sky, was the enormous Deathbringer that had supposedly left Earth three months earlier.

Sadeem gaped up at the thing, his Mullah ranks speechless beside him.

"They were supposed to leave," Sadeem said. "Why didn't they go?"

Clara looked inside. And in one gestalt leap, she knew the answer in full.

"Because this time it's different," she said. "This time, they *can't*."

GET THE NEXT — AND FINAL! — BOOK IN THE INVASION SERIES!

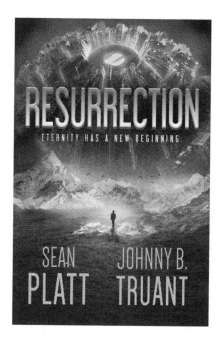

SterlingAndStone.net/book/resurrection

LEARN THE STORY
BEHIND THE BOOK

Want to know how this book was written? *Back Story* is our
podcast where we talk about the creation and writing of
all our books. **Follow the link below to hear how we took**
***Extinction* from concept to completed work.**
It's like DVD extras, but for books.

Go here to get the Back Story:
SterlingAndStone.net/go/extinction-backstory/

ABOUT THE AUTHORS

Johnny B. Truant is an author, blogger, and podcaster who, like the Ramones, was long denied induction into the Rock and Roll Hall of Fame despite having a large cult following. He makes his online home at SterlingAndStone. Net and is the author of the *Fat Vampire* series, the *Unicorn Western* series, the political sci-fi thriller *The Beam*, and many more.

You can connect with Johnny on Twitter at @JohnnyB-Truant, and you should totally send him an email at johnny@sterlingandstone.net if the mood strikes you.

Sean Platt is speaker, author, and co-founder of Realm & Sands. He is also co-founder of Collective Inkwell, home to the breakout indie hits *Yesterday's Gone* and *WhiteSpace*, co-authored with David W. Wright. Sean also publishes smart stories for children under the pen name Guy Incognito, and writes laugh out loud comedies with Johnny under the pen name Max Power. You can see Sterling & Stone's complete catalogue at SterlingAndStone.Net/Books. Sean lives in Austin, Texas, with his wife, daughter, and son.

You can find Sean at SterlingAndStone.Net, follow him on Twitter at @SeanPlatt, or send him an email at sean@sterlingandstone.net.

For any questions about Sterling & Stone books or products, or help with anything at all, please send an email to help@sterlingandstone.net, or contact us at sterlingandstone.net/contact. Thank you for reading.

44010650R00218